STORMING

Join the discussion: #storming

STORMING

K.M. WEILAND

Published by PenForASword Publishing.

Printed in the United States of America.

ISBN: 978-0-9857804-7-0

Dedicated to my beloved Savior,
who sets us free in His truth.

And to my sister Amy.
I write for her before I write for anyone else.

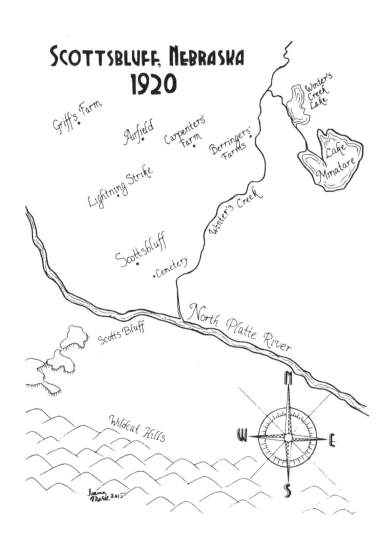

CHAPTER 1

AUGUST 1920—WESTERN NEBRASKA

FLYING A BIPLANE, especially one as rickety as a war-surplus Curtiss JN-4D, meant being ready for anything. But in Hitch's thirteen years of experience, this was the first time "anything" had meant bodies falling out of the night sky smack in front of his plane.

True enough that flying and falling just kind of went together. Not in a good sort of way, but in a way you couldn't escape. Airplanes fell out of the clouds, and pilots fell out of their airplanes. Not on purpose, of course, but it did happen sometimes, like when some dumb palooka forgot to buckle his safety belt, then decided to try flying upside down.

Flying and falling, freedom and dependence, air and earth. That was just the way it was. But whatever was falling always had to be falling *from* some place. No such thing as *just* falling out of the sky, 'cause nothing was up there to fall out of.

Which didn't at all explain the blur of plummeting shadows just a couple hundred yards in front of his propeller.

He reacted reflexively, pulling the Jenny up and to the right. The new Hisso engine Earl had just installed whined and whirred in protest. Hitch thrust the stick forward to push the nose back down and flatten her out. This was what he got for coming out here in the middle of the night to test the plane's new modifications. But time was short and the stakes were high with Col. Livingstone's flying circus arriving in town tomorrow for the big competition.

Hitch and his team were only going to have this one shot to win the show and impress Livingstone. Otherwise, they'd be headed straight from broke to flat broke. And he'd be hollering adios to all those big dreams of running a *real* barnstorming circus. If he and his parachutist Rick Holmes were going to pull off that new stunt they'd been working on, his Jenny first had to prove she was up to new demands. A little extra practice never hurt anyone—even him—but falling bodies sure as gravy wasn't what he'd had in mind for his first night back in the old hometown.

In the front cockpit, Taos turned around, forepaws on the back of the seat, brown ears blowing in the wind, barking his head off.

Hitch anchored the stick with both hands and twisted a look over his right shoulder, then his left, just in time to see the big shadow separate itself into two smaller patches of dark. A flower of white bloomed from first one shadow, then the other—and everything slowed down.

Parachutes. Some crazy jumpers were parachuting out here at night? He craned a look overhead, but there was nothing up there but a whole lot of moon and a whole lot more sky.

Then the night exploded in a gout of fire.

He jerked his head back around to see over his shoulder, past the Jenny's tail.

The arc of a flare sputtered through the darkness, showering light all over the jumper nearest to him. Beneath the expanse of the white silk parachute hung a dark mass, shiny and rippling, like fabric blowing in the wind.

What in tarnation? Parachutists didn't wear anything but practical jumpsuits or trousers. Anything else risked fouling the lines. And everybody knew better than to hazard a flare's spark lighting the 'chute on fire.

He circled the Jenny around to pass the jumper, giving a wide berth to keep the turbulence from interfering. Below him stretched the long metallic sheen of a brand spanking new lake—presumably from irrigation runoff—that had somehow appeared during the nine years since he'd left home. He was only fifty or so feet above the water, and the air currents were already playing heck with the Jenny. She juddered again, up and down, as if a playful giant was poking at her.

Another flare spurted into the night. Thanks to it and the light of the full moon, he could see quite well enough to tell that what was hanging from that 'chute was a woman—in a gigantic ball gown.

When you flew all over the country, you saw a lot of strange stuff. But this one bought the beets.

This time, the flare didn't fall harmlessly away. This time, it struck the woman's skirt.

His heart did a quick stutter.

He was almost parallel with her now. In that second when the Jenny screamed by, the woman's wide eyes found his, her mouth open in her grease-streaked face.

"Oh, brother, lady." The wind ripped his words away.

He couldn't leave her back there, but he sure as Moses couldn't do much from inside the Jenny.

He careened past the white mushroom that marked the second jumper. A large bird circled above the canopy. This jumper seemed to be a man—no big skirt anyway. He should be fine landing in the lake, if he could keep from getting tangled in his lines. But judging his capacity for brains from that blunder with the flare, even that might be too much for him to handle. Unless, of course, he'd shot at the woman deliberately.

Hitch circled wide around the man and chased back after the ball of fire.

This time when he passed the woman, he shouted, "Cut loose!"

She was only twenty feet up now. It'd be a hard fall into the water, but even that'd be a whole lot better than going down in a fireball—a flamerino as pilots called it.

He zipped past and looked back at her.

She couldn't hear him through the wind, but if she'd seen his lips moving and his arms waving, she'd know he was talking to her. And, really, what *else* was he going to be saying right now?

In the front seat, Taos leaned over the turtleback between the cockpits. His whole body quivered with his frantic barking, but the sound was ripped away in the rush of the wind and the howl of the engine.

The woman had both hands at her chest, yanking at the harness buckles. And then, with one last jerk, they came free. She plummeted, a whoosh of fire in the darkness. She broke the glossy water below. The flames winked out. She disappeared.

A third flare blinked through the corner of his vision, too late for Hitch to react. It smacked into the Jenny's exhaust stack and erupted in a short burst of flame.

Even the dog froze.

If the flame touched the wing, varnished as it was in butyrate dope, the whole thing would go off like gunpowder. But the flame sputtered out. The stack started coughing black smoke.

This was bad. Not as bad as it could be maybe. But bad.

Smoke and the stench of burning castor oil chugged from the right side of the engine. When Earl saw it, he'd lie down and have a fit. Here was the brand new Hisso, all set for the big contest with Col. Livingstone's air circus, already choking.

No engine, no plane, no competition. That was simple barnstorming mathematics.

Not to mention the fact that the show hadn't even started and Hitch was already leaving bodies in his slipstream—although that, of course, was hardly his fault.

He swung the plane around and pushed her into a dive. She stuttered and balked but did it anyway, like the good cranky girl she was. He took a low pass over the lake, then another and another. The fall hadn't been far, only twenty feet or so. Provided the jumpers hadn't hit at a bad angle, it wasn't a horrible place to bail out.

Of course, there was also the little fact of the woman having been on fire. But with all that material she'd been wearing, the flames probably wouldn't have had enough time to reach skin, much less do any considerable damage.

Out of the night's list of featured ways to die, that left drowning. If she couldn't swim, she was out of luck.

Beneath the Jenny, the white expanse of the man's parachute spread over the surface of the lake. The man himself wasn't to be seen.

Hitch dipped low for another flyby and leaned out of the cockpit as far as he could manage, searching for the other parachute. "C'mon, c'mon."

Taos squirmed around to stare at something ahead of them. Hitch looked up.

There it was. And there *she* was.

Head barely above the water, the woman dog-paddled a couple dozen feet out from the shore.

Thank God for that anyway.

He resisted flying over her, since his turbulence wouldn't help her overcome the soggy deadweight of that load of skirt she was wearing. But he waggled his wings once, in case she was looking, then turned around to hunt for the nearest landing spot. So much for a nice encouraging practice run.

A dirt road up past the shore offered just enough room to put the plane down. No headlights in sight, which wasn't surprising for this time of night. Most folks would be rocking on their front porches, enjoying the cool of the evening after long hours sweating in the corn and beet fields. He shut off the engine and jumped down to dig a flashlight out of his jacket pocket. Calling Taos to him, he started off at a jog, back toward the lakeshore.

The few cottonwoods growing around the water's edge were young, proof the lake hadn't been in existence long. Around here, trees—especially moisture hogs like cottonwoods—only grew near water.

He crashed through the brush, Taos trotting behind him, and followed the yellow beam of his flashlight to the approximate spot where the woman jumper might have emerged from the water. A scan of the area showed only white wavelets nibbling into the sand. The water stretched away from the shore, its ripples unbroken as far as the flashlight's weak beam carried.

He trudged down the beach. His leather boots, laced all the way up the front, sank into the wet sand and left the only footprints he could see. She'd been almost to shore when he had flown away from her. Surely she couldn't have drowned just a few feet out.

He stopped and swung the light in a broad arc, from shore to trees. "Hey! You guys all right?"

Only the rustle of leaves answered.

If either of them had made it to land, he'd practically have to fall over the top of them to find them in the dark. And if they hadn't, their bodies wouldn't wash up on shore until at least tomorrow morning. He stopped. Ahead of him, Taos snuffled into the brush.

Maybe the big question here wasn't so much where they had ended up as where in blue thunder they'd come from in the first place. He swung the light up to the sky.

The beam disappeared into the darkness. It was a clear night, playing host to a bare handful of big fluffy clouds. The moon was a huge one, just a few days past full. It cast a giant reflection against the lake and sheeted the world in silver. A thousand stars blinked down at him.

Like enough, the stars had a better view than he did of wherever these people had jumped from.

Had it been another plane? He might not have heard its engine over his own, but if it had flown right above him, the moon would have cast a shadow. And anyway, what kind of idiots went parachuting at night?

She had to be part of another flying act. Lots of acts would be coming into town for the weekend show, what with Col. Livingstone in the area. Hitch wasn't the only pilot desperate to get work for his people by piggybacking on a big circus's publicity—or better yet, beating the tar out of the competition and earning enough money to expand his own circus into something worthy of the name.

It was just possible these two had followed him out here. He chewed his lower lip. They could have botched it with the flare, since there was no sense whatever in that guy lighting his own partner on fire. What if he'd been aiming at damaging the Jenny the whole time?

That was beyond dirty. Hitch shook his head. To be honest, it just didn't feel quite right. Something else was going on here.

Even if these two had somehow jumped on accident, that still didn't explain why Hitch hadn't noticed hide nor hair of another airplane. He lowered the flashlight's beam and toed a piece of driftwood. It rolled over, and a crawdad scuttled out.

In the brush upshore, Taos barked once.

Hitch turned. His light caught on a footprint, then another.

They were fresh enough to still be wet and crumbling around the edges. They weren't particularly small, but they were narrow enough they pretty much had to belong to the woman.

He scratched Taos's ears. "Good dog."

The light showed the tracks emerging from the lake, as if she were some mermaid who'd grown legs and taken off running. After that, the prints disappeared in the brush, headed through the trees toward the road.

He started after them. "Ma'am? You hurt? I'm the cloud-buster you about crashed into a minute ago."

The cloudbuster you may have just knocked out of the most important competition of the year. But he swallowed that back. For now, it was miracle enough she was alive.

"If you want, I can give you a ride out of here so you're closer to town." Assuming he could get the Jenny up in the air and back to Earl.

Off to the right, forty feet ahead of him, the brush crackled.

He swung around to follow. But the crackling kept going, headed away from him. Pretty soon, what was left of the trees separated out onto a road. He peered in both directions and listened for more crackling.

Nothing.

"Ma'am?" What was she anyway, mute? "Look, if you or your buddy are hurt at all, holler out."

A restlessness shifted through him. He should just go. Seemed to be what they wanted after all. Fact of his life: his leaving usually made things better for other people, not worse. Certainly, it had worked out that way for Celia, whether she had ever believed it or not.

"Look, lady, I gotta go. I've got folks waiting on me."

More nothing.

He glanced at Taos.

The dog, a border collie cross he'd picked up in New Mexico five years back, cocked his head and stared at him, waiting. One brown ear stuck straight up; the other flopped at the tip.

In the fine dust at the edge of the road, his light snagged on another set of footprints.

He stopped and knelt. This set was much larger, definitely

the man's. Like the woman's, a little of the wet shore sand clung to the edges. The strides were long and didn't look to be hindered by any kind of injury.

He followed them with the light, across the road, and into a hayfield.

Well, then. Two parachutes, two jumpers, two survivors. And whether they'd intended it or not: one bunged-up plane.

CHAPTER 2

ITCH NURSED HIS ship back to the airfield north of town. It wasn't really an airfield, just an empty hayfield some farmer had been talked into renting out for the duration of the show. But even this early in the week, pilots and performers were coming in from all over. He and his crew hadn't been the first to arrive, and they wouldn't be the last.

Col. Bonney Livingstone and His Extravagant Flying Circus was one of the biggest in the business. The shows he put on were tremendous spectacles compared to the little hops Hitch was doing. With a dozen planes and twice as many pilots, parachutists, and wing walkers, Livingstone was able to haul in huge crowds and pay out even better purses. More than a few pilots' ears had perked up when word had gotten around about the big competition Livingstone was staging in Nebraska's western panhandle.

Below, bonfires speckled the field, bouncing light off the tethered planes. Hitch banked gently and swung around for a landing. As he pulled to a stop at the end of the strip, the sound of singing and the pluck of guitars drifted over. From beside the nearest fire, Lilla Malone waved at him.

He climbed out, snapped his fingers at Taos, and walked over to where his crew lounged around their fire.

"Howdy, handsome," Lilla said—more to Taos than to him.

He'd found Lilla in Denver some eighteen months back. She wasn't exactly part of the show, since he would hardly risk her out on the wings or in a parachute, even if it ever dawned on her to volunteer. But it was handy to have an extra person to drive Rick's car, which he insisted on dragging around from stop to stop. More important, she was as pretty as they came, in a bouncy, sloe-eyed way. Her job was to ride in the front cockpit, waving and smiling, when they buzzed the towns for customers. Then later on, she'd hold the sign, take admissions, and convince folks that if she could survive in that rattling flying contraption, it *must* be safe.

She pushed up from her seat on a blanket, knee-walked over to Taos, and hauled him halfway into her lap. He licked the underside of her chin, and she leaned back, giggling. "You missed all the fun. We've already had a dance and an arm wrestling match."

"Which you won, I hope."

She looked confused. "I just watched and cheered. But Rick almost won."

On the other side of the fire, Rick Holmes balanced a tin plate of boiled potatoes and cornbread on one knee. "The reprobate cheated." He rubbed his right biceps.

"Sure he did," Hitch said. "Only way you could have lost. Now where's Earl?"

"Why?" Rick narrowed his eyes. "You haven't already demolished that new Hisso, have you? I heard it protesting when you flew over."

"Ran into a little difficulty." If you could call a hail of bodies *little*.

"I warned you not to take it out at night."

"Gimme a break. I could fly our whole routine blindfolded, much less on a moon-bright night. Had to make sure everything was running smooth before you try that high-altitude jump for Livingstone."

Rick looked him in the eye. "If you mean you would also probably have demolished the engine at high noon, that's no doubt true."

Rick was a bit of a dapper dude, in his pressed pants and embroidered suspenders. He'd greased his dark hair back, widening his forehead in comparison to his chin.

He smirked at Lilla across the fire. "Too much power for our esteemed employer."

She glanced at Hitch, eyebrows up. She'd never been too fluent in sarcasm.

Hitch gave his head a shake. "Where's Earl anyway? Crazy stuff just happened."

"Oh, indeed," Rick said. "Please tell me it involved discovering a pirate's buried cache. Because the only bit of news I would be interested in right now is that I'm about to receive the wages you've been promising for the last six months."

Lilla clucked. "Did you forget, darling? He's told us over and over we're all going to get paid after we win this show."

"And if we fail to win the show? Then what?" Again, he directed a flat gaze at Hitch. "The skills I bring to this show are already worth twice what I'm *supposed* to be receiving in remuneration."

Hitch stopped looking around for his mechanic and turned to face Rick down. "We're going to win this one."

"Certainly. Win with two planes, one parachute, no wing walkers, and a demolished engine. Once again, your business acumen astounds me."

Hitch swallowed a growl. "How many times we going to have to go over this?"

"Yes, please, don't fight," Lilla said. "It's all right. We trust Hitch, don't we, darling?"

"Don't we though."

"If he says everything's going to be fine, I know it's true." She dazzled Hitch with one of her smiles. "Right?"

Sometimes he blessed her for her blind faith. Other times, it turned his stomach inside out with panic. Lord knew owning his own circus was all he thought about when he was lying awake at night, staring up at the underside of his plane's wing. Part of his reason for wanting that was so he'd be able to take care of his people. These days, they were just about the only family that would claim him, and he would do whatever he had to do to keep them afloat.

But sometimes the knowledge that they were all depending on him clenched inside of him and made him want to whistle to Taos, jump back into the Jenny, and take off into the blue yonder all by himself. He needed their help if he was going to build a circus like Livingstone's, but the more people he had to take care of, the less free this life of his started feeling.

He made himself nod to her. "Never starved yet, have we?"

Rick clanked his plate onto the ground. "It's been a narrow margin." He rose from his crouch and brushed past Hitch. "If we don't finish choreographing this sensational new act before the colonel arrives, we're routed even if Earl *is* able to repair that wreck of yours again."

Hitch watched him go.

"It's all right." Lilla retrieved Rick's plate and offered it to Hitch. They couldn't afford to let the food go to waste right now. "Rick's upset because he says we don't have enough money to get married yet."

To that, Hitch could only grunt. Lilla, bless her loyal heart, hadn't been gifted with the most capacious of upstairs accommodations. Still, he hadn't known how truly cramped they were until she'd fallen for Rick.

Rick flew the other Jenny and did parachute drops. He'd been with Hitch for almost a year, which was almost a year too long for anybody to have to deal with an ego that outsized.

The whole thing had worked—barely, but it had worked—until a competition last month in Oklahoma when Rick had announced, in front of half a dozen other pilots, that he'd been the first man to do a successful handkerchief pickup. That, of course, was downright hogwash. The trick—of flying low over a pole and using a hook attached to the bottom wing to snag a handkerchief off the top—had been around a whole lot longer than Rick Holmes.

Without thinking, Hitch had snorted a laugh and called the lie for the malarkey it was. Rick had gotten about as red in the face as it was possible to get without exploding every single one of his blood vessels. He'd stomped off without another word—but Hitch had been hearing about it ever since. Rick wasn't about to leave without getting paid, and Hitch couldn't fire him until he had the money, but that day was coming and they both knew it.

For now though, he still needed Rick. Good pilots were hard to find these days, much less jumpers skilled enough to pull off this high-altitude stunt they were planning for the competition.

Behind him, footsteps crunched through the grass. "Well, how'd she fly? Like a dream?"

Hitch turned around. "You're not going to believe what happened up there."

Beneath the upturned brim of his baseball cap, Earl Harper grinned. "Won't I though? How about that speed? Didn't I tell you? We more than doubled the horsepower. You should be getting ninety miles an hour, maybe a climb rate of five hundred feet per minute." He smacked his hands together. "And with that reinforced frame I gave her, you know she'll take a whole lot of beating. Hot dog, boy. They're going to have a hard time trouncing us this week."

"About that . . ."

The shadow of a day's worth of black whiskers froze around Earl's grin. "About what?" He glanced at Lilla.

She turned to sit primly, knees bent, eyes studiously on the fire.

Earl looked back at Hitch. "You *busted* it? Tell me you haven't already busted that beautiful, brand-new Hispano-Suiza?"

This was where it got tricky. Hitch paid for the planes. Hitch flew the planes. But once Earl got under the hood of anything with oil running through its veins, he thought it belonged to him.

Hitch held out both hands. "Okay, look, *I* didn't bust it. But there was this woman—"

"Lilla?"

"No, not Lilla . . ."

Earl lowered his chin. He looked like a bulldog, thick all over and more than a little rumpled. "That's what this is all about? I told you to wait until morning to take it out, but, no, it had to be tonight." He turned around and talked to the darkness, both arms raised. "He wants to fly back to his hometown after nine years, he says. He wants to take the new engine out at night, he says. It's all perfectly innocent, he says." He turned back and prodded Hitch in the chest. "I thought you were done with the dames in this town!"

Lilla turned her head. "You have a girl?"

"She's not my girl!" Hitch said. "She plummets out of the sky, 'bout smacks me out of the air, turns into a fireball, then falls into some lake I've never even seen before."

Lilla sighed like it was the most romantic thing she'd ever heard. "Ohhhh."

Earl just stared.

Hitch waited. It was a good story. Better than his big wreck out in California, better than the guy who'd had to chase his unpiloted Jenny around the airfield until he could finally sever her fuel line with a shotgun, even better than that crazy Navajo who had dreamed up the stunt of hanging by his hair from the landing gear.

Earl tipped back his head and bellowed a laugh.

Hitch huffed. "C'mon."

When Earl finally wiped away the tears, he slapped Hitch's shoulder. "Where do you come up with this stuff?" He shook his head and started toward the Jenny.

Hitch strode after him. "I didn't come up with it. It happened. I'm flying along, and the next thing I know *bam!* Here are these two jumpers, right in front of my prop. And if that's not enough, the girl's wearing a cotton-picking evening gown— or, you know, one of those great big dresses your grandmother would have worn."

"Sure she did. And where'd she fall from? The moon?"

"Now, there, right there, that's what you should've asked in the first place. *That's* the question. I've been over and over it in my mind. Mine was the only plane out there, I'm sure of it."

Next to the Jenny, Earl pulled a flashlight out of his jumpsuit pocket and shone it on the engine.

Hitch stood over his shoulder. "And then the other jumper— he was a man, and a crazy lunatic, I might add—he starts shooting flares. Three of 'em."

The guy must have been reloading the second two by the light of their predecessors. You'd have to be pretty handy to manage that while hanging from a parachute in the middle of the night.

"One of them hit her, and another one caught the exhaust. I'm still trying to figure which he was aiming at and which was an accident. If it was some sabotage job, it's the most mixed-up thing I've ever seen."

Earl walked around to the plane's other side and shone the light into the exhaust stack. "Dagnabbit, Hitch. You can't fly this ship now! Why do you have to go and do these crazy things?"

"You think I'm going to do anything to endanger the plane *or* the engine right now, with everything we've got riding on this?"

Earl ducked under the plane and crossed back over to Hitch. "Look. I know you're trying to do your best here—for all of us. But this is no time to be going crazy."

"If we're going to win, we *need* to be faster and crazier than anything any of these people around here have ever seen."

"You keep busting up your bird and you can be as fast and crazy as you want, but it ain't getting you off the ground."

Earl had been with Hitch longer than anybody—going on six years now. They'd hooked up during a stopover in a little Texas town, where they'd gotten falling down drunk. By the time they emerged from their hangovers, Earl had somehow become the first member of Hitch's little flying family.

Earl got distracted by experiments too often to be the best mechanic running, but he was as true blue as they came. Every month or so, he'd start talking about leaving the circus to settle down somewhere, but it was just talk. Earl wouldn't leave, not as long as he reckoned Hitch needed somebody around to keep him from pitching head on into trouble.

That was why Earl, of all people, should know when Hitch was yarning and when he was dead serious.

Hitch leveled a stare at him. "You don't believe me."

Earl waggled the flashlight. "Do I believe some parachutist in my grandma's dress jumped out of the night sky and blew up in a ball of fire? No."

A wave of disappointment poked Hitch in the gut. He propped his hands on his hips and hung his head back.

Earl sighed. "Now I know this town ain't where you want to be right now. A bad marriage and a dead wife—that's not something any of us want to come back to."

That history was long, long over. But Hitch's stomach still rolled over on itself.

"Something must have been out there, because something sure hit your engine, I'll grant you that. But it was dark and you were going fast." A grin pulled at the corner of Earl's mouth. "Faster than you've ever gone before in this heap. You got the jitters? Fine. Maybe you were even sleepy. We pulled some mighty long hours trying to get here on time."

Had he been drifting off? Hitch thought back. What *had* he been thinking about before the parachutes appeared in front of him? He'd had a lot on his mind, that was sure. If he hadn't needed to be in Livingstone's competition so badly, coming back home would have been way down on his list of priorities. With any luck, he wouldn't run into too many folks he knew from before. Most of them—including Celia's sister and his own brother—wouldn't be too excited to see him. And there were a few he wasn't too excited about seeing himself—mainly Sheriff Bill Campbell.

That's what he'd been thinking. No dozing about it.

And then *it* happened, in a blur of adrenaline. His memory wasn't giving him too many clear pictures, just general blasts of color. But he was sure. You didn't just imagine a girl in a ball gown plummeting out of the night sky.

He rubbed his hand through the short ends of his curly hair. "If I say I'm sure, I don't suppose that'll get you to stop looking at me like I belong in the nuthouse?"

Earl snorted. "That ain't likely any day of the week. Not the way you fly."

Hitch looked at the plane, then back at Earl. "Can you fix it?"

"'Course I can fix it."

"Can you fix it in *time?*"

Earl put on his grumpy face. "Why is it always up to me to work the miracles around here?"

"Because you're the only smart one of the bunch."

"You know I'm going to need some money for supplies."

"Money I haven't got." Hitch chewed his lip. "Maybe somebody in town will have a quickie odd job. Or . . . I could sell something."

"And what have you got that's worth selling?"

He mentally rooted through his rucksack. "My old Colt .45

maybe. It's still in good shape. Somebody might give me more than a couple bucks for it."

"Better hope so." Earl hesitated. "And maybe we can take Rick's car and drive out to the lake, see if we can find any traces of these folks. You're pretty sure they're not hurt?"

"Yeah, I'm sure. They walked off just fine. They didn't much want to meet up with me." And he didn't blame them. "I just can't quite figure where they *came* from."

Earl clicked off his flashlight. "Same place all jumpers jump from. No mystery there."

Hitch stayed where he was and looked up at the moon. Seemed like the old girl was winking at him. Might it be she knew something they didn't? What secrets did she hold within all that silence?

Chapter 3

WALTER LIKED THE early mornings, especially in the summer—
with the full moon still hovering near the horizon, on its
way to setting. It nestled, white as a heifer's face, against
the blinding blue of the morning sky. He craned his head back.

Maybe there'd be a real live airplane up there today too. The
posters for the big show had been plastered all over town for
weeks. His insides jigged at just the thought of it. He couldn't help
a grin, and he pulled in a deep breath.

There was something about the air at this time of day, all shiny
with the mist rising off the dew-speckled cornfields. Even in a bad
drought, everything smelled wet and alive. This late in the summer,
the cornfields should have been towering far over his head—they
should have been up over even Papa Byron's or Deputy Griff's
heads. But thanks to the dry weather, the corn was barely taller
than his four feet five and a quarter inches.

Cane pole over his shoulder and wearing only his patched overalls, he ran through the crabgrass and the purple alfalfa flowers that
bordered the road to the creek. The dampness of the earth under
his toes crinkled up his legs, straight to his head.

As Mama Nan would say, good sweet angels, wasn't this the life!
Seemed like the right moment to do a war whoop and a dance, for
the fun of it. Problem with that was it involved saying something
out loud. He opened his mouth, loosened his throat muscles, and
waited. But speaking up felt wrong, even out here, where nobody
could hear him. It would be kind of like cheating, since everybody
wanted so much for him to say something back home.

He hadn't said hardly a thing since that day four years ago, half his whole life past. That was the day he'd gotten so scared and let the bad thing happen to the twins down by the creek. Evvy and Annie had been just babies then. He was supposed to have taken care of them. But he hadn't, and they'd just about died. And Mama Nan . . .

Sometimes her face from that day still flashed through his mind. Her eyes had been huge, her mouth open, gasping, like somebody had whacked her across the shins with the biggest stick they could find. She just stared at him and stared at him. And then words started coming out of her.

He didn't remember exactly what she said. But whatever she said had been right: it had been his fault.

He had stood there, wet and shivering, on the creek bank. Nothing would move. No part of his body would work right. Not because anything was wrong with him—he wasn't the one who'd just about died—but just . . . because.

And then he'd stopped talking.

But he didn't like to think about that. Much better to enjoy the sunshine and the morning. Maybe one of these days, he'd finally say something again—and make Mama Nan happy with him. But for right now, it could wait.

He set down his pole and rolled a somersault. Surely, God would know a somersault meant the same thing as a war whoop anyway. It was a sort of a thank-you for early summer mornings like this, when Mama Nan and Molly were baking and Papa Byron was starting up his rusty old tractor. If everybody was too busy to notice him, that meant he got to go fishing.

When he reached the Berringers' mailboxes—one neat and whitewashed and the other huge and rusty—he turned off the road into the trees that fringed the creek. His secret spot was on top of a flat boulder about a half mile down from the road. The rock had a round, hollowed-out spot on top, just perfect for sitting on.

Nobody else ever came out here. Well, maybe the old Berringer brothers, since it *was* their creek, but they never came out in the early morning. They wouldn't mind him fishing here. Or at least Mr. Matthew wouldn't. Mr. J.W. though, he was kind of grumpy and scary sometimes, like when he'd shot at Mr.

Matthew's prize hen and spooked her out of laying for a whole month.

Mr. J.W. hadn't known Walter was hiding behind the fence post. Then, when he walked by and saw Walter, he winked and gave Walter a penny for hard candy. Walter still had the penny in a sock under his bed. Didn't feel right somehow to spend a present from Mr. J.W. when he was afraid of him.

That was another reason he liked to come out here in the early mornings. Less of a chance of meeting Mr. J.W. or anybody else—like all these murdering sky people everybody in town was talking about lately.

Walter wasn't supposed to know about that, of course, but he'd heard Mr. Fallon from the dry goods store telling Mama Nan. In the last few weeks, five dead people had been found roundabout. Nobody knew who they were, just that they were dressed funny—old-fashioned, kinda like Grandpapa Hugh back when he was alive.

Two days ago, old Mr. Scottie, who always spent all day sitting inside Dan and Rosie's Cafe on Main Street, swore up and down he'd seen one of the bodies fall straight out of the sky. Everybody laughed at him like they didn't believe it. They all said maybe it was one of the pilots here for the show, who'd gotten drunk and crashed his plane. But they'd all started talking about the sky people after that.

Why *not* sky people? Walter peered upwards. Better that than the gangsters and bootleggers in the radio programs. A shiver lifted the downy hairs on the back of his neck. Now that the airshow was in town, maybe the sky people would be scared off.

He clambered up onto his rock. The coolness of its pitted surface, still protected by the morning's shadows, tingled against his feet. He settled down cross-legged, pole across his knees, and reached for the can he'd strapped around his waist. The piece of canvas tied over the top had kept the worms from falling out during his somersault.

Something splashed. And not a splash from a fish or a splash from a frog, but definitely a splash from a person.

He froze, then looked up.

There, on the opposite side of the creek, a few yards down

from his special rock, was a lady. She crouched on the bank, leaning forward to drink from the water. She was wearing a big blue dress like people wore in some of Evvy and Annie's storybooks about fairies and queens. But it was all torn on the bottom, maybe even burned in places.

She looked up and saw him.

He stared back, not even daring to breathe.

Her face was like a face out of the storybooks, pale and kind of glowy. Her hair was long and light brown, but it seemed shriveled, almost melted, at the ends.

She tilted up the corner of her mouth, and then she grinned full on at him.

His heart flopped over in his chest, and he grinned back. He even dared a wave.

She laughed, and it sounded like the creek gurgling past, only deeper. "*Zdravstvuyte*," she said. "*Prekrasnoe utro, ne tak li?*"

She didn't look like anyone around here, so it made a sort of sense she wouldn't talk like anyone either.

He shook his head.

"Mmm." She rose to her knees and gestured to her clothes. "*Mne nuzhna novaya odezhda.*" She mimed taking off the dirty dress and throwing it away, then pulling on a shirt and a pair of pants. When she was done, she shrugged her shoulders almost to her earlobes.

Now *this* was a conversation he knew how to have. The only question was where she could get a new dress. Mama Nan could give him one, but she might not be happy about it. She'd told Molly the other night that she'd have to be more careful about keeping her dresses mended, since only the sweet angels knew where they'd get money for a new one. Molly hadn't much liked that.

But still, maybe Mama Nan could give him one to *borrow*, until the lady could find her real clothes.

He set his pole down on the rock and stood. He repeated her gesture of putting on new clothes, then pointed to the road. If she could walk over there, she could climb onto the bridge without having to wade through the stream. Her dress was so long she'd get it all wet if she tried to cross here.

She turned her head to follow his pointing finger, then pushed to her feet. "Umm . . . tonk yuu." She bowed her head to him and disappeared into the brush.

So she spoke real words after all! He gathered up his pole and worm can and ran back through the trees to the road.

But when he got to the bridge, she wasn't there.

He climbed up to stand on the railing. From that height, he could see down the creek on one side, and on the other across Mr. Matthew's hayfield to the top of the fourth-story tower on Mr. J.W.'s house.

She was nowhere.

For five minutes, he waited. Then he climbed down and scouted back up the creek on her side of the bank. Still no lady.

But maybe she wasn't a lady. Maybe she was one of the sky people. He leaned his head back to look past the tree branches at the blue glitter of the sky. She looked too nice to murder anybody. So maybe . . . maybe she was one of Mama Nan's sweet angels come down for real.

CHAPTER 4

T HE WOMAN'S FOOTPRINTS led Hitch right up to the two mismatched mailboxes. On the smaller one, *Mr. Matthew G.
Berringer* was painted in square black letters. On the larger
one, nail heads formed the words *JOHN WILFORD BERRIN-
GER, ESQUIRE.*

So those two old buzzards were still at it, tooth and claw,
determined to outdo one another or die trying. Some things
around here hadn't changed, at any rate.

He shook his head and knelt to look at the woman's footprints in the thick dust on the side of the road. A set of much
smaller footprints had joined them, then veered off down the
road behind Hitch. A child's?

He looked over his shoulder, squinting against the early
morning sunlight.

Sure enough, a kid in overalls—cane pole over one shoulder—was tearing off down the road. Late for his chores, no
doubt.

Hitch remembered the feeling well.

He stood up and surveyed the lay of the land.

The Berringer brothers lived only a mile or so away from that
big lake, and there wasn't much in between, so it made sense
that one or both of the jumpers would have ended up here.
From the looks of the footprints traveling on into the green
sway of the hayfield, it seemed the woman was now alone.

After some cajoling, he had talked Rick into dropping him
by the lake before Rick and Lilla drove on into town to see the
sights. Unless Scottsbluff had changed a whole bunch since

Hitch had left, they wouldn't likely find much to see. But he hadn't told them that. He needed the ride, and no matter what they saw, Rick would be dissatisfied and Lilla was almost sure to be pleased.

Hitch had located the woman's footprints from the night before and followed them back to the road. In the daylight, he found his bearings right away. This was where he fished trout and hunted coyotes as a boy. The Berringers had always been willing to let him fish their creek as a bonus for his work. They would hire him for odd jobs whenever his old man gave him time off from the farm work. They paid good—outbidding one another to see who would hire him. And if he said so himself, he was pretty skilled at getting them to keep the bidding going.

Of course, looking back, the question was whether they had known all the time what he was up to.

And now here he was again. The rail fence surrounding Matthew's hayfield looked different somehow, smaller, even though Hitch had been more than full grown by the time he left home. A wave of something—not exactly homesickness, but a kind of sad queasiness—washed through his stomach. He'd left because he had to, as much as because he'd wanted to, and there wasn't anything for him here now. He'd known that after Celia had died.

He gripped the dry, splintery wood of the top rail. "Home again." But not for long. Home, with his feet in the cornfields, was a prison. Flying—that's where his happiness was.

He climbed the fence and crossed the field.

While he was here, he might as well stop in and say hello. The Berringers had always liked him. In contrast to some other folks in the valley, they might be willing to give him a quick job so he could afford those parts for Earl. And maybe they might have noticed a strange woman wandering through their yards.

On the far side of the field, he climbed another fence and started up Matthew's drive. J.W.'s drive was right next to it, ten feet away. Their houses sat side by side, across the property line from each other. Matthew's was a modest clapboard, white-washed, single-storied, with a roofed-in porch across the front. J.W.'s was a monstrosity, and he'd built it smack-dab between

Matthew and the view of the Wildcat Hills to the south. It looked like something some maharajah had rejected: three stories with two jutting towers and four chimneys. It was close to being the biggest house in the county, even though J.W. lived in it alone. Definitely, it was the most outlandish.

Hitch squinted at the sun. Probably only 7:30 or so, but both Matthew and J.W. might already have left for their respective fields by now. Crazy farmers and their early-bird ways.

Hitch took the three steps to Matthew's porch in one stride and thumped on the screen door. Nobody answered, so he crossed to the other side of the porch and jumped down. The ground was so dry, the dirt puffed up around his feet. He'd almost forgotten how bad the droughts could be here. Without the irrigation, nothing much would grow in these parts—and even then, it was a struggle whenever the weather refused to cooperate.

Around the back corner of the house, the wash on the line flapped into view. Faded long johns, dungarees, and a voluminous blue gown wafted in the breeze.

He stopped short.

The dress was shiny, sateen or something, with black lace up the front. One side of the skirt hung in charred shreds, and the whole thing was about as rumpled and dirty as you'd expect after having been dragged through a lake.

He scanned the yard.

And just like that: there she was.

She wore a white shirt and a pair of overalls, which she must have pulled off the line before putting the gown in their place. They were Matthew's, of course, so they were about ten sizes too big for her slim frame. She had rolled the sleeves up past her elbows and the pant cuffs above her bare ankles. She stood at the water barrel beside the house, with her back to him. She had a big knife in one hand and was systematically hacking off her tawny hair.

"Hey," he said.

She spun around, going into a half crouch, the knife out in front of her. "*Zhdi zdes.*" A charred wisp of hair floated from the blade to the ground.

"Err . . . what?"

She shook the knife at him. "I . . ." Her face wasn't streaked with grease anymore, and her skin was pale, almost transparent under the morning sun. Her eyes were big and wild—with fear or maybe anger. Either way, she appeared more than ready to use the knife.

He raised his hands, trying to appear peaceable. "Look, it's okay. No speakum English, I get it."

"I . . ." she said, "am . . . having sorrow." She tapped the coveralls on her chest. "But . . . need."

"Okay, do speakum English." Or something like it.

She sure didn't seem likely to be part of a flying crew. So what did that leave? That she'd maybe been *thrown* out of that plane or whatever it was? That maybe that guy from last night had been shooting his flares at her on purpose—and not at Hitch?

"Look, why don't you give me that knife? Nobody wants to hurt you, and I'm sure you don't want to hurt me." He could hope anyway. "Matthew'll lend you what you need to wear, but he's not going to be too happy about losing the knife." He took a step and held out his hand.

She hissed, sort of like an angry cat, and jumped away. "You—back."

He walked his fingers across his palm. "I followed your tracks out here, understand? I wanted to make sure you were all right." And satisfy his own curiosity. Which currently was very far from satisfaction.

Her eyes shifted, and he could almost see the whir of her thoughts as she sifted through translations. "Follow me?" She didn't sound too impressed by his chivalry. "Kill you I will—you follow me! *Plohoi chelovek.*" She spat to the side and came back up glaring.

He dropped his arms to his sides. "Listen, sister, I ain't here to cause you any trouble. You want me to go, then after we explain to Matthew what's going on, I'll go. But it looks to me like you need a translator if you're going to go wandering around these parts."

She stared.

Not only had his plane nearly been hit by a human being

out of nowhere, she was a human being whose nowhere sure as gravy wasn't from around here. The gibberish she was yabbering wasn't anything he'd run across in his travels around the country. That ruled out Spanish, French, and probably Chinese.

If he went back to camp with this story, Earl would tie him up in the front cockpit and fly him straight out of here. There had to be a sensible explanation to it. Sensible-ish, anyway.

He opened his mouth. How did you ask someone who didn't speak English if she'd done something that wasn't possible?

The fluttering dress caught his eye. He pointed at it. "That. Where'd you get that?"

She shook her head, vehemently.

"Is it yours? Did you find it someplace, same as you did the overalls?" He wiggled his own shirt collar.

She sidestepped, past the wash line, into J.W.'s yard.

"Just tell me if you're from around here. Maybe I could help you get back to your family."

She almost seemed to get that one. Her eyes narrowed, as if thinking hard. She gave her head half a shake.

Finally, he just bit the bullet. "Where—do—you—*come*—from? Savvy?"

She straightened, and her hold on the knife eased. With her free hand, she pointed one finger straight up.

Oh, *that* answer was sure going to make Earl think he was sane. "You're saying you, what, live in the sky?"

She dipped her chin, once, and then her whole body froze. She whipped her head around, eyes scanning overhead, as if she heard something.

Like enough, it was a diversion. Get him to look too and then find a good hunk of muscle to sink the knife into.

But two could play that game. He lunged at her, caught her knife hand by the wrist, and forced it clear of his own body.

She screamed and struck out at his head with her free hand. She didn't have much meat on her bones, but she was tall and surprisingly strong. He caught that wrist too, and she started kicking at his shins.

"Ow! Just quit, will you? Drop the knife, and you can go. I'll even pay Matthew for the clothes. You don't have to stay to talk to him."

She shouted words at him, and they didn't sound too much like endearments. Up close, she smelled like engine grease, lye soap, and lake moss. Her eyes locked on his, and in back of all that fury, he saw fear. She was just a lost girl in a strange place, trying to keep her head above water.

Either that, or she was a foreign spy trained to kill people by kicking them to death.

The ball of her bare foot landed another thwack on his shin, just above his boot.

And then he heard what she'd heard: the buzz of plane engines, lots of them, maybe about five miles out. Had her people come back to pick her up? He risked a glance away from her, toward the sky.

That was when the shooting started.

The first shot smacked into Matthew's water barrel, and the report of a .22 rifle echoed. "Goldurn it, Matthew Berringer! Didn't I tell you to stay out of my tomatoes?"

Hitch ducked and yanked the girl down with him, barely keeping the knife away from his ribs. All around them, the red gleam of tomatoes peeked from behind brown-edged leaves. He pushed her backwards, tumbling them both behind a steel water tank.

Still hanging onto her knife-holding hand, he cocked his head back against the tank. "J.W., this is Hitch Hitchcock! It ain't Matthew, so for the love of Pete, stop your shooting!"

Another shot plinked into the tank and sprinkled water over their heads.

The girl tried to pull her hand away.

Hitch caught it fast in both of his. "Stop it, I tell you!"

"Eh?" J.W. said.

Matthew's back door slammed, and he came tromping out, shotgun under one arm, pulling up his overalls strap as he came. "Why do you have to go shooting everything up this time of the morning? I told you I locked my chickens in!"

"Maybe not chickens, but there's sure something in my tomato patch! If them tomatoes are ruined, you're accountable."

Overhead, the plane engines thrummed louder.

Hitch leaned sideways, trying to stick his head out enough for

Matthew to see him around the wash on the line—but not so far that J.W. could shoot it off. "Matthew—"

The girl released the knife and yanked her wrist free. She jumped to her feet and bolted.

Instinctively, he dove after her. "Wait, you idiot. You want to get shot?" He caught her rolled-up pants cuff and brought her down.

She scrambled back to her feet, and he barely managed to snag her waist. With another one of those non-endearments, she turned on him, both kicking and clawing this time.

He caught first one hand, then the other. "Just wait a minute!"

To either side of him, running footsteps tromped through the tomato patch. Next thing he knew, two gun barrels were pointed at him. Not at *them*. Just at him.

"Now hold up, sonny," Matthew said.

J.W. prodded Hitch with the .22. "Let her go. Don't know what Matthew's got to say about this, but I won't have no manhandling of ladies on *my* property."

Hitch's chuckle sounded forced even to him. "Let's all calm down here, shall we? You remember me? I used to work for you when I was a kid."

Matthew leaned his head back and surveyed Hitch through the round specs perched low on his nose. He was closing in on seventy, but his face was still smooth and hardly jowly at all.

"Well, bless my suspenders, so you did." He, at least, lowered his shotgun. "Hitch Hitchcock. Never thought we'd be seeing you again. How long has it been?"

Hitch huffed a sigh. "About nine years, I reckon."

Matthew glanced at the girl. "And who are you?"

She wasn't fighting anymore. She stared, first at the guns, then at the sky. The planes were almost overhead now.

"Don't know who she is," Hitch said. "But she's crazy. And she doesn't speak English."

J.W. gave him another poke in the ribs. "Let her go anyway."

The years hadn't been quite so kind to J.W. The top of his head was almost completely bald and peeling with an old sunburn. He still had his mustache, but it was stone gray now and in need of a trim.

"You heard me right enough," J.W. said. "I won't have no manhandling around here." The way he had of jutting his grizzled chin made him look like a badger on the prod.

"I don't think letting her go is such a great idea," Hitch said. "She already tried to stab me."

"Might be she had good reason, eh?"

Hitch glared. "I didn't do anything. *She* came in here, stole Matthew's clothes, and about scalped me."

"You're bigger'n her. Seems to me that evens the odds."

"Let her go," Matthew said. He looked at her. "You won't run, will you, miss?" He reached to tip a hat brim that wasn't there.

She stared at him, then at J.W., then finally at Hitch. She licked her lips and nodded.

"Fine, but you boys are asking for it." Hitch released her wrists.

She took off like a whitetail deer—but not toward the knife. In long-legged strides, she hurdled the water tank and bounded into J.W.'s yard.

"Watch the tomatoes!" J.W. shouted.

She reached the house and jumped to catch hold of the ornate porch railing that ran all the way around. Like some kind of squirrel, she hauled herself onto the railing, then shimmied up the support post to the porch roof.

J.W. started running. "What do you think you're doing? Get off my house, woman!"

Hitch and Matthew followed. By the time they reached the yard, she'd already clambered past the second-story balcony's roof and was half-running, half-climbing up the steep roof to where the third-story gable joined with the jutting tower.

Hitch stopped beside the house and shaded his eyes. "Get down! You want to kill yourself?"

The planes were shrieking into view now—Jennies most of them, all painted red, white, and blue. Little stars-and-stripes banners flew from their wingtips.

Col. Bonney Livingstone and His Extravagant Flying Circus had arrived—just as audaciously as they had all those years ago in Tennessee when Hitch had first worked for him.

His heart gave an extra pump.

"We have to do something," Matthew said. "She'll get hurt up there."

She didn't seem to share their concern. Wedging herself between the tower and the chimney, she practically bounced up to the tower window. Another second more and she was on the tower roof. She hung off the lightning rod, one foot braced at its bottom, the other dangling into nothing.

The planes buzzed past—over her head, on either side of her. The pilots waggled their wings and waved. Their turbulence whipped her oversized clothes and her chopped hair. She flung her free hand out to them and laughed. It was a crazy thing to do, but she actually didn't sound that crazy. More like delighted.

Which made no sense at all if somebody in an airplane had tossed her out last night. If it hadn't been a plane she'd been tossed out of, then . . . what did that leave?

CHAPTER 5

THE BUZZ OF the engines began to fade back out. The girl dropped her waving arm to her side and watched the planes until they were specks on the blue horizon.

"Now get back down here," J.W. said. "Before you fall off and break your durn neck."

Whether she understood or not, she lifted her shoulders in a sigh, then swung around the lightning rod to face them.

"Careful!" Matthew said. He looked at Hitch. "Maybe one of us should go up and help her."

Hitch gave a little groan, but took a step anyway.

If the girl was aware of their gallantry, she didn't seem too flattered. She dropped to the seat of her pants and slid down the steep roof as unconcernedly as she'd gone up.

Hitch lunged to the porch railing. "Hold on!"

She caught herself on the eaves and swung around until her bare toes found the tower windowsill. Half a minute later, she'd scrambled back down to the porch railing. She stood on the balustrade and looked them all over, eyebrows knit. She was probably wishing she'd kept the knife. But a little of the wild look from before had faded. Her eyes shone, as if the sight of the circus had filled her up with both adrenaline and joy all at once.

She definitely wasn't scared of the planes.

"Well," Matthew said. "Since we're all still in one piece, how about some breakfast?"

"Good luck getting her to stay," Hitch said.

She cocked her head. "Brakk fast?"

J.W. looked at Hitch. "Thought you said she didn't speak English."

"I think she understands more than she can say." Hitch imitated forking food into his mouth and chewing. "*Breakfast.* You know, food you eat in the morning." He offered her a hand down.

She contemplated his hand for a moment, then gave him a good hard look. Considering she'd only just gotten over thinking he was a threat worth knifing, her distrust made a fair amount of sense.

"I don't bite," he promised. "And I'm sorry about the scuffle."

She grunted. Then, ignoring his hand, she hopped the remaining five feet to the ground as if it was nothing.

He took a step back to get out of her way.

At first glance, she hadn't seemed like much to look at. Pale, almost transparent. But up close, she was pretty enough. She had high cheekbones, a sloping jaw, and a straight nose that might have looked harsh on someone else. But on her, it was tempered with an overall softness—a buoyant sweetness.

Of course, that sweetness was less than convincing in light of his throbbing shins.

She raised an eyebrow at his scrutiny, practically daring him to go on looking.

He gave her a wink and stepped out of the way.

Matthew turned back to his house. "C'mon."

"Hold onto yourself," J.W. said. "What gives you the right to go hogging the company?"

"The fact that I already have the skillet on. Mind your tomatoes, why don't you?"

J.W. snorted and stayed where he was.

Inside the sun-washed kitchen, Matthew propped his shotgun against the stove and set about cracking eggs, frying sausages, and flapping jacks. "Have a seat and tell me where this girl comes from. Where you come from, for that matter."

Hitch let the screen door bang. "Heard this big flying circus was coming to town. Decided it was time for a visit." He left it at that and held a chair out from the table for the girl. "As for her . . ."

She settled gingerly onto the edge of the chair and sat with her back straight, her fists knotted in her lap. She darted quick glances around the kitchen. When she caught both Matthew and Hitch watching her, she jerked her gaze down to her hands, then right back up: fear followed by defiance.

"I am having knowledge about you," she said. "Groundsmen. I am having knowledge how you are treating each other— even your people who are related." She jerked her head toward J.W.'s place.

Hitch took a chair across from her and turned it around so he could straddle it. "So you *do* speak English?"

"Ingleesh?" She leaned forward, as if trying to read his lips. Then she touched her mouth. "This?"

"What we're speaking, yeah."

"Um, yes. The *Sobirateli*—the . . . Foragers. They are where I am hearing from." She knit her eyebrows and stared at him. Maybe trying to ask if he understood her.

"And who are the Foragers? They're . . . Groundsmen?"

"*Nikogda.* Never."

He tried a different tack. "But they taught you English?"

"No. Teaching they are not." Her eyes flashed. "*Being allowed* to be knowing this Ingleesh is not for me. Just hearing them, and reading."

"You mean you read books in English? Taught yourself to speak it?"

She nodded. "Yes. But—" She tapped her ear. "Different from how—" She pointed to her eye.

He had to think about that for a minute. "It sounds different from how it looks?"

She nodded again.

Matthew put a pan lid over the crackle of his eggs and sausage. "Takes a heap of brains to do that."

If anybody knew about brains, it was Matthew. He'd always been the sort to read books most other folks had never even heard of. He was smart enough to have been more than a farmer—just not rich enough. Or maybe brave enough.

Matthew brought the first plate of flapjacks over to the table and set them next to a small blue ceramic pitcher of maple syrup. "Here you are, my dear."

"Tonk you." She looked at the plate, then picked up one of the flapjacks. It was so fluffy it compressed by nearly half between her fingers. She tore off a piece, glanced questioningly at Matthew, then dunked it in the syrup pitcher.

"Whoops, not like that." Hitch reached across the table and poured the syrup over the top of the flapjacks, then handed her the fork.

She took a bite of the pancake. When it hit her tongue, her eyes lit up. "*Prekrasno.*"

"You don't have to look so surprised," Matthew said.

Hitch hiked his chair a little closer. "So . . . where do you come from?"

She kept right on eating and pointed toward the ceiling.

Hitch glanced apologetically at Matthew. "She keeps saying she's from the sky." He turned back to her. "Meaning you work with flyers?" Or maybe just meaning she'd snorted a little too much water when she'd hit the lake last night.

Her delight in the airplanes flying over just now might not be the reaction of somebody who was afraid of them—but it also wasn't the reaction of somebody accustomed to spending a lot of time around them.

Matthew turned all the way around and gave her an appraising look.

"What about your friend?" Hitch asked. "The trigger-happy fella from last night? What happened to him? And how come nobody taught him about not using flare guns around a silk parachute?"

She flashed a look up and clenched her fist around her fork. "He is not friend."

"Okay." So the guy *had* been trying to light her on fire. "What happened to him?"

She curled her lip and shrugged. "Everything, I have hope."

Hitch glanced at Matthew.

But Matthew seemed absorbed in his own thoughts, shooting the girl a sideways look or two. In a moment, he put a folded towel down in the center of the table, then set the pan of sausages and eggs on top of it. After he'd pulled up his own chair, he served first Hitch, then himself.

Hitch got up and turned his chair around so he could eat.

The girl looked at each of the three plates, then at the empty fourth spot. She pointed at it, then at the door, toward J.W.'s place. "What about . . . *gromkiy chelovek?*"

"My brother prefers to eat in his own kitchen."

She didn't seem to quite get that, but Matthew didn't volunteer anymore and Hitch didn't blame him.

The Berringer brothers had been feuding for as long as he could remember. Something about a girl—Ginny Lou Thatcher, a fiery redhead of a gal. The story went that both of them had been crazy about her, but their competition to win her hand had spilled the bounds of brotherly affection. As it turned out, neither of them got the girl.

After their father died, they split the farm in two. Matthew kept his family's old farmhouse, and J.W. built that crazy mansion across the property line. Life had been a competition ever since, although J.W. seemed to take it a mite more seriously than Matthew.

Matthew poured milk for each of them. "I'm afraid my brother and I aren't exactly on friendly terms."

Footsteps stomped on the porch. Rifle still in one hand and a basket in the other, J.W. loomed outside the screen door. "If we ain't friendly, I reckon it's because certain parties think they can hide away the pretty misses at their table. Now, what's your name, girl?"

She stopped shoveling in the pancakes and licked a drop of syrup off her lower lip. She looked around the room, stopping to study each of their faces.

Then she swallowed. "Jael."

"Name like that, I'd say she's not from here," J.W. said.

Matthew had grace enough to refrain from pointing out they'd already covered that. He didn't invite J.W. in.

"You got any family around here?" J.W. asked. "Friends?"

She shook her head.

"You headed someplace?"

"To home."

Hitch stabbed another medallion of sausage. "Great."

"What's so bad about it?" J.W. asked.

Matthew salted his eggs. "She claims she lives in the sky."

"So what?" J.W. jutted his chin at Hitch. "You're a birdman, aren't you?"

"Not *that* good a one."

Jael finished her last bite of pancake and ran her finger around the edge of her plate to catch the remaining syrup. She licked it off, then looked at Hitch. She hesitated, her eyes dark with something: fear, uncertainty, desperation maybe.

She pointed at the floor. "Groundsworld." She pointed at the ceiling. "*Schturming*. To Groundsworld I am falling. Now I am *having* to go home before time is too late. Please. But you cannot be talking of this—to any persons on ground."

Hitch cleared his throat. "Right. Well, we won't say a word." He glanced at Matthew and J.W. "But in the meantime, you got any place to stay?"

She shook her head.

"She could stay here," Matthew said. "A bit of company wouldn't go amiss."

J.W. scoffed. "Where would you keep her in this mousetrap? I'm the one who's got plenty of empty rooms."

"That, J.W. Berringer, is your own fault."

"Like thunder it is."

Hitch swiped up a dollop of yolk with the last of his sausage. "Maybe she should stay closer to town. In case somebody she knows comes looking for her."

Matthew thought for a second, then nodded. "You're right. The gossips wouldn't find it proper anyway, a girl like her staying out here with two old bachelors."

J.W. harrumphed.

Hitch rocked his chair back to its hind legs. "Well, then, you know somebody who will take her?"

"You're the one that found her, son," Matthew said.

"Me?" He looked at her, then at J.W. and Matthew in turn.

"If she's from upwards, that would certainly seem to be more your purview than anybody's, don't you think?"

"Probably," J.W. said, "she's with that fancy flying outfit that just buzzed over. You best take her over that way and see if she belongs."

Hitch shook his head. "She's not a flyer." She wasn't a jumper either, unless he missed his guess. "So when I get her out there to the pilots' camp and nobody has a notion who she is, what do you think I'm going to do with her then?"

"Find her a place to stay."

He laughed. "I haven't got time for that. I've got to make some money. You wouldn't know of any day jobs around, would you?"

"That ain't the point here," J.W. said. "The point is you found this girl, so you gotta do something about it."

Hitch didn't have time to deal with this. He could barely find bedrolls and meals for his own crew, much less an addled girl. "I found her in *Matthew's* backyard."

She looked at him from across the table, steadily. Who knew if she understood what was going on, but those smoky gray eyes seemed to look right through him—still fearful, still distrusting.

And that was ever so slightly irritating. Most girls thought the devil-may-care lifestyle of a gypsy pilot was the most romantic thing ever. But of course, most girls weren't crazy.

He stared back at her. *Was* she crazy? Or was she smart, like Matthew said, and just as sane as he was?

Of course, Hitch's family—and Celia too—wouldn't have said sanity was his strongest point. He was a pilot after all.

But he'd seen enough of the world to know what crazy looked like. And this girl didn't look crazy. Wild, like an unbroke filly, definitely. Maybe a little reckless, judging from the way she'd scaled J.W.'s house without a second thought. But if flying had taught him one thing, it was that reckless and crazy didn't have to be the same thing, so long as you knew what you were capable of.

This girl wasn't crazy. She was lost and she was scared. After last night, who wouldn't be? There was no reason to think the guy with the flare gun wasn't still around—and still trigger-happy. Reuniting Jael with him obviously wasn't an option. But if Hitch could find the guy, that just might answer a lot of questions—and give him a lead on what he could do with her.

He thumped the chair back onto all fours. "Fine. I'll take her with me. Maybe somebody'll know where she comes from." He stood and beckoned her to follow.

She stood up warily. "To where do you go with me?"

"To town. See if we can find somebody who can help you get home."

Her eyes lit up at that, but then she bit her lip.

"Look," he said. "You don't trust me—that's fine. I can spare you a little help *if* you want it. But I won't make you say no twice."

She shook her head, slowly. "You are Groundsman."

"No, I ain't." He gave her a grin. "The sky's my home too."

"Then . . . you will be helping me to go to home?"

"Well, we'll see if we can find somebody who *can* help. And I'll get you someplace safe to stay in the meantime. Best I can do right now."

She tucked her chin in a nod. "Then, yes."

"All right." He gestured her toward the door. "But I swear, if you kick me one more time, that's it."

She wrinkled her nose, confused, as J.W. opened the screen door for her.

"Hitch," Matthew said—then paused a moment until she was out of earshot. "Wait just one second. Before you go on with her, there's something you should know." He pushed his old man's bones up from the table and circled around. He dropped his voice. "I want you to understand me: wherever it is she's from, I think she needs help. But . . . you've heard about the bodies, haven't you?"

"Bodies?"

"Five so far, I think. Mostly out around Lake Minatare, a few in some pastures nearby. Nobody knows who they were. But ol' Scottie Shepherd—you remember him?—he's been swearing up and down he saw one fall."

Gooseflesh creased the skin on the back of Hitch's neck. "Fall from where?"

"That's the sticker, ain't it?" And just like Jael had done earlier, Matthew pointed a finger at the ceiling. "Now, you tell me. How's that possible?"

The chill spread. "How should I know?"

"You're a flyer. You know what's up there."

He shrugged. "Sky, clouds—occasionally me. C'mon, Matthew, people don't fall out of nowhere." He felt like he was parroting Earl's rebuttals from last night. "They had to come from a plane."

Matthew regarded him. He didn't look convinced. "Her too?"

Hitch looked through the screen door to where she stood listening to J.W. going on about the drought or some such.

Part of him just wanted to say *yes*. Yes, she jumped from a plane. Yes, all these bodies had been chucked out of a plane.

But it wasn't as if planes were exactly common around these parts. Before this week, there was no reason at all why pilots should be flying over Scottsbluff, Nebraska—much less tossing people out at five thousand feet.

He might have dismissed the whole notion of the bodies even having fallen at all—except for her. He'd *seen* her. And night flight or no night flight, he'd still swear up and down his Jenny had been the only plane out there.

So what did that leave? That she'd jumped off a cloud?

Obviously not. But maybe the question here wasn't *how*, but *why*? Somebody'd been after her, that was clear. But again: *why*?

He looked at Matthew and shook his head. "You want answers that make sense? Don't ask me. I gotta tell you, I ain't ever seen anything like this one."

But if he could find Jael's attacker, that might put a period to a lot of questions. If the man was anything like her, he was going to stick out in Scottsbluff like a society grand dame at a county fair.

CHAPTER 6

B Y THE TIME they reached town, the noon sun was pouring heat on their heads. Scottsbluff had grown considerable since Hitch left nine years ago. Main Street was still dirt, but the raised sidewalks were paved now. The rows of cottonwoods were long gone, together with the buggies. Now, dusty Model Ts chugged up and down, and a six-story brick building—Lincoln Hotel painted across its front—dominated the row of stores and cafes. They even had electric lampposts and, on one corner, a drinking fountain.

Strange how things moved on without you.

He hooked his hands in his pockets and squinted down the street. "Wouldn't even know it's the same town I grew up in." He looked over his shoulder at Jael.

She was busy twisting the drinking fountain's knob. When the water started trickling out, she laughed. Her gaze flashed up to his, delighted.

They must not have these admittedly newfangled things up on her cloud. He grinned back at her.

Just like that, her delight faltered into uncertainty. She deliberately looked away and cupped a handful of water to start cleaning the dirt from her bare feet. Matthew and J.W. hadn't had any shoes that would fit her, so she'd walked barefoot all the way into town. The soft dirt on the roads had been easy enough on her feet, but now she was a dusty mess.

Several ladies in flower print dresses and cloche hats passed by, watching her from the corners of their eyes.

Hitch winced. "You know, maybe we should find you someplace else to do that."

She straightened, then turned the knob once more. "Very beautiful, this thing." It was about the first full sentence she'd said since leaving Matthew's, despite Hitch's best attempts to make conversation.

"Yeah, it's pretty nifty." He turned back up the street and surveyed his options.

"Where do you go to?" she asked.

"Have to find someplace for you to hide out, have to make some money, and then I have to hightail it back to camp. Those planes you saw go over—they're why I'm here. There's going to be a big airshow, like nothing anybody here has ever seen before."

She shook her head, obviously not picking up on much of what he was saying.

He beckoned. "C'mon."

He selected a dry-goods store—Fallon Bros.—halfway down the street. He didn't recognize it, or the name, so maybe the folks inside wouldn't recognize him either. All things considered, he was likely to get more for the gun from a stranger.

He pushed through the door, Jael treading softly after him. The big front room was whitewashed and airy. The shelves along the walls and the island counters down the center offered everything from ready-cut dresses to stick horses to electric fans. A modish clerk with slicked-back hair and a half apron stood behind a glass-fronted case.

Hitch pasted on a grin and approached. "Howdy. Would you be interested in swapping?"

The man—one of the Mr. Fallons probably—smoothed his hair. "Not exactly my line." He watched Jael retreat to the back of the store, his look somewhere between doubt and interest.

Hitch leaned against the counter. "Wouldn't want a pretty girl to go without lunch today, would you?"

Fallon looked back to Hitch. "That hard up, are you?"

"Just temporary. I've got a Colt .45. It's in good shape." He pulled it from the back of his waistband, popped the empty cylinder, and handed it over, grip first.

As soon as the gun left his hand, he had doubts. If ever he found the flare shooter, he just might want a gun of his own. He looked back at Jael.

She stood with her hands clasped behind her back, peering at a display of mustache cups.

Thing was, if he didn't find her a place today, he was going to need that extra cash a sight more than he currently needed the gun.

He turned back.

Fallon grunted as he examined the revolver. "Not from around here, are you?"

"Not recently. I'm here for the big airshow."

"Oh, yes, I saw the posters around town." Fallon glanced again at Jael. She was now out of earshot. "She in the show, is she?"

Hitch kept the grin going. "Not officially."

The front door opened with a rush of heat and a tinkle of the bell.

Behind him, someone inhaled sharply.

"Morning, Mrs. Carpenter," Fallon said.

Hitch's stomach clenched. His grin slipped entirely. He straightened away from the counter and turned.

Three women stood framed in the sunlight from the two big display windows. The two in front were Celia's older sisters—Nan and Aurelia. The slender third, red wisps escaping from beneath her straw hat brim, must be Nan's girl Molly, all grown up.

"You," Nan said. She clutched her handbag as if it were his neck.

Of all the people here, Nan was the one most likely to hate him until she died of it. Her—and maybe his brother Griff. He'd known that. He just hadn't figured it'd hit him in the gut quite so hard.

He fitted his hands into his pockets. "Hello, Nan. I guess I've come home."

"It's ten years too late for you to come home, Hitch Hitchcock."

Molly shot her mother a wide-eyed glance.

"Oh, it's all right." Aurelia wafted over. She was as pale as ever, her eyes unblinking. "I remember you. You married Celia, didn't you? Poor Celia. She's dead now. Did you know that?"

Hitch's heart stumbled just once. "Yeah. I . . . know."

"I remember you gave me half a taffy in the schoolyard, and you tied my sash to Laura Everby's in Sunday school. How charming." She extended her hand, bidding him kiss it.

Aurelia had been stuck in some kind of fairyish dream ever since she'd fallen out of the haymow when she was twelve.

He squeezed her hand gently. "You still look like a princess, Aurelia."

She laughed and twirled around. She was wearing a violet scarf as a shawl, and it spread around her elbows in diaphanous wings.

He turned back. His mouth was as dry as the drought. Nan was still glaring Black Death at him, so he turned instead to her daughter. "This must be Molly. You probably don't remember me. You must be, what? Fifteen by now?"

The girl dropped her eyelashes in a slow blink. It looked like an expression she'd practiced in front of the mirror more than a few times. "How d'you do? You're a pilot, aren't you? That's awfully ducky." She extended a hand.

"Stop it," Nan said. She was trembling, and her eyes were huge, almost with outright panic. There was a fair share of anger too.

"I'm sorry." His words came out before he even had time to think them. Lord knew he'd thought them plenty often in the last nine years. "I should have come back for her funeral."

"You shouldn't have left in the first place."

Nan's dark hair was pinned in a simple bun at the back of her neck, beneath her hat. She had been the prettiest of the sisters—more color than Aurelia, smaller features than Celia. But the years had weathered her skin and drawn fine lines around her eyes and her mouth. She was rail thin, the muscles in her tanned forearms ropy and hard.

She stared into his eyes. "You ruined Celia's life when you left."

From the first moment he'd heard Col. Livingstone was holding his show in Scottsbluff, he'd known this was coming. People around here would hold him accountable for what had happened to Celia. And maybe, in more than a small way, they were right.

Regrets weren't too valuable, so he didn't keep them around. But this one had stuck anyway, year after year, despite his best attempts to justify what had happened. He couldn't have stopped Celia's dying, not even if he had risked staying here while Sheriff Campbell cooled off. But there were too many other promises he'd made her that he hadn't had enough time to keep.

"I never knew she was sick," he said.

"Of course you didn't." Nan's voice squeaked, the way it always did when she was beyond angry.

"You act like I was never coming back."

"You never did."

"After she died, I didn't have a reason to." He tried to bite back the defensiveness. Nan was Celia's sister. If he'd hurt Celia, then of course he'd hurt Nan too. "And besides, other things were going on you didn't know about." Things like Bill Campbell threatening his family and wanting to throw him in jail.

"You were *married* to her, Hitch!"

That was the crux of it, wasn't it? No one could have blamed him for her death. But he *had* married her—in a summer of folly. And when it came right down to it, maybe the thing he felt most guilty for was the little bubble of relief that sometimes surfaced and broke. Because if she'd lived and he'd had to live with her, wouldn't they all have been the more miserable?

Nan clenched her handbag harder, almost hard enough to stop the trembling. "You couldn't just settle down and work a farm, like everybody else?"

"You know that's not who I am. It's never who I've been."

The look of fear swam up to the surface of her eyes once again. "Which means you're not planning on staying now either."

Anger, he understood. He'd expected anger—deserved it in some respects. Anger, he could deal with. But what cause could she possibly have to be afraid of him? He had no ways left to hurt her. She had to know that as well as he did.

His leaving again couldn't hurt her. If she hated him as much as all this, then surely that would be what she wanted anyway.

He cleared his throat. "I'll be going at the end of the week. Soon as the show's over."

"Of course. The airshow." Her mouth stiffened. "I should have guessed you'd come back for *that*."

His stomach turned over again. "I never meant to hurt you, Nan. You or Celia—or anybody else."

She held his gaze for a long moment. "That makes it worse, I think." Then she glanced past him. Her face hardened again.

He followed her gaze to the back of the store to see Jael and Aurelia standing next to a rack of dresses.

Admittedly, Jael did look more than a little bizarre, with her uneven haircut and her muddy feet. Matthew's clothes were so big on her she was practically falling out of them. She had to keep hiking the overalls strap back over her shoulder to keep the whole thing on.

Next to her, Aurelia was murmuring happily and holding dresses up to Jael's chin. The wild filly look still backed Jael's eyes, but she seemed to understand Aurelia was no threat. She stood quietly, letting Aurelia have her fun, while she, in turn, studied Hitch and Nan, brows knit hard.

Hitch turned back to Nan. "That's Jael. She's a . . . friend."

"I can see that." Nan's tone said she was seeing more than was actually there to be seen.

Molly edged out from behind her mother. She smiled at him. "Must be awfully exciting, flying all over the world like you do. Aren't you in constant danger up there?"

"It's a lot safer than you might think. If you've got a good pilot." He glanced at Nan.

If she could see the life he'd built—*was* building—for himself, would there be some small part of her that would understand why he'd never come back after Celia's death? He was plenty good at what he did, even if it had never mattered much to the folks back here. He might not own a farm or have a family any longer, but his life was a long shot from the waste they all wanted to believe it was.

He turned back to Molly. "I'll take you up sometime this week. If your mother says."

"Absolutely not," Nan said.

Hitch took a breath and gave it one more try. "Then why not come out and see the show Saturday." It would give him another reason to win. If she could see he wasn't just some worthless tramp, maybe it would help her understand he *hadn't* up and left Celia.

He hadn't left her out of irresponsibility. He'd left her because staying only would have hurt her—would have hurt all of them. Then, after she'd died, he'd stayed out there with the planes, because . . . it was the only place in the world that had ever felt *right*.

Nan shook her head, hard.

Fine. He'd give her the space she wanted. But he was here for a week. Before he had to leave again, he'd make things right—or right*er* at any rate. If he could fly a Jenny upside-down and only a foot off the ground, then surely he could do this one thing and make this better for her before he left for good.

Nan took Molly's elbow and drew her back a step. She raised her voice. "Aurelia, come along. The sooner Mr. Hitchcock returns to his red flying machine, the better."

Jael had wandered over, near enough to hear that last part. Her mouth came open, and she jerked forward half a step.

Nan caught Hitch's eye as she turned away. "We'll leave you and your charming *companion* to finish up on your own."

"Give me a break. You've got a right to take your spleen out on me. But don't go chucking mud on her."

"Oh, certainly, because any woman in your presence is instantly above reproach."

He held the silence for a second. "That's way below you, Nan."

She had the grace to blush, a hard line of red along either cheekbone. "Then who is she?"

"Don't know. Found her out at the Berringers' this morning." He gestured for Jael to come forward.

She eased away from the print dress Aurelia had followed her with, but she barely looked at Nan. "Red—flying? That is you? Like—" She made engine noises and gestured as if her hands were planes. "Out at two men's who try to kill each other?"

Then she hadn't connected him with the plane she'd about smacked into last night?

"Yeah, I fly a plane—a red one."

"*Fly?* But you are"—she looked at the women, then back at Hitch—"you are Groundsman. You are not having fear for this?"

"Well, I admit I ain't so keen on heights, but that don't matter so much when you're in a plane." He caught Nan's suspicious expression and cleared his throat. "Look—"

Jael came near enough to touch his sleeve with her fingertips. She lowered her voice. "*You* could take me home!"

Her home in the sky wasn't anything he wanted brought up in front of Nan. He cleared his throat. "Yeah, well, we'll talk about that later." He looked at Nan. "Her English isn't all that great. She needs a place to stay. Don't suppose you'd have one for her?"

"What she *needs* are some decent clothes."

"Don't think she's got any money."

Nan glanced at the counter. "You do."

Fallon, standing back a few discreet steps, had laid a handful of bills beside the .45. He stepped forward. "The piece is a bit banged up. Afraid I can only give you fifteen dollars for it." He nodded toward Jael. "Ten if you want the dress and fixings while you're here."

Fifteen was a few bucks more than Hitch had hoped to get for that old piece, and he wouldn't need quite all of it to buy Earl's parts. He looked back at Jael. She *did* appear more than a mite disreputable. Likely, she'd have a better chance of finding some place to stay if she got some clothes that were the correct size.

"All right. Let her pick out what she wants." He glanced at her and gave his own shirt a tug. "Clothes. Find yourself some clothes that fit."

Aurelia clapped her hands and turned to sort through the dress rack once again.

Nan pulled Molly toward the door. "Aurelia, we're leaving."

Molly cast Hitch a half-embarrassed look. "Awfully nice to have met you."

"Aurelia," Nan called.

Aurelia growled, then thrust the dress into Jael's arms and turned to skip back across the room to the door. She patted Hitch's shoulder as she passed. "Goodbye, dear man." She reached Nan and looped her arm through her sister's. "Isn't that girl the charmingest thing? Violet is her color, I am sure."

"Mmm." Nan pushed the door open, letting in another gust of heat. She paused. "Miss—" She waited until Jael met her gaze. "Be careful."

Jael had draped Aurelia's dress back over the rack. She raised her eyebrows, not understanding, then looked from Nan to Hitch and back again. "I have knowledge of how Groundsmen are." But the expression she turned on Hitch was more puzzled than anything. "Maybe I have knowledge."

Hitch watched Nan and the others go. Jael's knowledge sure seemed to be doing her more good than everything he'd *thought* he knew about his folks back home.

He never would have realized Nan would still be hurting so badly over this. Even if she blamed him for all of it, it had been *nine years*.

Didn't seem to be much she wanted to let him even try to do to make it right. But he'd have to do something. Last time, he'd left without being able to say goodbye to anybody but Celia. Maybe landing back here at home meant this time he could put it all to rights before moving on again.

The first thing he had to do here was figure out how to remedy his other little problem.

He looked over at Jael. "Find some clothes. Then we've got some ground to cover if we're going to get you back to *your* home."

CHAPTER 7

OUT ON THE street, Hitch studied Jael's new outfit. "I think maybe you'd have been better off staying in the overalls."

Back in Fallon Bros., she'd emerged from behind the dressing stall's curtain in breeches, knee-high boots, and a loose cream blouse that hugged her hips. With her hair tied back in a turkey-red handkerchief, she looked like some kind of pirate queen. He'd sputtered a protest or two, but paid up, even when Fallon tacked on an extra dollar for the boots.

He stepped around in front of her so he could give her another once over. At least the clothes fit—and her chopped hair and bare feet were covered. Still, she didn't look normal. And around here, folks who were good enough to take in strangers liked those strangers to at least have the decency of looking like everybody else.

"Why didn't you take the dress Aurelia gave you?"

She firmed her mouth in a prim line. "Was being too short for . . . properness."

"Properness?" What she was wearing now would probably give the local ladies heart failure. Nice country girls didn't wear breeches. If they were being extra practical, they wore overalls in the fields, but that was about it.

"And what is it you wear normally?" he asked.

The corner of her mouth lifted just a bit. "I am not being proper mostly." A twinkle lit the back of her eyes. "I wear . . . like this." She gestured at her new outfit. "Only all one."

"A jumpsuit? And what about that great big ball gown thing you had on last night?"

"That was for special day. Like, everybody come together and have fun."

"Celebration?"

The twinkle died. "Only was not for me. The—what you call ball gown—had no belonging to me. I was taking it for . . . so people would not be knowing me at *celebration.*" She pulled in a big breath, as if dispersing the memory. "Red plane you are flying? *Oplata*—um, payment—I will be finding. Groundsmen, they are doing anything to get payment. I have knowledge for this."

"You might want to consider you don't know as much about Groundsmen as you think you do."

He started down the raised sidewalk. He needed to be getting the money for the parts back to Earl pronto. And then there was Jael's buddy from last night. He cast a glance up and down both sides of the street. Could be the guy had his plane—or whatever—stowed someplace near town. He wasn't likely to be anybody Hitch had already seen at the pilots' camp.

"I have knowledge enough about your Groundsworld," Jael said. "Going home is what I *must* do."

He raked a hand through his hair. "Home's a place where people want what you don't have it in you to give them. And then they blame you for not having it to give to them in the first place."

"Yes." She trudged along behind him. "This I am having knowledge about Groundsmen too."

"What's that?"

"Your families you are not liking. You take no care for them."

He stopped short, just outside of Dan and Rosie's Cafe. "There, right there. That's one of your snarled-up facts. First of all, I'm not exactly typical of Groundsmen." Not that she had been near enough to hear most of his conversation with Nan about Celia. "Second, I didn't say anything about not loving my family. I'm just not good at pretending I belong someplace I don't."

"This pretend—this means what?"

"Means acting like something's real when it's not."

She fiddled with her cuff. "This pretending, it is not better than never to be belonging?"

He shrugged. "Everything comes with a price."

The greasy smell of fried chicken wafted out of the cafe's open door.

Jael's stomach rumbled audibly.

He looked through the open door.

From inside the cafe, Lilla leaned back on a red counter stool and waved at him. "Hitch! Come inside! They have the most fabulous orange phosphate."

He felt the remaining dollars in his pocket. His own middle felt pretty pinched at that. It had been hours since Matthew fed them breakfast.

He gestured Jael to walk in front of him. "C'mon."

The cafe was just one small front room, filled with square tables. A counter with swiveling stools separated the dining area from the cash register and the shelves of dishes. Beyond that, the kitchen was visible through the serving window in the wall.

Behind the counter, a short, balding man in a stained apron stopped polishing a mug and squinted. "I'll be dogged. Hitch Hitchcock, is that you?"

Jael shot Hitch a narrow look, both eyebrows going up.

He tapped her arm to guide her forward. "It's all right, I knew him back when."

Still, she walked slowly, her weight on the balls of her feet, her hands loose at her sides, like she was ready to run—or more likely fight—if one of the old codgers inside decided to wave a fork at her.

He took her elbow, as much to keep her from doing anything stupid as to reassure her.

Dan Holloway raised the empty mug he'd been polishing and grinned. "Well, so it is. The prodigal back after all these years." He looked at the room at large. "Didn't I tell you he'd be back?"

Hitch glanced around. He recognized most of the folks dining at the checked-cloth tables. Two oldsters by the door—Scottie Shepherd and Lou Parker—didn't look a bit different from how they had when he'd left. According to Matthew, Scottie was the one who'd seen one of those bodies fall out of the sky.

Lou dabbed his mustache with the end of the napkin stuck in his collar. "And aren't you the spitting image of your daddy?"

He gave Hitch's arm a slap as he passed. "Bless his soul."

Hitch's insides twitched. His dad's was another funeral he should have come back for. But he and his old man hadn't parted on good terms. For that matter, they hadn't been on good terms since Hitch's mother died when he was eleven. His dad never quite understood how flying could be so much better than farming.

Hitch managed a grin. "But handsomer, right?"

Scottie turned in his seat to watch Hitch cross the room. A day's whiskers covered his cheeks and ketchup stained his overalls' bib. "Well, you surprised me, son. We heard all kinds of rumors about you running off with some kind of shipment you were flying out for Sheriff Campbell. If that's the truth, then I'm surprised you're back at all."

That *would* be what Campbell would have them all believing.

"Calling me a thief, old-timer?" He managed to keep his tone light—barely.

Scottie shrugged. "Eh. Rumors is rumors."

"And you believe them?"

Scottie grinned. "Might've—if you hadn't ever come back."

Lou didn't look quite so convinced. "I expect the sheriff generally knows what he's talking about, don't you?"

At the counter, Hitch stopped and looked back. "Campbell's not still sheriff, is he?"

Scottie's eyes twinkled. "Ain't he though? Why'd we kick the best sheriff we ever had out of office? Older they get, the better they get. Ain't that right, Lou?"

Oh, gravy. That was bad. Hitch's smile grew more and more wooden. He turned to take a seat next to Lilla, with Jael on his other side.

"You look poorly," Lilla observed. "Have an orange phosphate." She stuck another straw in hers and passed it over.

How stupid could he be? Nan's anger—that he could deal with. But Bill Campbell was another matter altogether.

There were lots of reasons he hadn't come home when Celia died, but if you rooted around to the very bottom of it, what you'd find was Bill Campbell. Folks must still have no idea what Campbell was capable of pulling behind their backs.

Sure, Campbell was a good sheriff. The *reason* he was so good was that the only rules he played by were his own, and one of those rules was making sure people like Hitch never got a second opportunity to defy him.

Dan slung his towel over one shoulder. "Don't worry about Campbell. Your brother will fix it all, I expect."

"My brother?" Hitch looked up. "What do you mean?"

"Why, Griff's a deputy now, didn't you know?"

His little brother was working for Campbell? His ears buzzed. Griff knew better than that. He'd always been the smart one—the straight one.

"When did that happen?"

"Oh, about seven years, I reckon. He's a good deputy too. You haven't seen him?"

"Not yet."

Dan picked up his notepad and pencil. "Well, what'll you have, lady and gent?"

"Um." Hitch ordered from memory. "Roast beef, mashed potatoes, and green beans." Except in his memory, he'd been a lot richer. "Or wait, just two cheese sandwiches and two cups of coffee."

Lilla took her glass back. "You're missing out. The orange phosphate is delicious. I'm waiting for Rick. He finally found a station to put gasoline in the motorcar. He thought the first two places were disrespecting him."

"What'd they say?"

She shrugged. "I didn't notice."

Probably because there hadn't been anything *to* notice.

Lilla leaned forward to see around Hitch. "Hi, there. I'm Lilla Malone."

On the other stool, Jael sat about as easy as a broncbuster on a confirmed outlaw. She gripped the edge of the counter and kept looking over her shoulder. She eyed Lilla, then glanced at Hitch.

He nodded. "It's all right. Lilla works for me. This is Jael."

Lilla reached past Hitch to offer her hand. "How do?"

Jael looked at it.

"She's not from around here," Hitch said.

"Oh, well, that's all right." Lilla pulled her hand back. "I'm new here too, come to that. Your kerchief is lovely."

Jael touched her head, then smiled. Her whole face changed when she smiled. The hard angles faded, and the silver specks in her eyes sparkled.

"Tonk you."

"So you're a friend of Hitch's? From when he lived here?"

"Not exactly," Hitch said. "I kind of found her this morning. I'm trying to get her a place to stay."

"Oh, that's no problem. She can stay with us."

"No, she's got to be here—in town—so that when her friends come looking for her, they'll know where to find her."

Jael snorted. "Friend? No. If someone come, he is not friend." Then she actually turned her head to the side and spat on the floor.

"Hey!" Dan dumped the two sandwich plates onto the counter. "What kind of establishment do you think this is?" He flipped his towel into her lap. "Get right down and clean that up."

Her eyes got dark. She stood up from the stool and tensed the arm holding the towel, *that* close to snapping it back in Dan's face.

Hitch caught her arm. "Now just you wait."

She tried to jerk away.

"Hold up a minute. The man's not asking you to do anything unreasonable. You got to understand that around here, spitting inside—especially *ladies* spitting inside—ain't exactly the thing."

Behind him, Scottie scoffed. "*Lady?*"

Lilla twirled her stool around. "Hey!"

Jael tried to twist free again, but uncertainty edged her face.

Hitch lowered his voice. "Trust me."

She hesitated. Then she dropped to her knees and swiped the towel across the planks.

Before she could come back up, a familiar roar howled down the street outside.

Hitch's heart revved like it always did at the sound of a plane engine. He joined the general movement to the windows.

A star-spangled Jenny buzzed the street, so low her landing gear cleared the lampposts by only a yard. People outside ducked as the winged shadow sliced overhead. They came back up, hollering and waving. In the rear cockpit, the pilot held out his own hat—a white Stetson.

Col. Livingstone himself had come to promote his circus.

The man was a heckuva showman. That was why he owned one of the biggest airshows in the country. But he wasn't half the pilot Hitch was. And *that* was why, before many years more, Hitch would end up owning an even bigger airshow.

Winning this weekend's competition would be a start. What he really needed was to get Livingstone to strike a deal, hiring Hitch's crew to do their act as part of his circus for a while. Although it wasn't a long-term strategy, that kind of regular work would give them the start they needed. But *first* he had to figure out the right kind of stunt to get Livingstone to notice him to begin with.

The plane whipped on by. Then the engine cut out. No doubt Livingstone was putting her down in an empty street so the folks could come out and see the plane for themselves. Nothing was so sure for luring customers to a show—and nothing mattered more to Livingstone than the luring of them.

"Whooee!" Lou said. "I wouldn't ride in one of them contraptions if you paid me." He cast a sideways glance at Scottie. "A feller might fall out."

"You wait," Hitch said. "Before the week's out, you'll be paying me to take you up."

"I'd go up there with you," Scottie said. "People been fallin' straight out of the sky lately, haven't you heard? Somebody needs to go up there and see to what's happening."

Hitch glanced at Jael beside him.

But she wasn't watching Scottie—or the plane. She was staring across the street. Her face had gone as pale as alkaline soil, and she gasped, fast and hoarse.

"What's the matter?" Hitch asked.

"Zlo." And then, out of the back of her boot, came Matthew's knife.

"Whoa, now." He jumped away. "I thought we were past all that!"

She turned toward the door and, in her haste, smacked into Lou. He backpedaled, arms windmilling. His feet tangled with hers, and he fell backwards, pulling her down with him. She landed on top of him, her elbow in his stomach, the knife only inches away from his mustache. Behind his specs, his eyes bulged.

Dan dove into the fray. "What in tarnation? Get this crazy woman off him!" He reached for her knife hand.

She flipped over like a cat, rolling away from Lou and coming up in a crouch. She held the knife out in front, the other hand groping behind her for the door. Her teeth were bared in a snarl, but her eyes were big and afraid.

Hitch eased toward her, palms extended. "Calm down. Nobody's going to hurt you. Just give me the knife. You don't need a knife."

"Now, I don't know," Lilla said, from over his shoulder. "A girl never knows when a knife might come in handy."

"Shut up, Lilla."

Dan and Scottie backed Jael up against the big window.

"Wait a minute," Hitch said. "She doesn't mean anything. She's scared, can't you see that?"

"You think Lou *ain't?*" Scottie said.

Dan grabbed a chair and held it up, like a lion-tamer. He lunged forward, and Jael lunged sideways. One of the chair legs caught the corner of the window and went all the way through. The whole thing shattered in a rain of glass.

"Oh, great," Hitch said.

Jael ducked around the corner of the open door and disappeared.

Lilla pushed Hitch. "Well, go after her."

He followed Jael down the sidewalk and around the corner.

She had stopped and turned back, and she practically plowed into his chest.

The knife was still out, so he caught both her wrists and pushed her back against the wall.

She struggled. "*Pozhaluista, pozhaluista.* Here he is, I must be gone. Please!" She looked up at him, desperate, pleading.

He wasn't about to let her go. Not after what she'd pulled

out at the Berringers'. But he loosened his grip. "Look, it's all right. Nobody's going to hurt you. We'll go back to the cafe. Everything'll be fine."

"No!" She bucked against him. At least, she wasn't kicking. "If he sees me— He cannot see me! I will be not having breath—I will be *mertvaya*—I will be dead!"

"It's the other jumper from last night?" He looked over his shoulder, saw nothing worth seeing, then turned back. "Who is he? How come he shot that flare at you? And at me too, come to that?"

She only shook her head, panting. "Help me to leave far away from here! Please!"

This was not a good time for him to leave town. The one thing he needed to do this week was impress Livingstone. And Livingstone was *here* in town. For the moment, Hitch had the man all to himself. If ever he was to get a solo opportunity to help Livingstone promote the show—and get in good with him—this was going to be it. But then again, even though Hitch was here, and Livingstone was here—Hitch's Jenny surely *wasn't*.

He glanced over his shoulder again.

People milled down the sidewalks. They all looked like ordinary Joes. Farmers, bankers, workers from the sugar-beet factory on the edge of town. Nobody seemed interested in Jael, much less champing at the bit to do her harm.

But he couldn't just leave her. For one thing, who knew what she'd do now that she was all worked up again. And for another . . . the kind of fear burning in her eyes didn't show up out of nowhere. In fact, it was kinda making the skin on the back of his own neck itch.

So much for giving her back to whoever she belonged to.

He sighed. "You're turning into a whole lot of trouble, you know that?"

She shook her head, not understanding.

If he was going to get her out of here, he needed a plane. If he was going to get Livingstone's attention, he also needed a plane. And the only plane around right now was painted red, white, and blue.

"Give me the knife."

She clenched it harder, her eyes boring into his, as if trying to get at the core of him. Then just like that, she let it go. It clanked to the sidewalk.

"All right." He left the knife where it was and let her up from the wall, keeping hold of one of her wrists. "I've got an idea. It's crazy, but it might work out for both of us."

It might work out *if* Livingstone was as big a sportsman as Hitch remembered him being—and *if* the ploy drew in the crowds like he thought it would—and *if* he didn't get arrested first.

He pulled her off the curb. "Stay close!"

They ran across two roads, dodging honking automobiles, and sprinted down the sidewalk to where Col. Livingstone had landed his plane. The man himself was standing a few yards off, pontificating to the gathered crowd. Nobody paid too much attention when Hitch snuck himself and Jael right on by. He loaded her into the front cockpit, started up the engine, and hopped in back.

Then people started paying attention.

Chapter 8

HOW COULD HE have thought this was a good idea? In the rather impressive list of bad ideas—or at least *semi*-bad ideas—Hitch had come up with over the years, this one would have to be written in the history books with red ink.

In less than the time it had taken him to taxi this heap of Livingstone's down that empty street, he had probably ruined any chance of even being *in* the competition, much less getting a job with Livingstone. His stomach turned all queasy and rolled over on itself.

He flew low over town, headed north toward the impromptu airfield. Half a dozen motorcars careened through the streets, giving chase. In the lead car, a man in a white suit brandished his Stetson. Hard to tell from here, but he looked a little red in the face.

A crowd was following him. That much, at least, was going right. Now Hitch just had to make Livingstone see it that way.

He turned forward again.

In the Jenny's front cockpit, Jael rode like she was born to it. She sat up straight, neck craned to see the ground below, the tails of her red kerchief snapping in the wind.

He banked hard right just to see what she'd do.

She dropped a hip and rode the turn out like she'd known it was coming. Didn't so much as grab the cockpit rim. She seemed to catch sight of him out of the corner of her eye, and she turned her head and actually smiled at him. Whatever had scared her on the ground didn't seem to bother her much up here.

He grinned back.

The sky was like that. Up here, problems slipped away. People couldn't make demands when you were in a plane. Even if they were riding with you, you wouldn't be able to hear them. Once you spun that propeller and launched into the blue, fears and worries disappeared. Up here, everything was solid and fluid at the same time. Life was the buzz of the stick turning your hand numb. You held it, you controlled it. It was yours to keep or lose.

The only thing that even came close to experiencing that for yourself was sharing it with someone else for the first time.

Far ahead, the rows of parked planes glittered, mirage-like, in the sun. He banked again and dove low to cross the cornfields. From up here, they looked like a sea of green swirling in his prop wash.

A dark spot he'd taken for a blackbird suddenly flashed white: a small face looking skyward. A dark-headed kid in overalls saw the plane and jumped up and down, waving both arms. He started running, swiping the corn aside to keep up with the plane.

Hitch laughed and dove lower to give the boy a thrill.

In the front cockpit, Jael stood up. She leaned out, one hand on a support wire, and waved down at the boy.

Hitch's heart jumped into his throat. "Get down!"

She couldn't hear him, of course, and he couldn't reach her from here. So he waved his free hand, until finally she glanced back at him.

Her eyes twinkled. She knew she'd done exactly what she shouldn't have.

Consarn the girl.

She ducked back into the cockpit, and he yawed the plane a smidge to the right, enough to give her a push and tumble her into the seat. She was a gutsy little thing, he had to give her that much.

Once she was sitting again, facing forward, he let himself grin, just a bit.

They left the boy far behind and swooped in low over the airfield. From the back where he sat, Hitch couldn't see the ground ahead, but he lined up the landing as best he could. The plane glided in to about six feet off the ground, as nice and easy as you could want. He brought the nose up and flared, then settled the whole thing with a bump-hop, then another. He finally brought the wheels to the ground to stay, let the tailskid drop, and killed the engine. The propeller's noise died.

He slapped the turtleback between the two cockpits. "Are you crazy?"

Jael stood up. Her cheeks were flushed from the wind, and her hair was coming out from the front of her kerchief. "That was . . . What is your word for it? *Pole!* Like *Schturming*, but not same. Different."

"Passengers stay *in* the cockpit, you hear me?"

Earl came running over. "What in blue blazes? Where'd you get that thing? You've seen Livingstone? He let you fly his plane? That's got to be a good sign!"

"Yeah, well, about that . . ."

Earl drew up short. "What now? Or wait, don't tell me: You stole the plane."

"Yep."

"*What?*"

Hitch glanced over his shoulder.

Even now, a big cloud of dust chased the fleet of automobiles up the road to the field's entrance.

He hoisted himself up and swung his legs over the edge of the cockpit. "Look, it's not all *that* bad."

"You stole Livingstone's plane! How is that not bad? Tell me how that's not bad!"

Hitch's feet thumped against the ground. "You're right, it's bad."

Earl leaned his head back and groaned. "You did this without having any kind of a plan?"

"Of course I had a plan. It just might not be, on reflection, a very good one. I had to save this girl, see."

"What girl?" Earl whipped his head around to look at Jael standing in the front cockpit. "I *knew* there was a girl!"

"It's the girl from last night."

Earl didn't look convinced.

"She saw somebody in town, got scared—and then I had this thought."

"You should never have thoughts."

"We needed to make a splash with Livingstone—get his attention, right? So what if I was to do him a favor? You remember the man. What's the one thing in this world he loves better than flying?" He pointed toward the motorcars streaming in. "You cannot *buy* this kind of publicity."

"This is the kind of publicity that lands you right in the pokey!"

The cars careened to a stop a few yards off. Rick drove the first one, with Lilla waving gaily from the back.

Livingstone piled out of the front passenger seat. He smashed his Stetson back onto his head and gave his black string tie a tweak.

Hitch hooked his thumbs into his suspenders, trying to keep his posture both relaxed and confident.

"Well, well, well." Livingstone's words were calm enough, softened by the hint of a Georgia accent. The high pitch at the end of each word was the only tip-off he was peeved. "If it isn't Hitch Hitchcock. I do believe I haven't seen you since Nashville. When was that, '17, '18?" His nostrils flared, and he grinned wolfishly, the careful trim of his Vandyke beard curving around his mouth.

Hitch pasted on a grin that was just as wide. He came forward to shake Livingstone's hand. "You ol' bushwhacker. Took you long enough to get yourself out here." He gestured over his shoulder. "Quite the ship you've got."

Livingstone's smile widened, but he spoke through his teeth. "Isn't she?" He was still mad enough, that was clear. And he was likely to stay mad until Hitch did something sensible—like apologize.

"Thought I might help you drum up some extra business. All in good fun, right?" Hitch winked. "Showmanship, always showmanship, isn't that what you used to say?"

"And am I to understand you've pulled these shenanigans for no reason other than the benefit of my circus?"

"Why not?"

Bonney Livingstone could talk a man into picking his own pocket. He was as phony as they came and that much crookeder. Plus, he cheated at cards.

But he was no fool. What Hitch had done could either drown his circus in the excitement of a scandal—or raise it even higher with the anticipation of some good clean fun. Farm towns liked scandals well enough, so long as they didn't upset the equilibrium too bad. Good clean fun, however, paid the better by far.

And if there was one thing Livingstone was good at, it was getting paid.

The man shot a sideways look at the crowd gathering behind him, then back at Hitch. "My pilots will be hard to beat this week." He raised his voice so everyone could hear. "Do you think you're up to the challenge?"

He was going for the bait.

Hitch let a sigh of relief sift past his teeth. "And when have you known me not to be up to beating you?"

Livingstone slapped Hitch's shoulder, a little harder than he needed to. "My dear boy, you always were in the habit of biting off more than you could chew."

"Don't you worry about me. Earl here—you remember my mechanic?" He gestured to Earl, who managed a terse nod but didn't manage to stop scowling. "He's given my Jenny a reinforced frame and hooked her up to a Hispano-Suiza."

Livingstone straightened. He shot a look around the field, probably trying to spot Hitch's plane. "Is that so?" When his gaze came back to Hitch, he scanned him up and down. "Well now, that does sound interesting."

"Pulls like an elephant. More speed and power than half your boys would know what to do with." Hitch reined up a smidge. "Excepting you, of course."

Livingstone glanced around the field again. He smoothed a hand over his Vandyke. "This Hispano-Suiza of yours just might put a new light on things."

An uncomfortable feeling knotted in Hitch's middle. He looked back at Livingstone's Jenny. "What things?"

Jael had stayed in the front cockpit this whole time, leaning forward to peer at the hot click of the Curtiss OX-5 engine's exposed cylinders. She cast a nervous glance at Livingstone and Earl, then swung herself out of the plane and dropped to the ground. Gaze alternating between Livingstone and her feet, she sidled toward them, evidently headed for a closer look at the engine.

Livingstone swept off his hat and set it over his heart. "Well, now, my dear. If my ship must be commandeered, I can hardly complain if it is commandeered by a brigand as lovely as yourself."

She narrowed her eyes, but kept coming.

"May I have an introduction to your fair companion?" Livingstone asked Hitch. "A new addition to your act, I take it? What do you do, my dear? Wing walk, parachute?"

"She's not exactly part of the act."

Livingstone snagged her hand and raised it to his lips. "Charmed to the living end, my dear."

With any luck, she'd bat her eyes and curtsy and let it go at that.

Hitch gave her an encouraging smile.

Her eyes got big and shocked, and she yanked her hand back. *"Nikogda bez moego razreshenia!"*

Livingstone's smile slipped. "Well." He coughed. Probably, this was the first time his southern gentleman act had come up short. He clamped the smile back in place. "I'll give you this, Mr. Hitchcock, you've always had the knack for picking up the most interesting people. That *is* showmanship, sir."

Earl rolled his eyes. "Brother."

Hitch glared at Earl. Let Livingstone talk. The longer he talked, the better the chance he'd decide this whole stunt had been his own idea.

Livingstone straightened the lapels of his white suit coat. It was a crazy getup for flying in, but it had become his trademark.

He smiled, almost genuinely, at Jael. "It's quite all right, my dear." His gaze seemed to snag on something. "Now, that's an interesting piece."

Hitch turned to see.

On a chain around her neck, she wore a heavy brass pendant. Round like a compass and intricate with clockwork gears, it had a little crank in the center, the handle of which was shaped like a leaf.

She darted a look at it, as if shocked to find it there.

"Might I have a better view?" Livingstone asked.

What he was doing, of course, was asking her to let him save face after the rejected hand-kissing. Hitch knew it. Earl probably knew it. But in light of her record so far today, Jael was likely to take it as a threat and punch him in the face.

She snatched the pendant and held it against her chest. Her other hand tensed into a fist.

Hitch reached for Livingstone's shoulder. "You best leave her alone. She's a little . . . unsettled today."

"Nonsense. She wears it with pride. I'm sure she'd like to exhibit it." And then Livingstone actually reached for it.

Jael scrambled back two steps. "You stop! Or I—I kill you!"

Livingstone probably had no real interest in the pendant. But now it was a test of wills—and he had made his reputation winning those battles.

He laughed and followed her two steps. "Don't be ridiculous, child."

She threw a wild punch, all strength and no precision. Her fist clipped his Adam's apple, and his breath exploded in a noise too much like a hen's clucking to be good for his pride or anybody else's well-being.

Hitch ducked under the wing and snagged her free hand before she could swing again. He rose to his feet, facing Livingstone. "She didn't mean that."

Earl choked on something suspiciously like a laugh. "I'll say she didn't."

All Livingstone's blood rushed right back to his face. "You little— Is she mad? You're all mad!"

Hitch pushed her farther behind him. "Look, I'm sorry."

She put her free hand on his back, either to reassure herself he was there protecting her—or, more likely, getting ready to hit him too if he did something she didn't fancy.

"You scared her is all," he said.

Livingstone grasped his throat. "I am pressing charges for this one!" His voice sounded just fine, so she couldn't have hit him hard enough to do damage. "She can spend the rest of the week in custody, that's what!"

"Oh, c'mon." Hitch's own temper rose. "She hardly speaks any English. She didn't understand what you meant." He lowered his voice. "You really want the kind of publicity you're going to get for chucking a girl like this into jail?"

"You are not exactly in a position to be talking about who belongs in jail and who does not." Livingstone clamped his lips. Then, finally, he released his throat and straightened up. "Fine. But I want her off this field. You get rid of her, you understand? She is no longer a part of your act."

"She's not mine to get rid of. And anyway, you've got no right telling me who can be in my act and who can't." He kicked himself as soon as the words were out of his mouth. What was he doing? He didn't want the girl on the field *or* in the act. He needed to just let Livingstone have his way. Calm him down and get him off his back before it was too late.

But he said it anyway. "She stays."

Livingstone glared at him. Then once again, he glanced across the field to where the other planes were parked. "All right." With the backs of his fingers, he slowly knocked the dust from his hat. "If that's the way you want it, then let us reach a compromise. I will allow your"—he scowled at Jael— "*gamine* to stay, if you agree to a small wager I have in mind."

"What kind of wager?"

"You say you'll win the competition with your machine's new engine. But I will wager you do not, and if you do not, ownership of your plane will be transferred to me." He ran his tongue over his lower lip.

The knot in Hitch's stomach tightened. "And if I win?"

Livingstone settled his hat onto his head. "If *you* win, you get to be a partner in my circus."

A partnership in one of the biggest flying circuses in the country. Hitch near choked.

He looked over to where his Jenny's red paint gleamed in the heavy afternoon sunlight. That ship was his life. He'd picked it up for a bare two hundred bucks, still in the crate, when so many of them had been available for the taking after the war. She was a common little hussy, with more attitude than any woman had a right to. But she'd won his heart fair enough with her guts and her wild, willing spirit.

Lose her, and he'd be grounded for who knew how long. But if he won . . . he wouldn't have to scrape up the money to *buy* a circus, and he wouldn't have to tag along as a mere sideshow to

Livingstone's act. He'd have a ready-made circus handed right to him.

He glanced at Earl.

The man was almost as wide-eyed as he was—except his expression looked a lot like panic. Earl gave his head an insistent shake.

True enough the Jenny's engine needed some repairs, and true also that they barely had enough money to cover those repairs. But it was a better start than Hitch'd had on other bets he'd won.

He turned back to Livingstone.

That wolf-like look had spread from the man's mouth all the way up to his eyes. This had to be about more than Livingstone just saving face. This was about him trying to keep Hitch in his place. The only thing Livingstone liked about competition was squashing it. But if he was going out of his way to try to squash Hitch, then that seemed mighty indicative that some small part of him thought Hitch might just be able to *be* that competition for him.

Whether Livingstone intended it to be or not, *that* was a vastly encouraging thought.

"All right." Hitch let go of Jael and stepped forward to offer his hand. "You got yourself a bet. By the end of the week, you're going to have a new partner."

"By the end of the week, I'm going to have a new plane." Livingstone crunched Hitch's hand in his and grinned. "Seems to me I win either way."

CHAPTER 9

A FEW MISTY clouds gathered against the high blue of the afternoon sky as Walter ran barefoot through the cornfields, toward where the airplanes sat in an empty field. He reached the field and lay down flat to roll under the barbed-wire fence.

There they were, maybe twenty biplanes, all in four colorful rows. He drew in a deep breath. If anything was worth whooping over, this surely was, but the pilots might not like it if they noticed him here. And he needed them to like him, because more than anything in this wide world, he needed to sit in one of those planes. It could stay on the ground, and that would be enough. But he needed to sit in one once.

Not more than an hour ago, one of the red-white-and-blue ones had flown right over his head. A pilot had leaned out of the front driver's seat and waved at him. The engine thrum had rumbled all through his chest. It was like it had filled him up inside with floating air and near taken him off the ground.

Then it had flown on by, and he'd felt the warm dirt under his feet once more. If just seeing one could make you tingle all over like that, then sitting in one had to be ten times better.

The pilots were up and moving, some of them leaning over fires, getting ready to cook their suppers, some of them rubbing down their windshields and tinkering with their engines.

The question was, which plane to choose? He chewed his lip and scanned down the rows. It was important to pick the right one, and he might only get one shot.

A dog barked, and he turned to look.

A long-haired brown-and-white dog with one floppy ear

trotted over and sniffed his bare feet. Walter waited until he was done sniffing. When the dog looked up, Walter scratched his ears. The dog panted and wagged his tail.

Papa Byron had a dog to watch the chickens, but Walter and the girls weren't allowed to play with him. He was a working dog, not a boy's dog. That made a sort of sense, but, still, it'd be nice to have a boy's dog. A dog just like this one, as a matter of fact.

He patted the dog again, then looked back to the planes. The nearest one was as red as the barn after he'd helped Papa Byron paint it last summer. Nobody was near it, so he padded over. The dog trotted at his side.

The plane was just pretty all over, from its square metal nose to its wooden wing struts, all the way back to its tail. He stopped beside the wing and reached out to touch it. It was made of cloth, stiffened with some kind of varnish. He poked it once, experimentally, then gave it a gentle thump. A hollow strum resounded.

The tingly feeling in his chest wasn't quite as strong as when the engine had been roaring overhead, but it was close. He traced his hand up the wing and stopped next to the drivers' seats. They were too high up to see into, and he didn't dare climb onto the wing. He stood on tiptoe. Still nothing. Then he dropped onto all fours and peered underneath.

Two pairs of legs—one in laced-up boots and the other in grease-stained white pants—walked over.

"How long will repairs take?"

"That's all you're going to say to me? *How long will repairs take?*"

"What do you want me to say?"

"I don't know, something about how you've got some grand secret plan that's going to make winning this competition a cinch—seeing as how *everything* we've got is now riding on it."

"Not exactly a *cinch*. But we'll make it happen."

"Right. Just like that. Because beating Bonney Livingstone is always so easy."

"Can we go back to talking about how long you're going to take with those repairs?"

The other man harrumphed. "An hour or two, I reckon. But

I gotta go to town and dig up parts before any of that. You want to see if you can talk Rick into driving me?"

"You're better off asking him yourself, don't you think?"

The dog yipped and scooted under the plane.

The legs with the boots bent and their owner knelt to fondle the dog's ears. Then the man ducked his head and looked straight at Walter. "Well, now, seems Taos went and had a puppy. Where'd you come from, son?"

The man was long and lanky, his face square and freckled, and his eyes so pale a blue you almost missed them altogether. He looked older than Molly and younger than Mama Nan. He wasn't wearing a helmet and goggles or a leather jacket, like the pictures on the posters in town, but he was a pilot. He had to be. A real, honest-to-goodness pilot.

Walter's face went hot. This wasn't how he'd wanted to meet a pilot, not hunched over on the ground, as if he was spying.

"Come on out," the pilot said. He seemed happy to talk to Walter instead of the other man.

Walter clambered on through and stood up, hands in his overalls pockets.

"What are you doing under there?"

He shrugged.

"Cat got your tongue?"

The heat on his cheeks flared hotter. He watched the ground.

"Ah, leave him be, Hitch," the other man said. "He's just shy, I reckon."

"Come to see the planes?" the pilot asked.

Walter nodded. His fingers seized the wadded-up sock in his pocket. He'd brought Mr. J.W.'s penny. He wouldn't spend it if he didn't have to, but surely they wouldn't let people sit in a plane for free. He pointed at the plane behind him.

Hitch looked up at his plane. "I'm afraid this one isn't going anywhere right now."

The other man, the one in oily white coveralls, grunted. He scratched the days-old black whiskers on his cheek. "Let's just you and me hope it ain't a permanent condition. She may be ugly and cranky, but I'd hate to see her grounded for good." He ambled off, toward the nose of the plane.

Ugly and cranky? Walter craned his head to look at her again, then turned back to Hitch, eyebrows furrowed.

Hitch's face was straight, but something in his eyes twinkled. "What—you don't think she's ugly?"

Walter shook his head.

"Well, you're not so wrong. Planes are like people. If you love 'em, they're beautiful." He stood up. "I suppose you want a ride?"

Walter grinned and nodded.

Hitch chuckled. "I warn you, son, it'll change your life." His gaze got kind of far away.

Walter squeezed his penny again.

Hitch looked down. "You come on back tomorrow. My ship might be fixed up by then. And if not, somebody else around here'll be hopping rides."

Walter bit back the first wave of disappointment, but he nodded anyway. A ride tomorrow was better than no ride at all.

Hitch winked at him. "See you around." He walked off, slapping his leg to his dog. "C'mon, Taos."

He didn't seem to notice that Taos stayed where he was, only perking his ears.

So that was that. Walter heaved a sigh and backed up a couple of steps. As Mama Nan would say, when the pie comes out of the oven, you just have to go ahead and eat it the way it is. If the pilot said leave, Walter would have to leave. But maybe if he found something to do, so he looked busy and out of the way, nobody would notice he wasn't leaving in a hurry.

He walked away, the dog trailing him. He kept his eyes on the ground but peeked up around the corners so he wouldn't miss anything.

A dozen yards out from the planes, a woman stood staring at the sky. She wore pants and boots, and her hair had been bobbed short, in that new style Molly wanted so bad. She held one fist at her chest and swiveled her head back and forth, slowly, as she scanned the sky.

It was the angel lady! He stopped short and looked all the way up at her.

She glanced at him. A smile bloomed on her face. "Hello. It

is you, from by water this morning past?"

So she talked normal talk after all. Kind of. And even though she was wearing pants, she *looked* a lot more normal without her storybook dress.

He walked over. Hitch's dog padded along at his side, tongue lolling. Walter grabbed a handful of neck fur. The dog was real, and who knew what the angel lady was, so it might be just as well to hang onto something.

"I am Jael," she said. Her face, at least, still looked like something out of a storybook. Her eyes creased when she smiled at him.

He smiled back.

"Your name is what?" she asked.

He started to shrug, then changed his mind and squatted to finger his name in the dust.

She tilted her head to read it. "Walter." She pronounced it *Volltair*. "This is good name." She gestured to the dog. "Are you knowing this man Hitch?"

He nodded. If *she* knew Hitch, maybe she flew too. He pointed to the planes.

"Yes, they are very beautiful thing."

He raised both eyebrows and tilted his head toward her. Most people understood that meant a question.

Figuring it out only took her a second. "No, they are not mine." She leaned forward, as if sharing a secret. "I could be fixing them, but I could not be taking them into sky."

He let his shoulders sag.

"But Hitch would maybe be taking you."

He shook his head.

"You are not saying much, no?" But she didn't look angry or even confused, like some people did. "I am not saying much too. I am not quite knowing how to say how you say things here on ground."

She'd already said a whole lot more than he ever did. But he smiled and nodded back at her anyway. Not liking to talk wasn't something he could share with most people.

She touched his shoulder. "Come back again after time. You should be asking again, about planes. This man Hitch—he is man who likes to be saying no first. But I have thoughts that . . . maybe he will be helping if he can."

A random gust of wind hit their faces—and it smelled, strangely, just like rain.

She looked up, and she seemed almost scared.

What was there about rain to be scared of?

He followed her gaze. The sky was still blue overhead: no clouds at all. How did you get rain smell with no clouds?

He shivered.

The sparkles were gone from her eyes. Her mouth was suddenly hard. "Goodbye, Walter. Maybe you go to your home now. Maybe there is no safety now."

That didn't make any sense either. But that look in her eyes was real enough. He nodded slowly and backed up a few steps. When she didn't look at him again, he patted Taos one last time and turned to go. He'd be back to ride in the plane tomorrow—rain or no rain.

Chapter 10

THROUGHOUT THE AFTERNOON, Hitch did a good job finding reasons to stay away from Jael. But by nine o'clock, the sun had set behind the random clouds, turning the sky into a smoky haven for the rising stars—and he was starving.

He left Lilla and Rick at a neighbor's fire and meandered back over to their own camp to see what he could find in the way of chow.

The field was dotted with twice as many campfires as last night. Planes had kept flying in all afternoon, and this was still the beginning of the week. The show itself wouldn't start until Saturday.

Just beyond the shadow of the Jennies, Jael sat cross-legged beside a small fire, messing with one of the new spark plugs Earl had bought in town. Taos lay next to her, his chin on his crossed forelegs. Every few seconds, she'd reach over to scratch his ears.

Hitch dodged past her to Rick's plane.

Earl looked up from wiping his hands with an oily rag. "Well, you're sure the popular man around camp tonight, aren't you?"

Hitch managed a noncommittal grunt and stepped onto Rick's wing to look through the extra gear and supplies stowed in the front cockpit.

"Or could it be you're avoiding us?" Earl asked.

"Us?"

"Yeah, me and that girl."

"And why would I do that?"

"Maybe because you're scared of the both of us."

Hitch snorted a laugh and dug out some cold potatoes and cornbread left over from the night before. "Don't flatter yourself, old buddy." He jumped back off the wing and looked Earl in the eye. "Trust me. I am not about to lose my plane to Livingstone."

Earl shook his head. "What about that girl? You've dragged her into this now too."

"It was more or less the other way around." He turned to watch her silhouette against the fire. "She was lost and scared. What was I supposed to do? Somebody *did* light her 'chute on fire last night."

"Well, then." Earl still didn't sound entirely convinced on that point. "Maybe staying out here in the open like this isn't exactly the right thing to be doing with her. Not that I'm complaining. She's a nice little thing. Tad strange in the head maybe, but nice."

Hitch turned back. "Wait until she wallops you in the shins a couple of times."

"What are you going to do with her?"

"I'm not about to just throw her out, if that's what you mean. But folks who don't pull their weight around here don't eat."

"She knows what's what with engines." Earl nodded toward Hitch's plane. "Don't think she's ever seen a Hisso before, but she picked it up quick when I showed her."

Earl passed out compliments about as often as J.W. sent Matthew birthday presents.

Hitch stopped chewing. "Well."

"And here's something else." Earl stepped nearer and dropped his voice a shade. "She was talking about seeing 'ground people' fighting, killing each other in holes in the earth. Thousands of them, she said."

"The war?" Back when America had gotten into it three years ago, Hitch had given some thought to signing up as a pilot. Between experimenting with a new plane design, a fling with a girl in San Diego, and a busted arm, it hadn't happened. But he'd seen the photographs of the wasted battlefields furrowed with trenches.

Earl shrugged. "She talks like a foreigner. Maybe she's from over there. It's only been two years. She might have seen all that up close."

Or looked down on it from the sky. Hitch shook the idea away. Nope. No matter what she said, no fighter pilot in his right mind would have taken her up there.

"You've got no idea where she's from?" Earl asked.

"She doesn't seem to like talking about it. And what she does say doesn't make any sense."

"Why don't you go have a word with her. You're about the only person she knows here. Give her a tater, tell her things'll be fine."

"Ah-ha." Hitch grinned. "You do believe it'll all turn out."

"Hmph. What I believe is that the good Lord winks at the occasional well-intentioned lie."

Hitch left it at that and made his way over to the campfire. Taos raised his head and curled his tongue in a yawn. Speaking of crew who didn't earn their keep.

Hitch flipped him a wedge of cornbread anyway.

Without turning her head, Jael shot him half a glance. She kept right on working on the spark plug.

He held up a potato. "Hungry?" Lilla had boiled them last night, so they were already soft under their papery skins.

She kept her chin tucked and shook her head.

He ducked his head, trying to catch her eye.

Around her neck, the chain from that crazy pendant glinted. He wasn't about to ask about *that* right now.

In this light and this mood, she seemed a different person. The wild woman was gone, for the moment anyway. But maybe that had all been nerves. Getting lit on fire last night would be enough to shake up anybody.

And she did have guts aplenty. She'd been scared when she went after him at the Berringers', and then the boys at the cafe, and then Livingstone—but she hadn't cowered or whimpered. She'd flung herself right in their faces, and by the time she was done, darned if they all hadn't been a little bit more wary of her than she was of them.

He crouched near her. "C'mon, I know you're hungry. We never got a chance to eat those cheese sandwiches earlier." He wiggled the potato. "Trade you?"

She raised her chin and looked at him square. Her eyes charted his face, like she was searching for something. And maybe she found it.

The corner of her mouth lifted. "Tonk you. For earlier. I have sorrow for giving hurt to your leg."

"Ah well, shinbones of steel, don't you know?"

"You were right in what you said. You are not—none of you are not—what I am all my life thinking Groundsmen are like." She offered the spark plug.

He gave her his most charming smile and handed over the potato and a good-sized chunk of cornbread. "Afraid that's all the dinner we've got to offer right now."

"No, this is very much."

"Then you must not be in the habit of eating too good."

She shrugged without looking up from the cornbread. "Some do."

"But not you?"

"On bottom is where I am living."

"Earl says you're pretty good with engines. How'd that come to be?"

"Engines"—she pronounced it *ennjuns*—"are my work. Not like your engines." She held her hands far apart. "*Bolshoe*, and slower. But same still."

Big, slow engines. From something like a Sopwith Rhino tri-plane bomber maybe?

"They let you work on engines?" No matter how good she was, a female mechanic wasn't exactly most pilots' first choice. "You're in charge of them?"

"No, they are not allowing." She smiled, a bit sadly. "It is secret. I am having no family, not since long ago. So I am *nikto*—having no place. All through my life, I help Nestor with engines." She looked down at her potato. "But he is *merviy*—dead."

"What happened to him?"

She shrugged one shoulder. "He . . . was owning thing that is having importance. Someone had desire for it."

Meaning the "sky people" had killed him? Skepticism washed over Hitch, but then an image flashed through his mind: the falling body Scottie had talked about.

"I'm . . . sorry." He eased back to sit and propped one knee in front of him. "And how'd you end up here?"

"Was mistake."

"Your mistake . . . or somebody else's?"

"I took the . . ." She mimed putting on a harness, then made an exploding motion with her hands.

"The parachute."

Another shrug. "I had to go away from there. Before time had all vanished. The *ball gown* was a—how do you say?—a *mask*, but for whole body?"

"A disguise?"

"That. Because Zlo—he has celebration for what he has done." The lines around her mouth tightened. "He has thoughts that he has won."

"Zlo? That's the guy who lit you on fire?"

She tucked her chin in a nod.

"And what was it he did that was worth celebrating?"

"He changed everything." She blew out a deep breath. "Um, your word for it, I have no knowledge for. But he is—" She made a pushing motion with both hands, then glanced at him to see if he understood.

"He *pushed* you? Lucky thing you had your 'chute already on."

"And I—" She added a pulling gesture.

"Ah." That explained why they'd been hanging onto one another before their canopies opened last night. "And you're sure he survived the fall too? He's the one you saw in town?"

She nodded.

None of this made a lick of sense. They were having a party up in the sky someplace, so she put on an old-fashioned dress to escape notice—and then ran away with a parachute, only to be tackled and sent hurtling through the night? If Earl had thought last night's story was crazy, this one plumb ran away with the farmer's daughter.

"Well, that's not so good," he said carefully. "Why'd he push you?"

Her face stilled, and she pulled back, retreating into her secrets once more.

For a few minutes, they ate without talking. Taos edged closer and propped his chin on Hitch's leg. His eyes followed the food from Hitch's hand to his mouth. Hitch fed him a few crumbs off his fingertips.

Jael broke the silence with a soft laugh. "I have not seen this—what you call this animal?"

"You've never seen a dog?"

"No."

Where did someone spend her whole life without ever seeing a dog?

"I had small, very small animal." She cupped her hands. "Much hair, long tail. His name was Meesh."

"A mouse?" he guessed.

She shrugged again. She looked at the fire, then back at him. "I am also having sorrow for what I did to man with mouth hair. If I gave trouble to you, I am having sorrow."

"Yeah, well." He fed Taos the last potato skin. "If you gotta give trouble to somebody, might as well give it to me. I should know what to do with it if anybody does. What happened with Livingstone this afternoon was more my fault than yours."

"And this *custody* he said? He will not do this to you?"

He stood up and dusted off his pants. "Oh, I doubt it. Unless he gets his dander up again."

"But you have brother who will help?" She stared up at him. "The man with orange phosphate and cheese sandwich—he said you have good brother who is deputy? This is custody man, yes?"

"Oh, Griff. First I'd heard of that. To be honest, I don't much like it." He rubbed the back of his head. "Despite what folks think, I know for a fact the law around here isn't exactly . . . Well, the sheriff ain't a custodian, let's just say that."

"Would they do custody to Zlo?"

He looked down at her. "Griff would." Unless Campbell had gotten to him, changed him.

Hitch looked west, to where his family's farm lay a few miles off. Like enough, Griff was still living there, though he could be married with little ones, for all Hitch knew.

He needed to talk to Griff now, before any more time passed. Seeing him wouldn't get any easier, and it might get a whole lot harder.

So much water had flowed under that bridge. When he'd left, Griff had been a skinny twenty-year-old kid, still working the fields beside their daddy. He'd always looked up to Hitch, always backed him—and, in that quiet, intense way of his, always seemed aggravatingly intent on reforming him.

He'd be a man now—and he'd have become that man without Hitch's influence. It was a strange thought. His kid brother had been making all his own decisions for almost a decade now. And somewhere along the way, one of those decisions had been to send Hitch a letter saying he never wanted to see him again.

And then Griff had apparently made the marvelously intelligent choice to go to work for the one man in this town Hitch would have warned him to stay away from.

Hitch rubbed his shoulder; it got stiff sometimes on account of the crash that had kept him out of the war. "Reckon maybe I'll walk on over there tonight." He was stalling, and he knew it. He glanced at Jael.

She had picked the spark plug back up, but she was watching him. "Tonk you."

He looked away, suddenly embarrassed. "You don't have to keep saying that. I really haven't done anything."

"You have been giving me help. You have been giving me"— she held up what was left of her cornbread—"what this is. In morning, I must go. I must go where Zlo cannot look for me."

"Yeah, well."

That probably was her best choice. Like Earl said, she was mightily out in the open here in camp. And the kind of chaos she seemed to trail in her wake wasn't exactly the sort he was equipped to handle, especially with Rick on the prod like he'd been here lately.

Trouble was she'd still be a sitting duck *wherever* she went. No job, no place to stay, no friends. And it wasn't just the language she had trouble with. There was also the little matter of basic, everyday social conventions.

"Look," he said. "You don't have to go just yet." He slapped his leg to Taos. "If they can find this guy and put him jail, then after that, it should be safe enough for you to go find your folks again."

A flicker of something kind of like hope passed across her face and almost—but not quite—dispelled the doubt.

He took a breath. "I'll ask Griff about it." He started walking before he could let himself change his mind.

———————————

Hitch wandered up the familiar dirt road, listening to the tree-lined creek that bordered it on the one side. He came around the bend into view of the single-story farmhouse he'd grown up in. Hardly anything had changed. Same white curtains, gone yellow after his mother's death. Same willow rocking chairs on either side of the door. Same sag in the bottommost porch step.

Lights shone from the kitchen window, so somebody was home. When he reached the black Chevrolet Baby Grand road-ster parked in front of the porch, dogs started barking. He stopped at the base of the steps and waited, Taos alert at his side. His heart was thumping harder than it had any right to. He hooked his hands into his suspenders, then put them in his pants pockets instead.

Inside the kitchen, a shadow moved against the curtains, and a voice quieted the dogs. A man's silhouette darkened the screen door, his face hidden in the shadows.

Hitch's mouth went dry.

The screen door creaked open, and there was Griff.

"So," his brother said. The dim light shone against the side of his face. "I'd heard you were back."

"Hullo, Griff."

Griff came forward and let the door bang behind him. The skinny kid was indeed gone. His shoulders had broadened, his voice had gotten a little deeper, and, beneath his rolled-up sleeves, his forearms were hard with muscle. Hitch had always favored their father, with his dark curly hair; Griff had got-ten their mother's tawny coloring and that sideways slip of the mouth that could telegraph either happiness or anger.

Right now, it looked like anger.

Quite a few words started running through Hitch's head. Words like: *I'm sorry. I missed you. I should have come back.* But none of them quite wanted to surface.

Better to start with business, feel out the water, then see what happened.

He cleared his throat. "Got a problem I thought you could help me with—"

"Nan came by," Griff said. "Told me you'd flown in for this big air circus." His tone was tight.

Great. Hitch might not have any of the right words for this. But anything he could say right now would have been a better way to start this reunion than whatever Nan'd had to say. She *was* scared of something having to do with Hitch, and folks who were scared didn't always say the most helpful things.

Nothing for it now. He took a breath. Should have started with this anyway.

"I got your letter." He left his hands anchored in his pockets to keep from uselessly moving them. "It's been awhile back."

Griff looked him in the eye. He had always been mild-mannered enough, gentle even. He was the one who took care of the orphaned kittens and calves. He was the follower; Hitch was the leader.

But right now, every muscle in Griff's body was cinched tight. His cheek churned. "Apparently, it was far enough back for you to forget what it said." He looked ready to pop Hitch one if he came a few steps closer.

Hitch kept his ground. "I know what it said. I thought maybe it was time to come back anyway."

"You're really going to stand there and tell me that? After nine years?"

Hitch dropped his hands from his pockets. "I'm here now, aren't I?"

"Was a time when people around here needed you." Griff came forward, the porch creaking under him. "But you weren't here, and it was pretty clear you had no intention of being here any time soon. So guess what? People moved on. I've no doubt that's hard for you to believe, seeing as you always thought life revolved around you, but that's what happened. Life moved on."

A bitter taste rose in the back of Hitch's throat. He'd been prepared for the anger. He could overcome anger, given enough time. But this was something else again. This was a door, barring him from his own past, from childhood memories, from the only true family he had left.

And like enough, it *was* his own fault. He'd let people down, no question about that.

"I didn't know," he said. "If I could have, I *would* have come back."

Griff huffed and shook his head.

"I figured you and Pop had each other. Then when I got word he'd died, so much time had passed. And then . . . I got your letter."

"You don't see it, do you, Hitch? You never have." Griff turned to the house. "You can't just dance back in here and expect everything to be how it was. There's penance to be paid, I reckon."

If Griff thought staying away from home for nine years had been nothing but larks and laughter, then he didn't understand penance. Hitch might not have wanted to *stay* in Scottsbluff. But it didn't mean he'd never wanted to come back. Likely, he would have come back, if it hadn't been for the sheriff.

His stomach cramped up. "So I hear you're working for Campbell now?"

Griff looked back. His frown tilted sideways. "Is that what this visit's for? I heard about the disturbances at Dan's cafe and the pilots' camp. If people want to press charges, don't expect me to interfere on your account. There's more important things going on in this town—"

"That's not why I'm here."

"Then why?"

Hitch cleared his throat. "Don't tell me you haven't figured out what Campbell is by now—behind all that strength and benevolence and 'what's right for the town' talk? Once he gets his hooks in you, it's not so easy getting them out."

Griff held Hitch's gaze for a moment, then leaned back. "Bill Campbell hasn't got his hooks in me. And I know exactly what he is."

"Then why work for him?"

"Maybe *because* I know what he is. You can't solve a problem by walking away from it, can you?"

Then Griff wasn't an idiot or a dupe. Hitch should have known better on that one.

Even still, the one thing Griff didn't understand here was that there *were* some problems that could only be solved by walking away. Griff wouldn't be standing on that porch if Hitch hadn't done as Campbell dictated and walked away. Their daddy wouldn't be buried on his own farm if Hitch had stayed.

The explanation for that stuck in his throat. Whether or not he'd left because he had to didn't change any of the accusations Griff was leveling at him. He could have snuck back for the funerals. He could have written. He could have explained.

But he hadn't. Because there had been that part of him—under the surface, where he didn't look at it—that had been plenty happy to go. He'd left the earth and entered the sky. In so many ways, he had gotten exactly what he wanted. And he'd never looked back.

Too late for explanations now.

He cleared his throat. "Well," he said, "what I'm here for right now is a good lawman. Guess we both know that isn't Campbell."

For just one second, Griff looked like the earnest kid he used to be—eager to help, eager to impress his big brother. Then his face hardened again. "Is it trouble you found waiting for you here, or did you bring it with you?"

"Not my trouble at all. There's a girl I ran into last night. She . . . not from around here. Doesn't hardly speak English. But she thinks some mug is after her. She's pretty worked up over it. Says his name's Zlo. She thought she saw him in town this afternoon."

Griff frowned. "Not much I can do unless he actually attempts a crime."

"I've been hearing about these bodies you've found around town. This guy Zlo might be tied up with them."

Griff's stance stiffened. "And what makes you think that?"

"Just a hunch, let's say."

They stood in silence. From somewhere under the porch, crickets sang. The breeze, still hot, carried the sweet smell of tall alfalfa.

"So was that it?" Griff asked.

No, not by a long shot. *It* was supposed to be reconciliation, maybe even forgiveness. Out of all the people he'd left, his brother was the one he loved the most. More than Celia, more than his father. Hitch had never really believed Griff's letter. No matter how stupid the scrapes Hitch had gotten the two of them into while they were growing up, Griff had always forgiven him. Could Griff really have learned to hate him somewhere in that long stretch of time?

"It doesn't have to be it," Hitch said. "I'm here now, and I'm sorry for messing things up. We could let the past stay in the past."

"It's not the past I'm worried about." Griff's tone was cool. "It's the fact it'll happen again if I give you half a chance. If I could, I'd throw you right out of the county."

"Right." That was all Hitch could manage to say.

Griff retreated to the screen door and screeched it open. "This isn't your home anymore, Hitch. You lost the right to call it that when you left us."

That truth was a fist in Hitch's gut. Because the truth was: Griff was right.

CHAPTER 11

HITCH WAS ALMOST back to camp when a huge cloud unexpectedly shadowed the moon. He stopped his amble down the dirt road and looked up, hands in his pockets. Tall fields of corn framed either side of the road. Somewhere far off, a cow lowed. He stared up at the cloud.

He was ten kinds of fool. Luck and charm had gotten him through most of his scrapes, so he'd more or less figured on them getting him past Griff's anger. Maybe nine years of silence was too much to overcome. He huffed wearily.

Beside him, Taos sat down, tongue lolling.

It was a crying shame people weren't more like planes. You loved a plane while you were with her, and all was right with the world. Then you left her to do what you needed to do to stay alive and sane, and she never held it against you. Fill her with gasoline and point her in the right direction—that was all she needed from you. But people . . . God help him if people weren't more complicated than any number of gears and pistons.

Especially the people that mattered. If he got right down to it, it sure seemed like he'd done a good job cracking up every relationship that had ever mattered. What did people expect? His foot had itched for as long as he could remember. He'd never lied about that, never pretended he was anything but what he was.

If Griff wanted it all to end, there wasn't much Hitch could do about it. But he could hardly let it lie either. He'd only be here for the week. If things didn't get put to rights now, they never would. He wasn't about to come begging—especially since he *had* left, in the beginning anyhow, to keep his family clear of his own troubles. There had to be some other way to get it all sorted out.

"Durn your stubborn hide anyway, Griffith Hitchcock."

He stared up at the gray-black underside of the cloud. It drifted on past the moon and released the light once more. Maybe it meant rain. From the looks of things, the valley sure needed it.

Taos gave a yip, as if reminding him they were getting nowhere fast.

He looked down. "Well, why not. Sometimes nowhere's the best place to be."

A smaller shadow zipped across the ground.

He looked back up.

A big bird, its wingspan easily a couple of yards wide, circled twice just above the low cloud. Then with a shriek, it soared up into the haze.

Another shriek echoed down: and this time it sounded suspiciously human.

Something—or some*one*—fell from the cloud and hit with a thump in the cornfield next to the road.

What in the sam hill—? Hitch blinked.

Taos gave a bark, and they both started running. Hitch clambered over the fence and elbowed through the heat-stunted corn. The body had fallen only a couple dozen yards away. He kept his face pointed in the general direction, pretty sure of being able to find it.

He cast a glance skyward. That cloud was wafting on by, faster than it had any business doing in a breeze this faint. And where had it come from anyway? Thunderclouds like that built up throughout the day. They didn't sprout out of nowhere, particularly in a place with so little humidity as western Nebraska.

He reached the spot roundabout where the body had fallen and peered into the night, listening. No moans. No sounds of life at all.

And then a head in an old-fashioned bowler hat appeared above the corn. The man turned, and his face flashed white in the moonlight. Beneath a broad forehead and an aquiline nose, a beard outlined his jaw. Nobody could be standing after a fall like that—thirty feet at least—but nobody else was crunching about in the field.

"Hey." Hitch swam toward him through the corn. "You all right?"

The man stared at him. He looked to be in his early thirties. His eyes were hooded and wary, lips pushed out in a thoughtful scowl. As the big cloud sailed on by, the flicker of the moon revealed that, even in the heat, he wore a brown coat down to his knees and a red scarf.

He shifted and gave Hitch a glimpse of the smashed corn at his feet—and the lifeless body of a burly man.

Hitch stopped short.

The bird—a strange-looking brown eagle—swooped low over their heads.

Hitch ducked instinctively.

But the stranger didn't budge from staring back at him. The bird, fully two feet from beak to claws, circled around. It landed on the stranger's hat, pushing the brim lower over his forehead.

It couldn't be a coincidence that somebody as obviously out of place as this gent was standing right over the top of the eighth body to fall from the sky. This was Zlo. Had to be. And even though Zlo obviously couldn't have pushed this man to his death, he was tied up in it somehow.

Hitch's heart rate started double-timing. Before he could think about it too hard, he lunged forward and caught the man's arm, whirling him around.

The idea was to get his arm up behind his back before Zlo had a chance to draw any weapons. But Zlo was at least five inches shorter than Hitch, and he moved like a greased pig. He spun with Hitch's momentum and kept right on spinning until his arm slipped free.

The bird squawked and flapped away.

Zlo pulled the flare gun from his belt and held it between them. "I have no fight with you." His accent wasn't as thick as Jael's.

Hitch stayed back, stance wide, hands in front of him. "Fine by me, brother." He pointed at the body. "All I want to know is where that guy came from."

Zlo grinned. "He is good sign. My people are finished with taking control."

"Control of what?"

"*Schturming.*"

"What's *Schturming?*" Hitch ran back through his brain for the biggest airplane he could think of. "A Handley-Page bomber? A hot-air balloon? What?"

"It is place where we pretend not to envy your world. But I think maybe it will be your world that will envy us."

"What does that mean?"

"It does not concern Groundsmen. Not yet." Zlo turned up the corner of his mouth. He seemed to be enjoying the fact Hitch had no idea what he was talking about.

"I'll say it concerns me," Hitch said. "You people keep falling on top of me!"

Zlo looked around, a smidge of theater in his expression. "I like your town. Very rich." He grinned fully, and his front teeth sparkled, as if they were capped with silver or gold. "When I return, I will not be falling this time. I can promise you that."

"Yeah, and do you promise you're not going to go shoving girls out in front of you?"

The grin disappeared. Zlo took a step toward Hitch. "This girl? Jael Elenava—you know where she is?"

Hadn't taken Zlo any time at all to grab *that* bait. Hitch stifled a growl. Probably should have let that one alone.

He moved to the side. "All I know is they found a body out by the lake this morning."

Another step forward. "She was not killed. I saw her footprints."

Well, it had been worth a shot. "Disappointed?" he asked.

Zlo shrugged. "I do not care if she dies or lives. If you want her, you can have her." He tapped the center of his chest. "All I want from her is this."

Her pendant? Hitch frowned and shook his head. "Maybe I can help you find it. My brother's a deputy sheriff. Lives down the road here. He'll help you retrieve what's yours and get you on back home."

"Deputy sheriff?" Zlo snorted. "I think not. But if you find *yakor* for me, I will promise you no more bodies will fall. I cannot leave you without it. I tell you that is no threat, it is just fact. I will even pay for it, yes? If you want *nikto* girl, she is yours too. And if you do not want her, I get rid of her for you. Is this deal?"

Hitch dropped his placating hands to his sides. "Look, you're going to stay away from that girl."

Zlo's features stilled. "Fine. *Idi i bud' proklyat.*"

That didn't sound too much like "farewell and good luck."

Zlo stepped forward, the flare gun still in front of him.

Hitch's choices had just rapidly narrowed themselves to one of three: get shot, turn and run like a scared rabbit, or take this guy from the front and probably still get shot.

He feinted to the right, then dove straight at Zlo. His shoulder caught the man's gut and bowled him off his feet. Zlo lost all his air in a hard exhalation.

Hitch caught the wrist of Zlo's gun hand and bashed it against the ground. The soil here was too soft to do much damage, and Zlo's grip didn't so much as loosen. Hitch hit it again with no luck, then looked back in time to take a fist in his ribs. His own breath whuffed out, but he managed to plant a knee on Zlo's throat.

He curled his fingers into Zlo's fist and pried the gun loose. "Now you're going to see the deputy, whether you want to or not."

Against Hitch's knee, Zlo's throat bobbed. "Maksim!"

The eagle hit Hitch from behind. Its talons skimmed the meat of his shoulder and knocked him off balance.

He lost the gun as he rolled, and it disappeared in the cornstalks. He turned around, jumping into a crouch.

Zlo was already up, fists clenched at his sides. The whites of his eyes shone in the dark.

Well, now Hitch had gone and made the man mad. Probably not a good sign, since to all appearances, he was already on his sixth kill.

Hitch rose, panting.

On the road, a motorcar puttered past. A woman's familiar laugh sounded over the rumble of the engine. Lilla.

And Rick with any luck. Never thought he'd be saying *that*.

"Rick!" Hitch kept his eyes on Zlo. "Lilla! Rick! Get yourselves over here before I end up dead!"

Behind him, the hard slap of the eagle's wings beat the air.

Zlo cast a glance at the road, then back at Hitch, hesitating.

The engine slowed. Stopped.

Lilla's voice floated across the cornfield: "I heard something, I know it!"

Hitch hollered again. "Rick!"

"It's Hitch," Rick said. "What's he want now?"

"Go see," Lilla urged.

That was enough for Zlo. He glared at Hitch, then whistled for the bird and turned to scramble back through the corn.

Hitch gave a thought to following. But in a cornfield at night, Zlo could hide five feet away and nobody'd ever see him.

The beam of a flashlight cut across the field. Rick and Lilla tromped through the corn.

"Oh, it *is* you!" Lilla said.

"Yeah, it's me."

"What is it this time?" Rick said. "We're on our way into town. There's supposed to be a speakeasy down on East Ninth. *Anything* to relieve the tedium."

"Well, how about this." Hitch pointed at the corpse. "That relieve the tedium?"

Lilla screamed.

Practically the whole crowd from the airfield came out to see for themselves.

When Jael eased forward to see the corpse, still lying in the circle of smashed corn, her face went whiter than ever.

Hitch looked at her. "Know him?" He pitched his voice low, so only she could hear him.

She tucked her chin in barely a nod.

"Whoa now," one of the flyers said. "Looks like somebody jumped without his parachute."

That was a whole lot closer to the truth than these folks knew. The gent in question was a big man, tall and lean with a muscled torso. He was bearded, had dark hair down to his shoulders, and wore loose pants and scuffed knee boots. A black leather apron covered everything down to mid-shin. On one hand, he wore a black leather mitten extending to his elbow. Both the apron and the mitt were smeared with oil and ash. Gelling blood coated his nostrils and ears, and he most certainly had about twice as many bones now as he'd had before his fall.

Hitch had offered the crowd a quick explanation about finding Zlo standing over the body. He left off the falling-out-of-the-sky part.

He watched Jael. "Who is he?"

She shook her head.

"Not a friend of yours, is he?"

She stared at Hitch for another of those long, studying moments, probably gauging whether she should tell him.

Then she shook her head. "He is Engine Master. Never is liking me. But is not bad man." She hung her head and huffed softly. "This is not how it is done."

"What do you mean?"

"This"—she flung an arm out at the field—"this is what we do with dead. Drop them to final sleep. But over water, not over Groundsworld. And not *before* death comes."

Okay. He glanced overhead. Not exactly what he had been expecting. If enough people died up there that they had *rituals* for taking care of the bodies, then it was starting to seem like more and more of a long-term place to visit.

Back at Rick's car, the voices grew louder.

Hitch looked over his shoulder. The talon cuts in his shoulder pulled and stung, and he winced.

Livingstone had arrived. He strode through the weak beams of the car headlights and held up both hands in a placating gesture. "Not to worry, ladies and gentleman, not to worry. Before leaving camp, I stopped at the farmer's house and was lucky enough to discover he is the proud owner of a telephone. I contacted the proper authorities. They should be here at any moment."

Hitch's heart sank.

Proper authorities meant Campbell. Maybe he'd send a deputy. Maybe he'd even send Griff since the farm was close by.

Assuming Griff also had a telephone.

Problem was—murder was a big deal in a sleepy town like this, especially with all the brouhaha of the airshow in town right now. If Campbell had any notion at all that Hitch might be part of that airshow? He'd be personally headed in this direction, sure as shooting.

If he did come, there was no way Hitch could get out of talking to him, since he just happened to be the chief and only witness.

Jael turned back to him. "Authorities? These are custody men—like your brother? You have talked to him?"

"Yeah, about that. It didn't go so well." He made himself stop poking at the cuts and drop his hand back to his side. "He didn't want to see me."

"He is your brother."

"That's mostly the problem." Hitch had never had any difficulty winning over strangers—only the people he cared about.

She frowned.

"In the meantime," Livingstone continued, "I suggest we do not sully the scene of the crime any further."

Even as he said it, headlights swiped across the field and tires crunched against the shoulder of the road.

"Ah," Livingstone said. "Admirably timed."

Hitch nudged Jael behind him and eased around to see the road.

Even before the big green sedan's engine stopped rumbling, Hitch started getting a bad feeling in the pit of his stomach.

The sedan's door opened, and Sheriff Bill Campbell slid his bulk out of the driver's seat.

Frustration rolled over inside of Hitch and rose back up, carrying with it more than a fair share of anger. Nothing left to do but face it. Now that Campbell was here, Hitch sure wasn't about to skulk around in corners, waiting to be hunted down.

He glanced back at Jael. "You stay back here. I'll keep you out of it if I can."

Her gaze flicked between Campbell and him, maybe not quite understanding what was happening. But she ducked her chin in a tight nod.

Hitch squared his shoulders and walked into the wind to meet Campbell.

They met at the roadside, a few paces off from the noisy crowd that had gathered around the body.

Campbell didn't look surprised to see him. "Well, now," he rumbled, his voice deeply graveled. "If it isn't the famous Hitch Hitchcock. Heard folks saying you might be back."

So it didn't matter after all that the dead body had fallen right on his head. Hitch wasn't sure if there was any comfort in that or not.

"Here you are," Campbell said, "one day back, and already you're my chief witness to a bizarre death. How's that happen, I wonder?" He rooted in his shirt pocket and came out with a match. He flicked the flame free with his thumb and cupped it in his hand to protect it from the growing breeze. As he held it to the cigarette in his mouth, he looked past Hitch to the crowd in the cornfield.

The death *would* have to be a bizarre one. Campbell might not have bothered coming out himself if it hadn't been.

"Same way it happens to anybody," Hitch said.

Campbell was a hulking man, as tall as Hitch and maybe fifty pounds heavier. His face had gotten craggier in the last few years, but the same faint, knowing smile lurked around his lips, never quite pulling them tight.

"I was just walking by," Hitch said, "coming back from seeing Griff."

Campbell took a puff on the cigarette, then let the breeze blow out the match. "Sure you were, son. I know you wouldn't get yourself mixed up in something like this. Tell me about it, why don't you?"

Campbell, of all people, wasn't likely to believe the truth. But it *was* the truth. If this murder was going to get solved, that truth would have to be told by somebody.

"I think he fell."

"From where? A tree? In the middle of the cornfield?"

"I know you've heard about Scottie Shepherd saying he saw a body fall out of the sky."

"Scottie Shepherd's an old man. He don't see good and he likes attention."

"But do you believe him?" The answer could either make things easier for Hitch, or a whole lot harder.

"I believe *something*'s going on." Campbell studied him. "And I believe *you* know more'n what you just told me. You think Scottie's right? Something's up there, in the clouds, killing folks?"

"That just sounds crazy, doesn't it?"

Campbell regarded him for a moment, then leaned in. "I heard about the stunt you pulled this morning, stealing that plane right out from under Livingstone's nose. *That's* crazy. Only you—that's what I said when I heard about it. Only you."

Hitch tried not to tense up. "That's got nothing to do with anything. I'm not lying about this. If it's a murder, then I take it as serious as anybody."

"Of course you do. You're not the type to take the law lightly. You're just the type to go hightailing when a job don't go right and you lose a man's money."

And there it was. Campbell liked to dance around the truth, but it never took him long to stick in the first jab.

Hitch looked him right back in the eye. "I'm not the type to take the heat for smuggling stolen goods when the man who hired me didn't tell me what they were."

"What they were was none of your business. Still isn't. You should have trusted your sheriff a little more, son."

"What I've learned over the years is that the folks telling you to trust them are usually the last people who deserve it."

Campbell shrugged. "Glad to hear you learned something along the way. Learn your lessons and pay your dues, I always say. That shipment you lost cost me a cool five hundred dollars. When I heard you were home, naturally I figured you'd finally decided to do the right thing and pay me back."

"I don't owe you anything—even if I had that kind of money."

"The way *I* see it, either you owe me five hundred dollars, or I should be investigating those stolen goods you got caught with nine years ago."

If Campbell wanted to put Hitch away for a crime he was guilty of himself—a nine-year-old crime, at that—he'd do it.

Even still, paying Campbell off wasn't going to be more than a short-term solution, at best. If that's all it would have taken,

Hitch wouldn't have had to scram out of the state.

Back when he'd taken Campbell up on his job offer—hauling goods over the state line—he had still bought into the whole idea that Campbell was an upstanding public servant. It was only after the cops in Cheyenne figured out the goods were stolen, and Campbell tried to pin the whole thing on Hitch, that he figured it all out.

Campbell had promised he'd clean up the whole mess *if* Hitch paid for the lost goods. Hitch hadn't had that kind of money, even back then. When he'd tried to tell the mayor what Campbell was pulling under his nose, Campbell had threatened Hitch's family—Celia, Griff, and his pop.

So Hitch had gotten into that plane and scrammed.

And now he was back, like an idiot. He'd never dreamed Campbell would still be in office.

"All right." He forced the words. Going to jail wasn't any better an option right now than it had been before. And this time he *wasn't* going to run. "I'll pay off. After I win the show."

First prize was only $500, which left a big fat nothing over to pay off the crew. But if he won the show, he won the bet. Once he was managing Livingstone's circus, the money would start rolling in. Earl and Lilla would understand the stakes here.

Rick wouldn't. But Rick didn't understand much.

"You always were a cocky son of a gun." Campbell dropped the smile and watched Hitch. "I'll tell you what. I like you, I've always liked you. So I'll make this easy for both of us. I don't need your winnings."

"What do you mean?"

"I got a little job. Nothing tough." He smiled. "Nothing stolen. Just moving a little booze across the state line. It's a special gift for the governor in Cheyenne."

"So you can add bootlegging to the charges?"

This crazy new Prohibition thing was a roaring mess all through the country. Why not here too? Campbell had always had an eye for a good on-the-side opportunity.

"Not if you do it right," Campbell said. "In fact, you do it right, and I'll not only cancel the debt and drop all charges, I'll even give you something extra. Say a hundred dollars."

A hundred dollars would come in handy like a new engine would come in handy. But that's exactly what Hitch had thought the first time he'd talked himself into working for Campbell.

"You'll get your money," he said. "After I win the show."

Campbell pursed his lips. "It's a limited-time offer. You think about it. You got until the end of tomorrow to make up your mind."

Hitch's mind was already made up, but he left it at that. If Campbell wasn't going to arrest him on the spot, the best thing he could do was keep his mouth buttoned up. He managed a tight nod.

Campbell took one step toward the cornfield, then stopped and looked over his shoulder. "Suppose you been out Carpenters' way? Seen the kiddies?"

"Not planning to." Hitch flexed his hands to keep from fisting them. "Nan made it pretty clear I'm not wanted."

"Did she now?" The almost-smile flickered across Campbell's face. "I'll be seeing you. Tomorrow, I hope." He lumbered over to the cornfield's fence and stopped to shake Livingstone's hand.

Livingstone immediately started talking and gesturing toward the corpse with his walking stick. That was one handy thing about having Livingstone around. He was always more than happy to take all the attention onto himself.

Hitch breathed out. That could have gone better. Could have gone worse too. But getting himself mixed up in this murder wasn't good. Campbell could use it in any number of ways to twist Hitch's arm up behind his back. He wasn't likely to find any legitimate suspects now that he'd just dismissed out of hand the fact Hitch had *seen* this guy fall out of the sky.

He looked up at the stars. The big cloud no longer obstructed their glittering.

Speaking of people who thought they had seen things in the sky . . . He looked back down to find Jael lurking in the shadows at the edge of the crowd. She deserved to know what Zlo had said about her.

He strode over to her and beckoned her to follow. "C'mere."

Once he had her off a ways, where she didn't have to see

the dead guy and the others couldn't hear her, he ducked his head down to her level. "The guy I fought with, that *was* Zlo, wasn't it?"

Her mouth was tight. "How you describe him is sounding like Zlo."

"You were right about him being dangerous. He tried to shoot me."

Her eyes got big. "*Shoot* you? *Gospodi pomiluy.* That is very, very bad. Only the *Brigada Nabludenia* have shooters. Zlo is Forager, not . . . Enforcer."

This morning, she'd said the Foragers spoke English. That explained Zlo's handle on the language.

"Well, it wasn't a regular gun. It was that same flare gun he was using on you the other night. He's after that pendant of yours, you know that, right?"

Her hand darted up to touch the bulge of the pendant beneath her blouse. She looked toward the east, and the breeze floated tendrils of hair around her face. "Then they are coming."

"I don't suppose you could just give him the pendant? Save yourself the trouble? He said he wouldn't hurt you if you gave it to him."

"No. I cannot be doing that. The danger is too much."

"Why? What's it for?"

She shook her head. "It is control for all of *Schturming*, because of *dawsedometer.*"

"Because of what?"

"It is not mattering."

"Please don't tell me it's not Groundsmen's business."

She shrugged. "Taking it back to home is what I *must* be doing before Zlo can go there before I am."

"Home to the sky. Right." He scrubbed his hand through his hair. "Well, I don't see how he's going to manage that, so I think you're safe on that score for now.

Across the field, Campbell straightened up from his preliminary investigation of the corpse. Several more cars arrived in the road, and deputies got out. Campbell gestured them all forward. He caught Hitch's gaze just once, and that almost-smile pulled at his mouth.

Hitch breathed out, slowly. The way things were going, keeping Zlo out of the sky might be the *only* thing they were safe on.

Chapter 12

Hitch was dearly hoping to wake up to some sunshine. Aside from the fact that clouds were turning out to be bad luck around here, he could just plain do with a little cheer after last night's goings-on.

But, nope. Even before he stuck his head out from under his canvas bedroll, the light was all wrong. So he kept his head right where it was for another forty minutes or so—until Earl's clattering about with the engine finally destroyed his ability to even pretend he was sleeping.

He reared up on one elbow and squinted out from under the edge of the Jenny's lower wing.

Heavy gray filled the sky. Yesterday, there hadn't been a cloud in sight—except for that big thunderhead in the middle of the night. Now it was almost starting to look like rain, and lots of it—which was surprising. To hear folks around here tell it, they hadn't been in a drought this bad for ten years.

The air didn't smell like rain though, and the wind wasn't ruffling so much as a leaf on the cornstalks.

He flung back the bedroll and reached for his boots.

The whole field was pretty quiet. Barnstormers only rose with the sun when they had rides to hop or places to go. Earl was the exception. He'd always been an infuriatingly early riser. Right now, he was banging on something overhead.

Rick and Lilla weren't to be seen. Hitch looked around. Jael either, for that matter.

He knotted his boot laces midway up his shins and rolled out from under the wing to gain his feet.

Earl was standing on the Jenny's rear seat, checking a wing strut. If the racket Hitch had been hearing meant anything, Earl had to be almost finished with the repairs.

Earl acknowledged Hitch with a glance from under his cap brim.

"Well?" Hitch asked. "Good as new?"

"Good as next to new, I reckon." Earl swiped his hands across the front of his white coveralls, then gave Hitch a longer inspection. "You look about as fresh and happy as a funeral bouquet. Not so good with the sheriff last night?"

"Could be worse."

"What'd he want?"

Hitch ducked under the wing to take a look at the engine repairs. "Nothing much. Just five hundred dollars."

"What for?"

Hitch grunted. "Doesn't matter. Not right now anyway. This thing ready to fly?"

Earl swung out of the cockpit and onto the ground. He faced Hitch, eyes narrowed. "Don't change the subject. What about you and this country copper? You know him from back when?"

"Yeah, I know him."

"And you owe him five hundred smackers?"

"Not exactly, but that's what it's going to cost me to get out of town. But never mind. We'll worry about that later."

Right now, Hitch's main concern was more immediate problems: like making sure the plane could still handle the altitude they'd need for Rick's special drop. Qualifying rounds were tomorrow, and he desperately needed to get Rick into the air for a little practice.

If they bailed on the first day, they could say goodbye to the prize money and goodbye to Hitch's Jenny. Of course, losing the Jenny might not matter so much by then, since Campbell would heave Hitch into jail and toss the key into the North Platte River. That *probably* wouldn't go very far in helping Griff and Nan forgive him for past wrongs—such as they were.

"Just tell me about the plane," he said. "Is she ready to go?"

"Yeah, she's ready. But maybe not in this weather. If that wind kicks up like it looks like it wants to, we're going to have to tie everything down."

Hitch squinted at the sky. It didn't look so bad. The clouds seemed socked in, and the wind wasn't going more than maybe ten miles an hour. "I only want to take her up for a quick one, make sure she's purring, so you can tweak any last problems." He turned back. "Where's Rick?"

"Said something about going to town for supplies."

Hitch raised an eyebrow. "Where's he getting dough for that?"

Earl shrugged. "Looking for credit, I suppose."

"Hah. Like every pilot here isn't trying that. These storekeepers aren't going to give us credit for just the week. And Rick knows it. More likely he's after gin. Didn't he say something yesterday about finding a speakeasy?" Hitch pulled on his flying jacket and swiveled to look around the field. "For the love of Pete, he knows I can't take him up if he gets gassed."

Earl peered at him. "Why am I getting the sense that if we lose this one, we're in deeper trouble than usual?"

"'Cause that's exactly the sense of it." He dug his leather helmet out of the front cockpit. There was an apple in there too. Leftover from Earl's breakfast probably. "But don't tell Rick and Lilla just yet."

"If the weather goes bad on you and you crack up this ship again, I won't have to tell them."

"I'll have her back in one piece in less than twenty minutes." He took a bite out of the apple and looked around again. "Where's Jael?"

"Dunno. Saw her headed out across the field. She looked like she knew where she wanted to go."

Maybe Hitch should have gotten up earlier and checked on her. But she'd seemed all right last night when they'd returned to camp. Honestly, for all that she was obviously—and rightly— scared of this Zlo guy, she didn't seem like the type to rattle easily.

Hitch frowned. "I thought she agreed to stay here." But then who knew what went on in that head of hers? Her English wasn't that bad, but it left more than a few holes to be tripped into.

"Which way did she go?" he asked.

Earl pointed southward, toward town.

"Why didn't you stop her?"

Earl raised both eyebrows. "Didn't exactly ask my permission, did she now?"

No, she wouldn't. And last night she *had* said she needed to go someplace where Zlo wouldn't find her. Hitch made himself breathe out. She wasn't his responsibility—just like he'd told Matthew and J.W. yesterday morning. But having her wandering around in the open wasn't something he'd choose for anybody in her circumstances.

'Cept Rick maybe.

He huffed. "Well. If she starts knifing people again, there's going to be trouble." He squashed down the impulse to go after her. He'd told her she could stay. What more could he do? "If she doesn't want to stay, that's her business I reckon."

The corner of Earl's mouth twitched, and a twinkle surfaced in his eyes. "Yeah, good riddance to her."

"Well, she was a nuisance."

"Oh yeah, I know how you're always glad to see nuisances go. Especially when they're as cute as that."

Hitch scowled. "I mean it. She's done nothing but cause trouble."

"Yup."

"She tried to stab me."

"Yup."

"Never mind." He buckled his helmet under his chin and hauled himself into the rear cockpit. Maybe he'd fly south just to keep an eye out for her. "If you see Rick, give him black coffee and tell him to stay put. Assuming your repairs get me off the ground, I'll be back before it starts raining."

———

The weather held up only until Hitch reached the edge of town.

Out of nowhere, a blast of wind smacked into the Jenny's nose. Raindrops spattered the windshield and peppered his face, dry like rice kernels. The already low cloud ceiling dropped rapidly, and, just like that, visibility went to zero.

What in tarnation? He pushed the plane into a dive to get beneath the cloud and back into sight of the ground. Where were these clouds coming from? This storm cycle was like nothing he'd ever run afoul of. Clouds could roll in fast enough, sure, but they always *rolled*. You saw them coming, a mobile barricade scudding across the sky.

Fortunately, Earl's repairs worked fine. The Jenny refrained from even her normal grumbling as Hitch pushed her down. The Hisso snarled steadily, and the reverberation thrummed up the stick into his hand and all through his chest.

The haze parted around the forward windshield, and the wide stretch of a shorn hayfield flashed below him, only a couple hundred yards away. He dropped another twenty feet, then leveled out. He was just beyond the outskirts of town, where the crop fields were bordered by a scattering of houses.

He looked over his shoulder. Toward the center of town, the overcast was even lower. No blue streaks to indicate rain, but thunder rumbled darkly from the cloud's interior.

Time to get back to the field before he broke the plane, his promise to Earl, or both. He started to swing around.

To either side, movement flashed—on the ground to the left and in the air to the right. He looked up first.

Through the haze, something rose. It was too small and the wrong shape to be a plane, and if another motor was running nearby, it wasn't loud enough to hear over the Hisso. Whatever it was, it sure as shoeshine didn't *move* like a plane. It was going straight up, almost like one of those elevators they had in some of the big city hotels. Color flashed within it and—maybe—a face?

He blinked hard.

The ground movement to the left caught his eye again, and he spared it a glance.

Someone was running full-tilt across the stubble in the hayfield, headed toward where the elevator hung suspended. Someone small and lithe. Someone wearing a red kerchief on her head.

Earl was right: Jael looked like she knew exactly where she wanted to go.

That was more than *he* knew at the moment. He hesitated between destinations. Jael couldn't outrun the Jenny, and, in the wide-open of a hayfield, she'd be easy to find if he came back to her in a bit. Whatever was up there in the clouds wouldn't necessarily give him the same consideration.

He stepped on the rudder pedal and moved the stick to turn the plane.

A flash of brown darted alongside him.

It was a big, brown eagle, like the one Zlo had called Maksim last night. The bird flew level with his cockpit for a moment, easily keeping up with the Jenny's fifty or so miles per hour. Then, with a scream, it tilted its wings and dove toward Jael.

Great. Rabid birds on top of everything else.

Holding the plane steady, he leaned over the cockpit's edge and scanned the ground.

Jael was all alone in the middle of the field, running hard in long-legged strides, fast and surefooted. If she heard the eagle's screech or the plane's engine, she didn't so much as tilt her head.

Then from the edge of the field, a man in a bowler hat and a long coat jumped the narrow irrigation ditch and gave chase.

Oh, gravy.

Hitch swung the plane around and dove low. Precious little he could do to help her from up here, save maybe whack Zlo in the head with the landing gear. With luck, the roar of the engine would distract the man from his pursuit.

Or not.

Zlo didn't even look back. He caught Jael's waist with one hand and spun her around to the ground.

Hitch swooped on by, then hauled the plane around for another pass, even lower this time.

On the ground, Jael and Zlo struggled. He clawed at the collar of her blouse, going for the pendant no doubt. Flat on her back, under the man's bulk, she was at a major disadvantage. Still, she punched him in the eye, then managed to squirm free, crawling backwards on her elbows.

Hitch zoomed past once more and craned his head to watch behind him.

She got a leg up and kicked Zlo square in the jaw. Then she was on her feet and running again, one hand clutching at the pendant under her blouse. She looked up at the Jenny, tracking it through the sky. She waved at Hitch with her free arm.

He dove as low and slow as he could, leveling out only a couple yards off the ground. He could hardly escort her to safety in the plane. But if he could get a sense of the field's condition, he might be able to set the Jenny down right here.

The ground looked smooth enough, so he lined up and set the wheels down. He rolled up beside Jael just as the tailskid touched the ground.

"Fly!" she shouted. "Go back to fly!" As soon as the wing reached her, she grabbed hold of a strut. The whole plane rocked with her weight. The hoop-shaped skid on the wing's underside nearly bumped the ground.

He scrambled to right the plane before she pulled the whole thing over. "Get off! What are you doing?"

She kept right on coming. Her momentum had given her enough of a start to grab hold of a wing strut and haul her legs up. As soon as the plane was more or less level, she squeezed through the first X of guy wires that stretched between the two wings.

If she put all her weight on the wing's unsupported canvas, her foot would go right through, and then the jig would be up for all of them.

"Step on the ribs!" he hollered into the wind.

She walked the wing like she'd been doing it all her life. Her face was tight, her eyes huge. But her movements were sure and steady—no shaking as she switched handholds from wire to strut to wire. She'd scaled J.W.'s house without a second thought, so this was probably nothing.

She motioned forward and looked him straight in the eye. "Keep going!" The heavy pendant swung free from her blouse.

The plane still had momentum enough so that it needed hardly any coaxing to pull it back up into the air.

Jael scanned the ground, peering back at Zlo, then looking ahead.

Hitch craned his head around to see what had happened to Zlo.

Either Jael hadn't kicked him all that hard after all—or Zlo had an iron chin. He was up and running, his ragged coat spread out behind him. He didn't run like a man panicked—more like one who was determined to get someplace and get there in time.

Hitch scanned ahead. Nothing. He leaned sideways to see around the front cockpit.

Ahead, the cloud had dropped almost to the ground. Wind rolled off it and plastered another round of rain against his goggles.

Not good. A fog like that meant zero-zero: no visibility, no ceiling. Wind and rain only made it worse. He had to get the Jenny back on the ground and fast. He threw the stick hard to the right and pulled the plane around to head in the opposite direction. For that one moment when his momentum and direction were matched up just right with the wind, he heard Jael's cry.

Halfway up the wing, where her weight was a little easier for him to balance, she had stopped and braced her back against the crossed guy wires. She stared toward Zlo, and once again she curled her hand around the pendant.

Hitch shot a look over his shoulder.

At the bottom of the cloud, the elevator car had emerged. It was a square metal basket, the sides open except for a crosshatch of iron. A man, wearing a red coat and dark goggles, stood inside. The basket dropped the last few feet to the ground, then bumped back up, and dropped again. The oscillation of a cable cut swathes through the haze above it. The man in the red coat swung open one of the basket's sides and beckoned with both hands.

Zlo had said he was going home. This must be his ride. But how had he signaled for it? Radio or something?

And what was up there to go home *to*? Hitch stared up at the cloud. What did that cable have at its other end?

A flash of lightning lit up the inside of the cloud. Thunder clapped immediately, loud enough to block the noise of the motor. Hitch flinched in spite of himself.

Zlo reached the basket, slammed the door behind him, and started waving his arms. The cable jerked tight, and the basket jumped off the ground so fast it nearly capsized the red-coated guy.

The eagle flew over their heads, spiraling around the cable.

Zlo peered up at the bird, then past it, to the Jenny. He tilted his head to his companion, speaking to him, then looked straight up and circled his finger in the air.

Jael's weight on the wing shifted fast, shaking the plane.

Hitch muscled the Jenny back under control and shot Jael a glare.

She leaned toward him, over the last X of wires and shouted. Judging from the way the cords in her neck were standing out, she was bellowing with all she had. But the wind still whipped away everything but the ghost of a sound.

He rapped a fist against his helmet-covered ear. "I don't know what you're saying! What do you want?"

She pointed at the cloud in front of them, which either meant *go there!* or *don't go there!*—one or the other.

And he'd thought they had a communication barrier before. He shook his head.

She stopped hollering and bared her teeth, obviously frustrated. The wind howled past her, whipping her loose blouse and ripping through her short hair. The red kerchief had come off somewhere along the way. She stared at the cloud, and her eyes streamed tears into the wind.

Then suddenly, she was turning again. She swung herself under the wires, so they were at her back. Nothing lay between her and the front edge of the wing except air.

She didn't yell this time. She just jabbed her finger at the ground.

Now she wanted him to put it down? He looked. Too many hayricks. He couldn't land without running into one of them.

She pointed again, more insistently.

Maybe the hayrick was what she *wanted*. She was poised, like a diver, knees bent, shoulders forward. If he flew close enough to one of those piles of hay, she was going to jump straight into it. The trick wasn't unheard of. He and Rick had pulled it a couple times, when they'd wanted to thrill an audience with the old "scorning a parachute" gag. But except for that plunge into the lake the other night, Jael had no experience with either jumping or planes. If she missed, he'd have another busted-up body to take to the sheriff.

Another glare flashed inside the cloud. The glow grew bigger and bigger, and then, with a static crackle, the lightning burst out. It sliced sideways across the sky, seeming to come straight at the Jenny.

Hitch jerked the stick, reflexively. It was a fool move, since he could hardly dodge a lightning bolt.

The shot of electricity crashed past him before he even finished seeing it.

That sideslip took him right over the top of a hayrick. On one side of him, the lightning started another build-up inside the cloud. On the other, Jael jumped.

The plane ripped on past the hayrick, and he swiveled around in the cockpit to see.

Hay puffed from the top of the twenty-foot mound. She'd hit it then, right in the middle. Lucky her. At the speed he was going, one hesitation would have crashed her into the ground.

In a flurry of limbs and hay, she scrambled to her feet, face raised to the clouds. She snapped her pendant free of its chain and held it up in her fist. Her mouth formed a round hole, the wind tearing away her yell.

At least she was safe—and off his wings—for now. All he had to do was put the plane down before the storm got any closer. Summer storms never lasted long around here. He and Jael could weather it out inside that hayrick. He started to face forward again.

The bolt of lightning that had been building inside the cloud streaked past his cockpit. A clap of thunder chased in its wake and rattled everything from his teeth to the instrument panel to the floorboards under his feet. The lightning zoomed straight for Jael's upstretched hand.

A gust of wind hit the plane, and the Jenny yawed to the side.

Hitch struggled to bring it back to level. All the while, he turned his head around as far as it would go to see over his shoulder.

The lightning slammed into Jael's upraised hand. It split around her in a blinding nimbus that, for a second, shrouded her from head to toe. The light faded out in a drizzle of sparks, and the hay at her feet burst into flames.

For one more moment, she stood there, staring in shock.

The next, she dropped like she'd been brain shot and rolled down the hay mound to the ground.

The clouds let loose the rain and doused the flames.

Hitch froze, open-mouthed. *That's* what that stupid pendant did?

Under his slack hand on the stick, the Jenny pitched her nose toward the ground. He twisted back around and pulled her up. In the turbulence—and now the rain—she was bouncing around like a half-deflated ball.

He did an about-face and zoomed low over where Jael had fallen.

She was out cold—or worse. She lay with her arms splayed above her head, the pendant a dull wink of metal just past her fingertips.

He'd seen people hit by lightning before. They'd all died. But it hadn't exactly looked like she'd been *hit*.

He squinted back up at the cloud. The elevator had disappeared.

Zlo had done this to her. Somehow, some way or another, he had brought this storm.

Hitch circled Jael again. Still no movement.

Automobiles were tearing down the dirt roads around the field, some from town, some from the farmer's house. Somebody'd be along to help her soon. He wouldn't be able to get the Jenny onto the ground sooner than their arrival.

That meant the only thing Hitch could do for that crazy girl was knock her buddy Zlo right back out of the sky. If nothing else, maybe that'd give Hitch a glimpse of what was up there and where it was headed next.

He turned the Jenny back into the storm.

Rain chattered against the windshield, and the wind buffeted the wings, first from one side, then the other. The plane wasn't built to take this kind of abuse—even with Earl's modifications.

But doggone if he was going to just sit here. He opened her up and sent her screaming into the cloud. Up and up. Visibility turned into a big, black nothing. After a bit, it was hard to tell up from down. Every little pull of his engine felt like gravity calling him earthward.

A gust of wind caught him from below and shoved the Jenny

straight up. The engine started choking, and the controls got mushy.

He gave her the throttle. "No, no, no, no."

No good. The engine sputtered and died. For a second, they coasted. The wind sideswiped them into a turn, then another upwards jump.

Through the haze, a tremendous shadow loomed. The Jenny's landing gear hit something. Hitch pitched forward and whacked his forehead against the front rim of the cockpit.

The world faded out in a blink.

It came back only slowly, heartbeat by heartbeat.

Voices whispered through his head, the words too far away to grasp.

"Ti s uma soshel? Chto mi budem delat s etim chelovekom? Luchse bi ego ubit."

Or maybe just too foreign.

He tried to drag his eyelids open.

"Ego budut iskat."

Footsteps clattered all around him, and the plane rocked as if hands had grabbed it.

He managed to squinch his eyes open a slit. The world swirled around him. He was still out in the storm? A little more squinching. Nope, it was his head spinning, not the plane.

The voices rattled on, at least two of them nearby and a lot more farther off. One of the men nearby sounded concerned, even a little hysterical. The other sounded somewhere in between ticked off and triumphant. He sounded an awful lot like Zlo.

That brought Hitch to faster than a cold dash in the face. He yanked his head upright. He was in some sort of a vast room. A long narrow passage, full of flickering darkness, stretched in front of him for hundreds of yards.

Nearby, the empty elevator basket leaned in a corner, its crosshatched door hanging open. Beside it, its cable pooled on the floor.

Dozens of men—along with maybe half as many women in long old-fashioned skirts and even a couple kids—worked feverishly at using ropes to lash to the walls barrels and bags and boxes upon boxes of canned goods. Most of it looked just like the stuff he'd seen yesterday in Fallon Bros.

Was that what this was all about? These guys had dropped into town on a shopping expedition?

Rain-speckled wind gusted against the side of his face, and he slid a look to the left. The storm stared straight back. The whole wall on this end was open. The Jenny wobbled on the edge. No way of telling how far a drop was below them, but her skid definitely wasn't resting on anything solid. She seemed to be balancing on her wheels and the end of the fuselage. One wing stuck through the massive doorway.

Two faces appeared on the opposite side of his cockpit.

A dark-haired kid in a red coat—the same one who'd beckoned Zlo into the elevator—had shoved his goggles up on top of his head. He had a doughy face, framed by cultivated sideburns, and big, puppy-looking eyes. He gaped at Hitch.

Apparently, it was a shocking thing to find an airplane pilot inside an airplane.

"*Ti!*" the kid exclaimed.

Next to him, his friend Zlo didn't look surprised at all. "You have come to join us, so?" He grinned, hard and determined. "Or maybe not."

If he'd had time, Hitch might have thought of a name to call him. But he didn't have time. He had no room to taxi up to airspeed even if he could find somebody thoughtful enough to pull the propeller. That left one chance of getting out of here—and even if it failed spectacularly, at least it'd look good.

He gave Zlo a salute. Then he hurled his weight to the left as hard as he could.

He didn't have to try twice. The Jenny, her balance already compromised, pitched straight out the door into the swirl of the storm.

CHAPTER 13

SURVIVAL RIGHT NOW depended on how many feet were between Hitch and the ground. There were a lot of other factors, but that was the only important one. Provided he had enough room to recover from the Jenny's spin and pull her into a glide, he could land her deadstick. Even that hayfield would look like a good landing strip right now.

He wrestled with the stick and the rudder pedals, fighting the stubborn Jenny—shorn of the Hisso's power—back to level. The storm had slacked off considerably. The wind was headed in just one direction, the clouds had lightened to gray, and the rain was barely spitting.

He eased the plane into a shallow dive and prayed for the clouds to clear before he reached the ground. God must have been listening, because the clouds broke apart a good two hundred feet above dirt. The hayfield wasn't anywhere in sight. He'd lost all his bearings up there, and who knew how long he'd been unconscious, although it didn't feel like it could have been more than a minute.

He swiveled his head all around, leaning over both sides of the cockpit. Without the engine running, all he could hear was the wind whistling past, thrumming the wing wires into that eerie song they sometimes sang. Thunder rumbled, but it was away off in the distance.

The broad swell of Scotts Bluff—the crag that gave the town its name—scored the horizon behind him. Town had to be just a dozen miles or so to the north. If it wasn't for the lingering clouds, he would have been able to see it.

A road, empty of traffic and wide enough to accommodate the Jenny, appeared to his right. He guided her over and held his breath as she glided lower and lower. He got her lined up just in time, dropped her to the ground, and let her roll to a dusty stop.

Ignoring the drum of pain in his forehead, he hopped out to check the engine over. The fuel line needed fixing. After that whole adventure, he was happy that was *all* it was. His legs wobbled a bit, and the ground felt funny underfoot—like it always did after a crazy stunt.

Nobody could tell him he wasn't lucky. He closed his eyes long enough to huff an exhale. Then he shook the jitters from his hands and got the fuel line straightened out. That done, he gave the propeller a couple heaves, and took off once more.

The hayfield was empty, except for the scorched hayrick, so he circled back to town and landed the Jenny on a backstreet. Scattered tree limbs and broken glass lay everywhere. The storm had hit hard, but the damage seemed to be mostly the result of the wind. No hail, at least.

He left the Jenny and started jogging. He'd seen a hospital on Main Street—a smart-looking three-story building that was brand new or close to. If there was any kind of good news about Jael, that's where they would have taken her. His stomach cramped. He should never have let her climb on his wings. He should never have flown close enough to that hayrick to let her even think about jumping off.

Unless . . . had she really pulled that lightning bolt toward her?

Why? To protect him?

That definitely made him feel better.

What had happened out there? What had he crashed into up in the storm? For that matter, where had the storm come from? And where had it gone?

As he reached the hospital, he scanned the sky. The clouds were already scattering. Blue peeked around their ragged corners.

Inside the crowded waiting area at the front, people packed the few chairs along the walls. More stood, supporting friends and relatives. There was crying and shouting. A harried nurse in a white cap manned the front desk. She seemed to be spending most of her time scribbling and shaking her head.

The place didn't look set up to hold more than a couple dozen patients, and judging by the glimpse through the door into the open ward beyond, three times that many already jammed the ground floor. Nebraskans were used to summer storms. But this one had upset everybody more than usual.

He leaned over two people to catch the nurse's eye. "Jael!" he raised his voice above the hubbub. "I'm looking for a girl named Jael! She was hit by lightning." Or close to it, at any rate.

The nurse gave him a harassed shake of her head.

He filled his lungs to try again.

To his left, a dog barked.

He turned.

On the far side of the ward, in the open doorway of what looked to be a single-patient room, Taos sat beside the dark-haired kid who'd come by yesterday for a ride. Nan and Aurelia loomed behind him. And behind them, sitting on the edge of a bed, was Jael.

She gave him the tiniest crook of a smile.

Thank the Lord for miracles. The breath he'd gathered left his lungs in a whoof.

He pushed through the crowd and weaved his way through the ward to her room. "You're alive . . . Shoot, kiddo, give me a heart attack next time, why don't you?"

She slumped, both hands braced against the mattress edge. Dark circles deepened her eyes. Her bobbed hair, light brown before, was streaked with silver.

Other than that, she looked downright scenic.

"You all right?" he asked.

She nodded. "*Now* am fine." She jutted her chin at something in the big room. "I have acquainted your brother. They are saying he brought me to this place."

Hitch glanced back.

Griff, his deputy's badge glinting against his shoulder, was working the crowd, trying to calm the folks down. He caught Hitch's eye, held it for five full seconds, then turned away. He looked beat. Who could blame him? He'd probably been up all night with the murder. And now here he was again, hard at it.

"And then I once more acquainted your friends from store." Jael nodded to Nan and Aurelia. She lowered her gaze and smiled. "And Volltair."

The little boy—he was about eight or so, with wide ears and a nose full of freckles—looked back and forth between Jael and Hitch. His eyes were big and excited. He kept one hand on Taos's head.

Nan reached for Walter's shoulder. She stared at Hitch, practically dragging his gaze back up to hers. "This is unbelievable. It's amazing she survived."

Hitch shifted his weight and pushed his hands into his pockets. "Yeah, well, thanks for looking out for her."

"I do what needs doing, Hitch Hitchcock."

"I know you do," he said. "You always did."

Her cheeks flushed, and for that one second, she looked, inexplicably, like she might burst into tears. She pushed Walter forward. "Come along." She beckoned for Aurelia. "We need to go check what's happened to the farm."

Aurelia patted Jael's cheek. She sighed. "I'm so sorry you don't have to stay in the hospital. I was going to buy you a violet nightgown." She looked at Hitch and tilted her head from one side to the other, considering. "I know something. But of course you wouldn't believe me."

"I might."

"Another storm is coming. I know. I was told. And if there is one storm, there will be two." She inclined her head, like a queen after a pronouncement.

He touched her shoulder. "That's true as true. I believe you, Aurelia."

She blinked benevolently, then wafted out after Nan and the boy.

Hitch closed the door and turned back to Jael. "This is nuts. You know that, right?" He felt like he was going to explode right out of his skin. His forehead pounded where he'd hit it against the cockpit rim. The whirl of his thoughts, most of them ending in question marks, didn't help one bit. "Everything that's gone on today—everything that's gone on since you about fell on my plane the other night—that stuff does not happen. All right?"

She pointed to his forehead and opened her mouth in what might have been concern.

"This guy Zlo," he said. "Who is he? How's he doing that stuff with the storm and the wind and the lightning? *Did* he do that? Did he send the lightning deliberately?"

She eased up off the bed and stepped toward him. "Your head. You have blood."

"What you did with the pendant, you did that on purpose. Didn't you? You took the hit on purpose?"

"It did not hit me. It just . . . was surrounding me."

Which explained why she wasn't all crispy.

"And how exactly does that work?"

She hesitated, then shrugged. "Lightning is giving much danger to . . . *Schturming*, just as much as Groundsworld. So Nestor is letting me make changes to *yakor*—to direct lightning—and maybe to give protection." She tilted a sheepish smile. "It is only half working."

"I noticed."

Heck, why not? After everything that had happened today, a lightning puller/protector *thing* seemed almost the most believable.

"Well," he said, "if it attracts lightning, then do me a favor and don't take it in a plane ever again."

She picked up a rolled-up bandage from the table beside the bed and reached to dab it against his forehead. It came away streaked with red, and she dabbed again. She raised her other hand to prod his forehead with a fingertip.

"Ow!" He grabbed her hand reflexively. What she was doing caught up with his brain. "You're doctoring *me*? You're the one who got hit—or surrounded—or whatever by lightning."

She positively blushed. Embarrassed she'd been caught fussing? Or embarrassed she was still alive when her insides should be scorched?

She pulled free and lowered herself to the bed's edge once more.

He backed up to lean against the door and watched her, arms

crossed. He made himself take in a deep breath.

Okay, so there was something up there that could command lightning. Probably not the best thing to have happening just before an airshow.

He dug around for the right words to frame this crazy question he had to ask. "I went straight up into that storm. Ran smack into something." He pointed to his head. "That's when this happened. And then I was in a long room full of supplies, and Zlo and a bunch of other people were there." He eyed her. "That was *Schturming*, wasn't it?"

She gave one tight nod, then busied herself straightening the tray of instruments on the side table.

"Well, what is *Schturming?*" It sure as Moses wasn't the big bomber he'd been halfway expecting.

More fiddling. Then she looked him in the eye. Her pupils were tiny, the silver of her irises practically engulfing them. "If Zlo has control, he will use power wrongly—against my people. He will make more days like today. Worse days, even." She stood back up. "I am going to go home. I must find way home on any plane, and I will give stop to him."

"Why? From the sounds of it, folks up there haven't been treating you too good."

She jutted her chin. "Zlo was killing Nestor. And . . . *someone* has to give stop to him."

Her determination was about as real as it got. But what was one woman—even one as apparently indestructible as she was—going to be able to do?

A thought occurred. "This all isn't your fault somehow, is it?"

"No."

But she was still headed back up there, sure as shooting. She'd get herself killed. People who could zap you with lightning weren't people you wanted to be messing with. She'd be better off staying down here.

"Maybe you should back up a little," he suggested. "Catch your breath. Most people would say getting hit by lightning is way above and beyond the call of duty."

"I did not get hit. And this I *must* do. If Zlo is able to do these things he did today, it has to mean he has at least killed our *glavni*—our leader—and Enforcement *Brigada*." She raised her chin; her nostrils flared. "I will never be free, I will never be happy, if I leave my people in danger."

He wouldn't know about that. His people were only in danger so long as he *was* around.

"Being free is a harder thing to find than you might think."

"Yes. But I will not ever gain it by running away."

In his experience, life wasn't in the habit of making things that clear cut. But he bit his tongue. "Who are your people? What are they flying around in up there?"

The glimpse he'd gotten from his cockpit had been of a legitimate *room*—plank walls and floors. And the people inside of it hadn't exactly looked like crew. Their outdated clothing hadn't been familiar, but it hadn't seemed to be any kind of uniform. That might mean they were closer to being passengers. But since when did passengers have to help with stowing the supplies?

The whole thing had seemed awful *permanent*. That explained her talk of it being "home" and the fact that people would be up there long enough to need burial rituals. Even still, flight and permanence didn't exactly belong in the same sentence.

She shook her head, almost apologetically. "I cannot tell you. It is not for Groundsmen to be knowing."

Right. He'd heard that one before. "Tell me this then—how do you figure on finding Zlo?"

She slipped a hand into her pants pocket and fisted it around something. "He will find me maybe."

Ah, that wasn't so good. After the airshow maybe he'd go hunting, just to satisfy his own curiosity. But right now, the last thing he or the airshow needed was a crazy madman in a cloud machine.

Truthfully, Zlo's coming back to find Jael didn't seem like the best thing that could happen to her either.

They looked at each other. From beyond the door, the bustle of the hospital filtered in.

His pulse beat a steady rhythm against his bruised forehead. His muscles all felt like they were starting to sag right off his bones. The excitement was almost gone, and all he was left with was a huge desire for his bedroll and someplace dry to unroll it.

She was probably wanting the exact same thing right about now. But she looked a far sight better than he felt.

He clucked. "Anybody ever tell you you've got some guts?"

She knit her brows and laid a hand on her stomach. "Guts?"

"Courage. Maybe a little more than your share of insanity too." He offered a grin. "But then I'm hardly one to call the kettle black."

The line between her eyebrows deepened.

He stood up from the door. "I'm just saying, you're a brave and crazy person. Smart too." Everything she'd done out there today had been calculated. She made her decisions—the right decisions, as things had turned out—and acted on them without a second thought.

For some strange reason, the image that flashed through his mind was of what Celia would have looked like if she'd been the one standing on the wings of his plane today. Part of him almost laughed. Celia had hated planes. Never wanted to go near them. Partly, she'd just been worried about her health—she was always worried about something. And partly, she'd been maybe a little jealous of them.

She'd never have been able even to dream of doing anything like Jael had just done.

He tamped the thought away. Celia'd been her own person, with her own strengths. She'd hardly been alone in not being able to count wing walking and lightning dodging amongst her foremost talents.

But Jael . . . There *was* something about her. She surely hadn't been born for a life with her feet nailed to the ground. True, she didn't know much of anything about anything. But she could learn. Earl himself had said she'd picked up the workings of the engine fast enough. With a little time, she might really be able to do something in the air that was worth watching.

He hauled himself up short. No, the last thing in the world he needed right now was another mouth to feed—especially a mouth belonging to someone who needed a heap of training.

Jael cocked her head and looked him up and down. "And you," she said. "You are brave man too." She pushed up from the bed and limped past him as he opened the door. She tossed him a half-teasing, half-knowing glance. "But not crazy."

If that was her way of saying everything he'd seen up there in the storm wasn't a hallucination after all, it was a sight less comforting than she probably meant it to be.

He could always pack up the Jennies and leave. But he didn't scare *that* easy. Besides, where something smelled this funny, there was bound to be opportunities on the rise. He'd never been one to pass that up.

As it turned out, he wasn't the only one who smelled an opportunity.

Back out on the street, people crowded around a white-suited man standing in the bed of a rusty truck. Livingstone. He was gesticulating—hat in one hand, walking stick in the other—and hollering something.

If anything, the storm would be bad publicity for the airshow, since the pilots could hardly be expected to fly if this weather persisted. As if Hitch's stomach needed any more encouragement to be queasy.

He took Jael's elbow and guided her over.

Matthew and J.W. stood behind the crowd.

As Hitch approached, Matthew glanced back. "Well, now, you two look a little worse for the wear."

J.W. didn't turn from watching Livingstone. "Don't we all?"

"What's the damage?" Hitch asked.

"Pretty much what you see," Matthew said. "Downed branches, broken windows. Heard a tractor got flipped outside of town. Some woman got hit by lightning."

Beside Hitch, Jael shifted.

Word was bound to get around, but nobody knew who she was, so if she wanted to keep it mum, she probably could. He nudged the back of her wrist as reassurance.

J.W. glanced over his shoulder and gave Jael a long glance, then he looked Hitch in the eye. "Something's not right about all this. Storm like that, out of nowhere? And folks are talking. Lots of strange people seen in town today. Fallon Brothers and a couple other shops got robbed."

"And you think these strangers *caused* the storm?"

J.W.'s gaze drifted back to Jael. Then he shrugged and faced forward again. "'Course not."

"Well, something *is* going on," Matthew said. "I heard more than one person say they saw these strangers rising into the sky, like angels on Judgment Day. After all these bodies they've been finding, it seems a mite too coincidental."

Hitch cleared his throat. "I'm sure there's a more practical explanation."

J.W. pointed at Livingstone. "That's what your popinjay friend thinks too."

"Ladies and *gen-tle-men*!" Livingstone drew out every syllable, like a carnival barker. "I propose this is no ordinary storm! I propose something is up there!"

Hitch frowned. What was Livingstone up to?

"I propose," Livingstone drawled, "to personally deduce the solution to this mystery. The aeronauts who have come into your midst will search the skies and penetrate the heart of this labyrinthine enigma!"

Publicity indeed. Hitch had to clap along with the others, out of respect for Livingstone's theatrics if nothing else. No way Livingstone was actually buying into the idea that something was up there. But it *was* too good a story not to take advantage of.

J.W. grunted. "Hmp. And I just bet he's behind it all."

The buzz of conversation rose even higher.

Along the sidewalk, the crowd parted, and Griff strode up to the truck. He gestured for Livingstone to get down. His voice drifted out to where Hitch stood. "This is all nonsense, and there's no reason to go upsetting people any further."

Griff faced the crowd. He was hatless, and his dark blond hair had fallen across his forehead. He looked young and earnest and tired, but his voice was weighted with confidence. "It's just a storm. Lord knows, we've had our share of freak storms before. So go on home, clean up the damage. It'll all be right."

The crowd responded. Most of them acted like they recognized him. They nodded to him and started to disperse.

Seemed his little brother had grown up just fine without him. Maybe all the better for Hitch's being gone. The twist in Hitch's chest was bittersweet.

"Indeed," Livingstone said. "Heed these good words. And allay your fears. My pioneers of the sky will safeguard your children!"

Speaking of opportunities . . .

Griff scowled at Livingstone and practically hauled him down.

"Well now, he's full of the blarney, ain't he?" J.W. said.

Hitch grunted.

Livingstone could have no idea there was really something to *be* found up there. But after a public declaration like that, he had just about granted hero status to any pilot who *did* find something.

Hero pilots got easy jobs and better money—as all the war veterans could tell you.

Had to be a way to use that to his advantage. Maybe Hitch *could* find the dad-ratted thing. If he could figure out what it was, maybe get it to land . . . *That'd* be publicity like Livingstone wasn't even dreaming of.

And if they could get Zlo arrested in the process, that would work out all the better.

As it so happened, Hitch was the only pilot who'd had his plane in the air this afternoon, and surely he was the only one who'd glimpsed *Schturming*—much less crash-landed on it.

That meant he had a head start on every other pilot. *And* he had Jael.

He turned to look for her. "What do you think?"

The spot by his elbow, where she'd been a second ago, was nothing but empty air.

He looked around, but she'd plumb vanished. She had a knack for that, seemed like.

Across the street, Griff stood speaking to people and guiding them to disperse. Every few seconds, he'd glance over slowly, as if he were just casually scanning the road. But he always scanned right past Hitch.

Might be he'd cooled down a bit after having his say last night. A man had a right to blowing off some temper after holding it for nine years. Hitch couldn't blame him for that.

But still Hitch hesitated. He needed to march over there and say something. But everything he'd had to say he'd said last night. Didn't seem it would make much of a difference saying it all over again by the light of day.

The last of the crowd filtered away, and Griff hesitated too. He leaned back on one leg, ready to take a step.

Now or never.

Hitch pocketed his hands and ambled over. "So . . . I hear you met Jael."

Griff eyed him, up and down. He looked like a man trying to keep his sternness all closed in around himself. "The girl who about got hit by the lightning?"

Hitch nodded. "She's the one I came to you about last night. And that guy Zlo I was telling you about? He was out there this afternoon. That's why she was in that field—she was running from him."

Griff frowned. "She didn't say anything about that."

"Her English isn't so good." Hitch weighed his words. Griff just might help with Zlo, since that was about Jael, not Hitch. All they needed to do was keep Zlo out of the picture long enough for Hitch to win the show—and maybe even long enough for Jael to help him make something interesting out of this opportunity with *Schturming*. But the specifics didn't matter. Getting Griff to help him with *anything* might be enough to break down this wall between them.

Hitch looked Griff in the eye. "Zlo's no joke. He was there last night where the body fell."

Griff frowned. "You didn't tell the sheriff that."

"I don't tell the sheriff a lot of things." He had to rein back anger on that one. "But you will keep an eye out for Zlo? If he comes back?"

"That's my job, isn't it?"

And Griff always did his job, was that it? While Hitch went gallivanting irresponsibly around the country?

Seemed like they'd covered that ground last night. He was losing the argument again—and they weren't even arguing.

He took a breath and tried once more. He nodded down the street. "I can see why you like deputying. You got a way with folks."

"I like people. I've always liked people."

"I know it. I don't suppose you remember how when you were nine or so we heard that the schoolteacher old Mrs. Bates, from on the other side of the river, was down with the gout again? You decided to make her chicken soup, even though you didn't know how."

Took Griff a second. Then he nodded. "Boiled the whole chicken in a couple gallons of water. Didn't even know enough to drain the blood or take the innards out first. Smelled rank."

"I should know. I helped you lug it over there. Cured her gout though, I heard."

The crease in Griff's forehead eased a bit. The corner of a grin touched his mouth. "I reckon she was too scared to admit she ever suffered it again."

Hitch laughed, and for just a second Griff laughed with him. The sound of it warmed Hitch right to the pit of his stomach. He quieted and smiled at Griff. "It *is* good to be home, little brother."

As quick as that, Griff's face closed up. He looked away, and a muscle in his cheek churned. Then he looked back, his eyes thoughtful. "It ain't that simple, Hitch. I told you that last night."

"And I reckon I heard you."

"I'm not the only one who's upset. Nan's fit to be tied." Griff chewed his lower lip. He seemed . . . conflicted almost. "There's things you need to know about. About Celia's dying."

"Then tell me."

Griff shook his head. "I don't know if I can. Not yet." He stepped backwards, up onto the paved sidewalk. "You decide to stick around long enough, and maybe you'll prove you deserve to hear it."

Hands still in his pockets, Hitch watched him go. Sticking around wasn't exactly in the cards, especially with Campbell huffing down his neck once more. Thing was, Griff probably had no notion of any of that.

Didn't seem like requesting help with Campbell was exactly the right thing to be asking Griff right now. Even if it was, getting Griff mixed up on the bad side of Campbell wasn't something

Hitch wanted to leave behind him when he had to go.

And he *did* have to go.

Would Griff think a week long enough for reconciliation? Because if he didn't, this whole thing might end worse than it'd begun.

CHAPTER 14

WHEN HITCH PUT the plane on the ground back at the airfield, the right wheel busted clean off. The Jenny skidded around in a wobbling ground loop and nearly pitched herself onto her propeller. He fought her back to a standstill, then jumped out to stare at the damage.

He might have started yelling about how he couldn't believe this had happened *again*. Except, at this point, he totally could.

Earl ran over. "You keep her safe during that storm, then come home and botch your landing?"

Hitch growled. "It happens, doesn't it?" He knelt beside the broken gear. This was the side that had plowed into *Schturming* when he hit whatever was up there. Three landings later, the axle was near sheared in half. At least it had gotten him back to Earl.

For all the good it would do now. It was fixable, but that wasn't going to be the main issue this time.

"How much is it going to cost?" he asked.

Earl squatted beside the wheel and shook his head. "More than you got."

Wouldn't have to be much to be more than what he had at this point. Earl had spent all but change on the last round of repairs.

Earl pushed his cap back and rubbed his hand across his forehead. "I tell you what, Hitch, I'm beginning to see why you left home. This ain't a lucky place for you, is it?"

Hitch shrugged and leaned back against the fuselage. His head throbbed. The only good parts of this day were the worse things that could've happened and hadn't.

Rick roared up in his motorcar and came jogging over. He took one look at the broken axle and its missing wheel. "You can't be serious!" He was walking straight enough, but his breath had a definite aroma of gin.

Hitch didn't bother to answer. Jennies were always busting themselves to pieces. Most of the ones still in the air were held together with parachute cords, chewing gum, and lots of earnest prayers. It was just bum luck *his* Jenny had decided to turn into a fainting damsel this week of all weeks.

Rick propped his hands on his hips. "Well. Where's the money coming from this time?"

"We could hawk your car maybe," Earl said.

"I'm not the one who keeps demolishing my airplane." Rick pursed his lips at Hitch. "I can hardly perform our routine by myself. If you don't get her back into the air, I suppose that means I won't be getting paid again, doesn't it? Or eating, for that matter?"

"You think I don't know that? What do you want me to do?" Hitch's mind raced. No money meant no repairs, period. No repairs meant no contest. That'd be the end of the line. The end of quite a few lines, actually. He huffed. "I can't conjure your money out of thin air."

Rick sniffed. "And don't I know it well. If you could, we'd not only all have been paid, you'd also have had the wherewithal to hire a decent-sized crew. If we had a wing walker, we'd have twice as good a chance of winning this weekend's competition."

"Wing walker." Hitch looked around. "Where's Jael?"

Earl shook his head. "Haven't seen her."

His mind jumped to Zlo right off. But, no, Zlo was skyside right now. He couldn't have gotten to Jael even if he wanted to.

"She was in town with me not long ago," Hitch said. "I lost her, so I thought maybe she'd bummed a ride back here."

"Maybe she went home."

"That I doubt." He chewed his lip. "I hope not. I have this feeling she would make a heck of an aerialist."

Rick scoffed. "Yesterday was the first she'd even been in a plane."

"Heights don't faze her. She's got good balance."

A grin played at the corner of Earl's mouth. "And she'd be pretty to look at up there, I reckon."

Hitch glared. "That ain't it."

"'Course not. But don't forget you're not going to get her up there at all if you can't get this plane off the ground."

Rick stared at Hitch. "You can't possibly be thinking of bringing her on board."

"Maybe. If she wants the job."

"Well, I say no, Hitch. She's no barnstormer. She's a wild vagabond!"

"There's a difference? Anyway, you said you wanted a wing walker."

Rick flared his nostrils. "You intend to pay her the same as the rest of us if we win?"

"Why not?"

"Then I deserve a raise. I'm a veteran member of this troupe. A pilot and a parachutist. That's worth more than a fledgling wing walker any day, as both of us well know. "

Hitch's head pounded harder. "Maybe, maybe not."

"What does that mean?"

"Means for what I'm paying you already I get an okay pilot, a halfway decent parachutist, and a whole lot of complaining." The words were out before he could stop them.

Earl, still crouched near the wheel, shook his head.

Rick's face stilled. "Your trouble is that you have consistently and *deliberately* underestimated and devalued me! You seem to believe you own Lilla, and don't think I'm not aware of your attempts to lure her away from me. And you insulted me to my face, I'll remind you."

Here it came then. This old beef about Rick's claim to have been the first to do the handkerchief pickup stunt.

"Called me a liar, I believe," Rick insisted.

"You *were* lying."

"Is that so, is it?" Rick started nodding, as if he'd expected no less. "Is that so? And that is truly all you have to say to me?"

What Hitch *truly* wanted to say wouldn't go over any better. So he just gritted his teeth. "Guess so."

"Fine." Rick turned to go and stalked off.

"Looks like you went and hurt his feelings," Earl said.

"He'll get over it." Or not. But it didn't matter. Rick was always upset about something. He could still jump out of a plane whether his ego was feeling up to full size or not. That was all that mattered.

Earl grunted.

Hitch shot another look around. "What about Taos? Did that kid ever bring him back?"

"Don't change the subject." Earl pushed to his feet. "Look, I hate to tell you this, but your good pal Rick is the least of your troubles right now. Qualifying rounds are tomorrow. I suppose we could all go get ourselves some honest jobs, but I don't think they'd pay out fast enough to do us much good. So unless you've got another couple of old pistols to sell . . ." He spread his palms.

"Yeah, yeah." Hitch gritted his teeth. The pressure made his headache worse, but even that was better than the only option left staring him in the face. That option had more than its share of reasons why it was a stupid idea. But it also had one very good incentive: $100.

With a sigh, he stood up from leaning against the plane. "If I tell you to stop worrying, will you?"

"Probably not," Earl said. "What are you going to do?"

"Something I'm likely to regret for a long time. But it'll give us enough money to get back in the air."

With any luck, it would also get him out of town with a partnership in Livingstone's circus and no fear of Bill Campbell ever hunting him down. This thing was already too far along for him not to do whatever had to be done to make that happen.

"I'll do the job," Hitch said. The words sounded like the hiss of a noose pulling tight.

Campbell wiped his mouth with his napkin. "Will you now?"

When Hitch had finally reached Campbell's house, half a mile outside of town, the time was along about supper. Campbell'd done all right for himself, living in this smart whitewashed place. Two stories topped with dormer windows, it was too large for one man alone, but likely that was exactly why he'd bought it. He was the big man around here, so he needed a big house, right?

Hitch stood in the spacious dining room, where Campbell sat at a long oak table eating salt pork and baked beans. Campbell's seat looked out of a tall paned window onto a view of the river and, beyond it, the rugged crag of the Bluff. Around here, that was a prime view.

On the wall behind Campbell, framed newspapers highlighted his many triumphs in cleaning up the town and conquering crime. Photographs showed him grinning with all his teeth and shaking hands with state politicians and city businessmen.

With barely a glance at Hitch, Campbell kept on reading his paper until he'd swallowed.

Then he cleaned his back teeth with his tongue and looked Hitch up and down. "Here you are being sensible and on time, both. Maybe you *have* learned a thing or two in the passing years."

Just inside the archway that separated the dining room from the front parlor, Hitch remained standing like some hapless Army private waiting for his captain to return his salute.

He hooked his thumbs in his suspenders and cocked a lazy hip, as if he was at his ease. "I'll do it on one condition."

"Condition." Campbell sucked his teeth, then turned back to his plate. He crumbled off a piece of cornbread and sopped it in the bean sauce. As he chewed, he sat back in his chair and regarded Hitch once more. "What condition?"

"My plane was damaged in the storm. If you want it in the air, then you have to pay for the repairs."

"And how much is that going to cost me?"

"Fifteen, twenty bucks."

"All right."

Hitch raised his eyebrows. "That's it? Just like that?"

"Why not? Guess that storm was a lucky one for me." Campbell's mouth twitched in that almost-smile. "Kind of galls, don't it? Thought you'd pull it all off by yourself. And now here you are needing my help as much as I want yours. Just like in the old days."

Hitch's shoulders tightened. "This isn't going to be like the old days. After this job, we're even." After this job, he'd leave Scottsbluff and never again give Campbell the chance of camping on his tail. After this job, there'd be no reason to come back.

Not unless some miracle happened and Griff decided to forgive him.

"Sure, sure," Campbell said. "I suppose you've heard what your Col. Livingstone has to say about this storm? Griff tells me he's issued a challenge to any of you flyboys who can figure out what's going on up there."

Hitch eyed him. "You don't buy into that, do you?"

"That's hard to say, son. But you know me, I always load all six cartridges."

Hitch made himself shrug. "The storm was just a freak. They happen all the time around here, as I recall."

"Maybe, maybe not. But if you get a condition on our deal, then so do I. I want you to do like Livingstone says and keep an eye out. Should you happen to find anything, you tell me before you tell Livingstone—or anybody else. You understand?"

Hitch frowned. "Even if something *is* up there, why would you care?"

"Something's going on here. I don't think either of us is dense enough to believe otherwise. Stores robbed in town today? All these bodies?" He shook his head. "What if our folks from around here, instead of these strangers, start falling out of the sky?"

For an instant, the image of Griff spread-eagled in last night's cornfield blasted through Hitch's brain. His heart missed a beat.

"Whatever it is," Campbell said, "it's a threat to this town and the people. And make no mistake. It's my town, and they're my people." He looked Hitch in the eye. "I don't take it lightly when something threatens what's mine."

Hitch stared back. "Neither do I."

Campbell eyed him—trying to read his thoughts maybe. "I don't trust this Livingstone jaybird any farther than I can throw him. For all I know, this is all something he cooked up to get folks interested in his doings. And you're going to keep tabs on that for me, aren't you?"

For all that this *did* sound like something Livingstone might have cooked up on one of his more creative days, he definitely wasn't at the heart of it. But let Campbell think that.

Saying yes to him on this was the only way to move forward in any kind of positive direction. Even if Hitch did figure anything out, Campbell would never know the difference if Hitch decided later that keeping his mouth shut was the better course of valor.

"All right," he said.

Campbell held his gaze, then nodded. "Good enough." He picked up his fork and hunched over his plate. "I'll let you know when it's time for the job. My housekeeper'll give you the money for the repairs."

"Fine." Hitch turned to go. He'd done what he'd had to do. But if he didn't do what he *still* had to do, he was going to end up in deeper trouble than ever.

Hitch trudged through the gnarled grove of apple trees that surrounded the Carpenters' farm. Nan'd skin him alive for coming here. But so long as her kid had his dog, he didn't have much choice.

He was in way over his head with this deal with Campbell. To pull this thing off, he needed to fix his plane, smuggle Campbell's booze, win the airshow, and find the flying mystery in the sky—all in less than a week.

A dog barked.

He looked up. "Taos!"

The dog didn't come bounding out of the trees. But a human head—the very same one that usually wore that red kerchief—poked around one of the trunks. The low profusion of branches sagged with green apples just starting to blush to red. Jael blinked out from the middle of them.

She straightened up from leaning against a sturdy branch. Almost self-consciously, she pushed her hair behind her ears. "You are here? Your friend Nan Carpenter tells me I am to stay with her now."

He stopped short. "What? Why?"

"I do not have knowledge. I tell her I do not work for you, and she tells me that was good."

"Ah." So long as Jael wasn't connected with Hitch, then she wasn't quite the no-account Nan had taken her for. He frowned. "I thought you liked it out at camp."

"I thought you did not want me at camp. You asked Nan Carpenter if I can stay with her."

"That was then. Didn't I say you could stay with Earl and Rick and Lilla and me for as long as you wanted?" It was stupid, but her leaving without a word felt like a dismissal. And after all the stuff they'd been through yesterday and today, he deserved at least a goodbye. "Where'd you run off to anyway? You could have told me—I mean, all of us—you were leaving."

She frowned. "I am in hurry. I must find pilot to take me home."

"I never said I *wouldn't* take you."

"Yes, you did." She jutted her jaw. "More times than once."

He bit back a retort. He was cranky and frustrated and more than ready for this day to end. And he *had* been dancing all around her requests for help getting back home. But how was he supposed to have known she wasn't crazy after all?

He made himself relax, and he put on his best grin. "Look, how'd you like to come back? There's a job for you if you want it. Wing walking in the show. You're a natural for it."

"Wings?" Her face lit up, and she stepped forward. "You are saying go up in plane? You will take me home?"

"Yeah, I'll help you go home, if you're sure that's what you want." The evidence seemed to indicate she'd be a whole lot better off down here, where Zlo couldn't electrocute her. "But maybe not right away. I mean, I could use your help. You heard Livingstone this afternoon. If we could find *Schturming* and make sure it doesn't damage the town again"—or even just explain what it was—"then that could be a big deal, for both of us."

That was going to be the pill for her to swallow. He kept his posture casual. In her excitement over going home, maybe she'd skip right on by that part.

She knit her brows. "You will not take me home now?"

Or maybe not.

She leaned back. "What is this you are doing? You are being"—

she waved her hand, searching for the word—"not real with me."

His grin slipped. "What?"

"You smile same at me as when you tried to keep Livingstone from giving you to custody man." She crossed her arms. "Why do you change your mind about taking me to home all of this sudden?"

"It's not exactly about changing my mind. I didn't know you before. Now I know you."

"You are wanting my help now for something. That is why you do this."

"Well—"

"You think because I do not say your language well that I am stupid." Red spots appeared on her cheeks and neck. "I am not. I see your face, I hear your words. I am not needing days to have knowledge of who you are. I have seen you this few days already, and I have knowledge of you."

Like tarnation she did. "And who am I?"

"You are man who gets into trouble. Maybe you do not mean to be causing harm, but you cause it anyway."

"Look, you do not know me. It's only been two days. You don't know anything about me."

"And you have no knowledge about me either." She tossed her hair. "But here is something both of us are knowing. I can do something for you that you want, and maybe I am only person who can do it for you. But what I want is something any pilot can do." She raised her chin. "And they will have happiness to do it for me, after what Livingstone is saying to them about finding *Schturming*."

He stared at her. She might have seen right through him from the beginning, but it seemed like he had barely scratched her surface.

She was right, more or less, about almost all of it. He *was* always getting himself into trouble—he could hardly deny that right now—and save for the fact that he sort of had dibs on her, he'd given her no absolute reason to help him.

"I don't think you're stupid. I never did." He looked her in the eye. "I think Matthew was right—you're heaped with brains."

She widened her eyes. Then she looked away, anywhere but at him, before finally settling her gaze on the ground between them. Carefully, she pushed her hair behind her ear again and peeked up at him.

Did that mean maybe she didn't think he was so bad after all?

He took a step. "Listen, I deserved some of what you said. I admit I don't have a *right* to your help. But I sure could use it. And you've only met the one pilot—and that's me—and he's downright likable once you get to know him. So why not at least think about this job? Until we find *Schturming*, you've got nothing to do in the meantime."

She slanted a glance at him, another one of those studying looks. But the furrow in her forehead was gone, and the corner of her mouth *almost* hinted at a smile.

Doggoned if she wasn't human after all. Except for the lightning and the dead bodies and the bruised shins, he might even be more than a little sorry when the time came to hold up his end of the deal and send her on her way.

He smiled back.

From the direction of the house, footsteps crunched through the grass.

A slender redhead—Molly—ducked a tree branch and stopped at the sight of them. "Oh. I was coming to say it was suppertime." She looked back and forth between them. "I'm sure you could stay for dinner, Mr. Hitchcock." She did that slow blink again. She'd probably modeled it after moving-picture stars like Clara Bow and Mary Pickford, but it was so obvious, it would have been worth laughing at—if it wouldn't have hurt the kid's feelings.

"You could regale us with your stories of the sky," she said.

"You can call me Hitch. Nobody I like calls me Mr. Hitchcock. And thanks, but I seriously doubt your mama would appreciate—"

"Molly, did you find them?" Nan ducked around the tree behind her daughter. She caught sight of Hitch and froze.

"I'm just leaving," he said. "Thought my dog might be out this way. He was with your son last I saw. Walter, I think his name is?"

Nan wrung her hands in the pink floral print of her pinafore apron. She came forward to stand beside Jael. "If your dog's a brown collie type, he's around someplace. Call him and I expect he'll come. You'd best chain him after this." She opened her mouth like she wanted to say something, closed it, then opened it again. "I allowed as Jael could stay with us now."

"If it makes any difference, you should know I'm giving her a job. If she wants it."

"That's her choice, I'm sure." Nan drew a breath. Her voice was grim, but her eyes weren't—quite. "I don't want to have to be hard about this, Hitch. But you're not welcome on this farm. It just . . . isn't the best thing."

"So I've heard." He turned to go, then glanced back at Jael. "Well, what do you say about the job?"

She looked straight at him. "I say I will have thoughts about it."

CHAPTER 15

TAOS DIDN'T QUITE seem to understand how the game of fetch was supposed to work. He'd bring sticks back all right. But every time Walter threw a small stick, Taos would come trotting back with a big one. This latest one was almost as long as he was. He bit it on the skinny end and dragged the rest behind him.

Walter huffed and shook his head. Of course, a dog couldn't be good at everything, just like a person couldn't be. Taos seemed good enough at the rest of being a boy's dog.

Walter leaned down to try to pull the stick away. Taos pulled right back, tail wagging.

Footsteps approached through the apple trees. "Taos!"

The dog dropped the stick and whirled around. He bounded up to his owner—the man called Hitch—and reared onto his hind legs, barking.

Hitch snapped his fingers. "Get down." He crouched to fondle the dog's ears, but he looked at Walter the whole time. "Ran away with my dog, did you?" His voice was serious. But his eyes twinkled just a bit. Maybe.

Without saying anything, it'd be kind of hard to make somebody understand the dog had run away with Walter more than the other way around. So Walter just pushed his hands into his overalls pockets and shrugged.

"Weeelll." Hitch drew out the word. "Taos must like you. He always did have good taste in people. Picked me out right away." He winked.

Walter grinned. If he was a dog, he'd have picked Hitch too.

People had been talking all over town today. Most of it was about the big storm, but Mama Nan and Aunt Aurelia had been whispering with Mr. Matthew and Mr. J.W. about what Jael and Hitch had done. Flown right into the storm, dodging lightning and everything. Like real heroes.

And Walter was going to get to go flying with them. Hitch had said Walter could go flying, more or less, and Jael had promised.

Walter pulled his hands out of his pockets and crossed his arms over his chest, feet wide, the way Hitch had been standing beside his plane yesterday. He pointed at the sky and raised his eyebrows. With any luck, Hitch'd understand.

Hitch stood. "You really like planes, don't you, son?"

He nodded, enthusiastically.

"Well, I'd sure be happy to take you up. But to be honest with you"—he scratched the back of his head—"your mama doesn't much like me."

Walter frowned his best confused face.

"Doesn't matter why," Hitch said. "Not to a sprig like you anyhow. But maybe you better figure on going up with another pilot."

That wasn't what he'd had in mind *at all*. Yesterday, it might have seemed one pilot was as good as another. But that was before he'd met Hitch and his plane and his dog. He let his shoulders sag.

Hitch reached out to ruffle his hair. "Never mind. There's plenty of good pilots around. You'll find somebody. Thanks for taking care of my dog." He turned to leave.

Taos hesitated, panting, then bounded after his master.

Walter watched them go, until they disappeared behind the apple trees and even their footfalls were gone. Then he turned and ran back to the house as fast as he could.

He'd have to make Mama Nan understand somehow. Didn't make any kind of sense why she wouldn't like Hitch. He was just the kind of person a pilot should be. He had to be ten kinds of brave to fly around in that storm today. And hadn't he rescued Jael from the lightning? Plus, he hadn't been upset even a smidge about Taos running off.

Walter swung himself around the pasture fence post, ran

through the dusty yard, and leapt over all three porch steps at once. He'd been trying to do that all summer, but no time to celebrate right now. He banged through the screen door into the kitchen.

Mama Nan stood over the cast-iron stove with a wooden spoon in one hand. "Walter, where have you been? Didn't you hear me call?"

The family was all gathered at the long table—Papa Byron at the near end, Molly and the twins on one bench, and Aunt Aurelia and Jael on the other.

He stopped short. *Jael.* She was here? She was staying with them? His insides flipped, and he gave her his full-face grin.

She smiled back. She wasn't as sparkly now as she had been before. Seemed like maybe getting hit by lightning—if you survived—should give you more sparkles, but she only looked tired. She leaned both elbows on the table and supported her chin against her locked fingers. Her hair had gone silvery in places, so it almost matched her eyes. But that was about the only other thing different about her.

"Sit down," Mama Nan said.

He rounded the table to sit between Aunt Aurelia and Jael.

Papa Byron—his dark hair still damp from the sweat of the day and his sleeves rolled up above his beefy arms—said grace, and then Mama Nan dished up the meatloaf and green beans.

Walter peeked at Jael.

She gave him the tiniest of nudges with her knee, and her smile turned up on the side of her face.

He looked at Mama Nan. Getting her to let him fly with Hitch wasn't just a matter of timing. There was also the matter of figuring out *how* to get her to understand she was wrong about Hitch.

Her face was flushed, her mouth tight. But it wasn't the angry kind of tight. It was the about-to-cry kind of tight. Not that she actually would cry in front of them, of course.

She finished dishing out the supper, then eased down in her seat at the far end of the table around the corner from Jael. "Byron," she said.

Papa Byron glanced up at her, chewing slowly. He never had

too much to say. "Slow, steady, and silent," he'd told Walter once. "Live that way, and you won't never have much to regret."

"Byron." Mama Nan always said his name twice, once to get his attention and once afterwards. "I don't want these children down with those gypsy barnstormers. Will you tell them that?"

Panic welled up hot and fast. Walter clutched the table.

Molly gasped. "You can't mean it!"

"Don't think I don't, young lady. And don't think I don't see you making sheep's eyes at Hitch. That'll be enough of that."

"Oh, Mama. He's a nice man!" She sighed. "That curly hair. He looks positively like Douglas Fairbanks."

Walter wrinkled his nose. Molly had taken him to see a Douglas Fairbanks picture once. He wasn't a speck like Hitch.

Jael looked back and forth between Molly and Mama Nan. "Who is this Douglas Fairbanks?" Her voice was quiet, sweet. It sounded kind of like how honey and butter tasted.

Molly blinked her eyes wide. "You don't know? He's a star in the moving pictures."

"And he is like Hitch?"

"He's dashing and exciting and has all sorts of adventures."

"Ah."

"And he's only quite the handsomest man ever."

This time Jael blushed bright pink. "Ah."

"Molly," Mama Nan said, "that's quite enough of this foolishness."

Molly hunched over her plate. "Well, Hitch *is* nice anyway."

Aunt Aurelia poured out her milk straight onto her beans. "Very nice. Do you remember, Nan, when he ate that grasshopper down whole?"

Evvy and Annie both giggled. Their red-gold curls were plastered to their faces with the heat. They were only six, so they didn't yet know Aunt Aurelia sometimes said the wrong thing. Walter didn't play with the twins much anymore—not since that day when he'd nearly let them die down by the creek.

Still, a whole grasshopper. Maybe he should try that later and show it to them.

Mama Nan carefully cut her food into little bits. She didn't take a bite. "Hitch Hitchcock is not the kind of man you want to ever go running after, you hear me? He's as heedless and irresponsible as the Lord knows how to make them. He brought nothing but grief to your Aunt Celia."

Walter didn't remember Aunt Celia. But if Mama Nan and Aunt Aurelia knew Hitch, it made sense Aunt Celia would have known him too.

"Celia, Celia." Aunt Aurelia picked up a string bean with her fingers, dabbled it in the milk, then popped it into her mouth. "She always looked so beautiful in violet."

"Now, Nan," Papa Byron said, "what need is there to dredge that up? You ever think maybe he didn't know she was sick?"

"That's what he told you, Mama," Molly put in.

"Never you mind," Mama Nan said. "You just stop this nonsense and act like a proper young girl should."

Molly sulked.

"This is not where Hitch is living?" Jael asked.

"No. He doesn't live anywhere, far as I know." Mama Nan stared at the mess she'd made on her plate. Then she looked up at Jael. She had that pinched-up expression like she did when she wanted to know something but didn't think she would like the answer. "You're going to take this job with him?"

"Maybe. I must have thoughts about it."

Molly cast Jael half a glance. She looked jealous.

But then, good sweet angels! Who wouldn't be jealous? Walter couldn't help grinning. If he was a little bit older—and if Mama Nan wouldn't forbid it for sure—maybe he could have gotten a job too. He gave a bounce against the hard bench, then bent his head to his plate and started shoveling in meatloaf, so's nobody would notice his excitement. He kept watching Jael out of the corner of his eye.

She ate a dainty bite. "Whyever you are angry with him, I can tell you he is not bad man."

She had something sort of magic-like about her. It wasn't just the sparkliness. It wasn't even that she looked like a storybook lady. Maybe it was partly that she'd understood how to talk to him, from the very first time he saw her. She knew things. Things about people. If anybody could talk Mama Nan into letting him fly with Hitch, she might be the one.

But Mama Nan didn't seem to believe her. She sighed, slow

and weary, then finally bent her head to her own meatloaf and green beans.

That was all anybody said about Hitch for the rest of supper. Afterwards, Walter took Jael by the hand and tugged her along, up the narrow stairs to Aunt Aurelia's bedroom where the girls had already spread out an extra hay tick on the floor and covered it with Mama Nan's trunk-creased patchwork quilts. He pointed at it, and Jael nodded.

She looked more tired than ever, but she didn't shoo him out. Instead, she crossed the room and raised the window. "Come." She hoisted a hip onto the sill and scrunched her legs around so they were dangling out. Because the roof here slanted down from the dormer windows, it wouldn't be a straight fall if she lost her balance. In any case, she didn't seem too worried.

He tiptoed over and stood next to her.

"Come up," she said.

Mama Nan would have a fit if she saw, but she'd be down washing dishes for a bit yet. He scrambled up and sat beside Jael, feet hanging out. He clutched the windowsill hard.

She laughed and let go with both hands. "Put up your hands. You want to be flying. This is flying."

He shook his head.

"You will not fall. I will catch you."

No, she wouldn't. She'd miss him and fall right down after him, and it'd be his fault again, just like it had been with the twins way back when. But if a girl could be as brave as all that, then he sure could too. He pried his fingers loose and let go. He kept his hands hovering above the sill, in case he needed to grab it again.

She grinned. "See? Flying." She spread her hands, palms up, and whistled through her teeth, like the wind blowing. Then she glanced at him. "I will tell you secret if you tell me one."

It wasn't like he had many secrets—except about Mr. J.W.'s penny and about Molly letting Jimmy Porter steal a kiss down by the creek that time last week. So he nodded.

"Your secret is first." Her face went still and soft. "Why do you not like to be talking?"

That was hard to explain. Sometimes he thought he might

like to say something again. But it had just been the way it was now for so long, it seemed too hard anymore. He shrugged.

"There must be reason." She nudged him with her leg.

He smiled in spite of himself, but he shrugged again. How could he even explain it? The day he'd let the bad thing happen to the twins and when Mama Nan had been so angry with him . . . the words just hadn't *been* there any longer. Ever since then, he'd always had this feeling of not quite fitting in. His family loved him well enough. But it was just . . . his world seemed to slant a little different from everybody else's.

Like hers. Her world definitely slanted a whole lot more than his even.

He eased a hand up from the sill and touched the overalls bib on his chest. Then he pointed at her and back again.

"You mean you are like me?" She still smiled, but her eyes got faraway. "I am *nikto*. That is meaning having no place to belong."

Nikto. He rolled the word around inside his head. He felt that way sometimes too.

She looked up at the night sky, where the white dots of stars were starting to appear. "All right. Now I will be telling you my secret. I used to think, when I was at my home, that the world was very small place. I thought I had knowledge all about it. But now I am seeing different. The world is not what we are thinking it is—or what we are thinking we will be in it." She reached over. Her finger was warm where it touched between his eyes. "Young Walter, I think your world is not what you are thinking it is either."

CHAPTER 16

RICK QUIT JUST before the competition's first qualifying round. In contrast to yesterday, the morning had dawned clear as a looking glass—blue so bright it was almost transparent, with only a few wisps of clouds along the round edges of the sky. The dew was a little colder and crisper than it had a right to be on a normal August day, but by ten o'clock, the sun was hot enough to melt a man's toes inside his boots. Whatever had been up there yesterday was sure gone today.

It was a perfect morning for flying, and Livingstone hadn't wasted any time in maintaining his contest's schedule. The show didn't officially start until Saturday, but the qualifying rounds were already under way—and Hitch's crew would be up any minute now.

Hitch faced off across from Rick, each of them standing with their backs to their planes.

The heat rising inside his chest wasn't just anger: a fair share of raw-edged panic surged in there as well. "You've got to be kidding me? Now? Just like that, you're going to quit *now*?"

"Yes, now. And, no, not just like that." Rick tossed his bedroll into his front cockpit, where Lilla was already sitting. He'd insisted on packing up right away even though he was only moving to the other end of camp, where he'd supposedly gotten a job with another crew.

Planes growled overhead. Near the road, a crowd had gathered to watch the pilots prove they had skill enough to compete in Livingstone's extravaganza.

"Why?" Hitch demanded. "Because I wasn't polite enough

for you yesterday? Because I won't admit you did something we both know you didn't?"

Rick buttoned his top shirt button and straightened his collar. "You want reasons? All right. I'll supply three." He ticked them off on his fingers. "One, the gentleman on the far side of the camp promises pay that begins now. Two, your claims of no money to pay our salaries wear a trifle thin when you continually manage to find the wherewithal to fix your own machine. Three, quite frankly, I don't think I can bear the sight of you for another day."

"That's mutual," Earl muttered from where he crouched, putting the finishing touches on the Jenny's wheel repairs.

Rick ignored him. "You were perfectly convincing yesterday when you indicated you didn't think my skills were worthy of your esteemed circus."

"I didn't mean you weren't a good flyer." *Just that you're an obnoxious fathead.*

"And then there's four. You attempted to bring on another crew member without our consent."

"Oh, darling," Lilla said. "Earl and I consented."

"And five, if you truly believe that madwoman is going to help you find some secret in the clouds, then you are also mad, and I have no wish to attempt perilous stunts with a lunatic at the controls."

Hitch glared. "All fine and good reasons, and you can add to them that I won't miss one second of your company either. But no honorable man would quit now, when we need you the most. You know full well what's at stake here."

"What's at stake here is entirely yours, and none of mine." Rick looked at Lilla and walked around to the propeller. "Start the engine."

"And what am I supposed to do now?" Hitch asked. "Livingstone's rules call for at least one pilot and one performer. What do you want me to do, put Earl up there on the wings?" For all that Earl was aces with engines, he was useless in the air.

"Not on my life," Earl said.

"Walk your own wings," Rick said. "That would be a good trick." He gave the propeller a spin and stepped back as the engine caught with a click and a roar. The plane rolled forward, and he ran around to clamber into the rear cockpit.

Out of all the options right now, kicking dirt, throwing rocks, or even spitting sounded pretty good. But Hitch just stood there and ground his teeth. Stymied. He could count on one hand the times he'd been truly stymied.

Rick's plane pulled away. On the far side, Jael stood watching, hands in her pockets.

Lilla waved at her jauntily.

Rick guffawed and shouted over the engine: "Come to help that fool hunt castles in the sky, have you?"

She turned her head, without expression, and watched him go.

Then she crossed over to stand in front of Hitch. "I have come for job."

His heart tripped.

From across the field, the latest contestant's plane landed and taxied to a stop.

Livingstone turned to shout at Hitch through a megaphone. "Next up, Captain Robert Hitchcock!"

Hitch's heart kept revving, and the adrenaline swept away whatever panic was left. He took Jael by the shoulders. "I don't know what changed your mind, but bless your hide, kiddo. Thing is, we gotta go up right now. Can you do that? All you gotta do is stand on the wing. That should be enough for today."

She chewed her lip. All that confidence she'd been brimming with yesterday during the storm seemed to have filtered right out of her. "Can we not give it practice first?"

"Captain Robert *Hitchcock*!" Livingstone bellowed.

Hitch looked at Livingstone doubtfully. "Well, we can ask." He let her go. "Stay here."

He jogged across the field. Every eye in the place followed him. The townsfolk fanned themselves with hands and hats, looking bored with the wait. The pilots were either frowning— probably thinking Hitch's plane was still busted—or laughing— probably thinking he wasn't showman enough to get his act together.

Showman, indeed. He ironed the creases out of his forehead and tried to look as nonchalant as possible.

Livingstone set his megaphone at his feet. With one hand, he took a spotless handkerchief from his coat and mopped his forehead beneath the Stetson. With the other, he checked his chained pocket watch.

"Well?" he said. "You are holding up these proceedings, sir. You have a suitable reason for this, no doubt? Something good for my publicity?"

"Could be." There had to be a way to spin this to keep Livingstone from calling the bet right here and now. "I had to make some last-minute changes in my crew. I've got a new wing walker, a woman." Best not to say *which* woman.

Livingstone curled his lip. "I have no place in my show for amateurs, sir."

"She's good, trust me, I've seen her work. But she's a smidge rusty. Can't you nudge me down in the round, so she can have a quick practice run?"

"There will be no changing of the order."

"Then give us ten minutes to warm up."

Livingstone eyed him. "Why should I?"

"'Cause it's good sportsmanship." He looked Livingstone straight in the eye. "And good showmanship. Ham it up to these people. Tell 'em she's taking her life in her hands for their entertainment. They'll eat it up." With any luck, it wouldn't end up being true.

"Hmm." Livingstone ran his thumb and forefinger over his mustache. His gaze flitted from Hitch to his Jenny and then to the spectators. "All right, but ten minutes only. And do it over here where the ladies and gentlemen can see you practicing."

Hitch breathed out his relief. "Thanks."

"And, Mr. Hitchcock." Livingstone waited until Hitch turned back. "Make it look good."

"No problem." He started running and cast a glance skyward as he went. *Please, no problems.*

He reached Jael and Earl. "All right, here it is. He says we get ten minutes, but we have to do it over there where people can watch." He looked at Jael. "All you gotta do is the same thing you did yesterday—except don't jump off and don't get hit by lightning." He crooked a grin, just to let her know it was a joke.

Earl pushed his baseball cap back farther on his head. "I don't know about this. All this rush and hurry—this ain't a good time to be pushing anybody into something like this. Maybe you should put a 'chute on her before she goes out on the wing."

"That's just as dangerous, if not more." If the parachute opened accidentally while she was on the wing, it could end up hauling her right through the wires and struts. If things got too ripped up, or she got tangled in the structure, they could both get themselves killed in a crash.

"She'll be fine." Hitch led her toward the plane. "Just stay on the lower wing for now, where you'll have plenty of stuff to hang onto. Later, when we can take our time, we can work on climbing up top."

"Five seconds!" Livingstone bellowed through the megaphone.

Hitch glanced at Earl. "Let's push the plane over to the runway. Jael can climb up when we get there."

They each took hold of a wing strut and started pushing. For all her bulk, the Jenny was surprisingly light: nothing but varnished linen over a spruce frame with an engine screwed to her front.

Jael walked on Earl's side of the plane. Above the rear cockpit, her head bobbed exaggeratedly up and down, as if she'd stepped into a badger hole.

Hitch frowned. The last thing they needed was her twisting her ankle right now.

They wheeled the plane around to the end of the landing strip. The ground was already dusty and grooved from many takeoffs.

"Ladies and *gen-tle-men*!" Livingstone shouted. "We now have something rather special for your enjoyment. Our next qualifier, Captain Hitchcock, will attempt to best all performances with his raw courage and, for the first time in this or any professional competition, an *untried* assistant. I ask you to please applaud this brave young woman who risks life and limb to attempt the impossible!"

Hitch's heart started doing hammerhead turns. He scrubbed his palms against his pants. "All right," he said to Jael. "Come on around here."

160 – K.M. WEILAND

Earl circled to stand ready at the propeller. Jael followed him, still bobbing, this time with a definite limp.

Hitch's stomach flipped. "Did you step in a hole?"

She shook her head. "It is not something to worry about. Getting that close to lightning has given me stiffness."

"Oh, heck. The lightning." It *would* be too much luck to ask for her survival and an immediate recovery all at once. He caught her arm. "You're not doing this. You're going to need balance and strength up there. It's not worth falling off and getting killed, not after you made it out of yesterday alive."

She scrunched her forehead. "Let me have practice. This I can do. If I did not think I could, I would be telling you."

Livingstone was still selling it to the crowd: "In light of these special circumstances, we will be giving Captain Hitchcock and his lovely assistant a ten-minute warm-up period—which will provide you a first-hand look behind the veil of secrecy that shrouds a barnstormer's carefully planned routine."

Earl snorted. "Carefully planned, my bunioned foot."

In this business, you either winged it—literally—and maybe died flying, or you stayed grounded.

Hitch looked at Jael. "I'm not getting you hurt."

"I have knowledge of what I am doing. Give me my own decision." Her eyes were clear. Except for the wrinkle in her forehead, she looked totally unafraid.

If she couldn't do this, he'd lose the Jenny right here and now. But even that was nothing to somebody's neck. He could start over if it came to that—eventually. He always seemed to land on his feet, one way or another.

But that look in her eyes. *She* believed she could do it.

Livingstone had fallen silent. It was now or not ever.

"We'll just roll around on the ground for a bit to start with," Hitch decided. "If you feel wobbly at all, or you've got any kind of notion you're not going to be able to stay up there in the wind, you tell me, you got it?"

She dipped her chin in a terse nod.

He looked at Earl. "Get her some goggles and gloves." He walked Jael right up to the wing, supporting her so her limp wasn't so noticeable. "Stay on the wing's ribs, all right? You're going to feel a wash from the propeller. Don't forget that once we're up, I won't be able to hear you and you won't be able to hear me."

"I have understanding. I am not afraid of height."

"You're not afraid of much, I guess." He pulled on his own helmet and goggles. "Be careful." He hauled himself into the rear cockpit and checked the fuel selector.

Jael accepted the goggles and gloves from Earl. Then she reached for a strut and started to step aboard. The back of the wing wasn't even a foot off the ground, but she had trouble bending her knee that far. She set her teeth, hard and unflinching, and put a hand under her thigh to pull her leg up.

This was bad. Really, really bad.

On the sidelines, Rick's high-pitched laugh carried. Standing beside him, Lilla jumped once and waved. Rick joggled her elbow to make her stop, his sneer never wavering in its aim toward Hitch.

Hitch looked back around.

Jael had made it onto the wing and was crouching on the ribs, balanced with one hand on the strut and the other on a guy wire. She nodded at him, all business, as if her joints hadn't about rusted shut on her.

In front of the propeller, Earl gave Hitch a strained look.

They were all in trouble. No way Jael could go into the air, and no way Livingstone would give him another chance if she didn't. But right now, the only thing Hitch could do was play along and taxi around the runway. She couldn't get into much trouble that way, even if she tumbled.

He nodded to Earl. "Let's do it."

"All right. Fuel on?"

"Fuel on!"

"Switch off?"

He checked the magneto switches on the panel. "Switches off!"

Earl raised a leg and gave the propeller a mighty heave, then another and another. "Contact!"

Hitch flipped the magneto switch. "Contact!"

Earl swung the prop once again.

One of the cylinders coughed smoke. A second later the whole engine caught, chugging at first. He opened the throttle a bit, and the noise rose to a steady roar. He checked the stick and the rudder pedals, then gave the Jenny enough juice to start her taxiing.

The crowd watched them, intent and quiet. Only Lilla cupped her hands around her mouth and whooped, oblivious when Rick turned his scowl on her.

Jael crouched, her back braced against a strut, and clutched the wires. She was panting, and her eyes were big and unblinking. But she still wore that determined grit of her teeth. It was a mighty familiar look: she was in over her head and too proud to admit it.

How stupid had he been to get himself—and her—into this fix? He growled deep in his chest. Right now a little anger was better than a whole lot of scared.

As they bumped down the runway, she slowly eased herself up to a standing position. Chin raised, she turned to duck under the wires, so she'd be facing the same direction he was. This time, there was no mistaking her wince. She might even have whimpered; it was hard to tell over the engine noise.

"Take it slow! Just go slow!" he shouted. So long as they were on the ground, she should still be able to hear him. "There's no rush here!"

She nodded.

At the end of the runway, he turned the plane around and started to taxi back. Now she was on the side of the field facing the crowd. Time to perform if ever there was a time.

She gave them a wave, then started to walk down the wing toward them. This time, her whole right leg gave out under her. She hit her knees, landing on a rib. The crowd's gasp was audible even over the engine.

He ground his teeth and kept on grinding them all the way back to the other end of the runway.

Once there, he shut off the engine and climbed out. "C'mon. It's all right." He reached up to swing her down.

Her breath came hard, but two hot splashes of color burned against her cheeks. Her eyes snapped, almost angrily. "Give to me time." Her feet reached the ground and she turned away.

"We may not have time." But he headed over to meet Livingstone halfway. "Let me have a few more minutes, will you? She's not ready."

Livingstone stared askance, past Hitch's shoulder. "So I see."

Hitch turned around. Jael was rolling somersaults in the dust, apparently trying to loosen herself up. Earl caught his eye and shrugged.

He turned back to Livingstone. "She was that close to getting hit by lightning yesterday."

Livingstone sniffed. "You have no witnesses to that."

"You want to give me a fair chance to win this bet or not?"

"That is what I am trying to do. No, I am sorry, sir, but this is your one chance to go up and qualify, just like every other contestant. If you cannot do so, then that's the bet right there."

"The bet wasn't about *this*. You really are a rat, you know that?"

"Yes, I am, sir. I find it is good publicity." Livingstone inclined his head. "Now, if you'll excuse me, I have a contest to oversee."

Hands on his hips, Hitch hung his head back. Then he turned and trudged over to where Earl waited next to the plane. "That's it. We're done."

Earl nodded. "Yeah."

Jael trotted over, wincing a little, but looking more limber. "I will go up. I am ready."

At the other end of the field, another pilot started up his engine.

Hitch shook his head. "We're grounded looks like."

She walked right up to him. She was on the tall side for a woman and she only had to tilt her head back a little to look him in the eye. "Let us go up. If we are high enough, maybe they will not have sight of what we do, and accept it for contest anyway."

"Can't hurt nothing now," Earl said.

That was surely true. And anyway, if they had to go out with their tails between their legs, then at least they could do it thumbing their noses at Livingstone one last time.

"She can stay in the cockpit," Earl said. "Just fly around a little."

Hitch dropped his hands from his hips. "All right. Let's do it."

Earl helped Jael into the front cockpit and hand-propped the Jenny once more. As it rolled forward, the crowd's attention split away from the other pilot and swerved back to them. Hitch picked up speed down the field and saluted Livingstone as he passed.

Livingstone scowled. He could holler at them through his megaphone if he wanted to, but then the whole place would know he'd lost control.

At the field's end, Hitch lifted the Jenny off the ground and pitched her toward the sky. They leveled out some eight hundred feet off the ground.

That was when Jael stood up in the front cockpit and started climbing onto the top wing.

CHAPTER 17

"DON'T YOU DARE!" Hitch shouted.

But just like he'd promised her, Jael couldn't hear a thing. She hauled herself up and over the top wing's edge and crouched there, hanging onto the strut wires that looped up from beneath.

The pounding of his heart filled his whole chest. Walking on the bottom wing was one thing. Down there, you had all kinds of stuff to hang onto and brace yourself against. But the top wing was a whole 'nother horserace. You wouldn't find anything but a wall of wind and a few small wires in which to wedge either your hands or your feet.

His stomach flipped. The cockpit was safe; it was solid ground. But up on top, there was nothing but a long, long fall.

He held the plane steady. He needed to turn around, get this heap back to level ground before Jael lost her balance. But he couldn't turn without the wind shifting around her and maybe pulling her over anyway.

"Get back in the cockpit!" he hollered so loud the words scraped his throat.

Maybe she heard him. She shifted one of her legs. But she didn't extend it back toward the cockpit. She raised it, bending the knee, until her foot was flat against the wing. She wiggled, squeezing her foot into the wire.

"No! Don't stand up!"

Slowly, slowly, hand still flat on the wing, she brought her other foot up and wedged it too. Then she started to straighten.

His lungs stopped inflating. Over the years, he'd worked with dozens of wing walkers. He'd seen more than a few of them break too many bones to survive. And none of *them* had about got hit by lightning the day before.

He braced the stick in both hands, feet against the rudder pedals.

She made it all the way up, body tilted forward, leaning into a fifty-mile-an-hour wind. And then, just like a pro, she raised her face to the sun and spread her arms.

She was doing it. She was *really* doing it. Of course, she could stop doing it any second. But for now, she was as good as any of the best of them. Her head started to move. She tilted it around, inch by inch, until he could see the corner of her eye. And then she grinned: a wide, exultant grin. The kind you grinned when you were as happy as you'd ever been in your life, and you knew you weren't likely to be that happy ever again.

Durned girl. He grinned back.

He dropped the right wing the barest of smidges and started a big circle. If she wouldn't get back into the cockpit, then he'd have to land sooner or later. Might as well do it under Livingstone's nose.

The other contestant's plane was in the air now, headed in their direction. Hitch gave it a wide berth to avoid the turbulence. As they passed each other, he offered the pilot and his staring parachutist a jaunty salute. Then he pitched down, still going slow to minimize the pressure on Jael as much as possible. By the time they reached the field, the Jenny was a bare twenty feet off the ground.

He gave her the gun and buzzed the field. Hats and scarves blasted away in every direction. White faces turned sunward to stare.

Let the Jenny crash and burn right now. It'd still be a heck of a way to go out. He laughed aloud.

Jael lowered herself to one knee and inched back until her hands could anchor themselves in the wires. He swung the plane around and came in low for a landing. Even above the engine, the sound of the whooping and clapping was colossal.

This girl was born to be an aerialist.

The wheels bounced. Jael bobbled and nearly fell over sideways.

His heart jumped into his throat.

But she righted herself and straightened up on her knees to wave one hand at the crowd. She was a natural, no question.

The crowd ducked through the fence or clambered over. They swarmed the field, despite Livingstone's megaphoned entreaties.

Wasn't everyday you worked a crowd into this kind of frenzy, especially with a relatively simple stunt. Still, crowds on the field were never a good thing. Even if they managed not to mangle their faces in a propeller, some of them had the not-so-charming tendency to grab souvenirs off the plane.

He tugged at his helmet and goggles and jumped out.

"Stay there," he told Jael.

Still kneeling, she braced her hands against the wing, looking like she'd topple if she didn't. But beneath her goggles, her grin sparkled.

Earl ran up. "I don't believe it!" He looked from Hitch to Jael and back again, then got a knowing gleam in his eye. He threw his head back and laughed.

Hitch slapped his shoulder. "Help me move the plane. Stand back, folks! Wouldn't want you to get bumped over."

Somewhere toward the back of the bustle, Rick stared. Even if he'd stuck around to do the parachute drop, they wouldn't have gotten a reception like this. And Rick knew it.

Livingstone jostled through to stand at Hitch's elbow. "Well." He looked abashed. But his mustache was trying to twitch away the fact that what he really wanted to do was grin. Hitch had just given the show another big fat plug.

Livingstone squinted at Jael from beneath his hat brim, then looked Hitch up and down. "You cannot follow rules to save your life, now can you?"

Hitch shrugged. "I try. The rules just don't follow back."

"Hmp."

"But we qualified, right?"

This time, the mustache twitch hid a scowl. "I could well disqualify you on any number of technicalities. But far be it from Bonney Livingstone to disappoint the expectant public." He raised his megaphone and turned to the crowd. "I am pleased to announce Captain Hitchcock and his team have qualified—

with much aplomb, I might add—for this weekend's competition. I am certain you all will return to watch him and his fearless flying companion tempt death once more!"

Hitch motioned to Earl, and they eased the plane through the crowd and back to camp. Behind, Livingstone's megaphone droned on, and another plane engine chattered to life.

As soon as they were parked, Earl ducked under the engine and clapped Hitch on both shoulders. "You sly son of a gun! You had even me fooled. I bet you knew this whole time Rick was going to up and quit. That's showmanship for you, boy!" He made the OK sign with one hand. "Those folks don't even know what hit them." He gestured up at Jael. "They think they just watched a cripple wing walk!" He turned back to Hitch. "Why didn't we think of this before? You're a genius, you know that?"

"Yep, a genius." He was a lucky idiot, but why mince words? He walked around to the back of the wing and waited for Jael to shimmy down into the front cockpit.

She caught his eye as she ducked her head under the top wing and swung first one leg, then the other over the edge of the cockpit. She moved slow and careful, but her whole face beamed.

He grinned back.

Earl smacked his fist into his palm. "I mean, this is great. Forget Livingstone's competition. This'll rake in the dough at every hop between here and San Francisco. What an act, brother!"

Hitch helped Jael step from the bottom wing to the ground. "Except it ain't an act."

"What?"

"It wasn't an act. I didn't plan any of it. All I did was hang on. She did it all." He raised her hand, as if introducing her to an audience.

She bit her lip, shyly, her eyes still dancing.

Earl chuckled once. Then his grin faded. "Are you kidding me?"

"Nope."

He looked at Jael. "Is he kidding me?"

She shook her head.

"Well . . . dadgum." Earl started laughing again and reached to engulf her hand in both of his. "Dadgum it is, sweetheart. You're a crazier fool than Hitch is, you know that?"

She inclined her head in a small bow. "Thank you."

"Well, come on, this is worth celebrating." He released her and turned to rummage through the camp supplies.

Hitch led her, limping only slightly now, to a rolled-up bed-roll she could use as a seat. "We got anything worth celebrating with?"

"Not much. I think Lilla left behind some orange sodey pop. Yep." He stood up with three of the ribbed glass bottles. With his sleeve over the heel of his hand, he snapped off the tops, then passed them around. Still standing, he raised his bottle. "Here's to our girl, who we may or may not let go back up again, but who definitely saved our grease-stained hides today."

Hitch tilted the spicy citrus bubbles into the back of his throat and took a long chug.

Jael sipped hers, licked her lips thoughtfully, then tipped her head back for a deep swallow.

He watched her until she came back up for air. "What made you do that?"

"You were needing help." She licked her lips again and raised a shoulder. "And I am needing to go home."

Yeah, right. Go home where nobody seemed to care what happened to her—except Zlo, who definitely cared that she ended up as a blob on the ground somewhere.

Finding *Schturming* and using the discovery to impress Livingstone was one thing. But it sure was seeming like Jael would be better off moving on from that place. She could stay here with his crew. With Rick and Lilla gone, she wouldn't even be an extra mouth to feed.

He watched her, trying to read her. "You have any idea how lucky you are not to have fallen off?"

"What is this lucky?"

"It's like when everything's going right, and you just know it's going to keep on going. Nothing can touch you."

"I like that. You have this lucky?"

"Luck. Yeah, sometimes." He smiled at her. "But listen, no

more of this. If you're going to work on my crew, then you have to understand I'm the boss. If I tell you not to do something, you don't do it."

"If you are boss, I understand this. But there is something *you* do not understand. If I have this feeling, inside me"—she laid her hand over her stomach—"that I must be doing something, like today, then I must be doing it."

"Why?"

"If I do not, if I think about it, that is when luck goes away. I maybe start believing I cannot be doing it, then I have fear. And then I cannot do it." She gave him a long look. "You understand this?"

What airman didn't understand that? "Even so, I don't want any more climbing out on the wing without you at least giving me a warning. Okay?"

She nodded once.

"I don't need you falling off just yet. We've got a competition to win and this *Schturming* thing of yours to find." *Finding* it would work out well for both of them. When it came time for her to think about actually going back to it, that'd have to be another discussion.

Earl clinked his bottle against Hitch's. "Hear, hear!"

The sparkle in her eyes faded. That wrinkle surfaced in her forehead again. "About finding *Schturming*. Last night, there is something I was not telling you." She traced her forefinger back and forth in the soft dirt beside her foot. "I cannot find it."

"What do you mean?" Earl asked.

"I cannot find it. It does not stay in one spot always."

Hitch lowered his bottle to his bent knee. "So it could be headed to Calgary now for all we know?"

She looked up. "*Schturming* will not be leaving far. It will be coming again." She fingered her pendant's chain. "But I cannot be telling you to what time or place."

He chewed his lip. "You know that means Zlo's coming back too? You just want to sit here and wait for him?"

"I must get back—to stop him. And how can I be going up without—?" She pointed to the Jenny.

"Look, I never said anything about helping you *stop* Zlo. If he comes down and we can get him arrested, great. But all I'm wanting is to get a good look at this *Schturming*—enough to give Livingstone something to make him happy." And satisfy his own curiosity. "I'll take you home like I said I would, but you're better off forgetting Zlo and moving on to where people aren't going to go around chucking you overboard."

The shy smile was gone from her face. She looked wan and haggard—a bit desperate maybe. "Yes," she said. "I am having understanding." She set her drink on the ground and stood. She walked, mostly steady on her feet, and disappeared around the far side of the plane.

Aw, shoot. He kicked himself for being an oaf. So her home was a touchy subject. *He* "had understanding" for that. He thumped his drink down on the ground and pushed to his feet.

Earl tugged his ear. "Where you going?"

"Where do you think?"

He eased around the nose of the plane, moving slow in case she was doing something dangerous—like crying.

But she was only leaning against the fuselage, fiddling with a sore spot on her finger. She looked at him. "Will you still give to me job?"

He huffed out a breath. As long as she stayed here, she'd be mostly out of harm's way. It'd give him a few extra days to maybe talk her down to a more sensible plan.

"'Course I will," he said. "Wing walkers like you don't drop in front of my plane every day."

That earned a grin. "I would be hoping not."

"Look, I'm sorry I didn't believe you about all this before. And I'm sorry I didn't take you home when we still had the chance." That was only half a lie. "You really think we won't see them again?"

She snorted. "Oh, we will be seeing them again. But only when it is right for Zlo and wrong for us."

"We'll figure something out," he said. "You help me win this competition, and I'll help you get home—or wherever else you may decide you want to go." Whatever he thought, it *was* her choice. She'd undoubtedly get where she wanted to go one way or another anyhow. "I promise."

She studied him. Something in her eyes said that, this time, she saw something different. She smiled. "Thank you."

He smiled back, then found himself strangely at a loss for something else to say. He looked at her hand. The left forefinger bore a long raw spot along its side. "What happened there?"

"It is from when there was fire—when I was falling."

From when Zlo had lit her dress on fire. "Should have told me about that before. We've got some salve for stuff like that." He went back to search through the supplies for the jar, then returned.

She bit her lip, but proffered her hand without protest.

It wasn't the hand of a lady of leisure. It wasn't even the hand of a farmwife, like Celia's. More like Earl's hand. Black oil lined the short nails, and heavy calluses edged her fingertips and the pad of her palm. It was a strong hand—a proficient hand, the fingers long and nimble.

"So," he said. "You mentioned you didn't have any family up there?"

She watched him smooth grease down the length of the burn. "Yes. I am *nikto*."

"That means what? Orphan?"

"Yes, but more."

He thought about that. "Outcast? Like other people don't want you around them?"

"Yes, that is it."

"Doesn't seem like this home of yours has much earned its way to being so important."

She looked up at him, surprised. "Where else do any people have to go except home?"

He finished with the grease, tucked the jar in his jacket pocket, and snapped out a narrow length of linen. "Whole big world out there, kiddo."

She scrutinized him. "That is why you did not go back to your home before now?"

"Something like that. Long story."

"But you have family. Nan Carpenter and—Griff. They seem very angry with you always. I wonder about Nan Carpenter." She knit her eyebrows above those silver eyes of hers. "Before you were leaving, was she . . . belonging to you?"

He darted up a look and laughed. "You mean, my *girl*? No, never. No, she's mad because of"—he concentrated on snugging the bandage around her finger—"well, because of Celia. That's her sister. She *was* my girl. They don't quite understand why it was I had to leave her."

"Why had you to leave?"

"The sheriff—I told you he wasn't a custodian—he was threatening them to try to get me to do something."

She gave him a small, encouraging smile. "You should be telling them this. That is not a wrong reason, Hitch Hitchcock."

"No, it's not." He knotted off the bandage, held her hand for one more second, then gave it back to her.

He thought about Griff and Nan—and the passel of kids Nan had gone and had for herself in the past few years. That boy of hers, the silent one, seemed a good kid. He played with Taos and looked at the sky like everything was a new adventure to be discovered. It was a pleasure to see that in somebody else's face for a change.

In some ways, it might have been nice to have someone like that through whose eyes he could have seen the world afresh. But a family would have staked him to the ground, and he wasn't fool enough to believe that being the stake was any better a life than being the one who *was* staked.

He looked at Jael and put on a rueful smile. "It could be I did it for the right and the wrong reason all at once. That's the problem."

CHAPTER 18

ARMS SPREAD LIKE plane wings, Walter careened through the kitchen, tilting to the inside whenever he needed to make a turn around the edge of the table. It wasn't a bit like real flying. It wasn't even as fun as *seeing* a real plane fly over. But it sure beat sitting in the corner, waiting for supper to be ready.

At the table, Aunt Aurelia perched on the bench. She held the tarnished sugar bowl in both hands. "I would like to have a sweet."

Mama Nan didn't even look up from poking at the corn ears boiling in the big pot. She swiped a dark strand of hair from her damp face. "No. We'll eat in a few minutes. Walter, stop running around like a wild man. Sit down."

He imagined plane noises rumbling in the back of his throat and banked hard around Aunt Aurelia's corner of the table. A cricket crawled along the seam in the floorboards. As high as he was in the sky, the cricket might be a cow or a tractor. He bent his knees and swooped lower to see if he could spook the cow.

Aunt Aurelia whimpered and thumped the sugar bowl against the table. "I want a sweet *now.*"

"Wait a bit, won't you?" Mama Nan said. "Walter, please!"

"Don't want to wait," Aunt Aurelia said.

"Well, you must." Mama Nan balanced a stack of plates on her hip and carried them over to the table. She set one at Papa Byron's place and reached to set another in front of Aunt Aurelia.

Walter rounded the corner again and clipped Mama Nan's elbow with his outstretched hand. The plate flipped off the edge and crashed against the floor. It broke into three big pieces.

"Walter!"

Oh, no. He stopped short and clenched both fists. Mama Nan's plates. And not just any plates. She was using company plates, because Jael was there.

"Oh, Walter." She pushed the rest of the plates onto the table and dropped to her knees to pick up the pieces. "Good sweet angels, sit down, can't you? And stop making that unholy racket!" Immediately, she bit her lip and flashed him a dismayed look, because, of course, he hadn't been making any noise at all.

He couldn't even apologize to her. Shoulders slumped, he dragged himself over to a three-legged stool in the corner and sat down.

He was stupid. He made everybody worry because he didn't like to talk. What he needed to do was say something. He opened his mouth and tightened his throat. But he just . . . couldn't do it.

Anyway, it wasn't the talking he needed to do to make everything right again. The real problem was that he was a coward. Whenever he got that scared squished feeling in his middle, he wasn't able to move either. Not even when other people needed his help. Not even when they were dying.

Someday he'd be brave. Maybe that would be the day he'd be able to get the words out again.

Aunt Aurelia sniffed at Mama Nan and hugged the sugar pot closer. "Serves you right. You should have let me have a sweet."

Mama Nan kept stacking the pieces. Her eyes seemed very tired. "Just please stop."

The porch creaked, and a shadow blocked the late-afternoon sun. Jael stood with her hands in her back pockets.

Mama Nan would say it was unladylike if she saw.

But Walter's heart got a nice warm feeling to it. Not too warm like the stove heating up the summer-hot kitchen. Just happy warm. He grinned.

Mama Nan glanced up, wearily. "You took Hitch's job after all?"

"Yes," Jael said. "It was right thing to do. I hope it does not give trouble to you too much."

Mama Nan shrugged and returned to the broken plate. "That's your business, not ours."

Aunt Aurelia sniffed again. "Don't be rid-dic-u-lous." She always said all the parts of a word when she was upset. "Of course, it's our business. After all, *Walter* wants to go flying with him, doesn't he?"

Mama Nan glared at her. "That's enough."

"No, it is not. I want a sweet, and Walter wants to go be with Hitch Hitchcock. And I don't see why not. After all—"

Mama Nan's eyes got huge in her face. "That is enough, you hear me!" She stood up fast and snatched the sugar bowl.

Aunt Aurelia let out a scream and tried to hang onto it.

But Mama Nan pulled it away and thudded it down on the back of the stove. She stood with her hands on her hips, breathing hard.

Aunt Aurelia screamed louder. She opened her mouth wide and squinched up her eyes. Once she got going in one of her fits, nobody could stop her. She rapped her knuckles together and then slapped the table and stomped her feet. Tears boiled up from the corners of her eyes. In another minute, she'd be on the floor, sobbing. Papa Byron would have to carry her up to bed when he came in.

Mama Nan heaved a sigh and turned around. "Aurelia—Aurelia, I'm sorry." Her voice got soft, like it only did with Aunt Aurelia, softer even than with the twins. "Please stop. Please don't do this." She leaned across the table to take Aunt Aurelia's hand.

Aunt Aurelia slapped her aside.

"I'm sorry, dear. I know you didn't mean anything. Please—"

The wail rose higher. In another second, it would start hurting Walter's ears.

The screen door screeched open. Jael walked right up to Aunt Aurelia and took her hand. "Come. Come beside me."

Aunt Aurelia tried to pull away, but Jael tugged again and made Aunt Aurelia look her in the face.

Jael smiled. "It will be right. Come." She nodded toward the door and pulled again.

Aunt Aurelia kept screaming, but she was looking at Jael—actually looking at her, not just staring off into space. She let Jael hang onto her hand, and then she started to follow her. She slid right off the bench and, still bawling, let Jael lead her onto the porch.

For a second, Mama Nan stared. Then she let her chin fall to her chest. "God be thanked for that."

This was Walter's chance too. He eased up from his stool and ran out the door after Jael and Aunt Aurelia.

They were halfway across the dusty yard.

Jael had let go of Aunt Aurelia, but was still leading her, walking backwards, her hand outstretched. "Come." She smiled big, like she had an honest-to-goodness secret to show them. Buried treasure or something.

Walter jumped off the porch.

At the hayfield's open gate, Jael turned around and started running. Her bones must not be hurting her like they had been this morning when she'd left.

Walter lengthened his strides and passed Aunt Aurelia. For a few steps, he ran backwards, gesturing with both hands for her to follow.

She'd stopped screaming. Tears glistened against her face, but she stared after Jael, eyes wide open and curious.

"Follow behind me!" Jael shouted. "You must be running!"

Walter gestured to Aunt Aurelia again.

She gurgled a shriek that sounded mostly happy and started running. She ran so fast she passed him, her skirt flapping around her knees. Her pale red-blonde hair fluttered. She wasn't a very *good* runner—she waved her arms around too much. But she was laughing, really laughing, all the way.

A laugh started building in his own throat, but he kept it sitting on his tongue, where he could savor it. The uncut Timothy grass wisped against his legs and pricked his bare feet. He stretched out his hands and caught handfuls of seeds. Papa Byron wouldn't like them running through his field, but he wouldn't get too mad once he heard Jael had stopped Aunt Aurelia's tantrum.

Halfway across the field, Jael threw herself down and disappeared in the sea of green.

Aunt Aurelia kept running. "Where are you now?" She laughed. "Where did you go?" Then with another happy shriek, she disappeared too.

Walter pumped his legs harder.

And then—there they were. They rolled in the tall grass, giggling.

Jael saw him. "Come!"

He plopped down and joined them. The grass was tall and prickly, but it bent under his body as he rolled. The broken stalks smelled sweet and . . . deep somehow, if deep could be a smell.

Finally, they rolled themselves still and just lay there, breathing. He turned his head sideways, so he could see Jael. She was awful swell. She wasn't a girl exactly, not like Molly and the twins. But she wasn't like grown-ups either. She wasn't like anybody.

She rolled onto her elbow and hung her head back in a sigh. "It is all so very beautiful."

Aunt Aurelia sat up, grass and leaves sticking out of her hair. "What is?"

"This, all things. Ground, plants—dirt." Jael grabbed a handful of the dark soil. She rubbed it between her hands, then held her palms to her nose and inhaled. "It is, how do you say it? *Otlichno*. It is like nothing I have ever had knowledge for." She extended her arm, gesturing to the whole field. "You are having these of such size to grow things. Where I am coming from, we are having only little rooms that are being made of glass. Not like this. It is very beautiful."

"But you like flying best." Aunt Aurelia straightened her skirt. She sat with her legs out in front of her and clapped her feet together. "You are flying with Hitch?"

"Yes, and that is beautiful too." Jael glanced at Walter. Maybe she knew he cared more about these things than Aunt Aurelia did. "He is giving me this job. I will go up on his plane, and I will walk on his wings."

It *did* sound beautiful. His heart pounded, a little painfully. If only he could go up. There had to be a way.

"*Nan* doesn't like Hitch anymore," Aunt Aurelia announced.

Jael shook her head, slightly. "I think he is . . . giving her fear. He is not bad man, and she must have knowledge for this. He is having much bravery. Maybe he is having—how do you say more than much?"

Aunt Aurelia shrugged, uninterested.

"Well. He is also giving to people, despite he has no things to keep for himself."

"And he knows how to fly," Aunt Aurelia added.

"Yes. His flying is like my home." Jael stared at the sky. "Only . . . with more excitement."

"If you have a home, why do you live with us?"

Because she was an angel, and God had sent her down to help them. But of course, that didn't make any sort of sense. Walter shook his head. If she was *really* an angel, she should've been able to say words right. And the first time he'd seen her, she wouldn't have been all dirty and her clothes all burnt.

He cocked his head, encouraging her to tell them.

She traced her forefinger through the dirt. "Oh, it is hard to say words about. It is secret, yes?"

Aunt Aurelia applauded. "I adore secrets!"

"For all my life, I wanted to visit your world, down here, on ground. I read about it, in many books we have."

"Storybooks." Aunt Aurelia nodded her head in encouragement. "What do they say?"

"I am now thinking they *are* stories." Jael hesitated. "They are saying Groundsmen take very little care for their families. That is why people are saying not to come down here. Because it will be bad for next children." She doodled some more in the dirt. "But I was never having family, so I do not know about that." She raised her head and smiled. "Our books are not right in what they are saying about you. Your families are good. Your sister, the way she gives care to you, it is good."

"And is this the first time you've been to our world?" Aunt Aurelia asked it primly, as if they were at one of those tea parties for ladies.

"Yes." Jael looked at Walter. "I am already having seen most of it from above. But this is first time I have ever been on ground. Hitch says I am his wing walker. This is truth. I am walking in sky all my life."

What did that mean? Walter looked up at the mountains of white clouds scudding through the blue sky. That she was a pilot too? That she *lived* in a plane?

In town yesterday, everyone had been sure something had *caused* the big storm to happen. He shivered. It was a very bad storm. He was shopping with Mama Nan when the wind started ripping through town. It gusted right through the open door of Mr. Fallon's store and scattered clothes and papers all over the place. It felt like being right in the middle of a twister.

Mama Nan had grabbed him and Aunt Aurelia and hustled them right over to the cafe, since it was built on top of a cellar where they could hide. While they were still on the street, the hail started hammering down. A stone the size of a strawberry had thunked his big toe.

Already, the nail was starting to turn black. He looked down at the bare toe and scooped up a handful of cool dirt to cover the bruise.

At least, he hadn't almost gotten hit by lightning, like Jael had. He looked at her sideways. If the people from her home had caused the storm, did that mean they had *made* the lightning that hit her?

"You don't want to go home?" Aunt Aurelia asked.

Jael shrugged. "What I want does not have so much importance. I must be going . . . to give help before Zlo is doing much damage to many places."

But if she went home, they'd never see her again. His stomach cramped.

She smiled at him. "Now that I am working with planes, your mother maybe would let you come to see them. You should ask her. Tell her I would be certain for your care."

It wouldn't work, of course. When Mama Nan made up her mind, that was that. He bit his lip, hard. But maybe—just this once—he might sneak out anyway. Once Mama Nan understood how important this was, she would see it was all right for him to go. She had to.

And, of course, good sweet angels willing, she might not find out at all. Jael wouldn't tell on him. It would be just once. After he rode in the plane, he'd come home and do all the girls' chores without anybody even asking him.

He gave Jael a firm nod.

Aunt Aurelia stared at him. The look in her eyes was serious. He'd forgot about her. She wouldn't tell on him either. But she might say the wrong thing without realizing it.

"It's coming back," Aunt Aurelia said.

What? He shook his head.

"Jael's home—it *is* coming back. The storm hasn't stopped. It's coming to get us, and I know all about it." She raised her chin, kind of like Molly did when she was spatting with Mama Nan. "People who fly, it will get them all. First, you." She brushed her fingertip against Jael's nose. "It has already gotten you." She turned to Walter and touched his nose in turn. "And now it will get you."

Aunt Aurelia was always saying stuff that didn't make any sort of sense. Her mind didn't work right, after all. Everybody knew that.

But he got cold all over anyway.

Jael's eyebrows came almost all the way together. She pushed herself up to sit. Beneath her rolled-up blouse sleeves, goose bumps appeared on her arms. "It *must* find me—I know because of . . . this." She fingered the strange pendant that hung around her neck. "But where do *you* have knowledge for this?"

Walter frowned. If her home was up in the sky and she was down here, how could she use the pendant to make it come back to get her?

He pointed at the pendant and then at the sky.

She was too busy watching Aunt Aurelia to notice.

Aunt Aurelia sniffed. "Oh, I do talk to people, you know."

"Zlo? Zlo told you this. You had sight of him?"

Walter's insides froze up.

Yesterday, when Mama Nan had been taking him to the shelter in the diner's cellar, Aunt Aurelia disappeared for a minute. Mama Nan stopped right in the middle of the sharp rain, her pocketbook over her head, and turned back to call for Aunt Aurelia.

Walter had looked back too.

Aunt Aurelia was standing in the door to Mr. Fallon's store, and a man with a great bird on his shoulder held the door for her. He looked like a tramp, and his teeth gleamed when he grinned down at her.

Then Aunt Aurelia came running and they all made it to the cellar.

Was that the man who had made the storms? The one who'd robbed all the stores in town? The one who'd hurt Jael?

And Walter had been *that* close to him?

A sick feeling swirled through his stomach.

Jael kept her face very still. Only a little muscle at the edge of her cheek flinched. "This," she said, "is why I am having fear."

She was afraid too? She didn't seem like she was afraid of anything. She rode on the *outside* of Hitch's plane.

On a different day, that might have made Walter feel better. But if she was scared too, then maybe this man really was coming back.

Aunt Aurelia tsked. "Oh, he was a *most* polite man. You have no need to be afraid."

"I am having fear because maybe many people will be hurt before I can stop Zlo." Jael looked up at Walter, not Aurelia. "But I have to be staying in this place, because how else can I be going *up* to him when he comes?"

Walter's stomach rolled over on him. He tried again to point at the pendant and then at the sky. It was the only way he knew to ask.

But she looked away again, and the ticking of the muscle in her cheek got worse.

Aunt Aurelia stood and stretched. She bent to pluck a long strand of grass out of Jael's hair, then she turned toward the house. Her gaze caught on Walter's face.

He could feel his eyes growing huge. He was clenching his teeth awfully hard.

She cooed and patted his head. "Aww." Then she started back across the field, swaying and humming along to whatever music she heard in her head.

She wasn't afraid anyway.

He watched her for a second. Maybe he shouldn't fly with Hitch after all. He looked at Jael.

"Have no worry." She smiled, but it was forced. "She has no knowledge of what she says. Her head is not correct." She stood up and reached out a hand.

That was true, of course. Mean people said Aunt Aurelia was loony; nice people just said bless-her-heart. If he let what she said after one of her fits keep him from riding in Hitch's plane, then *he* was the one whose head wasn't right.

He grabbed Jael's hand and let her pull him up. She put her arm around his shoulders, and he put his around her waist, holding on tight.

He jammed the fear down deep inside of himself, so deep he could hardly feel it. It was still there: beating like a baby bunny's heart after you caught it and held it in your hand. But if he didn't look at it, maybe, just maybe, it would go away.

CHAPTER 19

OR THE SIXTH time that morning, Hitch took off, gained about nine hundred feet, banked hard, and turned around to set the plane right back down. The show started tomorrow, which meant today was the big opportunity to make extra dough by hopping rides to paying customers.

Up, turn, and back was worth two bits a person.

The passengers in his front cockpit, a pimpled farmhand and his sweetheart—the farmer's daughter if Hitch didn't miss his guess—grinned at each other, wide-eyed. Most folks reacted that way the first time. Even if they got into the cockpit all stiff, hanging onto the sides until their knuckles went white, it usually only took that first stomach-bumping lurch into the air to win them over. Half of them might not ever get the bug to fly again, but they'd be telling their families about it for the rest of their lives.

Luckily for him, that made for good business. Not so luckily, business was a little *too* good to manage single-handedly at the moment.

He bounced the wheels back onto the strip and looked around. The crowd had been a couple hundred strong at dawn, and it'd only grown since. Even with almost every pilot here hopping rides, there were plenty of fares to go around.

But without Lilla to flash that smile of hers and direct traffic his way, every pilot but him was getting the lion's share. Even Earl had deserted him—not that he was much good at flashing winning smiles. He'd thumbed a ride into town to buy gasoline with the last of their payment from Campbell.

No doubt Rick was laughing his head off. Hitch craned his neck and squinted through his goggles toward where Rick was successfully operating on the far side of the field.

Just ahead of Hitch's propeller, Taos got up from lying in the shade of a lonely parked plane and ran, barking, across the field. And there, out of the early morning haze, walked Hitch's solution.

Jael saw him. She didn't wave, but her face lit up.

Speaking of winning smiles . . .

The dog jumped a good foot off the ground, still barking.

Hitch cut the engine. "All right, folks, thank you very much." He climbed out and came forward to help them down off the wing.

No other customers were clamoring just yet, so he pulled off his helmet and jogged over to Jael. "'Bout time you showed up. Haven't you figured out what 'crack of dawn' means?"

"I figured it." She stood easily, hands in her back pockets. "But I had to help Walter with eggs. The birds sit on them. Did you know this?"

He glanced down to where Nan's kid stood at Jael's side. "Yeah, I know about it."

The boy—Walter—bit his lip, uncertainly. But it only took half a minute for the light to start dawning in his eyes. He darted his gaze from Hitch to the planes, then back. He let go of Taos's scruff long enough to stick out his hand.

"This is Walter," Jael said. "You have memory of him?"

"I remember." He gave the kid's hand a shake. He had a firm grip for a skinny little guy. Then Hitch looked back up at Jael. "Nan said he could come out here?"

She glanced at Walter.

The boy tucked his chin in one hard nod. He didn't look too certain of the fact. But whatever the truth, it was too late now.

Hitch peered at Walter, trying to figure the right thing to say. "Well . . . okay then. Anyway, we've got to get to work."

Jael grinned. "Wing walking?"

"No, we'll rest you up for now and give it a try later today. Right now, we're hopping rides."

She did a little bounce. "Hopping?"

"*Giving* rides. To all those wonderful paying people over there. All I need you to do is stand there and look . . ." He cast a glance over her trim figure, long legs longer than ever in those breeches and boots. He cleared his throat. "Well, like you do. Your job's to convince these folks to come ride in *our* plane rather than somebody else's." And particularly Rick Holmes's. "You just smile and say, 'Right this way, ladies and gents. Only two bits a ride.'"

She wrinkled her nose.

"C'mon, you can do it. Your English is already better than it was when you first got here."

She repeated his words—only with her thick accent, they sounded more like, "Reekgt tis vay, ladhee-es aundt ghents." She stopped. "What is this 'two bits'?"

"Hmm." He looked at Walter. "How about you? Can you say it?"

The boy's smile faded. He shook his head.

Jael laid a hand on Walter's shoulder. "He is not liking to talk."

"Right." Hitch heaved a sigh and looked around for inspiration. "You know what, we'll just make up a sign real quick, and you can hold it, okay?"

Walter tugged his sleeve and looked at him expectantly.

"You can both hold it. Now, come on. Every five minutes we waste is twenty-five cents we don't earn."

The three of them ran around camp until they'd found a board about as big as Taos and a quarter of a can of whitewash. No brush though, so he used the corner of his shirt to streak the paint onto the board in broad capital letters.

"All right. Now you hold that." He handed it to Jael. "Fingers on the edge. Don't smudge the paint."

She looked bored already.

"You want Earl and me to eat tonight, don't you?" He took her shoulders and turned her around to face the crowd. "Now, give 'em a smile and act like you're having so much fun they'll scramble to join you."

She rolled her eyes.

"Smile."

"All right, I smile." She grinned wide, all teeth. Not quite

Lilla's effervescent allure, but it'd have to do.

Walter, on the other hand, seemed about ready to bust out of his skin, he was so excited. He stood next to her, one hand gingerly gripping the edge of the sign, the other petting Taos's head. He caught Hitch's look and stopped petting Taos long enough to give him an OK sign.

"See," Hitch said, "he's got the idea. You're doing fine, son, you keep that up." He cupped his hands around his mouth. "Over here, folks! No need to wait. We're ready to take you up right this minute!" He elbowed Jael. "Wave."

She got that shy look all of a sudden and bit her lip. But she lowered the sign enough to give a quick wave. Walter made up for it by jumping up and down and waving both arms above his head.

It was enough to start the crowd trickling in their direction.

"Good job." He pulled his helmet back down over his ears and headed toward the plane. "Now keep it up."

For the next five hours, he hopped rides pretty much non-stop. Earl and the gasoline arrived just in time to fill up the Jenny. They strained the gas through a chamois before funneling it into the tank, just to make sure there was no water in it. Then he was right back in the air.

With Earl helping the passengers in and out, Hitch didn't even have to climb from the cockpit between rides. A smooth takeoff, a sharp turn, and a bounce back to the landing strip. Then another customer clambered up the wing and into the cockpit. As fast as Earl could pack 'em in, they stepped forward to pay up. It was a terrific crowd—the kind that would keep you in food and fixings for a couple months, if you didn't have to share.

As it was, with all the pilots hopping every bit as fast as he was, the crowd finally petered out around one o'clock—judging from the ball of fire overhead. His backside had gone numb a long time ago, and his elbow was starting to ache from the thrum of the engine up through the stick in his hand. As he put the plane down for the last time, his empty stomach churned.

No more customers in sight, although Walter still held the

sign. Taos sat at his side. Jael had disappeared a couple hours ago.

Hitch cut the engine. "Where's Jael?"

Earl helped down the customer—a fat man in a black tie and a fedora—and guided him on his way. "Got tired of standing around, I guess. Went over to watch one of Livingstone's pilots fixing up his engine."

Hitch frowned. The barnstorming life wasn't *just* about flying and fixing engines. There *was* the business side to think about. Maybe she wasn't quite as cut out for this as he was hoping.

He raised his goggles and looked over at Walter.

Bareheaded in the sun, the kid stood tall, a hand on either side of the sign. Every time somebody walked by, he smiled and tilted the sign toward them.

"How much you think we made?" Hitch asked.

Earl jingled his jumpsuit pocket. "Oh, twenty bucks maybe."

"That ain't bad." Hitch dumped his helmet in the seat and swung out of the cockpit. "Give me one of those quarters, and then you can go rustle up some lunch. I'll be there in a minute."

"Sounds good." Earl handed over the quarter and ambled back toward camp.

Walter turned around to face the plane.

Hitch walked over and ruffled his hair. "You did a good job today. Couldn't have done it without you."

Walter beamed.

"You better get on back now, before your mama figures out what's going on. Here." He handed over the quarter. "Next time you're in town, you can buy yourself some licorice or something."

Walter took the quarter into his hot palm. He stared at it for a moment, then looked up at Hitch. Slowly, he held the quarter back out.

"No, it's for you. You earned it."

Walter pointed at the sign—25¢ for a Thrilling Ride in the Sky—then held the quarter back out.

"It's been a long morning, and I'm pretty tired and hungry. I'll give you a ride later, if Nan says you can have one."

Walter's face fell. He looked at the ground. Then he flashed his glance back up. Quarter still fisted in his hand, he reached into his overalls pocket and came out with a knotted sock. He set the sign down on the ground and worked the knot loose. He upended a tarnished penny in his hand. It clinked against the quarter. He held them both out.

Now what were you supposed to do in the face of something like that? Hitch stared down at him. The boy couldn't be more than eight years old. He was skinny as a rail, knobby around the elbows, black hair falling into big brown eyes that were as hopeful as all get out. And he wanted to ride in that plane so bad his insides were twisting. Hitch knew the feeling.

Surely, even if Nan didn't exactly know about Walter being out here, she wouldn't grudge the boy one quick ride. Walter would remember it all his life. Telling him *no* right now would be about like boxing his ears. Hitch's stomach hollowed out. If Nan wanted to do that, that was her business. But he couldn't.

"Alrighty," he said. "But you keep your money. This one's on the house."

Walter's eyes got even bigger. Then his smile faded, and his face stilled into a serious expression. He licked his lips and took a breath, like a parachutist nerving himself for the jump.

"C'mon." Hitch slapped his leg to Taos and bundled the dog into the front cockpit. "You want to ride in front with Taos, or you want to ride in back with me and learn how to fly?"

It was no contest, of course. Walter's serious look slipped into delight. He pointed at Hitch.

Hitch swung the boy in first. He settled the helmet on Walter's head, the too-big goggles bumping into the boy's freckled nose. Hitch took his time pointing out the various instruments and explaining what they did. From the look in his eye, Walter actually seemed to understand most of it.

"You sit there while I start it up."

Hitch hand-propped the Jenny himself. When the engine caught and the plane started to ease forward, he ran back.

Walter's eyes had gone wide, probably thinking the plane was going to take off with just him and Taos.

Hitch laughed and hauled himself in. He set Walter's hands on the stick and covered them with his own.

The boy sat on his lap, shoulders tensed.

They gained speed down the field, the dust clouding up from under the wheels. Hitch eased back on the stick, pulling it almost to Walter's chest. The Jenny's nose left the ground, and his stomach turned over for that split moment, like always.

All the tension melted out of Walter. He opened his mouth, and he laughed, just loud enough for Hitch to catch the edge of the sound. Then he seemed almost abashed, and when Hitch looked around to see his face, he grinned a tiny grin that took only a second to engulf his face.

Yup, he'd never forget this moment as long as he lived.

Walter got the longest ride of the day. Hitch stayed up, doing all the tricks he could manage: wingovers, Immelmann turns, spins, and even a heart-stopping deep stall that had the Jenny falling like an autumn leaf. Walter hung onto the stick the whole way. He kept his head up and watched the windshield for all he was worth—assuming he could see anything out of those goggles.

Finally, they landed. Hitch waited for the engine to sputter into silence, then leaned around to look at the boy. "Next time you can solo, right?"

Walter nodded. He sat for a moment, still perched on the edge of the seat, hands one atop the other on the stick. Then he breathed out a sigh.

Hitch patted the boy's back and climbed out. He swung Walter to the ground, and the boy immediately took off running. He ran all the way around the plane twice, then stopped and turned half a dozen somersaults. Taos, barking hard, wriggled in Hitch's arms and hit the ground running to follow Walter for another lap.

Hands on his hips, Hitch watched them run.

Nan could beef about this all she wanted, and, granted, it was her right. But he'd do it again if he had the choice. He couldn't give folks much. He couldn't even pay his own people what they were due half the time. But *this* he could give Walter.

It made him feel like his insides had fallen down a hole. After Celia died, he'd just wanted to stay free. But you lost a little something along that way. You lost this feeling.

Jael was right about that. Didn't make any kind of sense for an orphan—an outcast—to know so much about what it was like to have people in your life. But durned if she didn't.

The boy stopped, panting, in front of Hitch. Sweat trickled out from under the helmet. Above his grin, his cheeks were flushed with the heat.

"All right, Captain," Hitch said. "How about some lunch?"

They walked over to the pile of bedrolls and knapsacks. Earl and Jael were nowhere to be seen, but Earl had left them half a loaf of bread, a chunk of white cheese, and a slightly unripe apple.

Hitch split the food between them, and they sat on the bed-rolls while they ate.

Taos lay beside Walter, his head on the boy's leg. His eyes followed the food back and forth from Walter's hand to his mouth.

Walter fed him a crust. Then he looked up and gave the field a long, searching glance that finally ended on Hitch. He tipped his head and shrugged, asking a question.

Hitch bit a bruise out of the apple and spat it to the side. "You looking for Jael?"

Walter nodded.

"Like her, don't you?"

Another nod.

"You do know she's not staying, right? None of us are."

Walter nodded again, but his mouth bunched to the side in what was either a grimace or a thoughtful expression. He put his hands behind his neck, as if he were fastening a chain, then he pointed to the sky.

"Jael's pendant?" Hitch made a stack out of a slice of bread, a piece of cheese, and a wedge of apple. He chewed slowly. "What did she tell you about that?"

Walter shrugged, still pointing up. Then he made a blowing sound through his lips and gestured with his hands in what might have been supposed to indicate clouds rolling in.

Hitch shook his head, not following.

Frustrated, Walter sat back on his heels for a minute. Then he leaned forward and drew painstaking letters in the dust with his finger.

KEY TO HER HOME.

Hitch frowned. What was it Zlo had said about the pendant? That he couldn't leave without it?

What did that mean? The pendant was some necessary piece of machinery to get *Schturming* working?

The way Jael had handled that pendant during the lightning strike had been . . . strange. It *had* almost seemed like she'd been pulling the lightning toward her—and then deflecting it. If the pendant could do that, maybe it was somehow connected to *Schturming*. It might not be able to bring *Schturming* back, but it might be able to do *something*.

And if that were true, then that pendant around that girl's neck might be the last thing he'd want to be toting around the country with him.

"All right, let's finish up," Hitch told Walter. "We'll go see what she can tell us about this."

Chapter 20

When Hitch and Walter finally found Jael at the far end of the field, she wasn't alone. She stood near the road in the shade of Livingstone's rough-hewn bleachers. Across from her, Griff had one hand hooked over the bleacher above his head. With his fedora in hand, shirtsleeves rolled to his elbows, and his deputy's badge glinting against his shoulder, he looked mighty clean-cut.

He had that expression on his face—wrinkled forehead, unblinking eyes—that said he was dead serious about something.

"—not trying to butt in where it's none of my business, ma'am."

Instinctively, Hitch drew up and held out a hand to stop Walter.

The boy looked up at him, curious.

"I don't want to see you get into any kind of trouble," Griff said. "Not after having to bring you into the hospital after that lightning strike. My brother—he never was the kind who takes advantage. But this isn't a good business for a lady."

Jael murmured something.

"I don't know how close you are to my brother. If you're maybe . . . together?"

That got Jael to look up. She blushed up to the top of her ears and shook her head hard.

Hitch stepped forward. "Griff. Didn't expect to see you out here."

Griff looked back, first at Hitch, then at Walter. A strange expression—guilt almost—passed across his face. Then his mouth firmed, back to the same old resolute, righteous anger.

He put his hat back on and pulled the front brim down. "You mind what I said, miss. You decide you need help going home—or maybe just finding a decent job around here—you let me know."

She nodded, but kept her gaze resolutely forward and refused to look Hitch in the eye.

Griff passed her and walked over to Hitch and Walter.

Hitch's tongue itched with a demand to know what exactly Griff thought he was up to—riding in here on his white horse and acting like Jael needed saving. But he swallowed it back.

"Come for a ride?" he asked.

"Not exactly."

"Then what? Trying to lure away my wing walker?"

Griff was breathing a little harder than he needed to be. Every muscle in his body was tight. "You think she's like you, but she's not. She doesn't belong out here, and you know it."

That depended on what Griff meant by "out here." She *had* seemed a lot more comfortable at Nan's farm, with all the kids around, then she did here at camp, hawking rides. But Griff hadn't seen her in the air. Hitch had.

"She can make her own decisions, I reckon," he said.

A muscle in Griff's jaw hopped. He held Hitch's gaze for so long it started to feel like one of the staring contests they'd had as boys to decide who got the apple with fewer worms.

All right, so Griff was still mad. More than that, he was *determined* to be mad, as if that was going to finally teach Hitch some important lesson. He looked about ready to pop, like if he didn't say what he really had to say—if he didn't just take an honest swing at Hitch and get it over with—he might explode right here and now.

But he didn't say and he didn't swing.

What he did do was finally look at Walter. "Does Nan know you're out here?" His voice softened a bit.

Walter froze. He darted a glance between Hitch and Griff, then gave his head a tiny shake.

"Didn't think so. Come on, I'll give you a ride home."

The boy's joy filtered out of him and puddled at his feet.

It was partially Hitch's fault. He probably should have sent the kid home right from the start, before he could get found out. But what was wrong with letting him have one perfect day?

Griff laid a hand on Walter's shoulders and started to guide him away.

Walter stopped short and turned back to Hitch. He stuck out his hand in what could only be a heartfelt thank-you.

Hitch dropped to one knee and gave the hand a firm shake. "Tell you what. Why don't you take Taos along with you, play with him for the rest of the day. Jael can bring him back out tomorrow for the show. Or maybe you can talk your whole family into coming."

Some of the joy sprang back. Walter nodded and patted both thighs to call Taos. The dog leapt after him without even a glance at Hitch.

That guilty look burned a little deeper in Griff's face, and he clenched his jaw harder. But he didn't look any more prepared to tell the boy *no* than Hitch had been earlier.

Griff pointed Walter toward his motorcar, then turned back to Hitch. "Nan doesn't want him out here."

Hitch shrugged as he stood up. "All right."

Griff held his gaze for another second or two, then nodded and started after Walter.

And that was that. No mention of their chat the other day. No grin and slap on the shoulder. No indication anything had changed in the slightest. Hitch watched until they reached the car.

Doggone his stiff-necked, stubborn brother anyway. Yeah, Hitch had messed up—and he was sorry for it. But they couldn't go on like this forever. If Griff couldn't find it in himself to forgive him within the next couple of days, then, depending on how things went with Campbell, it could be *another* nine years before they saw each other again.

Hitch huffed and turned to find Jael.

She had hightailed it over to one of Livingstone's red-white-and-blue planes and was crouched beneath the engine, picking up tools—Earl's tools from the looks of them. She must have borrowed them. The pilot wasn't in sight. She kept her head down and refused to look at Hitch as he ambled over.

"What's the matter?" he asked.

Her head remained resolutely bent. Tawny strands of loose hair slipped past her ears and covered a little of the heat still on her cheeks. "The matter with me is nothing."

"Sure, it is." Had she been as embarrassed as all that by Griff's questions about what she was doing out here with Hitch? He pocketed his hands and leaned back against the fuselage. "Griff get to you, did he?"

"No."

Or maybe that clean-cut appeal of his was working on her. "C'mon. I *know* he's charming." He put on a grin. "It runs in the family."

She glared. "He likes to be bossing of people. That is also running in your family." She rolled the tools into a strip of canvas and stood up, nose in the air.

He couldn't help a laugh. "Wait. Wait, I'm sorry." He took her elbow and pulled her back. "Listen, there's something I want to ask you."

She shrugged him off but stayed put.

"Your pendant. Walter said something, and I got to thinking about it. There's more to it than what you did with the lightning, isn't there? You said that was just something you and Nestor were experimenting with. So what's it really do? Am I just imagining things, or is there some sort of connection between it and *Schturming*?"

She hesitated, then nodded.

"Maybe there's some way you can use it to find *Schturming*— or even guide *Schturming* back to you. Is there?"

She cocked her head, thinking. Then slowly, her eyes narrowed and her face got even redder. "You are thinking again that I am stupid."

"What? No, I'm not."

"Then you have all seriousness in asking me to pull more lightning onto my head?"

"Yes, more lightning." He kept a straight face. "We Groundsmen believe women as ornery as you must be hit by lightning at least once a week."

She gave him a deadpan stare, then turned and walked off.

He laughed again. "Oh, c'mon, you know I didn't mean it. I'm trying to help you get home."

"And to help yourself to impress Bonney Livingstone."

He followed. "Ye-es, that sure wouldn't hurt anything. How about we ask Earl about it? Maybe he'll know a way to jimmy the magnetic waves or whatever it runs on."

She kept right on going.

Was this about him, about Griff, or about the pendant? None of it seemed quite worth all this cold-shouldering and hoity-toitying, however amusing.

When a woman was upset for no good reason, the only thing you could do was either get mad right back—or laugh and let her be mad on her own until she got over it. And, anyway, she was so downright cute stomping around like this, it was hard *not* to laugh. Poking a badger with a stick was never a good idea, but it *was* irresistible sometimes.

He jogged to get in front of her, then turned around and walked backwards. "Is this because I made you hold that sign— or because of what Griff said about you and me?"

"It is both maybe. Now go away."

"Not until you come talk to Earl."

"No."

"Tsk. You leave me no alternative, kiddo." He caught her waist with one arm and swiped her right off her feet.

She uttered a squeal and squirmed. "Put me down, you *grubiy chelovek*! You are rudest man I have knowledge for!"

He lugged her, bent over in the crook of his arm like a naughty kid. "Considering you know that Zlo guy, that seems like pretty bad company."

"You *are* bad! Now, put me down! Put me *down*!"

He shook his head. "First, you have to take back this grubby chel-vek stuff."

"No!" She drew back one leg. The toe of her boot landed a resounding kick on his shin, square on top of the bruises she'd inflicted the other day.

Pain jagged up his leg. "*Ow!*" He dropped her.

She scrambled to her feet and turned to advance on him, fists clenched, eyes sparking. "*Skotina!*" That temper of hers was far

198 – K.M. WEILAND

gone for her to actually take a smack at him.

He caught first one hand, then the other when she tried again. "Why do you always have to be beating on me, huh?" She tried to bite his thumb, and he pulled her hands away from her face. "This is not how employees treat their employers, you realize that?"

She glared, huffing.

And then he realized how close they were. Only a few inches separated their faces.

She seemed to realize it too and froze. Her eyes got big. For one instant, her eyes dropped to his mouth, then flicked back. She clenched her teeth even harder.

She was mad at him, sure thing. And if he gave himself time to think about the new throb in his shin, he'd be mad at her too.

So he did the only sensible thing. He kissed her.

Maybe it was just because, at this moment, throbbing shin or no, she was about the cutest thing he'd ever seen. Or maybe it was because Griff was right: he looked in her eyes and he saw his own restless, wandering spirit.

He leaned back.

She gulped hard and stared at him, like she'd never been kissed before.

Maybe she hadn't.

Well, that's what he got for acting without thinking. A bit of heat crawled up his own neck.

He let her go—slowly, in case she had any more kicks in mind—and stepped back.

Blushing furiously, she bent her head to swipe the dust and grass from her clothes. After half a minute, she finally exhaled and raised her chin to look him in the eye.

Then she slapped him so hard his teeth rattled, and marched off.

He came up holding his stinging cheek. Yeah, okay, so he'd pretty much deserved that for manhandling her, even if it had been in fun. It hadn't been like he'd asked for a kiss. It wasn't even that he'd offered a kiss and she'd accepted it. Nice girls— or even nice hellcats, come to that—had a right to slap a fellow for thieving a kiss.

The grin faded a bit.

The kiss hadn't exactly been on purpose. So she'd gotten embarrassed when he'd overheard Griff's question. So she'd been too much fun *not* to tease. But Griff was right: he'd never had any intention of taking advantage of her.

Falling in love was something he did every now and then. But he had wings to fly away whenever it got too serious. Getting married, settling down, starting a family—that was a fork in the road he'd passed a long time ago. It was a road on the *ground*. And anyway Jael would soon be flying away to her own home. Unless he actually succeeded in convincing her to join the troupe long-term. Which, come to think of it, might end up being way more complicated than he'd first envisioned.

At the other end of the field, she rounded the corner of his Jenny and disappeared.

His stomach got that same hollowed-out feeling as before, when he'd watched Walter run laps around the plane.

All right, he admitted it: he'd miss her if he had to leave her behind. He chomped his lower lip.

But that was as far as this one could go. He hadn't come home to fall for some wacky girl who slapped, kicked, and tried to stab him. He shifted her—and her kiss—to the back of his mind and bent to pick up Earl's fallen tools.

Footsteps crunched through the grass, too heavy to be Jael's. He looked up.

"There you are." Earl hooked a thumb over his shoulder toward camp. "What's a matter with her?"

"She's just riled. She'll get over it."

Earl raised both eyebrows to the brim of his cap. "Riled, is it? The feeling I'm getting is that she doesn't know whether she's mad on purpose, mad on principle, or mad just for the show of it."

Sounded familiar. He dumped Earl's rawhide mallet onto the pile and started rolling up the canvas. His cheek tingled. "Take your pick. They all feel the same."

Earl held the silence for a second. "You get the idea she ain't seen much of the world?"

"Yeah, I reckon."

"Well, don't scare her off."

Hitch squinted up. "What's that supposed to mean? I don't scare women."

"No, but you get careless sometimes. All I'm saying is we need her right now—for the show. So don't do something dumb that's going to send her running."

Hitch tucked the bundle of tools under his elbow and stood. He sighed. "I know. I'll be careful." 'Cause Lord knew he didn't want to do something that was going to end up scaring himself either.

Earl held out his open hand. "How about this?" Jael's pendant, on its chain, lay in his callused palm.

"She gave you that?"

"More like slapped it into my hand. Isn't this what caused all the fuss the other day when she about tore off Livingstone's head?"

"That's it." He took it from Earl and turned it over.

It was about twice as heavy as it ought to be, even with all the little cogs and gears behind the glass cover. It clicked and whirred faintly, barely vibrating in his palm.

He looked at Earl. "What do you think?"

Earl shrugged. "Never seen anything like it."

"Would it be possible for something like this to, I don't know, *call down* lightning?" He explained about the storm the other day. "It's just a thought, and it's probably crazy. But if the pendant could pull in the lightning, and if that thing up there is causing the lightning, maybe we could use the pendant to pull in the whole kit and caboodle."

Earl took back the pendant. "I dunno. Maybe. Sounds like hooey, but then so has about everything else that's happened this week. Give me some time to look it over."

On the road, a dark green sedan slowed near the entrance to the field. It took the turn through the open gateway and bounced over the ruts, then stopped. The front door opened, and Campbell stepped out. He leaned back against the car and lit up a cigarette. Judging from the angle of his head, he was staring right at Hitch.

Hitch's stomach sank. "Oh, brother."

Earl turned to look. "What?"

"I gotta go." He handed over the tools. "I told the sheriff I'd do him a favor."

"What kind of favor?"

"The kind you get in trouble for these days, unless it's the sheriff who asks you."

Earl narrowed his gaze. "Please tell me it ain't bootleg liquor."

"It'll be all right."

"The more you say that, the worse your odds get."

"Just so long as the odds don't run out this weekend." He started toward Campbell, then stopped and looked back. "See if you can figure out anything about that pendant. If Jael will come with me on the job tonight, we can give it a try."

"No way I'm going to figure it out before tonight."

"Just try. And make sure Jael stays put until then."

CHAPTER 21

TURNED OUT JAEL had her own ideas about staying put. By the time Hitch got back from talking with Campbell and loading the goods into the Jenny, Earl reported she'd skedaddled. She was still gone an hour past suppertime.

Hands on his hips, Hitch stared across the crowded field, watching the road. In another couple hours, he'd have to take off with Campbell's present for the governor of Wyoming. Even if Jael was still mad at him, he could hardly leave her wandering around by herself. According to her, Zlo could come back at any time—which would be definitely bad for her and possibly good for Hitch—and either way she didn't need to be out there meeting him on her own.

"I'm going to look for her."

Earl kept on eating the rest of the loaf left over from lunch. "She can take care of herself, and you know it. What's stuck in your craw right now is the fact she smacked you one instead of falling at your feet."

"I'm going anyway."

"How, I'd like to know? You can't hike anywhere far and be back in time to fly out of here with that crate of Campbell's."

"I'll borrow Rick's motorcar."

"Sure you will."

Hitch slapped his leg to Taos, out of habit, then remembered he'd sent the dog home with Walter.

Across the field, Lilla jumped up from her campfire at the sight of him. "Hello, stranger! I was about to bring you boys a few of the buttermilk biscuits we got from that cafe in town."

204 – K.M. WEILAND

"I expect Earl would appreciate that. But I'm heading out. You seen Jael?"

"No. Is she missing?"

"Not exactly. But I need to find her." He looked around. "Where's Rick?"

She pointed. "He's over at Livingstone's camp. Card game."

"Think he'd let me borrow his motorcar?"

"Of course he would!"

Hitch kept his doubts to himself. "Thanks. I'll have it back before he even knows it's gone."

She beamed and lofted a tin plate with four fluffy white-and-gold biscuits. "And I'll run this over and make sure Earl doesn't eat your share while you're gone."

"You're a gem, Lilla." He walked backwards toward the car. "Anytime you get tired of Rick pushing you around, you come on back to the crew. Everybody's getting paid this week. I promise."

She laughed. "Ta-ta." She probably didn't even realize Rick *was* pushing her around.

He scowled. Reckon she had a right to marry who she wanted. But before Rick flew off with her forever, Hitch had a mind to corner him and finally put it to him straight. Lilla had been under his charge, for a while anyway, and she was way yonder too nice a girl to get stuck with that rat.

Hitch cranked up the black Model T and climbed in. It was ten years old: the pitted windscreen was held upright with cables attached beneath the headlights, and the steering column jutted out above the pedals on a long, exposed cylinder. The backseat, elevated six inches above the front, was half-shrouded under the folded-back top.

Along the edge of the horizon, clouds were starting to edge the sky, but the chance of rain didn't seem too likely—unless *Schturming* decided to return. He left the auto's top where it was and jolted across the field before Rick could spot him and squash Lilla's generosity.

Took him almost two hours, a full dozen stops, and most of Rick's gasoline before he finally crossed the bridge over Winter

Creek, headed toward the Berringers'. When he heard a woman laugh, he braked on the middle of the bridge and ducked to see beneath the railing.

Downstream, half hidden by drooping cottonwood branches, Matthew and Jael stood on the near creek bank across from J.W. on the far. Jael laughed again, high-pitched and happy, and a fishing line squiggled through the air. The hook plopped through the water, bulls-eyeing the center of its own round wavelet. The cork hit the surface behind it, bobbed once, then floated.

Hitch shut off the motor.

"Now, gently, just gently," Matthew said. "Keep your bait right there in that current."

"That's a nice way to catch nothing," J.W. said. His own line zipped in from the other side of the creek. "Haven't you been fishing here all your life? You ought to know better. Small creek with all this brush cover, you got to cast underhand, get her bait underneath the low branches."

"And snarl the line?" Matthew said.

Jael left her line where it was.

Figured. There Hitch was driving all over the county, worrying his head off about her. And here she was, relaxed as you please, fishing with these two old buzzards. He got out of the car and slammed the door as hard as he could.

That stopped their talking, although the trees kept them from seeing him.

He stalked down the bridge, swung over the slanted railing at the end, and skidded through the dry leaves to reach the creek bank.

He pushed aside a low branch. "You had me worried half to death. I been looking all over for you."

She watched her cork intently.

He missed a step, splashed one booted foot into the water, then climbed back up the muddy bank.

"You *trying* to scare all the fish away?" J.W. asked.

"Sorry." He made his way down the bank to peer around Matthew at Jael.

She still didn't look at him. Yup, still mad. Or maybe, with any luck, just embarrassed.

Come to that, he was starting to feel a little embarrassed himself.

"You could have at least told me where you were going," he said.

"Are you serious?" J.W. raised his fine bamboo pole and reeled in the line. "You've got her back up. Even an old man's eyes can see that."

Matthew glanced sideways from beneath his wide-brimmed hat. "In my experience, ladies always appreciate an apology."

J.W. snorted and recast his line. "And he's had heaps of experience."

Hitch shifted his weight. He cleared his throat.

Matthew gave him an encouraging nod.

"All right." He walked around Matthew, slogging in the water again, so he could stand in front of Jael. "I'm sorry."

She gave him a long look, then raised her chin and went back to staring at the creek. Her mouth was pressed tight, but a muscle in her cheek twitched in what *might* have been amusement.

Okay, so she wanted her pound of flesh. Fine.

He took a breath. "I'm really sorry. For making you mad . . . and for the rest of it."

"What rest of it?" J.W. asked.

He kept looking at her. "For the . . . kiss. Which you obviously didn't want."

Matthew tsked. "What's this?"

"She kicked me first and slapped me after, so don't feel too sorry for her."

"Seems like maybe she ought to slap you again," J.W. said.

Jael stole a tiny glance at Hitch. Her jaw was still tight, but a twinkle had surfaced in her eyes.

He took another step up the bank toward her. "Will you come back? We—Earl and me—we need your help."

The twinkle spread, and the barest hint of a smile peeked out. She thrust her pole into his hand and turned to Matthew. "Thank you for fishing. Maybe I will be catching something next time."

Matthew smiled. "Never you mind, young'n. Come back any time."

"That's right," J.W. said. "And anytime you want us to thrash this or any other young buck, you say the word."

Hitch kept his mouth shut on that one. If Matthew and J.W. ever decided to work together, they probably *could* thrash him.

She turned back to Hitch. "Yes. I will come."

That was it? Just like that? Maybe Earl was right and she *had* been mad just for the show of it.

She waved to J.W. and started up the bank toward the bridge.

Hitch stared after her for a second, then looked from J.W. to Matthew and handed over the rod. "See you."

"Mind yourself, son," Matthew said.

"I know, I know." He shoved his hands in his pockets. "But it surprised me as much as it did her."

Matthew harrumphed. "Might be it surprised you *more*'n it did her."

Hitch followed Jael back to the bridge and helped her into the car. After cranking the engine, he climbed in and backed up until the automobile was off the bridge and he could swing it around toward the airfield.

Sunset streaked the sky pink and purple, and the twilight crept in from the edges of the horizon, trailing violet darkness. Jael sat straight in her seat, only raising her hand every now and then to brush back her windswept hair. The silence stretched.

He glanced at her four or five times. What he should do was apologize again and spell it all out. The kiss hadn't meant a thing; it was a joke as much as anything, a fool trick he should have known better than to play on a girl like her. But the words stuck.

She looked at him sideways. "I have been having thoughts." She spoke softly, her voice barely audible above the engine and the tires on the road. "About *yakor*." She tapped her chest.

"The pendant? I saw you gave it to Earl. He didn't have any idea how to make it work after all."

"I am not having full knowledge for how it works either. But you are not wrong. It *is* connected to *Schturming*, in a way." She shifted to face him fully. "We should try it. It is . . . key, too. It can get us into *Schturming*, through any door."

The tires thumped over the ruts.

He shook his head. "When I said that, the last thing I was

thinking about was putting you in the way of another lightning strike." Speaking of which, she'd hardly limped all day. "How're the joints?"

"Better. I have hardly any bad feelings."

"That's something anyway, with the show tomorrow."

As bad as she'd been hobbling yesterday, it seemed miraculously fast for her to have healed up that quick. If he hadn't been a blockhead and she hadn't been so touchy, they might have been able to get in some practice time this afternoon.

He took the turn into the airfield and stopped the car in the gateway. He turned to her, one arm draped over the wheel. "I have a job I have to do this evening. I gotta fly some stuff over the state line to Cheyenne. It's only about an hour's flight each way, so I can finish it up tonight easy. And I was thinking, if you want to come along with the pendant, maybe we can see if Zlo decides to show up."

"I will do it."

"You sure?"

She raised a shoulder. "There is no storm now."

CHAPTER 22

THERE MAY NOT have been a storm when they left Scottsbluff, but by the time they finished unloading the crate at the Cheyenne airport, where it would supposedly wait to be picked up by the governor's people, the wind had started to blow pinpricks of rain.

Hitch pulled Jael's elbow. "This ain't good. We need to get out of here before the turbulence gets too bad."

Halfway back to the plane, something else gusted over. Maybe only fifty feet off the ground, it thundered above their heads like a train with a wide-open throttle. The waning moon, still fat and looking like a smashed headlight, blinked into darkness for five full seconds. A huge shadow blanketed the ground.

Hitch stopped short and craned his head. "What the sam hill was that?"

She clutched at his sleeve. "*Eto bil Schturming*! It worked! The *yakor* has been working."

"How can you tell?" Dumb question.

She took off running toward the plane. "Come! We can catch it!"

His heart sped up and he broke into a jog. "We need to push the plane around!" There was plenty of field in every direction, and he needed to take off with his nose to the wind if he didn't want the Jenny bucking into a ground loop.

Jael shoved hard, then clambered into the front cockpit while he heaved the propeller.

They took off into the wind, then circled around. With the wind at her tail, the Jenny and her Hisso engine careened through the air.

This was crazy, of course. More than crazy: *plumb* crazy. He leaned forward and squinted, trying to see through the darkness. Night flying was dangerous enough even when you had the whole sky to yourself. If that thing was still out there, they were likely to plow right into it before he even so much as saw it.

In front of him, the dark blob of Jael's head swiveled above the rim of the cockpit. The wing over her head blocked the sky from her view, but she leaned forward, neck craned.

He kept his own head rotating. The Hisso roared in front of him, and the wind slapped his head, front and back.

Fat chance of *hearing* the thing. It was either see it or nothing.

They flew for a good ten minutes.

In the dark, ten minutes was more'n enough to get lost in. He stopped craning his neck and dug his flashlight and compass out of his jacket pocket.

Below, the headlight of a train snaked through the hazy darkness. That at least meant they were close on target. The tracks would take him almost all the way back to the airfield.

He pocketed the compass and pointed the flashlight's beam skyward. Darkness swallowed the weak light a couple feet above his head. He clicked off the light and tucked it under his thigh.

To the right of the Jenny's nose, a great wall of white rose through the darkness.

A cloud.

But this wasn't like any cloud he'd ever seen. It was too dense, and in the darkness it was too white. Over the sound of the Jenny's engine, the *thwack-thwack-thwack* of a huge propeller thundered.

Oh, gravy. He hauled back on the stick and kicked the rudder pedal.

The Jenny roared into a climbing turn. The wind and the sound of something else—the thrum of tight canvas maybe?—tore through his hearing.

His airspeed was quicker than this thing, but it was climbing faster. He would run into it before he could get above it. Either that, or stall out trying.

He stepped on the rudder pedal and forced the Jenny sideways in a sloppy wingover. The good Lord willing, Jael'd had sense enough to buckle her safety belt.

By the time he leveled the plane back out, now heading in the opposite direction, Jael had shot up in her seat. If she'd had her belt on before, she sure didn't now. She turned around and leaned over the turtleback between their cockpits. The moon splashed her face. She opened her mouth wide, hollering something he couldn't hear.

He shook his head.

Frustration crinkled her face before the shadows engulfed it once more.

And then she was at it again—crawling *out* of the cockpit and leaning across the turtleback, her face jutting over his windshield. Her voice drifted to him, wordless.

"Get back, you little fool!" He leaned forward to be heard and ended up bonking his forehead against hers. "Get back, you hear me!"

"Turn around!" The wind strained her scream to a shrill whisper. "Fly underneath!" She raised one hand from its grip on the windshield. Brass glinted between her fingers: the pendant.

She obviously had something in mind. Something that hopefully didn't involve lightning—or her trying to climb on board that thing. But whatever else Jael was, she wasn't stupid. If she wanted to try something, he'd give her credit enough to try it.

He nodded. "All right!"

She slithered into her seat, and he eased the Jenny back around. The wind buffeted them from the right, and they slideslipped a good twenty yards or more. But the air was dry. No more rain, at least.

Two hundred feet below, the North Platte River glinted in the patchy moonlight. At least they had plenty of room to maneuver without ramming into the ground. The trick was not to hit anything up here in the *sky*. Just to be safe, he took the Jenny down fifty feet more before opening the throttle.

The plane chewed through a mile or two, and then the clouds opened and the moon lit up the night. Ahead, the huge not-cloud exploded into view. As big as a thunderhead—maybe a couple hundred feet long and almost as high—it coasted through the night sky.

Jael whipped around to look back at him, her face glaring

white in the moonlight. She brandished both arms, waving toward the beast in the sky. Her mouth moved. Telling him to get under it again, no doubt.

If that's what the lady wanted, then that's what the lady would get.

He dropped the Jenny into an angled dive and swooped under the not-cloud. Jael motioned with her hand: lower.

He increased the dive. Just in time too. Right above his top wing, something whooshed past. Too dark to see much, but it was easily as tall as J.W.'s house. His heart hammered his ribcage.

He straightened out the Jenny and then risked a look up at— nothing. But *something* was up there, because his vision had gone black as oil. No moon, no stars.

In the dark, *Schturming* was featureless.

Motion flickered in front of him. Jael was standing up. Still facing forward, she scootched rearwards to sit on the turtleback.

He groaned. This girl was going to kill herself one day, that was all there was to it.

She reached up to feel for the cutaway in the top of the wing, then levered one leg back until her foot was on the turtleback. Ever so slowly, she raised the other leg, then pushed herself up to stand.

He held both his breath and the plane as steady as he could.

Only her white blouse was visible in the dark.

He eased the plane down another couple feet. The last thing he needed was that black expanse up there taking her head off.

She lifted an arm, and, in her hand, the tiniest wink of brass showed the pendant.

She'd said one of the things the pendant functioned as was a kind of master key—but what sort of door was she thinking she could reach from here?

Her whole body flinched. And then she shrieked, the sound audible even above the double engine roar.

She'd touched the thing? His heart tumbled over itself. *Schturming* and the Jenny were matching speeds, which should have kept her from losing any fingers, but *should haves* didn't always work like they were supposed to. He ducked down another ten feet.

She stretched her arm all the way up, reaching for the sky, for *Schturming*, for something. Then as the plane dropped away, she started scrabbling for a grip farther up the top wing. She stood on tiptoe and then raised one foot from the turtleback.

He released the stick long enough to lean forward and snag her waistband. Before she could haul herself up onto the wing, he pulled her back and dumped her in the front cockpit.

"And for the love of Mike, stay there!" he shouted into the wind.

Whether she heard him or not, she huddled in the cockpit.

He poured on the coal, ducking low to follow the river until he could locate the railroad tracks again.

Behind, the not-cloud drifted higher and higher into the sky. Then it winked out in the darkness.

He landed back at the airfield, navigating by the light of the campfires. That kind of landing was always tricky, but he managed this one without as much as a bobble. His heart was pounding so hard it felt about ready to crack ribs. He cut the engine and swung a leg out of the cockpit before the propeller stopped puttering. When his feet hit the ground, his knees went all airy and tried to bend under him. He gripped the cracked leather pad that edged his cockpit and filled his lungs as full as they would go three times.

Then he stepped up onto the wing and practically dragged Jael out of the cockpit.

"Do you have to go and scare the living wits out of me every time I take you up? What on God's green earth *was* that thing? I about plowed into it twice! You and me and Jenny, we could be lying in a hundred pieces between here and Cheyenne right now!"

The firelight turned her face into a grim map of hollows and ridges. She was gasping harder than he was. "*Yakor* . . . I have lost *yakor*."

"What?"

She cradled her right hand against her stomach. A dark streak ran down the front of her blouse.

He reached for her hand. "Did you get hurt?"

On the far side of the fire, Earl propped himself on an elbow. "Now what?" Sleep clogged his voice. "If it's revenuers, I'm going back to sleep, and you're on your own 'til morning."

Blood covered the back of Jael's hand.

Visions of torn-off fingers skidded through Hitch's brain. "Get up and find some bandages."

Earl reared up a little farther on his elbow. "What's the matter?"

Hitch finished counting: all the fingers were there, even down to the fingernails. "She's bleeding."

Earl threw back his bedroll and scrambled to pull on his shoes and hook his suspenders over his short-sleeved undershirt.

Hitch guided Jael to sit beside the fire. Beneath his hand, her arm trembled.

"I . . . it pulled from my hand. I was holding it, and then it was becoming caught on something. The chain . . . it caught on bottom of *korabl*. There was door there—door in . . . floor. I could have been unlocking it, I could have . . ." She slumped on top of an upturned galvanized bucket. "I have lost *yakor*."

"I'm sorry. Anyway, it must not work the way we thought it did. No lightning, at any rate." And thank God for that, considering how things had turned out.

He dug out his own bedroll and crouched beside her to drape it over her shoulders. He had to guide her good hand—such as it was, since it was the one he'd bandaged the other day—around to hold the blanket shut against her throat.

Then he reached for her other hand and tilted it to the firelight. Blood streaked all the way down her fingers, but there wasn't as much of it as he'd first feared. Most of it seemed to be coming from her knuckles. With any luck, they'd just be scraped.

"Can you flex that for me?"

The hand stayed limp in his, so he bent her fingers under. She didn't so much as flinch. Then he prodded at each of the knuckles. She winced, but the bones all felt solid enough.

He breathed out. "Just a scratch, I think. What happened?"

Earl returned with an armful of ripped linen. "Had to get our supplies back from Lilla. She took them all with her when she jumped ship." He dumped the load at Hitch's feet and squatted to squint into Jael's face. "You look plenty shook up, girlie. What you need is a snort." He looked at Hitch. "Don't suppose you saved one of those bottles of Campbell's, did you?"

Hitch shook his head.

Earl pushed himself up. "All right, well, I'll run back over and see if I can rustle up what's left of ours. I expect *Rick* took that with him when he left."

Kneeling in front of her, Hitch dunked Jael's hand in their water bucket. He scrubbed off the dried blood and hopefully some of the grease, then wrapped it up in a strip of linen. It'd be sore tomorrow, but, once the blood was cleaned away, it didn't look bad at all. Better than what it *could* have been, that was for sure.

"Did you touch that thing?" he asked.

She stared at the white bandage and nodded.

"You're lucky you didn't rip off your hand, you know that, right?"

She kept staring.

He rolled up the rest of the bandages, watching her the whole time. In the last week, she'd fallen out of the sky, caught her dress and her hair on fire, barely avoided getting nailed by lightning, and then stood up on the top wing of a Jenny. None of that had so much as fazed her. Now, she looked like she needed smelling salts.

"I'm sorry about the pendant," he said.

She drew a shuddery breath. "You were not wrong about what you are thinking of *yakor*. I wanted to use *yakor* to bring Zlo back to here. So I could be stopping him from using the *dawsedometer* for his wrong purposes."

"*Dawsedometer*—what's that?"

"It is why *Schturming* is—why it was created long ago. It is how it is controlling storms." She shrugged. "I do not have knowledge really—even though I am worker in engines. Most of my people are not being allowed to know these things because maybe there is danger in it."

He chewed on that. "So something up there *did* make that big storm?"

"Yes. But *yakor* is there to hold it back. I think it was made in *caution* of someone like Zlo being strong enough to take *Schturming* from our leaders. That is why he wanted it. They would not allow him to be Forager anymore, because he is not following laws about staying away from Groundsmen." She bit her lip. "So he was coming to work for Nestor in engines."

"Your boss who died?" More than a boss, judging from her tone. A sort of adopted father maybe.

"*Dawsedometer* too was belonging to Nestor's charge—and *yakor*. Zlo wanted it. Because of its power."

"Because it can make these storms—and the lightning?"

She nodded. "He needed *yakor*. That is why he jumped after me on night when I fell in front of your plane."

"But what's the pendant do exactly?"

"It is like . . . anchor. *Dawsedometer* can have no power without it. When it is more than fifty *mili* away from it, there can be no storms. Without *dawsedometer*, *Schturming* can have no purpose for Zlo." She drew her knees up to her chin. She sat on top of the upturned pail, his blanket around her like she was a sad old Indian. "There was—what you would call—mutiny."

"You mean Zlo took control? So you grabbed the pendant before he could get it. And then you both parachuted out?"

"Yes."

"Let me get this straight. Zlo's in charge now. He's killed the only person up there you really care about. And now there's no way he's getting his hands on the *yakor* because it's who knows where. What possible reason do you have for still going back?"

"He still has *dawsedometer*. He could cause much trouble."

"But he doesn't have the pendant—which I thought you said he needed to make the thing work?"

She shrugged. "He does not need *yakor* to turn it on. He needs it only when he is ready to move away from here."

He thought back to approximately where Jael had lost the pendant. It was definitely within fifty miles of Scottsbluff, probably closer to twenty. So . . . that put a new light on things.

Between them, the fire clicked and popped. Sparks bounced high and winked out. Across the field, a guitar strummed faintly. Nearer, Earl's and Rick's voices grumbled, as they argued over the bottle of gin. A coyote yipped up by the river, and another wailed a long answer.

"It'll be all right," Hitch said at last. He looked over at her. Sitting on the bucket as she was, her face was a little higher than his and he had to tilt his head to look up at her. "We'll figure out a way to keep Zlo from causing trouble. I promised you that."

"Maybe there is no way." She turned to him, her chin cradled against her shoulder. "But I thank you."

He inhaled deep—wood smoke and gasoline fumes—then out again. Right now, all these ground smells were downright reassuring.

"Thank me when I've done something." He pushed to his feet. "Maybe I better go help Earl talk to Rick. You should get some sleep. The competition starts bright and early tomorrow. If your hands are up to it, we'll need you."

"Then you will have me." She tilted her head back to look at him. "And I thank you because you have already done something. I have no knowledge what would have happened to me if you had not helped."

Of course, he had almost *not* helped her—several times.

In the firelight, her eyes were soft and big. "You are good man, Hitch Hitchcock."

It'd been a long, long time since anyone had said that to him.

CHAPTER 23

THE FIELD WOKE up in a buzz of excitement. Pilots, mechanics, and performers ran all over the place, borrowing screwdrivers and pocketknives, topping off fuel tanks, and polishing their ships 'til they dazzled in the golden morning light. The dry air, already hot, carried the sounds of shouting, laughing, and plane engines revving. Motorcars had packed the incoming road two full hours before the show's start time.

Earl went over the engine once more, and Hitch did a walk-around, checking every surface. Today was not the day to have something fall apart on him.

Livingstone, wearing white jodhpurs and dapper red-striped suspenders, ambled over with his walking stick. "Well, my boy, here we are." He looked at the Jenny and smoothed his mustache. "She's mighty pretty, I'll say that for her. You've got her shined up brighter than a shoe button. Clip-wing, eh?"

Hitch nodded. Last year, he and Earl had swapped out the standard top wing, with its three-foot overhang, for another bottom wing. It made her a little wilder than even most Jennies, but on days when she was in good temper, she could outmaneuver a hawk.

"Well," Livingstone said. "I won't mind giving that a try after you've lost her to me."

Hitch hooked his thumbs in his pockets and flashed his most confident grin. "Maybe after you've made me your partner, you can talk me into giving you a free ride."

"Maybe, indeed." Livingstone pointed his stick toward where Jael was sitting cross-legged next to the fire pit, staring at the sky. "Your lovely wing walker seems a mite distracted this morning."

"Oh, that's just something she does. Helps her focus."

"Indeed. Well, good luck to you. You'll need it." Livingstone touched the brim of his hat and strolled on.

Hitch glanced at Jael.

She'd shaken off the squigglies since last night, and her hand seemed in good shape. But she'd woken up with a dark, almost desperate look in her eyes. Knowing her, that probably wasn't a good thing.

Behind him, a dog barked, and he glanced back.

Taos bounded up, Walter running after him. Bottom lip between his teeth, the boy grinned as wide as he possibly could.

Hitch grinned back. "So you got to come after all?" He leaned down to rub Taos's ears.

Walter nodded.

"Did your mama find out about yesterday?"

The nod became a shake.

That could only mean Griff hadn't told on them. That was something, anyway.

"How'd you get her to let you come today?"

Walter shrugged, then pointed at Taos. His eyes sparkled.

"Ah."

Nan probably thought Hitch sent the dog home on purpose to manipulate her into letting Walter come. Hitch looked up for her, but something else caught his eye: a green sedan bumping across the field and parking twenty feet off.

Through the driver's open window, Campbell watched him. That almost-smile played on his mouth.

Hitch guided Walter forward a step and pointed toward Jael. "Why don't you go say hi? Cheer her up a bit. She's had a rough night of it."

Walter lit up at the sight of her and ran off without questioning.

Hitch put on his best unconcerned look and ambled over to Campbell's window. "Heard from last night's satisfied customer yet?"

"I have." Campbell twisted in his seat, his broad shoulders almost too big to let him turn and face Hitch. "You did a good job. Much better than the last time." His eyes were bright and black, like a starling about to decapitate a worm. "Considering how well this job went, I might end up having another for you before you leave town."

"Nah, I don't think so. We're even now."

"Are we then?" Campbell kept on watching him. "And what about that thing"—he twirled his forefinger—"up in the sky. Any sign of that?"

"All that's up there is clouds—and not too many of them." Today, only a big thunderhead drifting in from the west marred the astounding blue of the sky. "Anything more is crazy talk. You and I both know that."

Campbell sucked his teeth. "I reckon. But you keep an eye on the sky." He reached to shift the car's gear. "Time for me to go enjoy the show. I'll let you know when the next job is." He pulled away.

No way there'd be a next job. Hitch hung his hands on his hips. He'd more than fulfilled any debt he had to Campbell. He'd fly out of here without looking back before he'd do another deal.

But the nape of his neck still crawled. Campbell had a way of twisting even straightforward situations until he got what he wanted. The sooner Hitch was out of here, the better.

He turned and scanned the crowd.

At the corner of the bleachers, Griff stood, watching him.

The skin on Hitch's neck crawled harder. He dropped his hands from his hips. No doubt Griff would jump to the worst conclusion possible, seeing him talking to Campbell—especially after Hitch had warned Griff off himself. But maybe, after all, the worst conclusion wasn't so far from the truth.

How had things gotten this snarled up? He stared at his brother and rubbed a hand through his hair.

A white-haired lady hobbled up to the bleachers, hauling a picnic basket about half as big as she was. Griff turned away from Hitch to tip his hat and take the basket for her.

Before the day was out, Hitch would track Griff down, make him understand for good and all. After that, it was Griff's business whether he forgave him or not.

"Hitch!"

He looked around.

Nan strode toward him, cheeks streaked with red. Her straw cloche was mashed low on her head, her black purse slung inside her elbow. Aurelia, Molly, and two little girls who looked like twins trailed twenty feet behind.

"Where's Walter?" she demanded.

He hooked a thumb. "Over with Jael, last I saw. I'm glad you let him come. This sort of thing means a lot to a kid like him."

"I *didn't* let him come. It's the last thing I wanted. You and that *dog* of yours." Her breath was shuddery. "He was supposed to let it jump out of the automobile."

"I told him to send the dog over with Jael this morning."

She crossed her arms. "Jael didn't come home last night."

"Yeah, we ran into some trouble—"

"I don't want Walter out here, Hitch." Her eyes bored into his, demanding but also somehow pleading. "How can I make that any more clear?"

He strained air through his teeth, fighting for patience. "Look, I do understand where you're coming from. But if you don't want him out here, then *you* make him stay at home. You keep acting like I'm going to push him into a propeller or something. I like the kid. He's smart, he loves the planes. I'm not going to kick him like a stray dog whenever he comes around. He reminds me too much of me at that age."

She went pale, all except for the hot slash up either cheekbone. "Hitch, you listen to me—"

"No, just listen to me this time." He closed the distance between them and lowered his voice. "This isn't about Walter, it's about me. I know that. If it was any other pilot out here, you wouldn't care a bit."

"Wouldn't I?"

"All right, maybe you would, but only because you're set against the whole breed just 'cause I'm one of them. But the point is, *why?* Why can't he hang around for a couple days? After that, I'll be gone." He hesitated. "Nan, I'm asking you to forgive me."

The corner of her mouth trembled. "I thought I *had* forgiven you. But . . . then you came back." She squared her shoulders

222 – K.M. WEILAND

and stepped away. "Even if I could forgive you, I still wouldn't let him near you." She shifted her gaze past his shoulder and raised her voice. "Walter, come here."

The boy hesitated, glancing at Jael as if for guidance.

"Now," Nan said.

He shambled over, Taos trotting after.

She took his hand. "It's time to go."

Walter's shoulders drooped, but he followed, footsteps dragging.

He *was* a good kid. And maybe Nan was right. Maybe Hitch was corrupting him. Before the airshow's arrival this week, Walter would probably have never even thought about disobeying her. A shiny red Jenny was an awful big temptation to put in front of any boy, especially one as lonely as that.

Nan should let him stay for the show. She should swallow her loathing of Hitch and give Walter at least that much.

But at the end of the day, it wasn't Hitch's decision to make. It was Nan's. She was the one with a husband and a family. She was the one with both feet on the ground. She was the boy's mother, even if she wasn't doing an all-fired perfect job of it.

Hitch slapped his leg, calling Taos back from chasing after them.

The dog hesitated, looking between him and the boy, then ran back obediently.

Walter cast a forlorn glance over his shoulder.

There had to be a way to make this all right. Hitch waved at the boy. Had to be. A little luck, a little skill—that could make anything right.

In the open field, Livingstone's band—consisting of a snare drum and a trumpet—struck up a circus march. Half a dozen plane engines roared to life, and the prop wash blew over Hitch, flapping his leather jacket and ruffling his hair.

"*Ladies and gen-tle-men!*" Livingstone bellowed through his megaphone. "Col. Bonney Livingstone and His Extravagant Flying Circus welcome you to the ex-*trav*-a-ganza of your lives!"

Hitch's blood started pumping. He took a deep breath and turned away from Walter and Nan. First things first: he had to win this competition.

He jogged back to the Jenny.

Earl gave the engine one more wipe with his rag. "You ready?"

"I'm ready. Let's push her over to the start line." He ducked to check the steel hook underneath the lower wing.

The first competition of the day would be the handkerchief pick-up. His heart pumped harder, and his thoughts started to clear, like always.

He looked around for Jael. By Livingstone's rules, if a crew had a performer, he or she had to be in the plane at all times, even if the event didn't require anything but flying.

She stood behind the wing, eyes on the red-white-and-blue planes taking off. She bent over and rubbed both thighs, like she was trying to warm them up.

"She's limping again," Earl muttered.

"What's this?" Hitch called to her: "You all right?"

She turned and nodded, mouth tight.

"You hurting again? I thought you were past all that."

"It is nothing."

"Nothing, my foot," Earl said. "You should stay on the ground, and we all know it."

She looked at Hitch steadily. "I will not stay on ground."

He looked back at her, trying to gauge how fit she was. "If you fall off and break your neck, I won't be none too happy."

She smiled, tightly. "There is no worry. I will go whether you say I can or not."

Earl turned around so she couldn't see his face. "Not if we tie her up, I reckon."

Just the thought of that made Hitch's shins throb. "If she wants to come, she can come. It's her call." When it came right down to it, she hadn't made a bad one yet. He nodded to her. "Let's go."

After a few events, it started to feel like maybe Hitch was the one Earl should have tied up and left behind.

They barely squeaked by in the pants race—where the contestants had to land the plane, jump out to struggle into a pair of oversize trousers, then jump back in and fly across the finish line.

They came in a poor third in the handkerchief pickup. It took Hitch two tries to swoop low across the ground and use the hook attached beneath the wing to snag the bright white handkerchief from off its pile of tumbleweeds. The only consolation was that Rick didn't even attempt the stunt—which seemed like quite the poor showing, considering this was the trick he swore up and down he invented.

Finally, Hitch found his groove in the acrobatics demonstration.

All barnstorming stunts were based on three basic maneuvers—the slow roll, the loop, and the snap roll. Hitch was good at all twenty-six variations. In a clip-wing Jenny with a Hisso engine, he was better than good.

He finished off his last loop with an inverted screech across the field. That was a trick in itself, since it was tough keeping the fuel pumping when a Jenny was wrong side up. Then he screamed around for a perfect landing. He didn't need Livingstone's grudging announcement of his name to know he'd won that one.

It was a start. A few more event wins today and most of tomorrow, and that bet was as good as won. He grinned.

"And now for something inimitably special!" Livingstone announced. "Our audacious pilots will race head to head, starting from right here in front of the grandstand, circling around the far pylon, and returning to land before your very eyes, where you may judge the winner for yourselves!"

Hitch taxied around to the starting line—newly chalked in the dust in front of the bleachers.

He leaned forward to tap Jael's shoulder. "You all right?" he hollered over the engine.

She nodded and smiled. Her eyes still had a pinched look, but her face was all lit up like starfire.

Well, flying *did* fix many an ill.

He lined up next to Rick's dusty blue plane.

Rick turned his goggled head and gave them a long look. "The way this morning is progressing, I can't say I much regret my decision to leave your employ."

"You can regret it later—after I take all the winnings." And he'd pay Rick off all the same, just to show him that was how folks around here did things.

"Ready!" Livingstone shouted.

The checkered flag fell, and every pilot on the line opened his throttle.

Hitch grinned. This was where the Hisso would prove its worth. He spared Earl a salute as they passed.

And then they were up. He pitched the Jenny's nose to the sky and poured on the steam. The Hisso, with its hundred and fifty horsepower, hit full speed and tore through the air. He glanced back.

Rick's plane was the closest—and it wasn't even in spitting distance.

Hitch laughed. So long as he could make the turn—and he *could*—there was no way they could avoid winning this thing by less than half a mile.

They reached the old telegraph pole topped with streamers, and he tensed his feet on the rudder pedals, ready to drop the left wing in a tight turn.

Out of the clear sky, pea-sized hail spattered the windshield and his goggles. He shot a glance up. Nothing but blue.

Head back down, eyes ahead. The Jenny careened around the pylon.

In front of him, Jael leaned back to see through the cutaway in the top wing.

He circled all the way around the pole and leveled back out toward the bleachers.

The other planes tore through the sky, headed straight at him. He raised the Jenny's nose to get above them.

Another spatter of hail rattled against the top wing.

And then a jagged gash of lightning smashed into the rear-most of the planes racing to catch Hitch.

The plane seemed to freeze, midair. The varnish on the wings reacted to the spark just like gasoline, and the whole thing ignited. The top wing folded up, the plane's nose pitched down. It hit the ground, and it exploded.

Hitch stared, open-mouthed.

That's when *Schturming* dropped out of the sun's glare and into plain view.

The expanse of white went on and on, for hundreds and

hundreds of yards. Last night, it had looked like a cloud. This morning, the sun showed different. White canvas—or more likely cowhide—was stretched against a massive rib structure and swelled tight with hydrogen. Beneath it, on a comparatively short tether, hung a long, ark-like ship, easily as big as J.W.'s mansion.

"Criminently." The wind ripped Hitch's voice away from his own ears. "It's a dirigible."

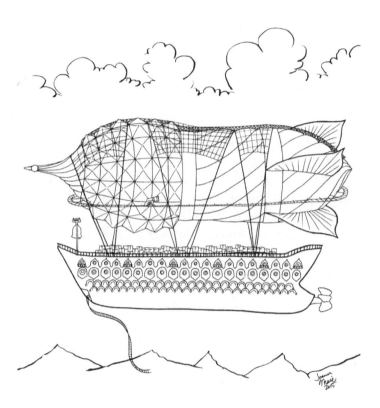

CHAPTER 24

HITCH HAD HEARD of dirigibles. They'd been big news during the war, bombing London and all that. But this was the first he'd seen of the beasts.

A double row of round windows lined the long side of the ship. On the back end, two massive propellers churned, thrumming like very big, very off-key bass fiddles. The ship's bottom flashed egg-shell blue, the color of the sky. No wonder nobody had spotted it before. It blended right in.

It sank lower and lower, right over the grandstand. People scattered just as if they were being blown away by the propeller blast.

All around Hitch, the racing planes kept screaming right on toward the pylon. He was the only one facing the field, so he was the only one who could see what was going on. None of the other pilots probably even knew the rearmost plane had gone down.

The Jenny pitched her nose one degree too many toward the ground, and his hand on the stick came back to life. He hauled her nose up.

In the front cockpit, Jael leaned forward and clenched the rim with both hands. She shot him an agonized look over her shoulder.

All right. So *Schturming* had come to them, just like they'd hoped. Now the trick was to keep the thing here long enough to get Zlo off, without getting anybody else electrocuted. His heart pounded its way up his windpipe.

First thing he had to do was move out of the way before Zlo or one of his buddies spotted him. Otherwise, he and Jael would be the next ones to end up toast.

He hauled back on the stick, slammed the throttle forward, and screeched skyward into the protection of the sun's glare. Then he banked wide around the end of the field and swooped in low to land behind the rows of parked motorcars. The Jenny didn't exactly blend in, but she'd be a whole lot less conspicuous there than she was in the air. With any luck, the dirigible's propellers would be running too loud for anybody to hear his own plane growling.

He cut the engine and jerked his safety belt loose.

Even before the plane stopped rolling, Jael squirmed around in her seat. She groped for his shirtfront, eyes wide. "What is it we are doing? We should fly to it!"

"Not yet!" He had to shout to be heard over the thrum of the big propellers. He jumped out and grabbed her arm to half-help, half-haul her out. "They'll stick around for a little bit. They've obviously got something in mind. No sense buzzing around and getting ourselves shot out of the air like that guy back there. First, we find Earl and figure out what they're doing."

And when and if Hitch went back up there, Jael was staying firmly on the ground—even if he did have to tie her up. No way he was going to risk her jumping out of the cockpit again.

"C'mon," he said. "And keep low!"

He hustled her through the motorcars, running bent over. In the bleachers ahead, people were screaming, fleeing.

One grizzled farmer in overalls shook his fist. "The Huns! The blamed Huns are invadin'!"

Hitch scanned for Griff. He'd be in the thick of the melee somewhere, trying to keep order.

Instead, Hitch spotted Earl.

Earl wasn't scrambling. He stood with his head hung back, staring straight up past the brim of his ball cap, open-mouthed. He was probably slavering over the kind of engine that could power those monster propellers.

Schturming kept right on dropping. By now, its sky-blue bottom was only a couple dozen feet off the ground. From this close, the thing looked like the hull of a pirate ship, planked and weathered—but without the barnacles. On the narrow end at the prow, two barn-sized doors split open and revealed a cavity with twenty or so men standing inside in ranks. Zlo, in his long coat and bowler hat, stood at the front. The eagle rode his shoulder.

Here it was then. Wouldn't be any kind of a surprise if these guys pulled Tommy guns and started mowing everybody down.

The propellers cut out, and the whole ship bobbed. In the booming silence, the screams and the stamp of running feet suddenly sounded tinny and small.

At the near end of the bleachers, Hitch stopped short. He crouched in its shadow and pulled Jael down after him. Earl was still staring, so Hitch took advantage of the all-around shock to stick two fingers in his mouth and whistle, loud and sharp.

Earl twitched his head around.

The durn fool was going to get himself fried for sure. Hitch motioned him over.

Earl came running and ducked around the corner to join them. He skidded in the dust and sat down, his back to the bleachers. He looked at Jael. "Okay, sweetheart, so you're not crazy."

She stared past him. "The *glavni*, the Enforcement *Brigada*. To be able to do this, Zlo must have finished with killing them all!"

Up above, Zlo took a megaphone from his lieutenant in the red coat. "I give you greetings, Scottsbluff! You are wondering who I am and what I am wanting. So I will tell you. I am Rawliv Zlo. I am master of *Schturming*, and that makes me master of you. If you do not as I say, I will destroy your city, your farms. I will bring floods, and I will bring hail. And lightning. The storm you saw last time I was here? It is but nothing. Can you understand that?"

People stared and murmured. The screams became low-pitched wails.

A man with hulking shoulders—Campbell—pushed through to stand at the front. He looked grim. "What do you want?"

"I want what you call ransom. And, oh yes, I want my *yakor*."

Hitch looked around at Jael.

She shook her head. "Then he does think I still have it."

Oh, great. Hitch scowled. "What's he going to do when he finds out it's somewhere between here and Cheyenne?"

She knit her brows, staring up. "It is not maybe. The way it pulled from me—it caught on something. What if it is still there?"

"Small chance of that." But still, he craned a look upwards.

She clenched her fists against her bent knees. "He is wanting it because if he has it, he can go to anywhere he wants. Do all things he wants. And things he wants are very bad."

"Well, even if he does have it, he obviously doesn't know it. And there is no guarantee it snagged on something up there. More than likely, it fell right to the ground."

She shook her head. "Then he can make storms nowhere but in this place. He will not like that. He will do his threats."

"Give to me *yakor* and eighty thousand dollars," Zlo shouted.

Jael put a hand on Hitch's shoulder and started to push herself up. "I should go—"

He grabbed her wrist and pulled her back down. "You can't seriously still want to go back?"

"No. My people—maybe they are letting Zlo do this thing, or maybe they cannot stop him. If it is first, then they are betrayers. If it is other, I can only help them if I help all of you."

"And you're telling me Zlo is a man of honor?"

"Honor?"

"Is he the kind that keeps his word, that gives a Lincoln penny about whether anybody down here thinks he's a good guy or not?"

She shook her head.

"I didn't think so. So you stay put. If he finds out you don't have that pendant, then he's got no use for you. He's likely to shove you right on out of there again. And this time you won't be wearing a parachute."

Her gaze flickered from him to *Schturming*, then to the people huddled in the grandstand. "But—"

"Look, I got enough on my mind right now. So just you promise me you're not going to go turning yourself over. Trust me when I say that's not going to do anybody any good. The man's a pirate. He's going to try to wring that money out of the folks down here whether you go up or not." He rattled her arm. "Promise me."

Her gaze came back. Her throat bobbed in a swallow. "I promise."

The next trick would be keeping everybody else from figuring out who she was and forking her over to Zlo anyway. He huffed.

Earl thumbed Hitch in the ribs. "You better pay attention to this."

One of Zlo's men kicked a rope ladder out the door. It unfurled with a snap and swayed a foot or two above the ground.

"What happened?" Hitch asked.

"The sheriff's going up to talk."

"Oh, well, that's swell."

Griff pushed through the crowd behind Campbell and spoke to him for a second. Campbell waved him off, took hold of the ladder, and started hauling himself up. Hands on his hips, Griff stood watching. He looked as happy about the whole thing as Hitch felt.

Campbell would do his best to bring Zlo to his knees. He wouldn't be satisfied with just getting the ship out of the county now. Zlo had challenged him, and like Campbell'd said, he didn't take it lightly when folks threatened things he thought belonged to him. That meant, from this moment on, Campbell would be dead set on bringing down *Schturming* any way he could.

If Campbell figured things out, that probably didn't mean anything good for Jael.

Hitch growled. There had to be another way around this. Something *he* could do. He was, after all, about the only person on the ground right now who knew what was really going on here.

He scanned the length of *Schturming's* gas envelope, then squirmed around in the dust to face Earl. "I'm going back into the air."

"What for?"

"To see if I can pop their bubble." He pointed at Jael as he got up. "You stay here, you cotton?"

She frowned. "You are going to do what?"

He left without answering. As soon as the bleachers were between him and *Schturming*, he straightened and started jogging toward the Jenny.

Two pairs of footsteps sounded behind him.

"What's your plan?" Earl asked. "Please don't tell me it's to ram it with your propeller."

"It's like a balloon, right? Stick a pin in a balloon and it pops." He reached the Jenny and hauled himself into the rear cockpit. "Give her a crank."

Earl scrunched his face. "What are you going to puncture it with?"

Hitch pointed at his left wing. "The handkerchief hook."

"Oh, fantastic." Earl rolled his eyes. "That's brilliant. You hook that hulk, and you'll rip your whole wing off. Anyway I don't think it's quite that simple. The air chambers are probably pocketed. You could blast it with a shotgun, and it'd still float. And even if it did work, you'd have to hope your exhaust didn't ignite the whole thing when the gas spurted out."

"Well, I gotta do something, so crank her."

Earl threw up his hands and walked around to the propeller.

A frown creased Jael's forehead. She gripped the cockpit rim. "I am coming with you."

"No sense both of us buying it if this doesn't work." And Earl was right. It probably wouldn't.

"I am part of what is happening here."

"There's nothing for you to do right now. Just stay out of sight."

Her brows came down, looking pretty stormy themselves. But the spin of the propeller and the cough of the engine kept her from saying anything more.

The engine sputtered and backfired once, and the propeller jerked to a stop.

Hitch circled his finger in the air. Earl spun it again. This time the engine caught with a chuckle that rose to a roar.

Overhead, Campbell's megaphoned voice shouted: "All airplanes have to stay on the ground! The man says if any more take off, he'll bring the storms!"

Hitch pushed the throttle forward anyway. Better to take a calculated risk and call Zlo's bluff than sit here and do nothing.

Jael flung herself at his cockpit again. "No! He will do it!"

Frustration cramped his throat. He hesitated, fist still tight on the stick. *Schturming* was in reach *right now*. If it disappeared again, Zlo could unleash all the storms he wanted from his invisible perch in the sky.

Jael shook her head hard.

But if she was right and going up only brought the storms that much faster, that'd hardly do anybody any good. He loosened his grip and reached for the switch to kill the engine.

Jael whipped her head around to look at the western sky.

Hitch followed her gaze, his hand hovering over the switch. He heard the rumble over his own engine's before he saw them.

The rest of the competitors were finally roaring in.

"That'll work!" He caught Jael's arm and pulled her in close enough to shout in her ear. "I can take off under the cover of their engine noise. Zlo'll never hear me."

She still shook her head, but the crease in her forehead eased a bit.

"Once I get up there and distract them, you and Earl see if you can't figure some way to mark that undercarriage! I'll try to force it lower!" So long as *Schturming* couldn't blend into the sky, they might have a chance of finding it again if it ended up getting away.

Overhead, the plane engines screamed in louder. The pilots would be wondering what was happening. Half of them would probably think the dirigible was some stunt of Livingstone's. They'd close in right over its top just to get a look. With any luck, they'd spot Hitch, realize what he was doing, and follow his lead.

Jael nodded and stepped back, out of the prop wash.

He exhaled, faced forward, and opened the throttle.

"Hitch!" She cupped her hands around her mouth. "Be careful of cannon!"

Cannon—? Even as the plane taxied past, he jerked a look back at her.

She was kidding. Surely, she was kidding.

Except Jael never kidded.

He faced into the wind again and tried to pretend his gut hadn't just done a snap roll.

CHAPTER 25

WALTER'S STOMACH TWISTED in pain. He was *that* scared.

Now Mama Nan really would be sorry she'd let him stay.

He clenched both fists over his middle. He should be praying—like Mama Nan was praying, out loud. But his mind couldn't seem to find any words. All he could do was stare and try not to huddle on the ground with his hands over his head as if he was a little baby like Evvy and Annie.

After she'd yelled at Hitch, they'd walked almost all the way back to the automobile before she looked at Walter with a sad face and sighed. "All right, Walter. We'll stay and watch, but only for a little while, hear?"

He gave her the hardest hug he could manage, then ran back to stand next to the Berringer brothers in the shade of the grandstand, where he could watch Hitch's red plane. And then, during the race, that *thing* smashed one of the planes out of the sky and stopped everybody cold.

It could kill them. It could kill them all right here and now. Inside his ears, his blood pounded.

Out of the corner of his vision, a red plane streaked from behind the grandstand.

Hitch's plane! It had to be. The knot in his stomach convulsed. That hurt too, but it was a better kind of pain. He pressed his fists together.

Of course Hitch would do something. *He* was brave. He was the only one here brave enough to do something. Even Sheriff Campbell might be giving in to the pirates up there. But Hitch—he was like the pilots in the storybooks.

The plane darted around the field, like a red wasp, and circled to join the oncoming swarm of racers. Hitch shot over the other pilots' heads and took the lead. He swooped so low over the white balloon that his landing wheel seemed like it might have skimmed the surface of the monster's skin.

That'd teach those pirates! Walter jumped and shook a fist. A whoop stuck hard in his throat, and that kind of hurt too. Death to pirates! They didn't stand even a little chance.

The air exploded. The balloon quavered, and near Hitch's tail, a black blast of smoke puffed.

Walter froze.

Everybody started screaming and ducking all over again.

Another blast pounded, and another, one after the other. Puffs of smoke chased behind Hitch's tail, like huge smoke rings from one of Mr. J.W.'s cigars. The red plane ducked and dived. It rolled all the way over, as it screamed down and then back up again.

Next to Walter, Mr. J.W. clenched his fists at his sides. "Durn furriners! They're shooting at him!"

Nan gripped Walter's shoulders with both hands and stared upwards. "Hitch, you crazy fool. You always did have more backbone than brains."

The crowd swarmed all around. Half the people ran to their automobiles to try to get away. The other half stayed, hunching over and wailing, probably scared too much to move. Deputy Griff and Col. Livingstone were shouting and trying to direct everybody. Nobody listened.

Clouds swirled out of the clear sky, and thunder blasted over their heads. Far behind, the twin propellers began blatting against the air.

From behind, Jael and Earl shoved through the throng. They'd know what to do.

Walter caught at Jael's hand.

She glanced down long enough to see him and stop. Her eyes sparked, afraid one minute, just plain angry the next. "Hitch cannot fly away from cannon and lightning forever!"

"He's doing a pretty good job so far," Mr. Matthew said.

Earl stopped in front of the Berringers and hollered to be heard, "He's going to see if he can force it a little lower. We have to find a way to mark that undercarriage, so we can find it again if it gets away."

"Mark it how?" Mr. J.W. asked. "Paint?"

Mr. Matthew shook his head. "Take too long to put enough paint on that to make it visible from far away."

Jael stared up, her whole body fidgeting. "If we could maybe be tying something to it . . ."

"Have to be something awful big," Earl said. "But not too heavy for us to lift."

Walter swung his head around to look. About twenty yards off, just shy of the grandstand, the scattered remains of the first lightning-struck plane still smoldered. One of its wings, almost as red as Hitch's Jenny, flashed in the fading sunlight.

His heart skipped and his stomach went all hollow for a second. He yanked on Jael's arm.

She turned her head—slowly, slowly, like the drip of sap in the crook of a tree—and finally looked at him.

Still hanging onto her, he pointed.

She followed his gaze, and then her face lit up. "Wing. He is right. If it is not burned, it is good color and not too heavy." She started running, but she was slow again, wincing with every step.

Earl and the Berringers took off after her.

Overhead, the plane engines howled. More explosions slapped the sky, each one like a punch in the chest.

The noise thrummed all through Walter's body. His palms tingled, and he clenched them. He should go with Jael and the Berringers. It was his idea. He should help them. But he couldn't make his feet move. Just like everybody else was screaming and carrying on from the outside, he was screaming on the inside.

Schturming's shadow shifted, and the sun poured its heat down on Walter through the only big crack left in the clouds. Sweat dripped off the ends of his hair and plopped against his face. He sucked in one deep breath and then another. If he didn't move right now, if he didn't *do* something, then he was nothing but a scared chicken.

One of the planes winked out of the glare of blue sky in

front of *Schturming*. It snarled through the air, the sound of its engine louder and deeper than the others. Hitch's plane.

Walter couldn't suck in enough air through his nose, so he opened his mouth and gulped.

The plane flew in from high above *Schturming*. Then, like the fall of an ax, it dropped its nose and dove straight at the open doors where Zlo and his men stood. Everybody inside, even Sheriff Campbell, scrambled. Zlo waved his arms. His bird got scared and flapped away from his shoulder. *Schturming* moved, dropping low and shifting sideways, trying both to avoid Hitch and to swing the cannon around to face him.

Far away across the field, Jael and the others ran, dragging the wing directly underneath the airship's huge shadow. *Schturming* hovered only twelve feet off the ground. Hitch had forced it down. It was low enough now.

What Hitch had done . . . it could have killed him. He was so brave he didn't even care about dying. He didn't care he was in a tiny plane and the bad men were in a huge airship. He didn't care they were shooting at him with a cannon or that they could light him on fire and knock him out of the sky with a bolt of lightning. Walter made himself unclench his fists.

But maybe he *would* care if he found out Walter was so scared he couldn't help anybody, couldn't even move.

Walter sucked in another breath through his open mouth. He lifted one foot off the ground. It came slow, and his other leg shook so hard he nearly fell over. He put his foot down in the dust, then lifted the other.

Mama Nan grabbed at him. "Walter!"

Now or never! He leaned forward, and he ran.

"Walter, get back here!"

She'd be mad at him again—and worried. But he'd make it up to her later. There were some things he just *had* to do.

He pumped his arms and pounded his feet against the ground. Jael and the others would need a rope if they were going to tie the wing onto *Schturming*. Papa Byron always kept one in the automobile. He ran back through the cars. People jostled and pushed him. Miss Ginny Lou Thatcher shrieked his name and tried to grab his overalls strap. He ducked free and kept running.

His hands shook as he hauled the rope out. But he could breathe steady now, and his heart pumped hard and firm. He turned and headed back. Across the line of the airship's shadow, the sudden cool engulfed his sweaty skin. He ran to the back end of the ship, just under the propellers.

Jael and the others crouched over the wing. She glanced up at him. "Rope! Good boy." She pointed up. "There is door in floor—we can tie rope to its handle."

Earl finished ripping a hole through the fabric at the wing's tip. He threaded the rope through and snugged the knot. Then he handed it to Mr. Matthew, who was the tallest of them. "Gonna have to get you something to stand on." Earl whipped around to look at Mr. J.W. "Get your car!"

Jael stood and used both hands to shove her blowing hair out of her face. "Walter can do it. He can ride on Matthew's shoulders!"

Mr. Matthew glanced at Walter. "How about it, son?"

Walter couldn't breathe again. He managed a nod.

Earl grabbed him under the arms and swung him up to sit on Mr. Matthew's shoulders. "You'll have to stand up, kid! Can you do that?"

Walter's head didn't want to nod, so he just planted both hands on top of Mr. Matthew's hat and pushed himself up. Jael grabbed one of his ankles and Mr. J.W. grabbed the other.

Earl handed up the end of the rope. "Loop it through that iron ring in that trapdoor. Pass the end back to me, and I'll knot it off down here on the wing again. Got it?"

"Bite it in your teeth!" Jael said.

He bit the rope hard. If nothing else, maybe it would keep them all from hearing his teeth chattering. He pushed up from Mr. Matthew's head, first one hand, then the other. Inch by inch, he straightened. Then he leaned his head back and looked up.

The endless bottom of the ship hung a couple feet above his head. Its wood was sun-bleached and weathered, the paint stripped off in long shreds. It smelled of dry wood, like the split-rail fences around the hayfield. The whole thing swayed, creaking. The taut skin of the balloon thrummed in the wind like a flat palm against a drumhead. All around, the plane engines shrieked. The cannon thundered rhythmically, joining the sharp scent of gunpowder with the gasoline fumes and the rain smell.

He reached up with both hands. *Don't move, don't move*, he wanted to tell Mr. Matthew. But it wouldn't do any good. Plus everybody would probably fall over from surprise because he'd actually said something. Then the plan really wouldn't work.

The tips of his fingers brushed the wood—smooth where it still had paint, rough where it didn't. He took the rope from his teeth, carefully pushing the rough weave out with his tongue. Then he raised his hand again. The rope slid through the iron ring. He pushed it all the way through, then reached for the other end.

Beneath him, Mr. Matthew wobbled. Walter clenched at the two ends of the rope and managed to stay upright.

"All right." Earl sounded like he couldn't breathe either. "That's okay. Good job. Now pass it on down. Easy."

The cannon cracked again, bigger and louder. Beyond the edge of the ship's hull, a blast of flame winked: a plane hurtled to the ground.

The tremor rattled all the way up through Mr. Matthew's body, and Walter swayed.

Earl grabbed the rope's end and hauled it the rest of the way down. "Get him off there! I can tie it now!"

"Wait!" Jael said. "Look up, Walter! Can you pull open door?"

He straightened back up long enough to wrap both hands around the large iron ring and pull on it. But it wouldn't budge. A three-inch slot—like an odd keyhole—notched the wood beside the ring.

"Look for my pendant! Is there anything you see?"

Mr. Matthew was already reaching for him, a hand on either leg to help him down. Walter scanned the whole length of the ship. A haze of smoke from the explosions and the plane exhaust filled the air. If anything was there, it blended in against the wood and the shadows.

The ship started to move. Ponderously, the tail swung around toward the grandstand.

"Get him down!" Mr. J.W. yelled.

Mr. Matthew hauled Walter off his shoulders and practically dropped him to the ground.

The airship's long shadow rotated, and the line of sunshine on the ground crept toward them.

Earl yanked the knot tight. "There!"

Walter stood up and turned to see.

The wing skidded through the dirt. Then, as the airship started to rise, the wing flipped up off the ground. The free end spun around, headed straight toward his head.

Earl leapt at him. "Watch it!"

The wing caught Earl's outstretched arm with a loud crack. The arm flopped, and Earl sprawled, taking Walter down with him.

CHAPTER 26

ANOTHER PLANE CAUGHT a cannonball square in the tail. It spun a full circle in the air, then pitched nose down, screaming until it hit the ground in a splash of wood and metal. Hitch swooped into an Immelmann turn and hauled his Jenny back around through the haze of smoke and exhaust. He swiped the heel of his hand across the oil sheen on his goggles. Right after that last pass, the engine had started leaking pretty good.

He couldn't get close enough to *Schturming* to hook it. All things considered, that might be a good thing. The way it looked from up here, Earl was probably right about that being a point-less way to die. But that left him weaponless. If he'd kept his .45, at least he could have popped some shots at the envelope. That would have made him feel better even if it didn't bring down the ship.

Schturming's propellers started chugging. The dirigible eased forward.

He circled prow-ward.

The rope ladder snaked around in the wind; they were letting Campbell climb back down, probably so he could carry their terms to the town.

As *Schturming* moved out of the way, Hitch could see a huddle of people on the ground, faces raised skyward. Looked like Jael, Earl, and the Berringers. Hopefully, they'd had a sight more luck than he had.

Schturming started to rise: it was leaving.

So far, he'd scored exactly nothing up here. Jael hadn't been kidding about that cannon. Through the smoke, it looked like some old piece from the early 1800s, wide-mouthed and mounted on a track that ran all the way around the lower side of the envelope. On either side of the prow, a big iron bell snuggled between the envelope and the ship. Whichever side he showed up on, that was the side where the bell started clanging. Everywhere he went, the cannon followed.

What he needed was a wingman. He swiveled his head to scan the sky. Most of the planes had disappeared once the shooting started. Of those that had stuck around for the fight, at least three had been shot down.

A flash of light blue, nearly blending with the sky, winked on the far side of the dirigible.

Rick. Not his first choice for a partner, but at least they'd flown together.

Hitch climbed over the top of the ascending airship and straightened the Jenny into level flight beside Rick. Beneath his goggles, Rick's grimy face was set in a determined look. Hitch motioned to him. During their six months together, they'd come up with hand signals so they could communicate in the air. Cannons and dirigibles had never figured into those signals, but they'd have to make do.

If one of them could distract that cannon long enough, the other could repeat the trick of diving at the open bay at the ship's end. It had worked before to get Zlo to lower the airship. Maybe it could work again, and this time they could ram the thing right into the ground. See how Zlo'd like that.

Rick pursed his lips, frowning hard. Either he didn't under-stand or . . . he didn't *want* to be a wingman.

Even Rick couldn't really be that petty and short-sighted. Hitch hadn't dinged his pride *that* hard.

"Ah, come on!" Hitch shouted into the wind.

As if he'd read Hitch's lips, Rick grinned and saluted with two fingers. Then he peeled off to climb skyward.

The cannon circled around to bear on Hitch again.

He dove hard and whipped under the dirigible. A floating red wing, like an amputated limb, flashed in his windshield, and he skidded to the right. The Jenny tore through the narrow tunnel of open space between the undercarriage and the ground. He dared one glance over his shoulder at the dangling wing. That had to be Jael and Earl's handiwork. At least this little sortie wouldn't be a total loss.

Wouldn't be any kind of loss at *all*, if he could help it.

He burst back into the sunlight and pulled the plane into as steep a climb as he could manage, engine whining. A few more yards and he'd be able to level out and charge straight into that bay. He leveled out, throttle all the way open.

Something hit him. Like a giant outstretched palm, something caught the Jenny and swiped her aside. He slid through the air and wrestled with the controls to try to keep her straight and level. With only a couple dozen yards between him and the ground, he had zero room to maneuver.

The something hit him again.

Ahead, Rick's blue plane floundered just as hard.

A cold rush of air bit into the side of Hitch's face. Wind. He craned a look over his shoulder.

Zlo stood at the edge of the doorway, one hand propped against the frame. He seemed to be grinning.

That dirty mug. He'd turned on the storm.

Only an hour ago, the sky had been blue as cornflowers, the few clouds searingly white. Now, thunderheads swirled in overhead. The wind tossed the plane like she was a baseball. If it got any worse, his wings could stall and smash him to the earth.

He had to land, and fast. The round was over. Zlo had won hands down.

He growled deep in his throat and let the wind grab the plane for a second. That was all it took to whip her around, away from *Schturming*'s heading. In his wake, the cannon boomed. But that was the least of his problems right now.

What he needed was another empty field where he could put her down.

The Jenny scudded on the wind, covering the miles way faster than she should have.

The black blot of a burnt haymow showed the field where the lightning had hit Jael the other day. It'd have to do.

He overflew it, then hauled the Jenny around. Landing with her nose to the wind was about the only way to keep any kind of control over her. She bobbled her landing anyway, skidding around in a ground loop, and nearly pitching over. The propeller chewed dirt and clanked to a stop, splintered to its hub.

In the sudden engine silence, he whooshed out a breath. His hands shook, and he looked around. From every direction, dark clouds tumbled in to close off the valley.

He climbed out and took a look at the engine. Other than the busted propeller and the oil leak, the plane was holding up all right. But "all right" wasn't going to get him back into the air. Even should the wind die down, she wasn't going to be able to fly back to camp.

A rusty jalopy, the bobbing headlights held on with baling twine, screamed up the road alongside the irrigation ditch. Jael drove, jerking the wheel dramatically every time she made a correction.

In the passenger seat, Earl hugged one arm to his chest. "Slow down! You trying to break my other arm? The brake—step on the brake!"

Jael must have stomped it with both feet. Dust boiled up behind the rear tires, and the whole car swerved, first to one side of the road, then the other. It skidded to a stop, left front wheel about two inches over the edge of the ditch. Both Jael and Earl bounced in their seats.

Hitch ran over. "What do you think you're doing? She can't drive!"

Earl's shoulders sagged. "You're telling me, brother." He still held his left arm cradled against his chest.

"What happened to you?" Hitch asked.

"Arm's busted."

"So you come tearing out here instead of finding somebody to set it?"

"You were about to crash my plane—*again*. You think I was going to just sit back there?"

Hitch opened the door. He reached to steady Earl's good elbow.

Earl dodged and, with a grimace, eased himself out. He hobbled over to the plane, his face the color of flour paste. "What'd you do to her this time?"

"Busted propeller and an engine leak. But this one wasn't my fault, and you know it." He looked at Jael. The wind splattered raindrops against his face. "We're in trouble now, aren't we?"

She swiped her hair out of her eyes and held it back with one hand. "Yes. You have no hurt?"

He looked down at himself. He hadn't stopped to check if he'd gotten hit or broken anything. Aside from the taste of castor oil in his mouth—and the beginnings of nausea from inhaling too much of it—and cramps in both forearms—and the fact he was still shaking all over and couldn't get enough air—he seemed fine.

Jael climbed out of the driver's seat and slammed the door.

"What about you?" he asked.

"I am fine." But she was limping worse than ever. She supported herself against the car as she hobbled around the corner. "We have put marking on underside."

"Yeah, I saw the wing. It about took my head off."

"The idea was Walter's."

"This *Schturming* of yours—" He dug around in his brain for the words to describe what he was feeling. "Whatever I was expecting, it wasn't that. Where'd it come from? It's not German. *You're* not German. It looks like it's been floating around up there for ages. But why? I don't get it. And these storms." He raised both hands into the wind. "Past time you brought me up to speed, don't you think?"

She opened her mouth, hesitated, then nodded.

"Doggone it, Hitch!" Earl hollered. "I'm going to have to carve a whole new propeller. I'd like to know how I'm supposed to do that with one arm!"

"Quit about the plane, will you? Get over here and let me set that arm of yours before it swells up bigger'n Rick's head." He looked around at Jael. "Whose car is that?"

"J.W.'s."

"Well, see if you can't find something in there to use as a splint." He tromped across the field and practically dragged Earl back. "Sit down and quit carping. Pretend you're the plane and I'm the mechanic."

Earl grunted in pain. "I wouldn't let you be mechanic on a Sopwith LRT."

Jael surfaced from the backseat with a couple plaid shirts and an old buck-bow handsaw.

Earl huffed through his clenched teeth. "Amputation's a little drastic, don't you think?"

Hitch ignored him. "That'll work. Tear up one of those shirts." He took the saw and stomped it apart. The crosspiece would be about the right length to support Earl's forearm. He shot Jael a sideways glance. "Tell me what happened up there. What *is* that thing?"

"You sure you can doctor and think at the same time?" Earl said.

"You, shut up." Hitch pulled his knife from the sheath in his boot and slit Earl's jumpsuit sleeve.

The arm was already swelling around a crooked bump halfway between the wrist and elbow. Definitely broken, but it looked pretty clean. He would immobilize it now, then let the doc in town set it.

Jael handed him the saw's crosspiece. "*Schturming* is . . . I don't know where to be starting."

"Who built it?"

"The *glavni*—the leaders." With both hands, she steadied the crosspiece against Earl's arm. "They made it and they launched it in year of one thousand eight hundred sixty."

"Explains the elderly cannon. How come you never updated it?"

She shrugged. "I have told you. My people they are not trusting your technologicals."

"We haven't got anything as technological as a flying weather machine."

"I think maybe they are afraid of that even. They see its power, and they do not trust even ourselves with it."

"When did you get on board?" Earl asked.

Realization hit Hitch between the eyes. "You were born there, weren't you? So was Zlo."

"Yes. All of us there now. It has never landed since one thousand eight hundred sixty."

Isolation. That explained things, partly—like why she thought of Groundspeople as practically another race, and maybe even why the descendants of the machine's inventors had ended up scared of the thing.

"How's that work?" Earl gritted out. "You gotta eat, you gotta fuel the thing."

"We send down what you called the elevators—so we can gain what we need."

"But why?" Hitch started winding the longest strip of torn shirt around Earl's arm. He overlapped the wraps and kept the cloth snug. "I don't get it. Why's it up there at all? It was an early army airship or something?"

"No." She frowned with her eyebrows. "*Schturming* was not made for war. It is for *nauka*—for science. The makers—they were men of studies. They made *Schturming* and took their families, so they could fly all across world and study weather. And I think, too, they wanted to protect their families from Groundsworld. They tell us all our lives that Groundspeople are ignorant, greedy, and having no responsibility." She shot a glance at both of them. "But in this I am seeing now they were wrong."

Hitch tightened the wrap over Earl's break. "You've been flying around up there for sixty years. How many people are up there now?"

"Hundred, more maybe."

Earl winced. "All up there in that flying sardine barrel?"

He had a point. It was a big ship, but not *that* big.

"That is being part of why Zlo has taken over it." She spoke in a low, even voice, as if she had to control each word. "Even in engines, I am hearing that changes are happening. People want to come to ground, and other people are thinking that is wrong and dangerous."

"And what'd Zlo want?" Hitch asked.

She snorted. "Zlo wants everyone *else* to go to ground, so he can be *glavni* of *Schturming* and gain for himself fame and richness. Once, I heard him tell Nestor that he is hating our leaders—even the first ones—for making us stay in *Schturming*. He was Forager. He saw your world. I think . . . I think he thought *Schturming* was like prison to him." She looked up at Hitch. "When Nestor let him see *dawsedometer*, he knew what he could do with it."

Hitch stopped wrapping. "That was your original mandate, then? Study and learn how to control the weather with the *dawsedometer*?"

He'd heard of such things before. During one of the bad droughts when he was a kid, some of the farmers had hired a quack out of Omaha to use his weather machine to bring rain. The whole thing had been hush-hush. Nobody had actually seen the machine: the guy had kept it barricaded inside a wooden tower. A few days later, when it rained in Morrill County to the east, he'd taken credit for it.

But for somebody to have come up with something like that in 1860—and something that *worked*, no less—that was more than a bit remarkable. Actually, the whole thing was jaw-droppingly impressive. Nobody'd ever heard of a dirigible of that size and power before the turn of the century. The Huns, with all the hullabaloo about their Zeppelins, had been decades behind the ball. And this one had held up for sixty years without ever touching ground.

"Weather is always controlling us," Jael said. "So now we could be controlling it instead." She gestured to the brown hay field. "There would be rain when growers needed it. It was never meant to do what Zlo is doing with it."

Hitch knotted off the last of the bandages and eased the arm back to Earl's chest. "So what happens now?"

Jael looked at the sky. "I think he is wanting to take from your world what he thinks he deserves because he has never had it. I think he is making prison of your valley."

"A barricade? With the storm clouds?"

Hard to see what was going on from down here, but it did kind of seem like the dark gray of the clouds was closing in from every direction. At least the clouds were drifting high enough that the visibility wasn't too bad yet. So far, the rain was only a spattery drizzle.

"What about your pendant?" Hitch asked. "If you don't have it, then there's nothing keeping him right here."

She handed him the other shirt. "That is maybe bad. Because he has no knowledge of that. If he has belief he cannot use *dawsedometer* anyplace but here, he will not stop harming your town."

Hitch slipped the shirt under Earl's arm and tied the sleeves around his neck.

Earl settled his arm into the makeshift sling and grunted. "I thought you dropped the pendant."

"I think it caught on bottom of *korabl.*"

Hitch met her look. "Maybe it did." He helped Earl scoot back into the passenger seat. "C'mon, let's get you to a doctor."

"And then what are you going to do?" Earl asked. "I reckon Livingstone's competition is over now. If we're going to try to fly through that storm to get out of town, we better do it sooner than later."

"I'm not getting out. I'm staying."

Earl raised both eyebrows. "You kidding me? Just like that?"

Hitch shrugged. It was hard to explain. There weren't even really words for how he felt. He'd left before because it had been the best thing for everybody. But this time he might actually be able to do more good for Griff and Nan if he stayed. This time, he couldn't just skip out. For once, maybe the skills of a wandering pilot might make the difference here.

He shut the door. "I need to stick around and at least see what happens. Then we'll clear out." He turned to Jael. "This could end up being a war, of sorts. You know that, right? A lot of your people could end up getting hurt."

"If Zlo is *glavni,* they are already hurt."

He pocketed his hands. This was dead serious, but he didn't want her to think it was a threat: "I need to know what side you're on in all this. Nobody's going to blame you if it ain't us."

She was watching him, with that deep, searching look. "It is not just your home Zlo puts in danger. If only way to save *Schturming* is to bring it down"—she lifted a shoulder—"then I will stay with you and help you to first save your home. I think you will save mine too, if you can." The steadiness in her voice held a daunting load of implicit trust.

Sooner or later, it seemed he always ended up letting down the people he cared about. But maybe not this time. Maybe this time, he'd not only stick it out, but actually do something useful in the process.

Take down the flying pirate and his crew. Save the valley. Make peace with Griff and Nan.

Sure. No problem.

He straightened away from the passenger door. "All right, then. Let's go."

CHAPTER 27

ITCH DROVE BACK to the airfield, towing the Jenny behind J.W.'s car. At the end of the runway, somebody had erected a big open tent against the spitting drizzle. Looked like half the town was crammed under it, all of them shouting and shaking their fists. In front of them, Campbell and Livingstone stood on top of something, head and shoulders above the crowd.

"Don't know about you," Earl drawled, "but them being in charge sure makes me feel a *whole* lot better."

Hitch parked the car and helped Earl and Jael out. They all made their way over to the back of the jostling crowd.

Everybody was hollering at once.

"I can't even pay part of eighty thousand dollars!"

"If they can send rain, they can send hail! My entire crop will be ruined!"

"They can't hold a whole town for ransom!"

"They've killed people already! This is war, I tell you! They're invaders!"

Campbell looked more like a granite crag than ever. He raised both hands. "Listen to me."

The hubbub continued.

His blue eyes lit up. "Listen to me!"

Most sensible people would shut up when Bill Campbell talked like that. Most folks here were sensible. Their cries quieted to a murmur. They shifted their feet, restless and scared, but also expectant.

"That's right," somebody dared to say. "You been up there, Sheriff. What's the score?"

Campbell kept his hands raised for a full second more. "You all just hold onto yourselves, and I'm going to tell you what's going to happen around here. Nobody's getting hurt. Nobody's losing their farm either, you hear me?" He scanned the crowd, stopping to look a few men in the eye.

"But what about the ransom?" a woman shrilled.

"We're going to pay the ransom." He waited for the inevitable rustle of whispers, then nodded his big head. "Everybody pays just a little. I reckon we can pay it off without anybody hurting too bad. We'll figure out what each household pays." The muscle in Campbell's cheek jumped, and his eyes flashed. "And if you can afford a little more, well, then maybe you can do that for your neighbors, huh?"

Must gall him to have to say that. Nothing got under his skin worse than somebody trying to strong-arm him. But he wasn't an idiot.

People shifted. They had to know Campbell was right. At the moment, the only choices were pay or fight. Most folks here couldn't even begin to fight a flying weather machine.

A man up front raised a finger to get Campbell's attention. "And what about the rest of it? This thing he wants us to find for him?"

Hitch stiffened.

Beside him, Jael inhaled sharply.

He forced himself not to look over at her.

Campbell straightened, his wide shoulders spreading even wider as he drew them back. "This thing our friend Zlo wants, it's some kind of pendant."

"How are we going to find it?" the same man asked.

"Somebody took this pendant from Zlo. We find that person, we find the pendant. I expect we're looking for someone new to the valley, somebody who don't quite fit in."

Of course, Jael fit in about as good as a coon in a henhouse. The hairs on Hitch's arms stood up. Not too many people had met her, much less heard her talk, but there'd been enough. And probably at least one of them was rat enough to turn her over.

Near the front of the tent, Rick looked over his shoulder. His gaze landed on Jael, and he scowled, obviously thinking.

Speaking of rats.

Hitch caught Jael's elbow. "Earl shouldn't be standing around here with that arm. Why don't you see if maybe the doc made it out here yet to treat casualties?"

She nodded, her face pinched and white. She turned to guide Earl out.

Earl stood fast. "The arm'll wait. I'm here, so I'll stay and hear the rest of it."

The thickhead. Hitch glared at him.

Earl glared back, then finally got it. "Ah, right." He faked a wince. "Ow! Yeah, I need a doctor. Pain's kicking like a horse."

Hitch patted Earl's shoulder. "Hang in there, old buddy. You'll make it."

They turned to go, Jael with one hand on Earl's back and the other supporting his good elbow. She looked at Hitch and inclined her head in a thank-you.

Folks in the tent were back to yelling.

Toward the front of the crowd, J.W. brandished his battered hat. Even in the shadows, the sunburn atop his bald head flashed. "Now, listen here! I don't hold with turning over no innocent person."

"Stealing a pendant ain't exactly innocent," Campbell said.

"Stole it from a man who's trying to kidnap an entire town! I don't know about the rest of you all, but I ain't taking the word of no man like that."

Hitch opened his mouth to back him up. Out of the pay or fight options, fight was looking a little better all the time. But then he saw Rick again and snapped his mouth shut. The less attention he drew to himself right now, the better. The last thing folks here needed to be remembering was his new wing walker and her strange way of talking.

Across from J.W., on the other side of the tent, Matthew caught Hitch's eye. He pursed his lips thoughtfully, maybe realizing Hitch's conundrum. The Berringer boys, at any rate, wouldn't have a hard time figuring out where Jael had come from.

Matthew faced Campbell. "How do we know this man Zlo will honor his agreement even if we pay his ransom?" His calm voice carried all the way through the tent.

"We *don't!*" J.W. hollered. "And the rest of you, including you"—he poked a finger toward Matthew—"and you"—a second poke, at Campbell—"can pay this ransom if you're fool enough to. But I ain't giving one red cent into that crook's sweaty palm. Put a shotgun in my hand and I'll shoot the gol-durn thing out of the sky before I'll pay for the privilege of living on my own farm!"

The whole place erupted—half the people shaking their hats and roaring in agreement, the other half shouting in dismay. J.W. kept right on yelling, even though nobody could hear him anymore. His face went even redder than his sunburn, and he jabbed his finger in his neighbor's face like he was about to start swinging punches.

Livingstone stepped forward, both arms extended. Except for the spattered mud up past his boots onto the knees of his jodhpurs, his white suit was still immaculate.

"Good people!" he shouted. "This is not a time to panic! This is a time for iron nerves, steely resolve, and steadfast action. Believe me when I tell you, you are not alone in this battle."

That got some of the folks—if not J.W.—to quiet down a bit.

"I regret that the simple joys of the airshow I intended for your pleasure should have been destroyed by so heinous a disaster. But I am *glad* that I and my stalwart pilots are here in your moment of need!"

That shut up even J.W.

"Now, listen." Livingstone hooked his thumbs in his suspenders. "In the face of this crisis, we must abandon the frivolous pursuits of showmanship."

Hitch almost rolled his eyes. For Livingstone, the show *always* went on.

"Instead, we will combine our skills and the horsepower of our many flying machines. We will face down this threat from above. We will not be content to sit on our laurels and wait for the enemy to come to us. No, sir! We will hunt down this sky beast."

The crowd started murmuring again, but this time they were calmer, maybe even a little hopeful.

"And to show the sincerity of my intent," Livingstone said, "I will personally dedicate the entire purse from our competition as an incentive for the man who finds the beast."

Everybody started cheering and clapping.

What was that old buzzard up to? Hitch frowned.

Before he could think on it too long, Aurelia pushed her way through the crowd, both hands held straight out. In front of whatever Campbell and Livingstone were standing on, she stopped and turned around. She hugged her violet scarf around her elbows. Her eyes were wide open and a little wild. The pale red-blonde of her hair fell out of the bun at her nape and wisped around her face. She started murmuring, too low to hear from the back of the tent.

Campbell and Livingstone exchanged a look, and Campbell leaned down, a hand on her shoulder to try to ease her away.

"No!" She slapped at his hand, then faced forward again. "I knew it was coming. I knew it was coming to get us all. I told you!" She looked around, maybe trying to find somebody she actually had told. "I told Walter . . ." Her voice trailed out again.

Hitch frowned. Somebody needed to go up there and fetch her before she started in on one of her fits. He looked around for Nan, came up empty, and started pushing forward himself.

"Come along, Miss Aurelia," Campbell said. "You're perfectly safe. You have my word."

"Your word can't change anything." She looked over her other shoulder at Livingstone. "Neither can yours!"

"Aurelia!" Nan's panicked voice cut through the tent. She sidled along the edge, headed toward the front, her mouth pinched. "Aurelia, that's enough!"

Aurelia didn't even glance at her sister. "It is coming to get you all, because you are all crazy." She tilted her nose. "I know because that man Zlo said it to me, back before the first storm. He was down here on the ground then, and he told me. Not any of the rest of you, just me."

"Aurelia!" Nan pushed through the last row of people and caught Aurelia's elbow. Her face was harried, her eyebrows drawn down in a deep V. "Stop this nonsense, dear. You must come along."

"I tried to warn you!" Aurelia's voice rose into a screech. "I told you! I told Walter, I told Byron, I told the postman!" The screech deepened into a frantic sob. "But none of you listened to me."

Nan hauled Aurelia away.

Dead silence held the crowd for two full seconds. Then pandemonium erupted.

A chill, like the fingertip of a ghost, touched the back of Hitch's neck. Aurelia was more than one egg short of a dozen, everybody knew that. But she wasn't a liar any more than Lilla was Madame Curie. What was it she had told him back at the hospital after Jael had been knocked out by the lightning? Now that there had been one storm, there would be two?

Maybe she *had* been trying to warn him. He'd said he believed her—and then brushed off the whole thing.

He filled his lungs and turned to go. He needed to get out of here, get his prop patched up, find a way to pay Earl's doctor bill, and then keep Jael under wraps until they could figure out how to knock Zlo out of the sky for good.

He ducked back outside into the drizzle and made his way over to where his Jenny was still tied to J.W.'s back bumper.

"Son! Hold up a minute, won't you?"

He looked up from the knot in the rope.

Livingstone walked over, mincing steps to avoid puddles. Behind him, people filtered out of the tent.

"You heard what was said in there, I guess?" Livingstone asked.

"Yeah, I heard."

"Well, then I know I can count on you to help me fulfill my promise to these people."

Hitch straightened all the way up. "Look, showmanship's all fine and good. I'm for it. But this ain't the time."

"Nonsense, dear boy. There's never a better time. Number one, it gives these people something to ponder other than their own panic. Number two"—he tapped Hitch's chest with the silver handle of his walking stick—"if we're going to be humanitarians, I see no reason why we cannot profit from it." He leaned in. "I hope you know without my saying so that I had nothing to do with this travesty. But I must admit it has presented what my business acumen tells me is the opportunity of a lifetime. I have no intention of wasting that. What we pilots must all do now is work together. Follow my lead, and this could end up being on every newspaper in the country. What do you think of that?"

Ah, of course. Livingstone didn't just want the publicity for bringing *Schturming* down. Wouldn't he be just *more* than ecstatic if he was to actually get his grubby hands *on* the thing? Hitch could see him now: making his grand entrance into every town between Seattle and Miami Beach, coasting in on that giant dirigible.

No doubt Livingstone would be equally delighted with the *dawsedometer*'s prospects. Lightning you could control? He could stage dogfights the like of which the war pilots had never even seen.

And of *course* he'd be as scrupulous as a white-gloved old lady at Sunday services. Wouldn't even *think* of using the threat of all that chaos to keep his pilots—and Lord knew who else—in line.

Working for Livingstone would be challenging enough as it was. No way Hitch wanted to be within five hundred miles of the man if he somehow shimmied past Campbell and got his hands on that dirigible.

"If you want me to tell you I'm going to go up there and try to find that thing and bring it down, then the answer is I sure am. But you're forgetting this is my home. What I do, I do for the people here, not for your show."

"Of course, of course. All the more reason you should come around to my way of thinking. I will bring down this threat to your home, and I tell you in all frankness that I *value* your skills in helping me achieve that." Livingstone lowered his voice. "You might yet achieve great things, Captain Hitchcock. You just need the guidance of an experienced hand."

In other words, Livingstone wanted a long leash on Hitch, so anything Hitch might do would ultimately be a credit to the Extravagant Flying Circus.

Livingstone smiled and stepped back. "I'm sure you realize that with the unfortunate demise of the competition, our bet will have to be abandoned. But I must be honest with you: I would still be pleased to offer you a membership in my troupe. *If* you should be instrumental in helping me destroy the airbeast, then perhaps I might consider presenting you that partnership after all." He shrugged. "My way gets you everything you desire. You get to free your town *and* journey on."

Had the old buzzard wanted Hitch as a partner in his show all along?

Hitch took a careful breath. "We'll see how it goes."

"Most excellent." Livingstone pursed his lips and tweaked the ring on his little finger. "And what about your lovely young wing walker? Seems I remember a pendant she was rather intent on defending."

Sudden heat burned away the chill on the back of Hitch's neck. "She's got nothing to do with this."

"Of course, of course. To be honest, I don't share your sheriff's interest in reconciling with these pirates. No glory to be had in that, is there?"

"Look." Hitch squared his stance. "We're on the same side in this. I respect your flying as much as any man's and I appreciate your offer. But I'll tell you this upfront—the only time I'll fall in line behind you on this is the time when I believe with all my heart that what you're doing is the right thing for the people here."

Livingstone's sharp gaze penetrated Hitch's. "Well." He touched a finger to his hat brim. "That may not be the *best* way to play this game—for anyone's sake. But I shall look forward to seeing what you come up with in this grand chase of ours. Happy hunting, Captain Hitchcock."

Hitch watched him go.

Livingstone wanted publicity, Hitch's Jenny, and a fancy new dirigible to add to his show. Campbell wanted to destroy *Schturming*, show Zlo who was boss, and remind Scottsbluff why he was such an all-fired swell sheriff. Jael wanted to save what was left of her people and get home. And everybody else just wanted to survive. That was an awful lot of juggling. If he dropped even one of those balls, he wasn't likely to walk away from this mess.

He hissed a long breath past his teeth.

So he'd juggle. If—when?—one of the balls fell, he'd have to hope it was the one that'd cause the least amount of hurt all the way around.

He stood in the wind, hands in his pockets, and watched the crowd.

Nan walked around the back of the tent, shepherding a weeping Aurelia. She saw Hitch and stopped short. Her eyes darted to either side of him, probably looking for a graceful retreat. Then she straightened her shoulders and trudged past him.

He took his hands from his pockets. "You all right?"

She nodded, even that gesture looking like it required half her remaining energy.

"Walter, the girls?" he asked

"They're fine. We're all fine."

Aurelia drew in a sharp, warbling breath. She wasn't having a fit, but her eyes stared at faraway things. She walked with her arms at her sides, shoulders slumped. Her violet scarf trailed in the thin beginnings of mud.

He leaned over to catch the scarf and tuck it around her cold arm. "It'll be okay." He couldn't stop his gaze from wandering over to Nan's as he said it.

Nan shook her head.

"I'm sorry," he said. "For what I said about Walter earlier. He's your kid. You got a right to raise him how you want. But I would never intentionally hurt him—or any of you."

She hesitated. "You frighten me, you know that."

"Me? Why?"

"You just do." Her eyes were red-rimmed, not with tears, just with the tiredness of it all. "Walter . . . Walter has some problems, as I'm sure you've noticed. There have been things that have happened to him, some I blame myself for, some I don't. I've tried all these years to *help* him, to give him a reason to talk again, to be a good mother to him."

"You are a good mother."

"I'm a good mother." She closed her eyes for a moment. "And you're an irresponsible adventurer. And *you've* helped him. I'd be a liar not to admit he's been different this week. I've never seen him like this, not since that day when I . . ." She inhaled sharply through her nose and straightened up. "Why you? Why does he respond to you?"

He shrugged. "Airplanes."

"It's not the airplanes. It's you. You have the gift for making people love you, Hitch." She didn't say it like it was a compliment. "I told Celia she was a fool to marry you."

Celia hadn't been the only fool, but he kept his mouth shut on that one. He bore a man's share when it came to blame there, and they all knew it.

Aurelia drew another shuddery breath. "I remember . . . Celia."

"Yes, dear," Nan's voice softened, almost all the way to tenderness. "She was our sister."

Aurelia's gaze roamed, but never quite made it back to the present. "Like you are my sister."

"Yes." Nan rubbed briskly at Aurelia's shivery arm. She looked back up. "Family means something to me, Hitch. I know it never meant much to you—"

"That's not entirely true—"

"—but to me it's everything. And I will protect it."

"I reckon that's as it should be."

"But . . ." Her mouth worked, almost like she had something to say and couldn't quite get it out. "You should know—"

He made it easy for her. "I'm here to see this through, and then I'll be gone again. I promise."

She closed her mouth, and the lines of her cheeks went hard—as if that added coals to her fire instead of making things better.

He tried again. "Looks like Livingstone's going to give me a job—a good one. Supposing we all survive this mess, then I'll be out of your hair for good." He tried to lighten his tone, but it came out a little creaky. "I may be irresponsible, but at least I'm consistent, right?"

"Yes." She drew herself up and tightened her arm around Aurelia. "That being the case, I think it only right I ask you again to do the right thing and help me see to it that Walter stays at home from now on."

Something under his heart twinged. He wasn't going to hurt that kid, even by leaving. People came and went in life all the time. That wasn't a bad thing to learn at any age. And unlike the last time he'd left, Hitch had never made a secret of the fact that this time he *would* be going.

The wind gusted against his back. Of course, there were other things that had changed. This was a battleground now. True enough that little boys didn't belong where there was nobody who could be looking out for them.

He nodded. "Fair enough."

"I know you don't understand, but believe me when I say this is the best thing for Walter. And that's all I care about."

He couldn't argue that. "Me too."

Something in her eyes shifted, but hard to tell what, since there were a *lot* of emotions swirling around in there. She tucked her chin. "Okay then." She herded Aurelia forward a step, then looked back. "Good luck up there, Hitch."

He touched his forehead in a small salute. "Yes, ma'am." He could use the sentiment, because truth be told, he didn't feel too lucky right at this moment.

CHAPTER 28

RAINDROPS SPLATTED AGAINST the wooden plank above Walter's head. He huddled under the front bleacher seat, knees against his chest, arms around Taos's neck. The dog sat quietly. Only the tip of his one floppy ear moved whenever he perked it at a new passerby. His long fur had kinked with the wet, and it smelled like a musty carpet.

Beside the bleachers, someone had backed two Auto Wagon Model As—with the back doors open—end to end and erected a blanket on poles over the top. The doctor, in his black derby hat, and a few volunteers worked underneath. The patients sat on one tailgate, and the doctor picked up his tools off the other one, so he only had to turn when he wanted something.

Right now, Earl was the one sitting there, sweat glistening on his face. He kept hollering at the doctor.

Jael stood at his side, a hand on his good shoulder. Every time he hollered, she patted him, like Mama Nan sometimes did when she was trying to make Aunt Aurelia hush without being obvious about it.

Really, though, it wasn't the doctor Earl was mad at. It wasn't the doctor's fault he was hurt. It was Walter's.

Walter leaned his cheek against Taos's neck. If he hadn't been so scared earlier, if he had dodged faster when that wing had started swinging, then Hitch's partner would never have gotten hurt.

The corners of his eyes pinched. One side of his mouth kept twitching downward. He rolled his lips in and bit them. Crying on top of everything else—good sweet angels, that *would* be too much.

His hands hadn't stopped shaking for even a little bit. People had died. Pilots had gotten blown up. And even Hitch hadn't been able to stop the outlaws in the ship.

Maybe this was what the Great War had been like. Some of the men who had gone across the sea to fight in it a few years ago told stories about planes crashing and people getting burned alive. When they told it, it had sounded bad, sure enough. But it always sounded like an adventure too.

Heroes liked adventures. They weren't scared of them, and they didn't sit around afterward, shaking and blinking back tears.

He blinked again.

He'd been scared all his life, ever since that day when he'd been so scared he'd almost let Evvy and Annie die. Maybe once you started being scared, you never stopped. That was the scariest thought of all.

Taos perked both ears.

Hitch strode in from the field, headed toward the motorcars. He glanced at Walter once, then again. He slowed, and then stopped. He looked at where Earl was hollering something new at the doctor. Then almost reluctantly, he turned and walked over to Walter.

If Hitch saw him like this, he'd know for sure Walter was a coward. He was just a little kid who couldn't stop shaking and wouldn't start talking—who didn't even fit in quite right at home, much less out here. He hugged Taos tighter and bit his lips harder. A hero like Hitch wouldn't want to be around him. Might even be ashamed to be seen with him.

Hitch stopped and stood over Walter. He looked around, almost like he was afraid he was going to get yelled at.

Then he looked at Walter. "What are you still doing here? Nan's going to be looking for you."

Walter shrugged. She probably thought he'd gone home with Molly and the girls, but he'd run back to make sure Taos was all right—and, also, so nobody would see him shaking like this.

Hitch wrinkled his forehead. "What are you doing down here?"

It was all too hard to explain—even if the answer hadn't been awful anyway. He shrugged.

Hitch shifted his weight from one foot to the other. Then,

with another look around, he lowered himself into a crouch and reached to scratch Taos's ear. "Well, I reckon this isn't such a bad hidey hole. Keeps you kinda dry anyway, right?"

A smile just wouldn't come. If he stopped clamping his teeth, he'd start bawling right here in front of Hitch Hitchcock. He turned his face into Taos's neck.

Across the way, Earl yelped.

Walter winced again.

"Don't worry about Earl," Hitch said. "He's as tough a bird as they come. You know, I heard it was you who thought up tying the wing to the bottom of the ship. It was a good idea. Not everybody can think that fast under pressure."

Walter had to make Hitch understand. It wasn't right to let him think Walter had been brave when he'd been anything but. He peeked up.

Hitch met his gaze and looked right back. "Scary, wasn't it?"

Was it written on his face that plain? His whole chin trembled, but he made himself duck his head in a nod.

"I was scared too."

What? Walter looked all the way up from Taos's neck.

Hitch let the corner of a grin slip. "Sure. Everybody's scared, don't you know that?"

Walter shook his head.

"Well, they are. And not just of big things like this. I'm scared every time I go up in a plane."

Was Hitch making fun of him? Was he trying to fool him just to make him feel better?

"Any pilot who's not a little scared when he gets in a machine that's going to take him a thousand feet above the ground is a fool. And I'll tell you this too—I don't like heights one bit. What Jael and Rick do, climbing out there on the wing? You couldn't pay me to do that. Inside a cockpit, it don't bother me for some reason. But the top of a high building"—he whistled—"that'll get me every time."

Walter's stomach stopped swirling around. If Hitch was scared, did that make him more of a hero—or not one at all?

"Fear's not a bad thing, son. Keeps us cautious. Also gives us that nice little thrill." He grinned. "If flying didn't scare me, I probably wouldn't like it so much."

Behind Hitch, Earl had stopped yelling. While the doctor tidied up for the next patient, Earl sat there cradling his newly wrapped arm against his chest and muttering.

Jael looked over her shoulder and spotted Hitch and Walter. She walked toward them—or rather she limped. She winced with every step and supported herself, first on the automobiles and then on the bleacher seats above her head. A few steps off, she stopped and listened.

Walter glanced back at Hitch.

"Let me tell you a secret." Hitch looked him straight in the eye. "There's no such thing as being brave. We're all scared, sometime or another—scared down to the soles of our boots—and all we want to do is curl up and cry and shake all over."

Walter clenched his fists. When had his hands stopped trembling?

"But if you *pretend* you're brave, well then, you are brave." Hitch reached out and ruffled Walter's hair. "And from what I heard, you did a good job pretending today."

A hot feeling filled his stomach. It was a good feeling—the hot-water-bottle-at-the-bottom-of-your-bed-on-a-January-night kind of feeling. The rest of the world might be all icy cold and howling wind, but you were warm and snug and safe inside. That kind of feeling.

His lip stopped wanting to droop, and he smiled.

Hitch smiled back. "You're quite a kid, you know that?"

The good feeling spread. Hitch Hitchcock was an explorer and a pilot, and if he *was* scared sometimes, then nobody'd know about it. And he liked Walter. He thought Walter was smart and brave.

Hitch must have seen Jael out of the corner of his eye because he darted a glance in her direction.

She was smiling too—that glowy smile of hers that lit her up from the inside and shone through all her scrapes and spatters. The way she looked at Hitch was kind of funny, like maybe she was saying things with just her eyes, like she was thanking him. She looked tired and hurting and pinched around the corners. But she looked hot-water-bottle happy too, like maybe what

Hitch had said to Walter had also given her the safe feeling.

Hitch didn't smile at her like he had at Walter. The back of his neck got kind of pink, though maybe that was from the drizzle making him cold. He cleared his throat and turned back to Walter. "Anyway, you better get home as quick as you can before your mama thinks you ran off again. We've got work to do now. It might not be too safe around here for a while."

When grown-ups said that to him, what they really meant was they wanted him out of the way. He slumped his shoulders and huffed. If he had to pretend he was brave, then he needed to *keep* pretending. Back home, there was nothing to pretend about.

"Hey, get rid of the long face, huh?" Hitch said. "You can still help us find that thing from home." He dug around in his jacket pocket and came out with a small pair of binoculars.

Walter's breath snagged halfway up his windpipe. A real *live* set of binoculars, like soldiers used.

"You take these, and you keep an eye on the sky. You see anything, you report it to Deputy Griff. Can you do that?"

Walter nodded. He cradled the binoculars in both hands, as if they were a baby bird, so Hitch would know he'd take good care of them and bring them back.

Hitch jerked his head toward the parked cars. "Now, get on with you."

Walter scrambled out. Hitch gave him a little slap on the back as he passed, and Jael laid a quick hand on his head. Walter watched the binoculars—scuffed black with shiny curved lenses and a leather neck strap. He was careful not to drop them.

Maybe Hitch was right. Maybe he had been just a little bit brave today. For some reason that made no sense, it suddenly seemed a whole lot easier to be brave out here where there really was danger, than it did back home with his family where everything was safe.

CHAPTER 29

ITCH WATCHED THE boy round the corner of the bleachers. Walter held the battered binoculars like they'd crack if he so much as jostled them. Crazy kid. He'd been the sharpest and the pluckiest of just about everybody here today—including Hitch. And there he was thinking he was some kind of failure. Did Nan *really* realize what kind of boy she had? With a nudge or two in the right direction, Walter would grow up to be some kind of man.

Hitch glanced sideways at where Jael was hanging onto the edge of the bleachers. She'd probably heard his whole conversation with Walter—and the days of hoping she might not have understood it were long over. His neck warmed a bit more, and he turned back to Taos. So he'd gone a little soft over the kid, so what? Couldn't exactly leave the boy crying in the rain under a splintery bench, especially if that was going to be the last time Hitch ever said anything to him.

Jael shuffled over. She clung to the bleachers and supported her weight on her arms with each step. She looked worse than she'd been even the day after the lightning. Earl's arm had been so obvious, Hitch hadn't given much thought to what might have happened to *her* during the attack.

"That wing didn't hit you too, did it?"

She shrugged. "No. It is the same hurt from before."

"I thought that was getting better?"

"Sometimes it is getting better, some other times it is not. There is no sense to it. It was very bad not long ago, but I think maybe now it is becoming better."

"You should sit down. J.W. seems to have forgotten his car's here, so I'll bring it over and give you a ride back to the Carpenters'."

"Maybe tonight I will stay here. I should be where I can see what is happening."

"What you should do is go sleep someplace dry and warm. This drizzle's not going to do anybody's joints any good."

He looked at the sky, then let gravity take his head and lean it all the way back on his neck. He closed his eyes. It wasn't really raining so much as sprinkling, and only a few drops struck his face. Sleeping somewhere warm and dry sounded awful good about now. His muscles stretched all the way down his chest and stomach, and he let out a groan.

"I'm sorry, you know," he said.

She shuffled a step nearer and leaned a hand on his shoulder to support herself. "For what are you sorry?" She lowered herself to sit beside him.

"I said I'd help you take care of Zlo so you could go home. It's not working out too well so far."

"It is not *not* working out. Not yet anyway."

He opened his eyes and raised his head. "It's not going to take long for people to figure out you're one of them. I'm sure Rick knows it, and Livingstone's figured it out. He's only keeping quiet so long as I play along with his heroics."

"You are good at heroics." The silver in her eyes had dulled to a pained gray. Her damp hair was crimping into curls, and she looked like a bedraggled little baby swan. "I was hearing what you said to Walter."

He looked down and thumbed mud from the corner of Taos's eye. "Yeah, I thought you might have."

"Thank you."

"Just being friendly."

"Do you know he thinks you are hero out of his book of stories?"

"He's a kid, he's got a big imagination. Nothing revs a boy's imagination like an airplane."

"Maybe this is true. But I think he needs to have heroes more than some little boys."

"'Cause he doesn't talk, you mean?"

She swiped a raindrop from her cheek with the back of her hand. "I cannot explain it, but he is sad somehow inside. At his house, his family, they love him. But"—she shook her head— "even with them, he is still somehow not *with* them."

"Well." What was he supposed to do with that?

The boy could sure have chosen himself a nice string of heroes better than him. That was certainly what Nan was always implying. Why not Griff? He was here. He obviously knew Walter and liked him. Griff would be a far better kind of man to look up to. Not as exciting, probably, but the kind that'd show you how to be there for people when it counted.

Not much Hitch could say about that, so he changed the subject. "You do realize all this talk of Campbell's and Livingstone's—and mine—could be so much hot air? Even with the dirigible marked, we'd have to stumble right onto it to find it. Zlo is still square in control of this game, no question."

She touched his shoulder again. Her palm warmed him all the way through his jacket. "We will think of something. Tomorrow will be different day."

"Heetch."

Somebody was saying his name funny. A woman. And she was poking him.

He shifted in his bedroll and eased his head out from under the blanket. The morning light—more gray than golden— zapped his eyelids shut just as fast as he opened them. He probably hadn't gotten to sleep until past midnight, what with all the to-do of cleaning up the field and trying to plan for tomorrow.

Or today, rather.

"Hitch. I have thought of plan."

He flipped over onto his back and squinched his eyes open.

Beneath the canopy of his Jenny's wing, Jael crouched over him, one hand still extended, ready to jab him again.

He groaned. "Oof. A plan. Right. A plan." The words circled in his brain, trying to find enough space to land.

She stabbed him again with two pointy fingers just under his ribs.

270 - K.M. WEILAND

"Ow! Stop with the poking already. Give me a chance to wake up."

"You are very slow with this waking up. Earl has been awake for many hours."

"Don't give him too much credit. He probably rolled over onto his busted arm."

"No." She rocked back on her heels. "He has been working on plane, to get it ready for when we need it."

"By himself? With that arm?" Hitch propped himself on his elbow and craned a look around at the front of the plane.

Where the propeller should have been, the naked shaft glinted.

"Matthew Berringer took him to his house to do this carving," Jael said.

"And he didn't wake me?"

She shrugged. "He said he did not need you. And that you are"—she squinted one eye, like she was trying to remember a word—"*bear*, when you are woken up."

"But you're not scared of bears, is that it?"

She scootched back on her heels, and when she was clear of the wing, she stood. "Walter has bear. It is furry and . . . sweet."

"Ri-ight." He pushed back his bedroll and looked around for his boots. "So what's this plan of yours?"

"I will tell you in car." She gestured to J.W.'s jalopy. "Should I drive?"

"No. You should *not* drive." He laced both boots all the way to the top and knotted them off. Then he raked a hand through his hair, grabbed his jacket, and crawled out from under the wing.

Uniform gray covered the sky, but it wasn't raining anymore. Along the horizon, the clouds darkened into black streaks that blocked sight of anything past Scotts Bluff.

He turned all the way around until Jael was in view once more. "So we really are blockaded. At least it's not raining here." He touched the Jenny's wing. It was only slightly damp from yesterday's drizzle. "If it got much wetter, we would've had to wait for the spark plugs to dry out before we could take off." He checked the engine, but Earl had already opened all the compartments to let her dry. "Guess that means the drought's broken, for what it's worth."

"You are very slow this morning," Jael said. She had rummaged through the grub sack and come out with what was left of Lilla's biscuits. She held up the plate. "For first meal. Now let us go."

"All right, all right." He leaned his neck to first one side and then the other to crack it, then trudged after her.

Today, she hurried to the car with barely a glitch in her stride and climbed into the seat, up and over, without bothering with the door.

He cranked the engine, then slid beneath the wheel. "Guess sleeping cold and damp agrees with your joints after all."

She grinned. "I thought of something that is very interesting."

"What?" He turned the jalopy around and bumped across the field toward the road. "That being around Earl is what makes you sore?" Earl would say it was Hitch who had the talent for making people sore.

She bit her lip, still grinning. Her eyes sparkled. All in all, she looked far too pleased with herself. "Not Earl. *Schturming.*"

"How's that?"

"Lightning is what made me hurt in beginning, yes?"

"Right. Although you're lucky to be feeling anything, if you want my opinion."

"Yes, but *how* it is hurting does not have sense. One hour it is almost all gone, and then I am hardly able to be walking."

He turned onto the road, headed toward the lake, and gave the car the gun. "You're the first person I know who's stayed around to tell me how it felt after getting that close to a lightning strike. Maybe that's just how it goes."

"Maybe. But I don't think so." She handed him a biscuit. "It is like you said yesterday. The weather makes people's bones to hurt. Well, *Schturming* causes weather, yes?"

He bit past the flour powdered on top and into the fluffy—if cold—insides of the biscuit. "And when are you figuring on getting to the plan part? *Schturming*'s making weather all over the place today."

"But I am not talking about *weather*, I am talking about *dawsedometer*. When it is near, I hurt. And since it is inside of *Schturming*, that is how we find it."

"That is . . . interesting, if it's true. Kind of like barometric pressure—which this *dawsedometer* thing probably warps like crazy."

She made a confused face.

"Barometric pressure. I guess you'd say it's part of what makes weather. At any rate, it can make people's joints hurt." He chewed his biscuit. "But even if that's true, what's it get us? You just want to drive around until you start hurting?"

She raised both eyebrows, mouth cocked. "You have better idea?"

"Not really."

"Then we drive." She settled back in her seat and pulled out another biscuit. "You will find it. You have luck."

"You can't trust luck."

She looked over at him. Her face was clear except for two serious little lines between her eyes. "I trust *you*."

"Well . . ." He dug around for the right thing to say.

What did he want to say anyway? He *had* wanted her to trust him. He'd wanted her to like him, almost right from the start. Well, now she liked him and trusted him—and he'd gone and kissed her, and who knew exactly how she felt about that now that she'd cooled down. At any rate, she wasn't too burnt up about it, from the looks of things.

He cast her a sidelong glance. "You do know you shouldn't count on me too much, right?"

"This 'count on'—what is that?"

"It means . . . depend on, to be sure of something."

"You are not sure of yourself?"

"Oh, I'm sure. It's just that what I'm sure of isn't always what other people *want* me to be sure of."

"You are very worried about disappointing people."

Most of the time, there weren't any people in his life *to* disappoint. It was only since coming home that the Groundsworld—as she called it—had started reaching out for him with its expectations and responsibilities.

He guided the car around a puddle. The left front tire hit the rut anyway and bounced hard.

"I'm not worried," he said. "There's things I've done—mostly long ago, before I left home—that I'm not proud of. I wish they could've turned out different. But the truth is, even if I had 'em to do again, they'd happen the same way. I am what I am, and I can't help it when people expect me to be something else."

She chewed on that for a minute. "You think you are still same person you were—before you left all this time ago?"

"Sure. People don't change." He gave her half a grin, trying to make it a joke. "It's a common myth."

She ate her biscuit slowly, watching him. Then she licked the crumbs off her fingers and shook her head. "People change. But it is slow. It is not that they decide tomorrow they will have differences. It is that they decide every day, for many days. Or maybe they do not decide—and it happens anyway, without them even having knowledge of it." She spread her hands. "It is not change. It is what you call . . . um . . ."

"Evolution?"

"Maybe. I do not know this word."

He steadied the steering wheel over a series of ruts. Maybe she was right. Maybe not. He wasn't entirely the person he had been nine years ago. Back then, he'd been as sure as shoeshine that running away was the only right choice. But now, a niggle of doubt surfaced.

What would have happened had he stayed? Maybe Campbell would have backed down sooner than risk his crooked dealings being revealed in open court. Maybe he *wouldn't* have gone after the Hitchcock farm like he'd threatened. Even if Campbell had held fast, maybe Hitch spending a few years in prison would have done less to hurt the people he cared about. Maybe Celia wouldn't have gotten sick and died.

He might have a family now. A little stability. A few bucks in his pockets. Would that have been such a bad thing?

His chest tightened. And leave the air? Let gravity chain him to the ground?

He shook his head. "People don't change. They want to, but they can't."

Jael drew in a pained little gasp.

He looked over at her. "Nothing personal."

"No . . ." She sucked in another breath, past her teeth. She sat up, rigid in her bouncing seat, both fists clenched in her lap. Her skin had gone tight over her face. Her eyes were wide, her forehead lined. "I am having pain again."

"What?" He hit the brakes hard, and the jalopy nearly swerved off the road. He leaned his head back and scanned the sky.

Nothing but clouds.

She leaned forward, wincing. "Move slowly."

He let up on the brake. "If you're right about this, you'll deserve Livingstone's prize all to yourself."

They crept down the road—four hundred yards, five hundred, then a mile. He alternated his gaze between the road ahead and the hazy sky that stretched out across the lake on one side and the unplanted fields of gray-green sagebrush on the other.

When you came right down to it, this was ridiculous. It was like looking for a mosquito smashed onto the Jenny's top wing. Maybe you'd find it if you looked long enough, but, even then, it'd be nothing but a fluke.

Jael snatched at his sleeve and pulled his arm, nearly turning the car into the barrow pit. "Wait!"

"Hey! Let up. You want to wreck us?"

Still hanging onto his arm, she dragged herself across the seat toward him. Her eyes strained for the sky. "Ssh! Engine—turn it off!"

He killed the engine and followed her gaze.

Even without sunlight, he still had to squint against the gray of the sky. "I don't see anything."

She leaned halfway over the top of him and pointed. "There."

He followed her finger.

High above, skating along the bottom of the clouds, something flickered. Halfway across the field, a speck about the size of his thumbnail blinked against the clouds. He squinted harder. He should never have given Walter his field glasses.

"It's probably a buzzard."

She gave her head a sharp shake. "No."

It flashed red and swung around. It didn't look like a bird circling. More like something swinging.

It was the wing.

He thumped the steering wheel. "Hot dog, girl! I do believe

you're right. Let's get you out of here and find me a plane!"

They careened back into camp to find Earl overseeing as Matthew and J.W. screwed the new propeller into place. Hitch skidded to a halt in a cloud of dust. In Nebraska, it somehow managed to be dusty even after it rained. He shut off the engine and started to climb out.

Jael grabbed his sleeve and leaned across the seat. "Hitch. I think Zlo would be having desire for airplane. He would want it for protection and attack, yes?"

Hitch didn't have to think about that for more than a second. "Of course, he would. Who's gonna be satisfied with a dirigible when you can have a plane too?"

"He would chase after you, I think." Her eyes sparked with the same excitement that was running all through his body. "If you were only plane he is having sight of—you could lead him to . . ." She gestured with both hands, trying to find the word.

He didn't need her to say it. "Ambush."

She grinned and nodded. "I would make you take me, but I can hardly walk when I am in nearness to it."

He winked at her and squeezed her shoulder. "You're already a genius. No need to be a hero too." He slid all the way out and slammed the door. Then he gave caution a good heave into the wind and leaned back over the door, trying to keep a straight face and failing. "You deserve a kiss, but I have to tell you, I don't want to get myself smacked again."

Her eyes flashed wide for a second. Then something that *might* have been a smile tugged at the edges of her mouth.

He turned away before she could respond—either way—and jogged off.

Livingstone had wandered over to observe the Berringers' work.

Hitch hesitated. If he told Livingstone about this, the man would want in on the hunt. But if every plane in his troupe went roaring out there right now, they'd lose any chance of surprise. Zlo would just rev those big engines—and that big cannon—and disappear again.

Better to leave now without saying anything, and let Earl fill Livingstone in after, so he could get the rest of the pilots ready when Hitch brought *Schturming* to them.

Hitch angled around to stay out of Livingstone's line of sight and stopped beside Earl, his back to the plane.

"Finally decided to get up, did you?" Earl said.

"I apologize right now for all the times I groused about you being an early riser."

Earl looked at him suspiciously. "How's that?"

"We found *Schturming*."

Earl's eyebrows sprang upwards. "That crazy wing idea worked?"

"Sure did. The plane ready to go?"

"She'll hold together, I reckon." Earl cradled his splinted arm and winced. "Where is it anyway?"

"Keep your voice down." Hitch shot a glance over his shoulder. Livingstone was already looking their way.

He turned back. "If I'm going to do this right, I need to do it by myself. I'm faster that way and a whole lot less likely to get noticed too soon. I'm going to try to sucker *Schturming* into following me. Ten minutes after I'm in the air, you tell Livingstone to head out and meet me at the Bluff. I'll lure it there, and if he's got enough pilots waiting for it, we can maybe maneuver it into crashing against the crags."

"You have thought this thing through, right?"

"Of course."

Earl glared at him. "Of *course* you have." His arm must be bothering him. He always got extra cranky when he wasn't feeling well. "And in all your thinking it through, I'm sure you spent a nice amount of time remembering that if you get this plane shot out of the sky again, all our plans are going to go up in smoke. You lose with Zlo, you lose with Livingstone, you lose with Campbell. And even if they don't scalp you amongst the three of 'em, you'll still be stuck here for a good long time. Now, are you telling me you're *sure* sticking your neck out for this little hick town is what you want to do?"

If he thought about it, he probably wouldn't be so sure. So he didn't think about it. "I'm sure."

Earl's grunt didn't sound too surprised. "Right. Just so we're clear." He jutted his chin. "Watch your tail."

"What?" Hitch turned in time to see Livingstone approach.

The man had a gleam in his eye. "Did I have the good fortune to hear you have accomplished the impossible in discovering our quarry for us?"

"Look, it's just a one-man mission to start with. Earl will tell you about it." He eased past Livingstone. "We send any more planes than mine out there, and we could end up with a sack full of nothing." He pointed at Matthew. "You want to give that propeller a heave when I tell you?"

Livingstone stepped a few paces away and snapped his fingers at one of the kids hanging around the planes. "Rally the pilots. Tell them I want them in the air in five minutes. We've found the sky beast."

Hitch turned on him. "You send twenty planes screaming out there, and Zlo'll see us coming a mile off."

"Piffle." Livingstone turned away, headed for his own plane. "You overestimate yourself, as usual. You'll need help, and we must stick together."

"And it'll look better in the papers, I suppose?"

"Now you're catching the vision, old boy." Livingstone gestured to Earl as he passed. "Since that arm unfortunately keeps you from any useful assistance, why don't you drive on down to the farmhouse and telephone the gentlemen of the press at the *Star-Herald* and the *Courier*?"

Earl watched him go, mouth open. Then he looked at Hitch. "I know we're supposed to be nice to him. I know I *told* you to be nice to him. But I hope you win all his publicity away from him, just for the principle of it."

"I'll settle for beating him to that field. If I can get enough of a head start on him to get *Schturming* to think I'm the only one, it might still work." Hitch clambered into the rear cockpit. "Let's go!" he shouted—and Matthew spun the engine to life.

Chapter 30

O N A FULL tank and with minimal headwind, Hitch gunned the Hisso for all it was worth. The prop chewed through the air and spat the miles back out behind them. He flew low, staying beneath the cloud ceiling and coasting over the ground. He kept one eye on the road, as a guide back to the correct field, and another on the sky. As he cut across the lake, the Jenny bounced a little in the air currents. And then—there she was.

The amputated wing fluttered, a red blot against the clouds. *Schturming's* keel separated itself from the gray as he raced in close. The wooden planks and their flaking blue paint materialized through the haze. He passed beneath the silent propellers and headed for the bow, where the cargo doors were located.

Over his head, the huge ship swung gently on its cables. High above, the envelope melded into the clouds. She was barely moving, just letting the wind take her. But she must have had some kind of engine running because a heavy thud reverberated through his chest, audible even above his own engine.

He slowed the Jenny to try to match pace enough to stay hidden beneath the ship. The Hisso choked a little at his tight hold on the reins. She'd stall out completely if he slowed her to under forty-five miles per hour, and from the looks of *Schturming's* hull racing by overhead, the dirigible wasn't going anywhere near that fast. He would run out of cover in less than a minute.

A few drops of oil spattered against the forward windshield, and one splatted back against his cheek. Apparently, Earl hadn't done such a great job with the oil leak. They'd filled it up last night, so Hitch would have enough oil to last him a while yet. And as fast as this job was going to have to be finished, it probably wouldn't matter anyway. In the meantime, it just stunk worse than usual.

He was only going to get one chance at this. If Zlo and his mugs didn't take the bait first thing, it'd be too late to get *Schturming* turned around to face Livingstone's ambush—such as it was. That would be the end of that.

Just a few more seconds and the Jenny would outstrip *Schturming*'s meandering pace. He glanced to the left. Out across the lake, two dozen planes tore toward him, their gaudy colors silhouetted in the silver water. Great. With throttles wide open, they'd be here in less than a minute. It was now or never.

With a whoop, he gunned the throttle, shot out in front of *Schturming*'s prow, and lifted the Jenny's nose to the sky. As soon as he had enough clearance, he flipped her back over and around—headed straight for the bay, where they sure enough *couldn't* miss seeing him.

The doors stood wide open, a gaping hole in the lowest level of the ship's front end.

That was the good news.

The bad news was that several burly, whiskery, rather astonished men wearing bowler hats and long coats were standing in the hole. Even before the Jenny bobbed into view, they had their arms extended, mouths open, pointing straight toward Livingstone's horde.

Their attention switched over to Hitch in a flash. Their open mouths got even rounder, and they started scrambling to close the doors.

In the two levels of portholes above the bay doors, faces— some of them women and children—stared out at him. Bringing this thing down was the top priority, but somehow he had to do it without endangering all these folks.

From the looks of things, there would be only two ways to bring this beast down. Either force her to ground from the outside—which hadn't worked out so well yesterday—or bring her down from the inside.

That would mean threading the needle to land in the big bay

that seemed to run down the length of the ship's lowest level. And then what? He'd extract himself from the wreckage and pummel two dozen guys? Great plan. Except it really wasn't a plan. Earl was right. He seriously needed to work on his thinking-things-through skills.

At any rate, the door slammed closed too fast for even a botched crash landing and left the Jenny skidding straight for a solid wall.

His battle scream turned into the real thing. He fought to pull the Jenny's nose into a sharp turn to swerve away from the doors before he slammed into it. The Hisso screeched all the way.

"Just do it!" he hollered into the wind. "I'll apologize later!"

If the Jenny had really been a woman, she would have crossed her arms and poked her nose into the air. Only at the last second did she deign to duck her propeller away from the doors. The wheels barely cleared *Schturming*'s hull.

Far away at the stern, the two vast propellers started inching into motion.

He leveled out and looked around just in time to see Livingstone's private flying corps howl in, headed straight toward him. He looped up and over in an Immelmann turn and matched speed and direction with them.

Livingstone's plane—white fuselage, red wings, blue engine cowl and tail—dropped into the airspace next to his. Livingstone grinned through his mustache and took his hands off the stick long enough to clasp them together in a victory shake.

Durn fool.

Hitch clenched his teeth. But then again, under the circumstances, it was just as well they were all here. He sure wasn't going to be bringing *Schturming* down from the inside today. The trick was going to be getting all these glory-hungry boomers to somehow work together. And he sure as Moses wasn't the ideal person to show them how to do that. Neither was Livingstone, come to that.

In front of him, *Schturming* strained ponderously forward. The propellers were taking their sweet time getting under way—and no wonder from the size of them. If she couldn't move, she couldn't maneuver. That gave the pilots a precious few minutes to hold the upper hand.

Fine. Great. Then what?

The propellers were the big enemy here. If he could bring them down, he could bring the whole thing down. He split away from Livingstone, headed toward the tail end of the ship. Luckily, for the moment, the cannon's track around the envelope hung empty.

Movement caught the corner of his eye, and he winced. That hadn't taken long. He turned to look.

It wasn't the cannon at all. Somebody was running on top of the envelope.

He swung in for a closer look. A walkway—made of a different material from the rest of the envelope, judging from its slightly darker color—ran the whole length of the gasbag. Cross-hatched railings guarded either side.

Huh. Missed that in all the excitement yesterday.

The man stopped in the center of the walkway and lifted a megaphone. An eagle circled his head.

Well, well. The dirty buzzard himself.

Hitch dove low, wheels centered over the walkway, and opened the throttle. The front half of the plane blocked him from seeing anything, so he kept her straight on faith alone.

Zlo failed to appear mangled in the propeller—which was probably for the better, since that would surely have wrecked Earl's repair job for good. When Hitch shot clear of the envelope, he looked back over his shoulder.

The bird had plunged down the port side. For a second, Zlo lay spread-eagled on the walkway, only to bounce back up. He leaned over the railing, shouting at his men through the megaphone.

Whoops, went and made him mad.

The cannon, on its track, trundled into view around the front end of the envelope. Almost before it stopped moving, orange flashed in its mouth. The ball ripped directly through the opening between Hitch's port wings. Way yonder too close for comfort.

He spun the Jenny around in another Immelmann turn, headed straight back for the dirigible. A cannonball was untold times faster than he was. But he was probably that much faster than the cannon itself. The safest place in the sky right now was directly behind the thing.

As he crossed over, Zlo followed his motion with his megaphone.

Right over the top of him, Hitch slacked off on the throttle. That cut the engine noise just enough for him to catch the bare outline of two bellowed words.

"—*weather now*—"

The first dash of rain hit his forward windshield like a handful of pebbles.

Oh, great. His throat tightened. That stupid *dawsedometer*. And Livingstone wanted Hitch to think it would be a good idea to add that to his show?

Since yesterday, Zlo had seemed content to leave the worst of the storms along the borders of the valley. Now, the wind grabbed the Jenny. One minute, the air was smooth as glass. The next, it yanked the plane like a dog on the end of a chain. The fuel got jerked out of the carburetor, and the engine sputtered for the longest second ever. Hitch's head snapped back, his vision blacking around the edges.

Then, just like that, the wind released the plane back into smooth air. He resettled his feet on the rudder pedals—and the wind smashed into him again. A torrent of rain washed over the windshield and peppered back against his face, too hard and needle-fine to feel damp. The roar of the rain against the wings thundered even above the engine chatter.

A crack of lightning lit up clouds that had gone dark purple. This was not good. Not good at all. The wind by itself was enough to do him in. If Zlo somehow managed to conjure hail, that would be about as lethal as if he started firing grapeshot out of that cannon of his.

The Jenny's stick had a mind of its own and kept trying to pull right out of his hand. He clamped it in both fists and gritted his teeth. Truth was, he had to get out of here too. Even his modified Jenny with its reinforced frame wasn't any kind of match for a crazed airship captain with a magic weather-maker.

He turned his head and squinted through the deluge. The rain, at least, had swept away the oil splatters and shined up his goggles.

Had to be a way to keep this day from being a total loss.

He could always crash the Jenny into the envelope. The whole thing would probably blow up. The leather skin would melt away and the spars would crumble. Whatever was left would plummet to the ground. He grimaced.

Noble, but maybe a tiny bit extreme, especially considering all the supposedly innocent people in there.

He turned the Jenny in closer to the dirigible for one more pass. The protection of the hulking envelope shielded him from the rain for a bit. Ahead, the cannon came clanking around the bow end of its track, headed straight for him.

He reacted almost without thinking. Throttle open, right foot on the right rudder pedal. The Jenny ducked sideways. She sailed in between the bottom of the envelope and the top of the ship. There was exactly no space to spare. His heart quit beating for a good long second.

Beneath him, a four-foot railing bordered a flat deck, loaded down with boxes and barrels of supplies, all of them lashed together. A few crouched men stared up at him, open-mouthed. One of them held a seven-foot stick; another squatted beside a pile of cannonballs; a third stood, with arms raised, hanging onto a rope that ran through a pulley system over his head.

A pulley system. That was how they were moving the cannon. He scooted the Jenny to the left. A few feet was all it took for him to line up the handkerchief hook on his bottom wing. As the Jenny screamed out the other side of the dirigible, back into the full force of the storm, he snagged the rope in the hook. A slight tug to the left told him it was secure.

His heart still refused to start beating. This here was the tricky part. If he'd snagged the wrong part of the rope, he'd catch the full weight of the cannon. He'd probably succeed in pulling it off the track—right before it jerked him out of the sky.

The wind pounded the Jenny sideways, and with every muscle in his body, he held her course steady. He watched over his shoulder. Through the cloud and the haze of rain, the rope unfurled behind him. Then, just as fast, it pulled loose. With a zip of spraying rain, it sped all the way free of the hook.

Time to get out of here and right *now*. His breathing came almost too hard to give him any oxygen. Push his luck any further, and he'd be a goner for sure. He turned the Jenny all the way around and zoomed over the top of *Schturming* for a look.

The cannon still sat on its track, solid as could be. Maybe that fool trick of his hadn't done a lick of good, except to give him a few gray hairs.

But the cannon wasn't moving. Beneath it, something dangled. The pulley system.

He'd completely unthreaded it. For the time being at least, Zlo's men couldn't move the cannon. That was something anyway.

As he whipped on past, something else caught his eye: the orange glare of a spark at the cannon's breech.

It was loaded, and it was lit, and without the pulley, they'd lost their ability to readjust its aim.

A heartbeat later, he was over the top of the envelope and out of sight of the cannon. An explosion tore through the storm.

He looked back.

Splinters and chunks of wood splattered up from *Schturming*. Her cannon had punched a hole down into her own hull. And straight through the *dawsedometer*'s heart with any luck.

He allowed himself a tight grin, then faced forward and opened the throttle, headed back across the lake.

CHAPTER 31

RAIN LASHED THE airfield as Hitch flew in. The wind was considerably slacker here. Even still, half the planes were skidding out in the crosswind, striking the ground with their propellers or flipping over. From the looks of it, at least one had busted its landing gear. Maybe only half the planes had made it back to camp at all. The rest were scattered in the fields between here and the lake.

Even without that cotton-picking cannon, Zlo and his storm had managed to wipe out half of Livingstone's impromptu air force. That might not bode too well for the future of the Extravagant Flying Circus—or Hitch's shot at a partnership.

Rick's blue Jenny streaked in front of Hitch, engine snorting black smoke. He flared for a hard landing. Parts splintered into the air. The wings caved in at the center, both ends shooting up like a broken teeter-totter.

To compensate for the wind, Hitch banked his Jenny a little and set his right wheel down first. The friction against the ground helped slow her some, and only then did he kick in opposite rudder to center her on both wheels. Her tailskid thumped down and dragged, acting as a brake. The wind caught her anyway, and she came *that* close to ground-looping and maybe even flipping over. Only the wooden hoop under the bottom wing, acting as another skid, kept the wing from tipping into the ground.

When she finally rolled to a stop, he sat there for a second. His ears were still buzzing, and his heart and his lungs pulled in opposite directions. That had been about as close as any bit of flying he'd ever had to do. He'd had his share of crashes, and had the scars to prove it, but not like that. Not with Death cackling in the front cockpit all the way.

People raced across the field, on foot and in automobiles, headed for the wrecks.

A man with a white scarf fluttering out of his leather jacket slowed as he passed. "You all right?"

Hitch raised a reassuring hand.

The man kept going. "They're saying the colonel is down!"

Bad weather could bring down anyone, didn't matter how good a pilot you were. But Livingstone was one of the best. It'd take a *lot* to bring him down. Hitch unfastened his safety belt. Served Livingstone right, of course—charging out there like some dumb media-hound palooka. But none of these pilots here today, including Livingstone, deserved to crack up like this.

He looked over at Rick's blue plane. Speaking of dumb palookas.

Hitch hauled himself out of his cockpit and crossed the field. The rain hadn't reached them in full force yet, which maybe indicated the limit of *Schturming*'s weather powers. But as soon as they finished rounding up the surviving pilots, they'd have to tie down and cover up what was left of the planes.

Rick hoisted himself up in his cockpit and fell out of it, landing on his backside. He clambered to his feet and started kicking at the wing and the fuselage. The wing spar bent, and a spider-webbed dent appeared beneath the back cockpit.

Hitch ran faster. "Hey, you idiot! Don't bust her up worse!"

Rick kept kicking. "I'll bust her if I please!" A line of blood trickled from beneath his goggles, but his face was already so red, the blood practically blended in. "Stupid plane! Stupid plan! What kind of a plan was this?"

"I'm wondering the same thing myself."

Rick wheeled on him, panting. "You smug ignoramus. This was your idea and your doing. Don't think I don't know it! And don't think I don't know this is all because of that girl you dragged in last week!"

Hitch stiffened. "Back off on her."

"Hah. Not likely. Not this time, *boss*." Rick jabbed a finger at him. "Don't fool yourself into believing I kept quiet about her this long because I was afraid of you. The only reason I haven't informed on your little skirt is because I was interested in the *reward*, not the *ransom*. And now I'm out of the running for that, aren't I?"

Most of the time, Hitch's rage was hot. But right now, it burned cold. All the adrenaline still running through his body razored his senses into focus.

Rick turned around and gave the wing another kick. "It's time for good citizen Richard Holmes to do his civic duty." He started to walk past Hitch.

Hitch caught his arm and hauled him back. "Don't."

Rick tried to pull Hitch's fingers free. "Get off me."

Hitch tightened his grip. "Listen to me. I know what you are—right down to your yellow backbone. You're an arrogant fool, you always have been, and you always will be. You don't deserve a girl like Lilla, you don't deserve that Jenny you just stomped, and you don't deserve any kind of reward."

Rick tried to sneer. "I deserve better than what I've gotten from you for the last year!"

"You squeal on Jael, and I'll give you more broken bones than if your 'chute failed on you."

Rick snorted in derision, but behind his goggles, his pupils shrank to pinpricks. Maybe he had never seen Hitch this way before, and maybe he didn't quite believe Hitch'd actually be dumb enough to kill him. But Hitch could beat his ugly mug into corn hash without trying—and Rick's belief of *that* was written all over his face.

Behind Hitch, footsteps pounded through the grass.

He held Rick's eyes for one more long second, then shoved him away.

Rick backed up, rubbing his arm. His lip was curled, but he didn't say anything, just turned and slunk off.

Filthy little skunk. He *would* be the one to walk away today when so many good pilots hadn't.

The footsteps stopped behind him. "There you are, you bushwhacker."

Hitch looked over his shoulder.

Earl hung his head in a relieved pant. "I was beginning to think you'd bought it like the rest of them. Look, I'll tie down the plane. That kid Walter came running in to get Jael and the Berringers. He's got some crazy aunt or something—she went missing as soon as the weather kicked up. He was pretty upset."

Aurelia again. Worry spurted in Hitch's chest. Back when he knew her, she'd been as docile as an old hound dog. Maybe she'd been getting worse with time. He cast a look around the chaos of the field. An ambulance—just a big truck with a canvas rigged over the bed—trundled in, bell clanging.

He should stay here, help with the downed pilots. But there were plenty of folks already doing that. Right now, Aurelia—and Walter—struck closer to home for him. He glanced at Rick's demolished plane. Besides, somebody needed to stick close to Jael right now. Rick was scared, sure enough, but he was still sulky enough to cause more trouble than not.

Hitch found Jael in the Carpenters' apple orchard. The rain poured down steadily, not quite in sheets, but more than enough to soak everything. He was wet clear through his leather jacket. Somehow the water had even gotten past the tight laces of his boots; his socks squished.

Jael made her way over to him—hobbling again, although not too bad. "Hitch." Her wet hair clung to her face, so dark with the rainwater that the silver streaks from the lightning practically glowed.

She reached him, slipped a little in the mud, and gripped his arm. She closed her eyes and breathed what sounded like a thankful prayer: "*O Bozhe*. I worried you would crash."

"Don't have much faith in my flying, do you?" But a lonely spot inside of him warmed, and he squeezed her hand on his arm. It'd been a long time since anybody cared what happened to him—except maybe Earl, and only then when he was in a good mood.

He looked around. "What's going on?"

Before she could answer, Walter appeared in a gap between the tree rows and beckoned them. His black hair was plastered around the edges of his white face, making him look as pale as a ghoul. He didn't wait for them to follow, just turned and ran.

Hitch followed, keeping Jael's arm in the crook of his elbow—*mostly* to steady her through the mud puddles. "What's this about Aurelia running off?"

"I do not have entire knowledge. Walter came for help to find her. Everyone is looking—his family, your brother. She has been gone since last night."

"In this weather? That ain't good."

"She is thinking we are all doomed."

"Maybe we are." He glanced down at her knit forehead. "Though I did take out their cannon."

She looked up at him. "That is not nothing."

"Yeah, but this weather's going to make it awful tough to get a plane anywhere close to it again, even without the cannon."

The lines reappeared between her eyebrows.

So much for polishing up the silver lining. He should probably tell her about Rick. But that'd keep for a bit. No sense dumping all the bad news at once.

Somewhere up ahead, through the iron gray of the driving rain, a dog barked. Taos probably, since he'd been nowhere to be seen back at camp. He must have run off with Walter when the boy came for help. Taos only barked when he was excited—which right now, probably meant he'd found himself an unidentified person.

Hitch pulled Jael forward. "C'mon."

They ran, slipping in the mud, until they reached the edge of the orchard. Half hidden under the branches of the outermost trees, an old pent shed had almost disappeared in the overgrowth of wood vines. The boards had weathered to a splintery gray, and on either side of the empty doorframe, the windows were all smashed in.

Outside the door, Walter hung onto Taos's scruff while the dog kept barking. Walter cast a wild look back at Hitch, probably scared to go into the dark.

"It's all right." Hitch let go of Jael and snapped his fingers at the dog. "Taos. Quiet." He patted Walter's shoulder as he passed.

The boy reached out and caught his hand, following him.

Hitch gripped Walter's clammy palm and ducked his head under the sagging lintel. "Aurelia?"

Despite the broken windows, the inside of the shed was dark. It smelled damp and rich with the earth and the rain, and a little sour with old cow droppings. Something shifted in the corner; someone whimpered.

He took one more step inside, then moved to the left, so he wouldn't block the light. "Aurelia? It's just me. It's Hitch Hitchcock—and Walter. And Jael's outside."

Another whimper. Definitely Aurelia.

He took one more step and tried to pull free of Walter, so he'd have both hands. But the boy hung on fast and followed him.

More straw rustled as he got closer. His shadow shifted, and the scant light fell across Aurelia's face. Even paler than Walter and a little blue around the lips, she stared right through him, like a blind woman. Damp glistened against her face. Dead leaves and old straw matted her hair. She lifted a hand, unseeing, and whimpered through her chattering teeth.

"It's okay." He crouched in front of her and reached for her with his free hand. "It's okay, darlin'. It's just me. I've come to take you home." He pulled her nearer, tentatively, then slipped a hand around her shoulders.

Her backbone was so sharp it practically poked through her dress. She remained stiff for a second. Then, with a stuttering exhale, she sagged against his chest. "I caused this—this storm. Did I cause this?"

He held her and patted her back. "Not a chance. You had absolutely nothing to do with this. The only thing you did was call it exactly like it was—which was a heap more'n most of us had the guts to do yesterday."

"But I knew. That man told me. I tried to tell . . . somebody. But they didn't believe me."

"That's not your fault, Aurelia. You tried, you did your best. It probably wouldn't have mattered anyway. I don't know that anybody could have stopped this from happening."

She reared her head back and looked up at him. Her bloodshot eyes were red almost clear through. They charted his face.

"I remember you. You're Hitch Hitchcock."

He smiled at her. "Yeah."

"You were . . . you were Celia's husband. Weren't you?"

"That's right."

In the straw beside him, Walter shifted. He looked back and forth between Hitch and Aurelia, wide-eyed and interested. So he hadn't known. He was probably too young to have met Celia, much less remembered her, so why *would* he know Hitch was his uncle? Nan had no doubt avoided talking about Hitch for all these years.

A shadow blocked the light, and Hitch looked back.

Jael stood there, cocking her head slightly like she did whenever she was caught off guard and trying to figure something out. The lines between her eyebrows deepened a little. Women never were very understanding about a man who would leave a woman—for whatever reason.

His throat tightened and he turned back.

Aurelia's bloodshot eyes looked up at him without anger, without blame. "I remember you," she said again. "You gave me a violet handkerchief."

"Yes, I did." Celia had washed it with his dungarees and it had come out purple.

Her lip trembled. "It caught on fire and burned up."

"Oh, well. I'll get you another one, how about that?" He tried to ease her up. "But first we have to get you home, all right? Nan and everybody's worried about you."

She darted out a hand and gripped his coat. "Wait." Her lip trembled still more. "Do you think it *is* true? Will the air beast kill us all?"

Walter watched him, as intent on the answer as his aunt was.

"Aurelia, listen to me." Hitch looked her in the eye. "You're scared, that's all this is. And that's okay." He put a hand on Walter's shoulder and glanced at him too. "We all are, I reckon. This is something nobody could have planned on happening. But the world keeps on spinning and people keep on living—through worse things than this. This is just a couple guys in an airship. It'll be over before you know it."

"Promise?" Aurelia asked.

"Reckon I can't quite promise. But I will tell you this. *I'm* sure. And I will bring it down."

"Even if it shoots at you?" Aurelia whispered.

"Reckon so." He shucked out of his sopping coat, draped it around her shoulders, and eased her to her feet. "Now, come on."

CHAPTER 32

HEN HITCH AND his group arrived in the Carpenters' muddy yard, the rest of the searchers were already there. Nan's husband Byron, Griff, and the Berringer brothers gathered beside Griff's Baby Grand roadster in the mud of the yard, talking urgently. A distracted Molly—her red hair plastered into clumps down her back—herded the twins toward the porch. Nan's urgent voice sounded from just within the house, as if she were speaking on the telephone.

As Hitch supported Aurelia on the way through the yard gate, they all looked up. Relief passed across most of their faces.

Only Griff's tightened.

Nan burst through the screen door and down the porch steps. She wore a plaid kerchief tied under her chin and a yellow slicker belted at her waist.

She reached for her sister and pulled her into a hug. "Aurelia. Thank God, thank God."

Jael and Walter both stepped back to give her room.

The rest of the group approached. Griff's eyes were darker than the thunderclouds.

And . . . this was where it got awkward. Hitch let go of Aurelia and stood with his hands in his pants pockets. He'd done a good deed, but he was still the black sheep. He was standing on property Nan had told him never to set foot on. And he was trailing her kid, who she'd told him, in no uncertain language, to stay clear of.

Nan lifted her gaze to Hitch's. Her mouth worked for a moment, as she seemed to consider all that. She'd sure *like* something else to be mad about. That was just the way she was. She'd love you forever until she hated you—and then she'd hate you forever. When he married Celia, he qualified for her love; when Celia died . . . well, there it was.

But if he'd ruined one of her sisters' lives, he *had* just rescued the other.

She eased the clench of her jaw and took a breath. "Thank you. I . . . appreciate it." The words sounded rusty as all get out, but at least she was giving him that much.

She started to turn toward the house, her arm around Aurelia's shoulders.

Griff, who had stopped just in front of them, reached to take Aurelia's other arm.

Nan glanced back. "Walter, come along."

This was probably the closest Hitch was ever going to get to her *not* being full-blown angry with him. If ever they were going to clear the air between them, this was it.

He took a step after her. He didn't look at Griff. "Nan—"

She turned over her shoulder. She bit her lip, her eyes big and a little afraid. For the first time in as long as he'd known her, she looked downright vulnerable—as if she knew what was coming and wasn't any more ready for it than he was.

He swallowed past the sudden scratch in his throat. "Nan, I'm sorry." He put all his energy into looking at her, not Griff. She was *almost* close to understanding, and shockingly it was somehow easier to say all this to her, instead of him. "Back then, I didn't see any other way than leaving, but if I could do it over again, I'd do it all different. I'm not asking you to forgive me. I'm just asking you to . . . to believe that."

She had always been indomitable, tough as a mud hen protecting her nest and just as stubborn. When they were kids, she'd been able to beat up most boys dumb enough to tangle with her—or, worse for them, her sisters. She and he had never quite got on; they'd rammed heads too often for that. But before he left, they'd at least been able to share some kind of mutual respect for each other's grit.

He'd never seen her weaken. Never.

The edge of her mouth quavered. "I . . . believe you." She

breathed out. Her voice was weary. "For whatever it's worth anymore, I believe you."

Griff closed up the hand he'd extended to help Aurelia. "What are you saying?"

Nan looked at him, and she gave her head a slow shake. "I'm saying I'm tired. I'm saying I have better things to do with my life than hate your brother for the rest of it. And so do you, Griff."

"No." He came forward. Rain ran off the back of his fedora's brim. He turned his fierce gaze on Hitch. "It's not going to work that way, Hitch. You can't just come back after nine years, stay a couple days, bring Aurelia home, and get everybody to absolve your sins."

Here it was then. At last.

Hitch looked him in the eye. "I didn't ask for absolution."

Griff kept coming. "You can't stand there and tell me some part of you hasn't always believed you're going to slide by, one more time, and still get what you want. Because you always have, right?" He stopped in front of Hitch, only a few feet between them. He was actually trembling. "You always slid by, with a wink and a nod, doing exactly what you pleased and nothing else. And everybody forgave you for it. Everybody loved you anyway."

Nan reached for Griff's arm. "That is not what's happening here. Griff—"

He ignored her. "*I* loved you, Hitch. *I* forgave you. Every single time. You'd go running off to chase your rainbows, and I would cover for you. I'd make excuses for you. That's my big brother, Hitch Hitchcock! Isn't he somethin'? And I *believed* it. Even after you left and let us all down, I believed it."

This was heading to a fight and fast. Hitch backed off a few steps, both to maybe mollify Griff and to get a little distance between them and Nan and Aurelia.

He tried to keep a calm voice. "Griff . . ."

"But guess what?" Griff closed the distance to barely a foot. "I stopped believing a long time ago. You've got no more excuses left." He spread his arms. "You think there's a person here you haven't hurt?"

Most of what he was saying was true enough. Hitch had admitted that from the start. But how long was this supposed to go on? He'd come home. He'd admitted he'd been wrong; he'd apologized with all his heart. *What more was there?*

His own anger flared. "I know I messed it up. And I'll shout it to the world if you want me to. But I can't take any of it back. It's *done*."

"Nothing's done! It goes on every single day. Every *day*, Hitch! You think coming back here fixed things? It didn't fix anything. You come back, and the whole world falls apart! Everything happening right now—to this town and everybody in it—is because of you. You cannot tell me you haven't had a hand in every bit of it!"

"It fell into my lap, same as it did yours. Back off, Griff."

He maybe deserved some of this, but not everything. And he was sick of it. So help him, it was time for all of them to let go of the past and cut their losses, one way or another. Nan was right about that.

He clenched and unclenched his fists. "You don't want to fight me, and you know it."

Griff's glare flashed. Something in his face seemed to snap. "Don't I? Things are different now, Hitch, and we're not kids anymore. Family is about being there when people need you. You weren't there for Celia, and you sure weren't there for me. You think when Pop was dying in that bed, he didn't ask for you?"

Hitch shook his head. "You don't—"

"And don't give me this about Sheriff Campbell! You shouldn't have gotten mixed up with him in the first place. And even then, how was running the right answer? If you stayed, you think I wouldn't have stood beside you? You think all of us wouldn't have? Nan may be willing to suddenly forget it all, but I'm not!" He reached for the front of Hitch's wet shirt.

Behind Griff, Nan started dragging Aurelia out of the way.

Hitch reacted without thinking, his own hand darting out to clench Griff's wrist. Every muscle in his body hummed. With the last ounce of will left, he held himself in.

He'd never seen Griff like this. Griff was the quiet one—the controlled one. Griff didn't start fights, and he was more likely to stop a brawl than finish one.

Hitch pulled Griff's hand free of his shirt and pushed him away. "Back off."

Griff threw a wide roundhouse that crashed into the side of Hitch's jaw.

Hitch staggered back. Blood thundered through his head, and his vision went black and then red. Even before he could make sense of what had just happened, he came up swinging. He clipped Griff's chin, but his brother had dived after him and was already raining blows. A punch caught Hitch in the cheek, then Griff started slamming Hitch's ribs and stomach.

Hitch scrambled upright. He got his feet under him and pretended the world wasn't tilting crazily. He closed with Griff and closed hard.

He had maybe an inch on his brother, but not much, if any, poundage. And Griff was right. This wasn't like when they were kids. Back then, Hitch could beat the tar out of Griff and they both knew it. Now Griff was big and strong and full-on mad enough to give Hitch a run for his money and then some.

Hitch hit hard and low. His fist connected beneath Griff's sternum, and Griff doubled over with a whuff.

Hitch stepped back and saw them all, frozen as if in a photograph. Himself, bleeding and dizzy. Byron and the Berringers, moving in to stop the fight. Nan with her arm still around Aurelia, shouting at them both. Walter staring on, wide-eyed. Jael, the lines between her eyebrows furrowing deeper than ever.

And Griff. His brother rose slowly, blue eyes coming up to glare right back at him. Griff wasn't done with this fight. He wouldn't be done until one or both of them were too woozy to climb up out of the mud. He was *that* mad.

That hurt.

Hitch had hurt him that bad. That's what this was really all about.

Something inside of him shuddered. Of *course* it couldn't be fixed in a few days. The kind of hurt that stuck around for nine years didn't go away just because the person who'd caused it wanted it to. Durn his ignorant, idiotic hide.

He pulled his punch in mid-swing and backed up, hands in front of him. "Wait—"

Griff hit him anyway, another ear-ringing blow right across his jaw.

"Hold up there, son!" Matthew said. He and Byron caught Griff's arms.

J.W., looking a little uncomfortable, stopped at Hitch's side.

Hitch righted himself, one hand on the thundering ache in his molars.

He blinked several times and found his brother's gaze. "Listen to me. What happened was never meant to be about you. I never once thought it would hurt you like it did. And I'm sorry."

Griff stopped straining against Matthew and Byron. The fury in his face flickered, for a bare second.

Then he shook his head. "You're sorry. Why shouldn't you be? You've got Campbell stuck on your tail for the rest of his life. I hear you practically lost your machine to that charlatan Livingstone. You got nobody left to call family in all this world. And you brought pirates right in on your hometown. You are sorry, Hitch. You're a sorry excuse for a man. And God knows why I ever looked up to you."

Matthew shook Griff's arm. "C'mon, son, you don't want to be lying awake tonight regretting all this stuff you're saying. Your brother's telling you he's sorry. Take his hand and put this all in back of you."

Griff drew in a breath so deep his shoulders lifted a full two inches. Then he dropped his gaze away from Hitch's and shook his head again. He pulled free of Matthew and Byron, picked his hat out of the mud, and limped across the yard to where his Chevrolet was parked.

And that, right there, was the end of Hitch's luck. He watched Griff leave, and, inside his chest, something broke open.

A hand slid around his waist.

Slowly, he looked to find Jael beside him.

Her face was carefully passive. She slipped her shoulders under his arm. "Come."

He tongued the blood from the corner of his mouth and looked up at the tableau he'd help create.

They all stood, frozen. They stared, not at Griff, but at Hitch. The eyes were wide and shocked and—almost sympathetic.

Why? Because they thought Griff had been wrong in throwing that first punch at him? Or because they knew Hitch had just lost his last reason for staying?

With a gentle hand, Jael guided him away.

He started to turn with her and, from the very corner of his eye, saw Walter standing alone, off to the side. The boy stared with big eyes. This was probably exactly what Nan wanted to protect him from. Hitch couldn't blame her. But it was as it was at this point.

He didn't look the boy in the eye. Instead, he looked down at Jael.

She raised her face, briefly. Her eyebrows were creased, partly with pain probably, but also with concern, chagrin even. She had no family—and she wanted one. Seemed like she shouldn't be too understanding of what had just happened here.

"Come." That was all she said. "I will be helping you."

He could only nod.

Together, they turned around, both of them hobbling. He left without looking back. Why not? Leaving was what he was so good at.

CHAPTER 33

IN THE GLIMMER of a lantern, Hitch sat beneath the canvas tarp they'd stretched between the Jenny's upper wing and two poles driven into the ground. The rain had slacked off considerably, but every few seconds, a raindrop still plunked against the tarp. Beyond, the encroaching darkness of night billowed with incoming fog. Nobody'd be flying tonight.

He felt the raw corner of his lip with his tongue and stared into nothing.

"Stop." Jael tapped his chin, barely avoiding the bruised spot where Griff's fist had slammed him twice. She scooted in closer, on her knees, and raised a damp cloth to the cut.

The warm wetness stung. He flinched away, then exhaled. He dragged his gaze over to meet hers. She'd seen him down to his core now—for real this time, and not just with that wondering stare she sometimes aimed in his direction.

But all she did was keep dabbing at his mouth. She looked at his face critically, then turned to re-dunk the cloth in the skillet full of water.

"C'mon," he grumbled, "just say what you're thinking."

Maybe she'd say it was all okay. That he wasn't such a jerk after all—which would be nice to hear even if it wasn't true. Or maybe she'd tell him to his face he *was* a no-account fool, and at least then he could lean into the pain.

She furrowed her brow and cocked her mouth to the side, as if cleaning up his face required a lot of thought. She didn't meet his eye.

"Reckon that all looked pretty horrible this afternoon, didn't it?" he ventured.

"All people are horrible some of times. Now, hold still." She finished off with a last dab, then wrung the cloth into the skillet. She turned back with a tin cup of hand-hot coffee. "Drink this."

He sighed again and took the cup without drinking. "It's over between me and Griff." He looked back out into the darkness.

Here and there, a blob of light marked other lanterns, and even a few campfires sheltered under tarps. Earl was out there somewhere, bumming gossip. Word was Livingstone had busted both legs in his crackup—and he was one of the lucky ones.

"When I came back here . . ." Hitch hesitated. He didn't talk about these things, not with anyone. But why not? Didn't make a lick of difference now. "When I came back, I kept telling myself I was only doing it because this was where Livingstone was hosting the contest. But I guess, deep down, I knew. It was time. Been time for a long while. I needed to know if they'd forgive me—or if I'd messed it up too bad." He snorted and raised the coffee. "Guess I know now."

The coffee—Jael's concoction—was darker than the night and swimming with grounds. He downed it anyway. When he came back for air, he swallowed with a cough and looked sideways at her.

She sat on her feet, knees bent, hands folded in her lap. She watched him steadily. Maybe she hadn't seen all there was to see after all.

"Why did you not come back sooner?" she asked.

He shrugged. "Scared, I reckon."

"That they would not give you forgiveness?"

"That, and . . ." Hard to put it into words. "Scared I'd get tied down again, I guess. I'm exactly where I want to be. I'm exactly *who* I want to be."

Except, of course, for those times when he hated it. When he couldn't believe that's all there was to life. He skimmed his gaze over the Jenny's ruddy skin.

The tarp over their heads flapped in the wind. A few raindrops blew in and spattered his face.

Jael pulled her legs out from under her and sat on the ground. As she draped her arms around one bent knee, her face tightened in a wince. Then she laid her cheek against her kneecap and looked up at him. "I did not have knowledge you were married." She didn't sound reproachful, like most women did when they found out.

Should have known he wouldn't get out of that one. He flung the remaining coffee grounds into the grass outside. "Yeah, well, you wouldn't if you hadn't lived around here ten years ago."

"Why do they say it is your fault she died?" Now she sounded more careful, like maybe his answer mattered.

He looked over. "Celia died because she got sick. Pneumonia, they said. She was always kind of fussy about her health. Mostly, I think it was a way to get people to pay attention, which mostly made 'em *not* pay attention. If I'd known she was sick, I would have come back. Do you believe that?" He tossed the words out casually, but something deep inside tensed. He needed her to believe him even if no one else did.

"Yes," she said simply.

"I left because I got mixed up with one of Campbell's less-than-legal sidelines. Smuggling stolen goods—though I didn't know they were stolen at the time. If I hadn't scrammed, he'd have sent me to prison to cover up for himself."

"You could not have told anyone who would have believed you?"

"Tried to tell the mayor. Turned out he was under Campbell's thumb. After that, Campbell threatened my dad's farm if I tried to open my mouth again."

"And people did not understand this?"

He shrugged. "Celia's the only one I actually told, and she probably put her own spin on it when folks asked her about it. And then I didn't come back for her funeral—or my father's. That's what really did it."

"How much time were you married?"

"About a year. It should never have happened. But we were young and stupid—and I guess I was bored. I'd known her all my life. And that's just what you're supposed to do, isn't it? Get married and do the same as your folks before you? I didn't know back then that something can be the right thing to do and still be a mistake." He rubbed his forehead. "I think maybe that's why Nan's really upset—I didn't love Celia enough, even before I left."

His stomach churned around the sludgy coffee. His head pounded from Griff's thrashing, and his ribs didn't feel none too great either. Dear God in heaven, what had he been thinking? He'd been nuts to believe any good could come of returning home. All he'd done was dredge up the dreary past and its regrets.

He ducked out from under the tarp and stood, hands on his hips. "If I had any brains in my head, I'd get out of town right now." Even trying to fight *Schturming* was turning out worse for his help than not. "This town feels like a cage."

Behind him, she shifted, getting up, slowly and a little awkwardly. Her hobbling footsteps brought her out from under the tarp to stand beside him. She held her hair out of her face with both hands and looked at the night. "I think . . ."

He looked down at her. "What?"

"I think . . . running away is also kind of cage, yes? How can we ever run far enough to run away *from* running away?"

All his running sure hadn't set him free. Nine years of fleeing this place—and here he was, right back at the beginning.

But staying put wouldn't be any better.

"When I stop moving," he said, "that's when I start feeling trapped. And if there's one thing I know, it's that I can't live that way. I don't understand how anybody stays put *without* feeling trapped."

She shrugged, almost apologetically. "That I do not have knowledge of."

She might not know. But somebody had to. People stayed put all the time. Folks might envy a gypsy pilot like him, but most of them would never want freedom bad enough to chase after it every single day. Somehow, most of them kept finding their freedom in the same place, day in and day out.

That was what he had to do. Somehow, some way, before he was too old and beat up, before he'd hurt every last person he knew, he had to figure out the secret. Otherwise, what else was he running away from but his own life?

Jael's teeth chattered. "It is good you *have* family. I think they love you, even though they are angry with you. They will always love you. I think it is better to have someone to love you and be angry with you, than to have no one at all. Maybe I would not have fallen from *Schturming* if there had been family for me there. In *Schturming*, if you are *nikto*, you have not even any quarters to live in. You must go from cabin to cabin to get your food."

"That's . . . harsh."

"Family, it is all there is, yes? That is worth this *staying put* for, I think."

"Surely there can't be many people up there without families."

"No, and most of those who do not"—she raised both shoulders—"well, they are often taking their final fall on purpose. I was having much fortune, because Nestor gave me hidden space." She crossed her arms over her chest and winced.

"Hurting again?" He tossed a glance at the low sky. No way to tell if *Schturming* was near right now. He looked back down. "Probably you're stiff from being out in the rain all day."

"M-mayb-be."

He ducked back under the canvas, snagged the lantern and a green wool coat borrowed from Lilla. "Here." He helped her put it on. "The rain's mostly stopped for now. Let's take a walk, loosen up those joints."

She slipped her arm through his, shoulder pressed against his side. "I do not know about these things you are telling me—if your family is right that you did what you should not have. I think if you *had* to go, you had to go."

"Sometimes you make choices and there isn't a good answer either way."

She hesitated. "When first I was knowing you, my thoughts said you were like I always was believing Groundsmen to be— what everyone else was saying you were. But that was before I had knowledge." For an instant, her head leaned sideways, against his arm, the touch of it almost an absolution in itself. "I said before that you are man who is causing trouble. But you are also liking to be stopping it. You act like you do not like people to need you. But you like to help them. You have helped me. If I can, I would like to help you."

The pit of his stomach warmed. She was just a tumbleweed who'd blown in. She didn't owe him any loyalty. If anything, she'd be completely justified in kicking free of him for any number of reasons. For once in his life, his pride had been squashed enough he could admit that, at least to himself.

He tightened his elbow, squeezing her arm against his side. "Thanks."

She stopped short, nearly yanking free.

He almost braced himself to be kicked again. "What?"

At their feet lay a severed wing—a red one with a rope looped through the canvas at one end.

Oh, gravy.

"Is that the marker you and Walter tied onto *Schturming?*" he asked.

"Look!" she hissed.

He lofted the lantern.

Ahead, almost lost in the shadow of a wrecked plane, a bit of material fluttered.

"It is one of Zlo's men!" Jael said.

The red flutter separated itself from the plane. The guy with the mop of hair and the dark goggles looked in their direction. Then he took off running.

Ground attack? That's what this was? Hitch snatched his arm from Jael's. Zlo had come back down to finish the job?

Hitch whipped his gaze skyward. "It *is* here. That's why you're hurting." He swiveled. The lantern bobbled in his upraised hand, pushing light only a few yards into the fog.

On the ground, Zlo could have only two goals: kill people or destroy planes. Since there were far fewer planes than people—and because most people would cease to be a threat without the planes—it was a good bet which he had chosen.

Jael gasped. "Your Jenny."

"You go back and make sure it's all right. Find Earl and whoever else you can. Tell them to do whatever they have to do to protect any planes that still work."

She nodded, then took off in a loping, limping run.

Somewhere in the darkness to the south, an eagle screamed.

Where the eagle was, Zlo would be. Hitch's blood fired and he started running.

Sounds of cracking wood and ripping fabric reached his ears

before his light showed a plane—or what was left of it. It was pitched forward on its nose. The tail hung free, like a broken bone. The wing fabric flapped in the wind. Zlo's eagle perched on the upended fuselage.

Zlo kicked at the lower wing, once, twice, until it snapped. Then the bird squawked, and Zlo spun around to face Hitch.

Hitch slowed and immediately cussed himself for it. Keep going, use his speed and surprise to bowl Zlo over, that's what he should do. Too late now. He approached slowly, lantern high, and circled around to get a clear angle at the guy.

Zlo bared his teeth, and the silver-capped ones in front glinted. "And so. The man who was so brave this morning." He spread his arms and sidestepped out from the corner of the wing. "I thought maybe you were not so stupid as you look." His tone was light, but his jaw tightened and something hot sparked in his eyes.

He was good and steamed, no question about it.

Hitch flashed a grin. "Liked my little trick with the cannon, did you?"

Zlo's eyes looked about ready to pop from his head. Veins stood out in his temples. Then he smiled—which somehow only made him look more dangerous. "You think you are smart man, yes? You think you are brave. You are hero!"

"If you want to start handing out medals, I'll be happy to accept 'em." Hitch sidestepped some more, going as much forward as he did sideways. With any luck, Zlo wouldn't notice. One more step, and then he'd charge—and pray God Zlo wasn't packing anything.

Zlo clucked. "No medals for you. That would be mistake. Your town does not give medals to fools who endanger them, do they? Your *glavni*—your Sheriff Campbell—he will see to that I think."

Hitch dropped the lantern and charged. His lowered shoulder caught Zlo beneath the breastbone, and they both went staggering. Zlo skidded underneath the plane's wing, while Hitch plowed right into it. The weakened wing frame cracked beneath his weight and gave way.

Behind him, the lantern must have been rolling, because the

light spun around in crazy circles. Tough to tell whether he was dizzy or the world was. He blinked hard and turned around.

Zlo loomed in front of him, a wing strut raised in both hands. His silver teeth flashed, this time in a snarl, and he swung the strut at Hitch's head.

Hitch backpedaled, arms windmilling. His heel caught and he tripped. The end of the strut barely caught the top of his head. But it was enough.

He hit the ground. The back part of his brain was still running, mostly just with the general shock of being consciously unconscious, but his body refused to move. He was going to get whacked again, his brain knew that much.

Footsteps crunched nearer. Then more footsteps, running in from far away. Voices shouted, hazy and wordless. Something that sounded a whole lot like a gunshot crashed through his head, and the pain pounded its way back through the darkness.

Warm, callused hands cradled his face. Jael's voice—muttering about *cheloveks* again—drifted in.

His body remained unresponsive, but he managed to crack open an eyelid.

She huffed and closed her eyes. "*O Bozhe.*"

"What happened?" His arm was working again now, so he pushed himself up. Instantly, pain spun around in his head. He flopped back down, head on her knees. That was much better anyway.

"We chased them all away," she said.

"Damage?"

She hesitated. "Earl and I—we saved your Jenny."

"And?"

Another hesitation. "That is all." She lowered her face a little closer to his. "Hitch, listen. If we give him *yakor*—if *I* give him *yakor*—he will go away from here."

Since when had she started caring more about saving the town than stopping Zlo?

"I am knowing he will," she said. "We have to find it. It is only way left."

Hitch might be dizzy and hurting, but he wasn't that far out of it. Throwing Jael at Zlo's mercy and then turning Zlo loose sounded like the worst idea yet.

He found her hand and gripped it. "Not happening." The words croaked a little.

He closed his eyes again and blocked out the murmuring and shouting of the gathering crowd. For just the moment, he let himself wish he and Jael were far away, some place where no one knew where they were—not Griff or Nan or Campbell, and definitely not Zlo.

It was a fruitless wish and he knew it. No way he was letting her sacrifice herself, no matter how stubborn she decided to be. But there was also no way, this time, that he could run away—which meant he could hardly take her away either, even if she'd go.

CHAPTER 34

WALTER WAS AS far from home as he'd ever been by himself. At least, not without somebody knowing where he was.

He stood in the prairie meadow between town and the Bluff. The tall grass tussocks had turned golden brown at the top with their prickly loads of seeds. They swayed and swirled in the wind, like a sea of green soda pop with golden fizz on top.

Somebody had to find *Schturming* before anybody else got hurt, and it didn't appear anybody besides him had thought to look out here. He clenched the binoculars Hitch had given him and looked ahead at the tan-colored spine of five dusty bluffs jutting maybe a thousand feet out of the flat ground.

His heart beat harder inside of him, and he looked over to where Taos was busy sniffing at a gopher hole. Walter slapped his leg like Hitch always did.

The dog looked around, pink tongue lolling, and trotted to Walter's side. Taos had stayed under the porch all night. Mama Nan hadn't known about it, and Hitch must have forgotten about him after his fight with Deputy Griff.

Walter's stomach tightened. At school, the big boys—and sometimes the little boys too—would fight. But never like that. Never like they hated each other so much they wanted to pound each other's teeth out of their heads.

And the things they'd said . . .

Deputy Griff was one of the best men in town. Everybody knew that. Mama Nan was always wanting Walter to spend time with him—go fishing or ride in his car when he did his patrols—

and Deputy Griff was always plenty nice to him.

But Deputy Griff hated Hitch.

And Hitch was Walter's *uncle*. They were related. Kind of, anyway. If Hitch had been married to Aunt Aurelia, *that* would have made him Walter's uncle, so that had to mean that being married to Aunt Celia—who nobody ever talked about—meant the same thing. If they were all related, it made even less sense why everybody was so mad at Hitch.

Walter frowned.

Maybe Hitch hated Deputy Griff too, but he hadn't looked like it. There at the end, his eyes had grown big and almost shocked-like. He'd stopped the fight himself, even though he'd gotten hit in the face an extra time for it. And he'd said he was sorry for whatever it was exactly he'd done.

Nobody was on Hitch's side. Except Jael.

And Walter. Walter was on his side.

When the family had all gone back into the house, after everybody else left, Mama Nan had huffed out the deepest breath ever. Then she buried her face in Aunt Aurelia's sopping collar and flat-out bawled. Everybody, even Papa Byron, stood there and stared. Mama Nan *never* cried. She got mad and hollered and sometimes sat at the table with her hands covering up her face. But she never cried.

Even though Aunt Aurelia was the one who'd near drowned in the storm, she patted Mama Nan's back and said, "There, there."

Walter curled his fingers in Taos's ruff, squared his shoulders, and started marching through the tall grass toward the Bluff. Deputy Griff had said this all was Hitch's fault. Walter frowned harder. There wasn't a lick of truth to that, of course. Nobody was fighting harder or was more brave than Hitch. Brave people didn't do bad things. Brave people were heroes.

This morning, when Walter sneaked out of the kitchen, Papa Byron had banged in through the other door, into the sitting room, and told Mama Nan the sky people had come down last night and ruined most of the airplanes.

"God help us," Mama Nan had said. "Have they found the airship yet?"

"No. It could be beyond the Bluff by now."

That's what had given Walter his idea. He had pulled open the kitchen door, nice and slow, so it wouldn't screech, then slipped out. He slapped his leg to Taos and started down the road. He walked maybe a mile, and then that Miss Lilla friend of Hitch's gave him a ride the rest of the way and dropped him off.

That'd been a good hour ago. If it hadn't been for all the clouds, the sun would've been way up past the horizon by now.

He followed the old wagon wheel tracks, embedded so deep from the pioneer days that they still striped the hard ground. The air was mostly calm, the clouds socked in instead of rolling—except along the horizon where the steely curtains of rain closed in all around the valley. Every once in a bit, a raindrop would splat against his face, and he'd wipe it aside with the back of his hand.

He walked with the binoculars held up to his eyes. They were a little big for his head, so he pressed one lens against his eye and squinted around the corner of the other. He followed the trail down into a gully near the base of the Bluff. A raindrop hit the main lens in the middle and spread out to wobble his whole vision.

He stopped and turned the binoculars around to rub the spot off on his overalls' bib. The material there, thick with his pocket, was too stiff to do the job, so he raised a knee and rubbed it there instead. That'd have to do. He'd forgot his handkerchief. Mama Nan was always telling him for goodness' sake remember your hankie, someday you'll need it. Guess that meant she was finally right.

At Walter's side, Taos yipped in the back of his throat. He perked both ears, although the floppy one wouldn't go all the way up. He was seeing something with his good dog eyes. But what?

Walter raised the binoculars and stood on his toes.

Only twenty feet away, nestled in the curve of the Bluff, plain as a coon in the corn, was the great ship hanging from its inflatable sail.

His heart scooted up his windpipe into his throat. He almost choked.

Breathe, keep breathing. Pretend to be brave. But the breath wouldn't quite come. He threw himself onto the ground, behind a spiny yucca. Breathe! He gritted his teeth and sucked air through his nostrils. A lot of dust came with it and scraped in the back of his throat. He swallowed hard to keep from coughing and hoisted the binoculars back to his eyes.

The ship was snuggled against the Bluff, where it'd be hard to see from any angle but this one. The pirates had brought it in low to the ground, only a couple dozen feet up. Men were running all around it, and their shouts drifted out to him. The words were hard and growly-sounding and sure not English.

His heart beat faster. He'd found it. *He*, him, he! Nobody else, just him. He could take the news back to town, tell Hitch, and Hitch would fly out here and beat them all up. Maybe that'd make folks stop thinking things were Hitch's fault when they weren't. Maybe that'd make them *both* heroes.

Little carts were being hoisted up and down between the ground and the ship, carrying men and boxes and burlap sacks of what might be supplies. Some other men were gutting a couple of mule deer. The cannon rested on the ground, half-hidden in the tall grass, while up on the balloon, men with ropes tied around their waists scurried around the cannon's track, making repairs. Men with revolvers stood guard in the gaping doorway at the front end of the ship.

Toward the back, some of the other men hammered away at a big hole. More of them worked on the propellers, which seemed different looking—wrong somehow. He squinted. Yessiree, the tip of one of the blades was missing.

It was broken! It couldn't move. Hitch could hunt it down right here.

Walter would just have to get up and run back down the trail. It would be easy.

He inched his legs up under him and crouched. His heart hammered. He looked over at Taos and patted his leg, but not loud enough to make a slapping sound.

Taos kept right on staring at the airship. He stood on all four feet, leaning forward, ready to run right at them.

Walter patted his leg again, a little harder.

Maybe Taos thought the slap was permission to go. He leapt the ridge of the gully, and he ran across the flatland, barking all the way.

Terror swallowed Walter up. He jumped to his feet.

Men started to turn and look at Taos. Some of them pointed; some of them hollered. Some of them got real still, and some of them started moving faster. Maybe they couldn't decide if the dog was just a dog, or if somebody big was coming for them.

One man, in a funny round hat like the one Papa Byron wore in his and Mama Nan's wedding photograph, stepped out from the shadow of the airship. It was Zlo, the lead pirate.

Zlo glanced at Taos, then raised his face, looking out across the prairie. He looked straight at Walter.

A chill hit Walter, and his skin shriveled up. He dove back behind the yucca. They were going to kill him now! They'd catch him and take him up in their ship and throw him off the very top.

"Boy!" The shout carried across to the trail.

He peeked through the long, sharp yucca leaves.

Zlo had caught Taos. He held the dog in both arms, trapped against his chest. Taos kept barking, both whining and snarling, but he was stuck fast.

"I know this dog! I know who has sent you. You must come out and talk to me. I will kill this dog!"

If they'd kill the dog, they'd kill him too. Walter didn't even have to think about moving his feet. They just ran. They carried him up the other side of the gully and fifty feet across the prairie. When he looked over his shoulder, the corner of the Bluff hid *Schturming*.

Taos! His feet stopped on their own.

He was no hero. He was a dope. He'd brought Hitch's dog out here without asking. And now he just ran away? His throat thickened, and tears pinched the corner of his eyes.

No crying! No running. What he should do was punch himself in his own face.

Pretend to be brave. Pretend, pretend, pretend.

He gritted his teeth. His feet didn't do anything on their own this time. He had to make them turn his body around, step by step, and creep back through the grassland to the gully. He clambered up through the dust and peered over the ridge.

The cannon dangled from a harness of ropes, slowly inching upwards. Three men straddled it like it was a horse and dangled the hollow deer carcasses off the sides by their hind legs. The rest of the men crowded into the elevator cars. Zlo stood at the front of one, empty-handed.

What did that mean? Walter's insides clenched up. Had Zlo let Taos go? Had he killed him already?

Walter scrabbled the binoculars up from where he'd dropped them under the yucca and raised them to his eyes. His hands shook, and he pressed the lens hard against his eye socket to hold it still.

Some of the men in Zlo's car shifted. Two of them held Taos upside down by his legs. A third man wrapped a handkerchief around his muzzle.

They were taking Hitch's dog. And it was all his fault.

CHAPTER 35

THE TOP OF Hitch's head felt about like a hard-boiled egg someone had smashed in with a spoon. That didn't do much to
make him hungry for the two sunny-side-ups staring at him
from his plate. He hunched over the counter at Dan and Rosie's
Cafe on Main Street and cradled his mug of lukewarm coffee.

What he needed at the moment was a plan. Any plan. Even
a stupid one would do—so long as it didn't involve Jael finding
that consarned pendant and turning herself over to Zlo. He
growled.

Dan stood in front of him, rubbing silverware on an already
damp towel. "Too runny?" he asked.

Hitch glanced up. "They're fine. Just fine." They weren't really
fine; they were just cheap. What he truly wanted this morning
was a steak—rare and bloody. Something he could stab with a
knife and then chomp with his teeth and rip into pieces.

Stabbing, chomping, and ripping. Those were about the only
things that'd make him feel better right now. If he could stab,
chomp, and rip that dirty no account Rawliv Zlo, why, that'd be
even peachier.

He tilted back the rest of his coffee, ignoring the pain in
his head, then thunked the empty mug back onto the counter.
Some little part of him wanted it to crack. Mug or countertop,
didn't much matter which.

Dan grabbed the mug. "Now, what was that for?"

A spark of penitence bounced through him. He reached to
run a hand through his hair, then caught himself before he
could make his headache worse. "Nothing. Sorry."

Dan eyed him. "Where're your friends?" He put the mug out of reach on the sill of the window that offered a peek into the back kitchen. Judging by the sizzle, his wife was frying hash browns.

"Out guarding the plane." And each other, with any luck. "I had to come in for a couple jugs of gas."

Behind Hitch, a chair squeaked. "We heard there was some trouble out there last night," said old Lou Parker. He and Scottie Shepherd had been sitting at their table by the boarded-up broken window when Hitch came in.

"You heard right," Hitch said.

"Well, what're you going to do about it?" Scottie asked.

"What makes you think *I'm* going to be able to do anything about it?"

"You seem to always be right there in the thick of it, don't you? Don't tell me you're giving up."

Why not? He'd sure like to about now. He picked up his fork. At the moment, plans seemed to be in short supply around here. So what did that leave? He stabbed the congealed yolk, and the soft yellow bled all over the whites.

After last night, what was there left to plan *with*? Zlo had left them with only one or two airworthy planes and maybe half a dozen salvageable ones. Hitch could take the Jenny out and fly around for days without coming anywhere near *Schturming*, even with Jael's pains acting as a divining rod.

A fists-in-the-face fight he could deal with. That's what he had stayed for. But slow and strategic wasn't his strength. Right now, the only thing he was good for around here was a whole lot of nothing. The wanderlust in the soles of his feet was starting to itch like crazy.

Maybe he should get out after all. Pack up Earl, Jael, and Taos and fly right through that storm and out of the valley. The storm couldn't be more than a couple miles wide at the very most. He could fly through that. Then they'd be out. The town wouldn't be a speck worse off than it was right now—and then maybe this crushing weight would lift from his chest. Free again.

Or not.

If he left his family right now, he'd never be free. He thumped the fork onto the countertop so hard his plate rattled. An answering thump of pain echoed through his head.

Dan gave him a narrow look.

"Well?" Scottie prompted from behind.

He swiveled on his stool and glared at the skinny old man. "Well, what? You got an idea, spit it out. Because right now I'd do about anything to end this."

Bill Campbell's broad shoulders filled the open doorway. "Is that so?"

Save for Rosie scraping a spatula through her hash browns in back, the cafe went still.

Campbell pulled out the toothpick he was sucking and entered. He looked at Lou and Scottie. "You'll pardon me, boys, for turning you out into the damp air, but I'd like a word with our prodigal pilot here."

Ah, gravy. Hitch resisted hurling his fork—or, shoot, the whole plate of eggs—straight at Campbell's head. Of all the things he did not need this morning, Campbell was way up there at the top of the list.

He glowered. "What do you want?"

While Lou and Scottie grabbed their hats and filtered out, muttering to each other, Campbell took a stool next to Hitch's.

He looked at Dan. "You too, if you don't mind, Holloway. Go on in the back there and give Rosie a hand with them dishes." He dropped a nickel onto the counter and turned the pewter coffee pot so he could grip the handle. "I'll help myself."

Dan gave a reluctant nod, flipped his towel over his shoulder, and pushed through the swinging door into the back.

"Well, son." Campbell righted one of the upside-down mugs from the back edge of the counter and filled it. "Hear we had some trouble last night."

"Seems everybody's heard."

"Well, here's the thing." He took two long swallows. Then he set the mug on the counter and leaned back on his elbow. "You and me, Hitch, we haven't always seen eye to eye. But I'm not about to let that jumped-up mercenary, or whatever he thinks he is, come in here and hold this town for ransom."

Swell. Save the town from Zlo and give it back to Campbell.

Out of the fire and back into the frying pan.

"Listen to me." Campbell's voice deepened. "When I went up there the other day, Zlo offered me a deal."

The hairs on the back of Hitch's neck rose.

"Said if I'd help him get this pendant thing he wants, he'd give me a quarter of the ransom."

Hitch shoved back his plate and stood. "Why tell me? If you think I'm going to help you help him, you're crazy."

"I'm telling you because I want no part of it. I'll tell you something else. I don't want him just chased out of this valley. I want him brought down. I want him and every one of those mother's sons up there in my jail. And I want you to help me."

"Why me?"

Campbell's mouth tweaked in that almost-smile. "Because you and me, we're friendly, Hitch. And because I hear you're about the only one left who's got a plane that'll fly."

"And I suppose you've got a plan to go along with my plane?"

"We'll figure that out. Right now, I'm here to get something straight between us. Whatever you do to bring down Zlo, when you're done, I want that big ship of his in my custody."

"You mean you want it for yourself." He couldn't entirely say which was worse: Livingstone using it to own the skies, or Campbell getting his hooks in it and using it to cement his ownership of this town.

Campbell shrugged a shoulder. "Who else around here has got a right to protect it and make sure it's used properly?"

Hitch snorted. "You're the last person I'd want to have it."

"You quit with your beefing, get your head on straight, and do this for me—and it could be we might finally be able to call it even between the two of us."

"I've heard that one before."

But his mind couldn't help turning it over anyway. Chances were good Campbell would actually uphold the deal this time. He wanted *Schturming* brought down bad enough for that. Hitch ground his teeth.

Find *Schturming*, bring it down, and let Campbell take care of it once it was on the ground. Then he could get out, back to life as he knew it, back to the barnstorming circuit. If Campbell

320 - K.M. WEILAND

took over *Schturming*, Jael wasn't going to have anything to go back to, so maybe he could talk her into joining the troupe for real. Maybe it was time to explore whatever it was that was happening between them.

Why not help Campbell and let Campbell help him? It'd sure solve everything.

Campbell was going to be in power here whether Hitch stayed or not. In fact, when it came down to it, Campbell'd probably take *Schturming* whether Hitch put his plane at his disposal or not.

But *help Bill Campbell?* His throat tightened. Whether Campbell ended up getting his claws into *Schturming* or not wasn't the point—particularly since he almost certainly would. The *point* was that Hitch's promise to Jael about getting her home would be a fat lot of worthless if he handed that home over to Campbell as soon as it touched ground.

He looked Campbell in the eye. "Can't do it." He turned to go.

Campbell let him get halfway across the room. "Why don't you get yourself on back here."

Two more strides and he'd be out the door.

"I told you the benefits if you do this right. Now I'm going to tell you the drawbacks if you don't."

In the doorway, Hitch stopped and looked back. He shouldn't have, but he did. Because Campbell had always had it in his power to wield a lot of drawbacks.

Campbell sipped his coffee. "That little gal of yours? Don't think I don't know exactly who she is. She could end up going straight back to Mr. Zlo. Your mechanic pal might end up breaking his other arm." He set the mug on the counter, and swiveled all the way around on his seat. "And you can bet my deputy's going to have to find himself a new job."

The anger, simmering in Hitch's belly all morning, finally came to a boil. "This doesn't have anything to do with Griff."

"Not yet, it don't."

Hitch shoved a chair aside and stalked back across the room. "I should have beat in your stinking head a long time ago."

"That ain't going to win you this fight." Campbell unfolded himself from the stool and stood. "You think you came home,

Hitch. But you're on *my* ground. Don't go raising no ruckus you can't finish."

Hitch kept coming. "You're wrong. You don't own this town, no matter how much you like to think people need you."

"I own you, son. That's all you need to worry about."

Campbell had to be closing in on seventy, but he still looked like he could take a beating without buckling—and give it right back with twice the force.

He eyed Hitch. "You always were a fool, Hitch, but don't do something you're going to regret. You're on my side on this one, even if maybe you can't see it. You take one swing at me, and whether it connects or not, I'll break you right in two, along with everyone you care about."

From the moment Hitch had opened his eyes this morning, his fists had been itching for a fight. In Zlo's stead, Campbell'd have to do. Yeah, Hitch would probably end up in as bad a shape as Campbell would. Yeah, Campbell would maybe take him apart afterward. But where did this end if not here?

Small footsteps clattered up the sidewalk outside.

Campbell looked past Hitch to the door. "Well, now, youngster." He turned back to Hitch. The hardness in his eyes put the lie to his friendly tone. "I reckon that's just in time."

Hitch took one more step, everything in him urging him on. Get to Campbell. Crack his face open. Have done for good and all.

But the sound of the panting behind him made him look back.

Walter ran into the cafe and grabbed Hitch's hand. His face was streaked red, from running or maybe from crying. He looked up at Hitch, eyes huge, the pupils little specks. His breath came so hard, he was practically wheezing. He yanked on Hitch, trying to pull him away.

Hitch attempted to free his arm. "You need to go home, kid."

Walter shook his head and pulled harder.

Still watching Walter, Campbell jutted his chin at him. "I know some other folks who might *benefit* if you don't get your head on straight. So what'll it be?"

Hitch clenched his fists, the tendons in his arms straining hard enough to hurt.

And then he backed down. Because what else could he do?

"We're going to finish this talk later," he said. "*Sheriff.*"

"You keep blaming me, son. But you're the one who got yourself into this."

And that, right there, was the gospel truth.

Hitch let Walter drag him to the door.

Once they were on the sidewalk, he got his arm free and shrugged his leather jacket back up onto his shoulder. "I'm in no mood for games right now. You and I both know you're not supposed to be around me anyway. So run home."

Walter shook his head hard and grabbed again at Hitch's arm. Hitch tried to shake him off, but Walter stuck out his hind end and dug in his heels.

"C'mon." Hitch yanked his sleeve free. "If something's the matter, go talk to your dad for a change. I got my own problems right now." He took two steps, then stopped and looked back. "Where's Taos? I thought he was with you last night."

Tears welled in Walter's eyes.

Uh-oh. This was bad. Something painful inside of him rolled over. That dog had been with him longer than Earl.

"What happened?" He walked back to face the boy. "Where is he?"

Walter stared at the sidewalk and shrugged.

"Just *tell* me."

Walter darted his face back up, as if he'd been slapped.

Totally, entirely, absolutely the wrong thing to say. Hitch had almost forgot the kid couldn't—*wouldn't*—talk. He exhaled hard.

Walter opened his mouth, shut it, then opened it again. His lower lip trembled. "Zlo—took Taos."

"*What?*" The word burst out before he really had time to think about it.

That snake Zlo had his *dog*.

And Walter had just said something.

Why was this happening now, with Hitch? This should be happening with Nan and Byron. They were the ones who had waited forever for Walter to start talking again. They'd know what to say, pat him on the back, make a big deal out of him.

Hitch's head pounded pain all the way down his spine. "What happened?"

Walter sucked in a shaky breath. He wasn't crying, but he was mighty close to it. "I—" His voice was tinny, unused.

Hitch was no good with kids, especially crying kids. "Come on now. Don't cry. Just tell me what happened. Where'd you see Zlo?"

"Out—by—the—Bluff." Every word was a gasp. "With his ship. It's broken."

Electricity zinged across Hitch's skin. "The ship's out by the Bluff?" He looked instinctively across town, even though the buildings blocked the view from here. He seized Walter's shoulder. "You're sure?"

"But they . . . saw me."

A deep growl welled in Hitch's throat. This was a lead, a solid lead. The first in days. If he could get out there in time, he could finish what he'd started the other day: bring the ship down and get his people and himself out of here before Campbell could rain down any more threats. And then he could put this whole big mess behind him. Coming home had been a mistake. He wouldn't make it again.

But only if he could get out to the Bluff in time.

He released Walter. "I got to go."

Shoulders slumped, the boy looked up at Hitch. His tears finally slid free. "I'm sorry about Taos." Then he turned and ran.

Hitch barely held back a groan as he watched him go.

He'd been too rough on the kid. He'd spoken too harshly, been too impatient. After all, Walter *had* come to fess up. And Zlo's taking Taos probably hadn't been Walter's fault to begin with.

He should go after him and tell him it was all right.

It *wasn't* all right. But what else were you supposed to tell a kid who was breaking his heart over a dog?

Except he couldn't, not right now. *Schturming* came first.

CHAPTER 36

THE JENNY TORE between the low clouds. Hitch guided her wide around the backside of the Bluff and over the top once more. If luck could hold on a little bit longer, and *Schturming* was still near where Walter had spotted it, that might give him enough time to keep Zlo from kicking those honkin' engines of his into high gear. That was the first thing that had to go right if this new plan had any chance of succeeding.

Below, two dozen motorcars roared up the mud-puddled road. Campbell and Griff drove two of them. Livingstone with his bandaged legs, and Earl with his slung-up arm, had somehow gotten themselves crammed together in one of the backseats, even though they were so much deadweight on this mission.

In the Jenny's rear cockpit, Hitch perched on the edge of his seat and danced on the rudder pedals to keep the plane straight. She kept trying to yaw left under the weight of the rope ladder hooked over her landing gear. Every second the ladder somehow stayed put was a second that made it a smidge easier to believe there might be enough miracles left in the world to make this actually work.

Because if it didn't, they were going to be out of options for stopping Zlo. And even if, by some miracle, everyone managed to pull together long enough for this to work out—Campbell still got the air machine at the end of it.

Not exactly a win-win situation, but getting *Schturming* on the ground was better than nothing. If they could make that happen, at least Hitch could leave home knowing it wasn't too much worse off than before he had come back on this misbegotten trip.

For whatever it was worth, at least there was a plan this time—thanks to Walter's discovery.

A stab of regret punched up through the adrenaline. Little Walter with his wide, trusting eyes and his fearless smile. The only wrong thing that kid had done was to pick Hitch as his hero.

The Jenny tried to drop her wing again. In the front cockpit, Jael twisted around and shot Hitch a questioning look through her goggles. She hung onto the huge piles of rope coiled in her lap.

She'd insisted her bum joints wouldn't keep her from doing what needed to be done here today. Plus, she "must be finding *yakor*." At any rate, she was the only semi-whole person left who wasn't mad at him and didn't have it out for him.

He yanked his focus back where it belonged, steadied the plane, and gave Jael a terse nod.

They bounced in the turbulence over the jagged peak of the Bluff. The bare limestone at the top melted down into patches of faded grass and scrubby cedars. A few hundred more yards—a few more seconds—and they'd be over to the other side. Then the luck of this plan would either pan out or it wouldn't.

"Be there." He gritted his teeth against the rain-flecked wind. "Just be there."

The Jenny swooped over the last ledge. The ground fell away and the wide-open sea of air rushed up to float the plane once more. Jael leaned over one side; Hitch leaned over the other.

He blinked hard, straining to see through his water-spotted goggles.

Rock, tree, rock, weeds, more weeds. Nothing that looked like a very large, very obvious dirigible.

And then—*there*.

Nestled in the corner of the Bluff, the vast, off-white envelope exploded into view.

His heart about exploded along with it.

Jael darted a look back and jerked her head toward it.

He spared a nod, and then dragged in all the air his lungs could hold.

Here went nothing. If this didn't work the first time, it probably never would. He eased the Jenny's nose down and dove, straight for *Schturming*'s propellers.

No time to go over the plan in his head. No time to make sure the cavalcade of motorcars were swinging around the end of the Bluff and bumping over the field into position. Hardly even time to think about what he was doing. They had to get in there and get in there fast. As soon as Zlo heard them coming, he'd rev those big propellers and the jig would be over.

Below, *Schturming*'s stern surged up fast. Jammed against the Bluff like it was, there was zero space to maneuver. Hitch slowed the Jenny as much as he dared, but the wingtip still reached the propellers a darn sight too soon.

One of *Schturming*'s prop fins was busted clean in half. *That* explained why Zlo hadn't beat it out of here before now. Looked like that cannon misfire yesterday had done some good after all. The dirigible would probably still be able to move, but not nearly as fast.

In another minute, with any luck, it wouldn't move at all.

As best he could, he angled toward the dirigible's props with the ladder on the landing gear.

"Hang on!" he shouted, more for the Jenny's benefit than Jael's. If he miscalculated this, it either wouldn't work—or his landing gear would get ripped clean off.

They zipped past the propeller.

He exhaled and craned his neck. The wheels were still there. So was the ladder.

He'd missed. To bring down the ship, they first had to knock out its engines. This was the only way to do that. And he'd missed.

On the walkway atop the envelope, a man stood and started shouting.

So much for the element of surprise. Hitch pulled up hard to keep from crashing against the ground.

The cannon sat on its track, down toward the bottom of the envelope, but it wasn't moving. Maybe Zlo hadn't had time to get the pulley system back together.

Jael looked at him again and twirled her finger in the air, like she'd seen Earl do.

He nodded. One more shot. Good Lord willing, there'd be time. He pulled back on the stick, and the Jenny shot straight up, all the way past *Schturming*, right to the point of stalling. Then, with a roar, he yawed the nose around into a hammer-head turn.

The sentry atop *Schturming* must have gotten word to the engine room. Slowly, slowly, the mismatched propellers started to turn. Even busted, they had enough power to inch the dirigible forward.

The Jenny swooped down once more. Hitch got her lined up with the propellers and pushed her in even closer. It'd be the landing gear or the ladder this time. One way or another, *something* was coming off and sticking to that thing.

In a whoosh, the dark bulk of the propellers shot past the plane. The Jenny's whole frame shuddered. The stick twitched in his hand.

In front, Jael, who had been watching over her shoulder the whole time, broke out a wide grin. Her laugh was almost audible.

His heart pounded so hard he could barely see straight. He dared a look under the plane.

The wheels still hung in place, revolving in the airflow. At least whatever else happened, Earl wouldn't kill him once he got back to the ground. He turned to look over his shoulder.

The dirigible's propellers still turned. But with every turn, they pulled the sturdy rope ladder deeper into the gears. A few more revolutions and the whole thing would be stuck fast.

If he'd had any breath left, he would have laughed too. But *that* had been the easy part.

He faced forward and pulled the plane up for a low pass over the field.

The two dozen motorcars were careening across the prairie meadow, some of them bouncing dangerously high over the grass tussocks. Half of them rumbled right under *Schturming*'s bow. The other half got in close to the stern. Twelve of them—six from each end—stopped long enough to spin all the way around until they were facing away from the Bluff and the other dozen cars.

Jael looked back again and raised her eyebrows, questioningly.

He gave her a nod. "Your turn, kiddo." Then he eased the plane around for another climb.

Jael tossed the end of one of the long ropes out of the cockpit and let it slip down off the lower wing. She fed it out and kept feeding it as the Jenny screamed back over *Schturming*'s choking props. By the time they reached the motorcars on the far side, Jael had come to the end of the first rope and tossed it out. It hung, beautifully, right over *Schturming*'s propeller shaft, both ends nearly touching the ground below.

He swung the Jenny around to make another pass. Jael waited until they were once again lined up over the propellers, then immediately started spilling the second rope.

Below, the men from the motorcars ran to collect the rope ends and secure them to their bumpers.

Jael dropped the tail end of the second rope, and more of the motorcar drivers raced to secure their ends.

Now to get the prow equally trussed.

Inside *Schturming*, barely visible in the crack between the bottom of the envelope and the top of the gondola, men scrambled, most of them headed aft toward where the propellers strained and groaned against the net.

The dark spot, where the cannon had been, had disappeared.

By the time the significance of that sank in, Hitch was already over the top of the envelope, headed for the bow.

The cannon appeared on the far side. It trundled up its track, headed straight for the Jenny. Two men clambered after it. They were taking no chances with their aim this time—or maybe the pulley system for moving it around still didn't work. At any rate, as soon as they saw the plane, they started shouting. The cannon stopped. One man reared it up to point at the Jenny. The other man fired her.

Hitch pulled on the stick. The plane pitched up. In the corner of his vision, the cannon exploded, and a great black ball hurtled at them. Every muscle straining, he willed the plane higher. An inch—just a bare inch—was all he needed to escape the dad-blasted thing.

With a mind-numbing thud of displaced air, the ball hammered past. From the feel, it was just beneath the fuselage. The

Jenny bobbled in his hand, but that was it.

He held his breath all the way up over the top of the Bluff, then turned around and swept back. If those mugs reloaded and started shooting at the drivers on the ground, this whole thing could get messier than mud in a bare second.

The first set of drivers had caught the ends of the two ropes over the propellers and were securing them to their automobiles. Some of the other men were hurriedly chaining car to car to create a better anchor.

But they were too slow.

Schturming's tremendous buoyancy hoisted her skyward. She dragged the two foremost automobiles right off their front wheels. Another two seconds, and she'd be floating away with both the cars and their drivers.

The men—Griff chief among them to judge by his slouched fedora—scrambled among the cars, fastening the locks on the chains.

Schturming kept right on going. She hoisted the first set of cars completely off the ground and hauled the second set forward yard after yard. The front wheels of the second set of cars inched off the ground.

Then the full weight of the train of twelve motorcars caught up with the dirigible. They yanked her to a stop. She bobbed for a moment, suddenly looking ridiculously flimsy for all her great size. The rearmost autos started up their engines, followed by all the rest. They hit reverse and started pulling.

Schturming's stern resisted for a moment, then slanted toward the ground. Her great bow tilted skyward, so that she hung diagonal in the cloudy sky.

That was Hitch's cue—again.

Two more passes, two more ropes—and his and Jael's part of the job would be finished.

They crossed in front of the high-ended front of the dirigible, and Jael dropped another rope to hang over the bowsprit projecting from the front of the ship. One more pass—one more drop—and that was it. Jael's fourth and final rope zipped out of her gloved hand, the end flying.

She hung over the edge of her cockpit and watched it go— without a safety belt once again, durn her.

He circled for a final pass. *C'mon, c'mon, c'mon.*

Zlo's men scrambled all over *Schturming*—up her cannon track, across the walkway on top, out over the side of the gondola with ropes tied around their waists. Every last one of them had a knife in hand and was sawing away at the thick ropes. Even if Campbell's crew got her on the ground, they'd have to secure her right away to keep Zlo's men from snapping the ropes and letting the ship drift skyward once more.

"C'mon!" Hitch shouted.

The team of cars assigned to the ship's front end secured the ropes. They'd already had the benefit of the time necessary to chain themselves together. In an instant, they fired up their engines and hauled *Schturming* back to level. And now she was well and truly stuck.

The four trains of motorcars lined up, six to each end of the ropes, and pointed themselves in opposite directions. They revved in reverse, tires throwing up mud, swerving a little—but hauling away nonetheless.

Schturming started to droop. Inch by inch, minute by minute, then foot by foot, she sank.

At last, the earth rushed up to meet her. With a solid crunch audible even over the Jenny's engine, she met the ground.

Hitch whooped and turned the Jenny around.

Now for the other tricky part. Zlo and his men were about as likely to give up the ship as Campbell was to play Santa Claus next Christmas.

Hitch put the plane down on the flat prairie—avoiding a few badger holes by the skin of his nose—then jumped out.

He jabbed a finger at Jael. "Stay there."

She wouldn't, of course, but he had to at least try. She wasn't likely to cotton to whatever ended up happening with Zlo, Campbell, and the pendant.

He didn't much cotton to it himself, but there it was anyway.

He firmed his mouth and ran through the tall, sparse grass to where *Schturming* lay hogtied, like a roped heifer. But she wasn't wallowing or bellering. She lay still—even her props were still—save for the creak of her buoyancy straining against her anchors.

The men who had been manning the cannon and sawing away at the ropes had disappeared. Matter of fact, the whole thing looked mighty deserted all of a sudden.

Except for the drivers of the cars—and Earl and Living-stone—the rest of Campbell's men had already piled out. Rifles and pistols in hand, they surrounded the downed ship and crept up to her.

Campbell looked over his shoulder at Hitch—then past Hitch for a second, which probably meant Jael was following after all. "Let's go," he said. "You got a gun?"

Hitch pulled his knife from the back of his boot. "This'll do."

They crept up to the main hangar doors, at the bow-end of the ship's bottom level. At a nod from Campbell, a business-faced Griff—who seemed to not even notice Hitch's presence—and three other men holstered their pistols and moved forward to haul the doors open.

The doors gave without a catch and rumbled open to reveal the dark cavern into which Hitch had crashed the Jenny during the first big storm. It was packed with supplies, but they had all been lashed to the walls and ceiling. Only a box or barrel here and there had fallen and spilled open during the tussle. Nobody showed his face.

Hitch's back crawled. He flexed his grip on the knife.

Campbell nodded again to Griff.

"Wait," Hitch said. "I'll go."

Griff stepped back and let him, without so much as a glance.

So that's how it was going to be.

But not for long. Soon as Zlo was under lock and key, Hitch was gone. If Griff wanted to forget about him then, so be it. Hitch could do his own share of forgetting.

He inched up to the corner of the door and looked inside. The whole thing settled a little farther, listing to starboard, so the door hole was a good four feet off the ground. Timbers groaned. But still nothing man-sized appeared inside.

He hoisted himself up through the hole—and about got whacked in the face.

CHAPTER 37

A TWO-BY-four whistled past Hitch's head, and he barely ducked in time. He got his feet moving even before he had time to straighten up and catch a full glimpse of what he was facing. He churned forward, arms wide, knife in front of him.

His arms closed around a body. He thudded to the ground with his shoulder in the guy's gut, and together they skidded down the slope of the floor. He kept his knife hand wide to prevent it getting pinned. From out of the shadows, footsteps thundered all around him. Outside, Campbell's posse hollered and charged.

Hitch squirmed on top of his victim. With his free hand, he pinned down the wrist holding the two-by-four. He used it to brace himself and jumped a knee up to land in the guy's stomach. The whoofed exhale sounded mighty familiar.

He pushed the knife against the man's throat.

Sure enough, Zlo glared right back at him, his mouth drawn in a snarl.

"You lowdown snake," Hitch said. "Where's my dog?"

"Your dog is gone. I have dropped him out of *Schturming*."

"I don't believe you. Why would you bother?"

Zlo managed a shrug. His throat bobbed against Hitch's blade. "What you call . . . practical? I will strike my enemies any way I can."

A growl built in Hitch's chest. He tightened his hand on the knife. "Believe me, you're not the only one."

Zlo jutted his chin.

Footsteps clomped up from behind. "That'll do," Campbell said.

Hitch blinked hard. He looked back. The sounds of the skirmish had already died down. "What happened?"

Campbell pulled him up and snapped handcuffs onto Zlo. "Seems these boys don't put up much of a fight after all. We had 'em outnumbered right from the start."

It was over? His brain struggled to catch up to speed. How could that be? He looked around. Nestled in the corners, between barrels and boxes, white faces with whiter eyes stared out at him. Dozens of them at least. Strips of ripped cloth covered their mouths.

Looked like Scottsbluff wasn't the only thing Zlo was holding hostage.

Hitch skidded down the slant of the floor to the first of the victims, a middle-aged woman with a purple kerchief knotted over her hair. Everyone's clothing was strange—foreign but also old-fashioned. The women wore wide skirts down to the ground, like Jael had been wearing when she'd jumped out over the lake.

The woman's eyes got even wider as he approached. She started fighting the rope that tied her hands behind her back. A nearby man, about her age, made a lunge at Hitch.

Apparently evil Groundsmen were still worse poison than Zlo.

Hitch stopped and raised both hands, the knife still in one of them. "Whoa. I'm not going to hurt her. Just going to cut her loose."

Campbell clamped a hand on his shoulder. "Leave 'em be. Save us from cuffing them again until we can get this all sorted."

"You're going to leave them tied up? They're sure not on Zlo's side."

"I don't know that yet, and neither do you." Campbell gestured for the posse to come forward. "Get these folks out of here. We'll take 'em all to the jail."

"You better have a mighty big jail."

Campbell stopped one of the approaching deputies. "Start searching the upper levels. And watch yourself. Chances are Zlo's got more men waiting up there."

It took them another couple of hours to completely clear the ship. A few of Zlo's men popped out of corridors, but Campbell's posse managed to overpower them with only a few busted knuckles and noses. No sign of Taos—or the revolvers Jael seemed to think Zlo's men would have.

It was almost like Zlo had wanted to be caught. Or maybe not *wanted* exactly. But at any rate he'd resigned himself to the situation. He knew Walter had seen them out here, so he knew trouble was probably coming. If he couldn't get out of here with that busted prop, then he might have figured out something else. Like give up quick and easy and make some other play. But what?

Hitch proceeded down the slanted floor of the second level. The corridors on this level were tight and dark, despite the round-windowed doors every twenty feet or so, which led to little observation decks. It was a homey, lived-in space. Big, if ugly, portraits hung on the walls between doors. Long rugs stretched down the hallway, tacked down so the wrong angle of the floor hadn't budged them. They'd been thick once; now they were threadbare, patched with bright reds, greens, and yellows.

The rooms, which he'd helped check, were mostly living quarters and mostly tiny. Thin-mattressed beds folded up against the walls. Round tables, inlaid with garish flowers, bore the remnants of family life: children's wooden blocks, old-fashioned quill pens, china plates and cups that had fallen and cracked when the ship rolled. Big silver ewers—full of strong-smelling tea—hung from a trio of small chains fastened to their bases. That tea wasn't spilling no matter how bad the turbulence got.

This was where Jael came from. He touched the leaf of a houseplant bolted into a porthole sill. And this was where Campbell would make certain she couldn't return. Only the good Lord knew why she'd want to, from the sounds of it. He frowned and headed back down to the cargo bay.

He got there just as Jael dragged herself over the edge. The deputies must have kept her back, or she'd have been here before.

Zlo still stood in the corner, where Campbell—balancing against a crate—talked to one of his men.

Jael caught sight of Zlo, stopped short, then slid down the incline toward him. She slapped him square in the face. "*Chtob ti sdoh.*"

Zlo didn't even flinch.

Campbell shoved her back and looked at Hitch. "Get her out of here."

The corner of Zlo's mouth twitched in what might almost have been a laugh. "*Zakroi rot, dura. Dumaesh voiny konchautsya? Oni beskonechny.*"

Jael looked ready to slap him again.

Hitch grabbed her arm. "C'mon, it's over. Where's this *dawse-dometer* of yours?"

She nodded toward the back of the room, where a regular-sized door looked like it would lead them farther aft.

"What'd he tell you?" Hitch asked.

She snorted. "That wars are never over." She pulled her arm free and hobbled ahead of him, through the door into another large room.

Towering pistons—to drive the propellers no doubt—took up the back half. They were silent now, bent like weary workmen leaning against their shovels. In front of them, a tall rectangular form, about the size of a chest of drawers, stood shrouded in tarps. It hummed gently.

Jael stopped short and gasped, painfully.

He glanced at her. "That it?"

"Yes. It hurts."

"Stay here. I'll shut it off."

"No." She gripped his forearm. "I must see it ended."

He helped her limp across the room, then tugged off the tarps for her. Underneath, a suitcase-shaped bronze box sat on top of a wooden cabinet. Three reflective panels on adjustable hinges topped it. The backside was a forest of punctured pipes—kind of like what you'd find on an organ. A panel of round buttons, like typewriter keys, and two funnel-shaped exhaust ports finished it off.

"Looks worse'n J.W.'s jalopy."

She started poking buttons. "It emits gas of chemicals into sky—and this causes rain." She pointed up, to where a skylight showed a blink of gray clouds. They were in the very back of the ship, where the bottom level jutted out from under the top tiers. "That is basic ingredient. From there comes other weather."

"And you can turn it off?"

"I can make it stop making gases."

"And the storm'll quit and the clouds'll go away?"

"It will stop *making* storm. Then wind must blow away clouds, like with all weather."

The machine's vibration changed ever so slightly. In a moment, she closed her eyes and let out a relieved sigh. The pained lines in her forehead slacked off a little.

He leaned an elbow against the edge of the bronze box and relaxed enough to let a few of the jitters shake their way out of his system.

He watched her.

He'd expected her to look like she *fit* here—like this was the puzzle where her piece belonged.

But she didn't, quite. She looked more like she belonged back in town than she did here.

What was this like for her? Maybe this would provide closure—permission to move on. Hopefully it would work out for her a little better than his trip home had for him.

"This must be kinda hard for you," he said.

"You mean, to see *Schturming* like this?" She looked up at the slanted roof. "I suppose yes. I have never seen her on ground."

"With her wings busted?"

"Yes." She eased out a smile. "But she will be flying again."

Maybe, maybe not.

He shifted. "Did you find any friends?"

She shrugged. "There is no one to find. I lived down here." She pointed to a tiny room in the corner. "But it was secret. If Engine Masters found out, they would have put me in custody. Only Engine Masters are allowed here. *Nikto* are not allowed anywhere but corridors. Nestor made exception for me."

Hitch strolled over to peek inside her room. Another one of those thin mattresses covered most of the floor. Tools poked out of a tarpaulin bag. A khaki jumpsuit with flowered yellow patches at the knees hung from a nail. A green bottle woven inside of a basket dangled from the same sort of contraption as the ewers upstairs. The walls were covered in woodcut illustrations torn from books.

"Snug." He turned back to her. "But kinda lonely, I reckon."

"I was not being *not* happy." She looked back up at the skylight. "I could always be seeing sky."

He chewed his lip. Campbell was going to make sure she couldn't return here, even if she still wanted to.

But she didn't. He could see it in her eyes.

So what did that mean? That she'd come with Hitch in a second if he snapped his fingers? She had no roots at all. She had even less to hold her back than he did.

But he didn't want to just snap his fingers. He didn't want to promise her something he might not be quite ready to give. He didn't want to complicate things between them right from the start.

Of course, it already was complicated to some degree.

A troupe member—a wing walker—that was one thing. But she was already more than that.

"So," he said, "now what?"

She shrugged. "I . . . cannot say. I have never had that question to be asking." She pushed a flyaway piece of hair behind her ear. "Now Groundsworld must be my home."

Not quite the answer he was looking for. The ground wasn't *his* home, that was sure.

But when she spoke the word, a small little thread of something that was almost, but not quite, longing trembled through him. Longing to *stay*? Just because she was going to stay here—in the one place he'd always been happy to escape? So now he was going to do, what? Stay with her? Just like that?

That made about as much sense as letting Lilla fly the Jenny.

Still, for a second, something in his windpipe hurt.

He cleared his throat and thrust his hands into his pockets.

He was the one who was complicating matters here. She'd stay or she'd go and she'd do it all on her own accord, because that was how she always did things. He'd already more or less told her she could join the troupe if she wanted. Should she decide to stay, that'd sure enough take care of his problem for him. He wouldn't try to talk her out of it. If coming home had proved nothing else, it had proved that trying to talk them through only tended to make things more complicated.

"Well," he said, "I'm glad we got this *dawsedometer* thing turned off for you anyway."

She offered a little smile, then sobered. "Just now, I did try to speak to people here—those who are not Zlo's. I was telling them everything will be right, that Groundsworld is not like we are thinking. But I am not best person to be talking to them. I do not think they believed me."

He crossed back over to her. "It does seem likely Zlo still has something up his sleeve. But whatever it is, it's a last-ditch gambit. Once Campbell's got him in that jail, there's not much Zlo can do."

She chewed her lip. "What I am not understanding is why they were not using the Enforcement *Brigada*'s weapons."

That *was* the lump in the gravy here.

He reached for her elbow. "Reckon we better mention that one to Campbell."

They left the *dawsedometer* uncovered and headed back. Jael still limped, but already her breathing came easier.

In the cargo bay, Campbell's men pawed through the boxes and bags. Griff, in the corner, glanced up once, caught Hitch's eye, then looked away.

Hitch held his sigh and followed Jael to the doorway.

On the ground below, Campbell directed the mopping up.

Schturming's passengers—more than a hundred of them in all—stood in a bunch a couple dozen feet from the ship. Somebody'd seen to taking off the gags, but their hands were still tied. Another ways off, twenty or so of Zlo's boys sat on the ground, handcuffed. They looked somber and nervous, but not quite desperate.

Zlo stood behind Campbell, flanked by two stout deputies. He'd lost his hat in the tussle, and his bird was nowhere in sight. Beneath his scruffy beard, his face was set in hard lines.

Hitch squatted on the edge of the door. "Hey. Where are all your firearms?"

Zlo pursed his lips. He looked up at Hitch, like he was examining an interesting bug.

Jael gripped the side of the doorframe and leaned out over the edge. "*Gde pistoleti?*"

Campbell took a step nearer. "What's this?"

"Jael says these people should have been armed," Hitch said. "No sign of their weapons anywhere."

Campbell turned to Zlo. "How about that? Where are the guns?"

Zlo ran his tongue over his silver-capped front teeth. "Will you believe what I tell you?" He shrugged. "These people— they do not like being tied up. They fought us and threw away the weapons." He looked at Hitch. "Like I threw away your dog."

Hitch looked at Jael. "We searched the ship already. Any hidey holes we could have missed?"

"There are places." She glared at Zlo, and her nostrils flared. "But I know them all."

Campbell took a step back and hollered into the ship, "Griff! Take this girl and look around in there. We may be missing some artillery!"

Jael shot a glance at Hitch, then ducked back inside and slid down the incline of the floor toward Griff.

Hitch stood to follow, then stopped.

Griff took her arm without a glance at Hitch.

She looked back, almost apologetically.

He stayed where he was. If there really was anybody left in here, Griff would take care of Jael. Anyway, there was something else Hitch needed to do, while Campbell was occupied. He sighed and swung over the edge of the door, back to the ground.

"You are wrong," Zlo said as Hitch brushed past. "There is nothing there to be found."

Hitch clucked. "Maybe I'll find something else."

The ship had rocked far enough over on its side to allow him to stand up straight underneath its high edge. He followed the keel aft. The weathered boards, peeling flecks of blue paint, were splintered here and there—but they were smooth enough for the most part. Too smooth for the pendant to have caught and stuck like Jael thought it had.

He kept walking. He craned his head back, scanning the huge canted bottom.

A dull glint of brass caught his eye. He walked two more steps, then stopped and looked back over his shoulder.

Couldn't be it. Crazy he was even out here looking for it. But he stepped toward it, reached up to a deep splinter in one of the planks and closed his fingers around something cool and hard. He pulled it out and lowered his open hand. Jael's pendant, still on its chain, lay in his palm.

At least he could give that much back to her.

Footsteps crackled through the grass behind him. "Well," Campbell said.

Hitch closed his fingers over the pendant.

Campbell's eyes met his. "Find something, did you?"

Hitch looked up at the hull. "What happens to *Schturming* now?"

"*Schturming* stays with me, where I can look after it. We'll get that propeller of hers fixed up right off."

"What happened to destroying it? Because it's such a danger to the people?"

Campbell seemed to consider. "That all depends on who's flying it, now doesn't it?"

"It surely does."

"I know what you have there, Hitch." Campbell held out a broad palm. "And I don't believe it's yours."

"Don't reckon it's yours either." Hitch nodded toward the ship once more. "What are you going to do about the *dawse-dometer*?"

"I'm going to keep this valley safe." Campbell still didn't crack a smile. "That's my job. Just like it's your job to keep your own folks safe." He lowered his voice. "You held up your end, obeyed my orders. So I'm going to make it easy for you. I can acknowledge who that girl is as easy as not, and she'll go to jail with the rest of her kind. This place ain't her home anymore—and that ain't her pendant."

Hitch tightened his fist, and the pendant's gears dug into his hand. "Why do you want it? You don't need it."

"Don't I now? I know what it does. I know this boat'll be on a pretty short leash without it."

So much for that. "Zlo told you? Why?"

"Back when I first talked to him the other day, he figured it might give us a little more incentive to give it back to him if it was the only way he could leave. And so it did." Campbell held Hitch's gaze for five full seconds. "Well, son. What'll it be? She can have her pendant or she can have her freedom."

Far behind Campbell, Jael's booted legs appeared outside the door. She dropped to the ground, Griff right behind her. They stood talking and shaking their heads. They must not have found anyone hiding. Maybe Zlo really had tossed them and the guns overboard.

Hitch looked back to Campbell.

Right now, either Hitch handed the pendant over to Campbell and hoped for the best—or he kept the pendant and waited for the worst. Filthy choices both of them, but they were the only ones he had.

Campbell probably *would* use *Schturming* to protect the valley. His personal vagaries and corruptions aside, he *was* a good sheriff in a lot of ways. Maybe it would all work out. Maybe this was the best victory anybody was going to get.

Funny how this had all turned out. Here he was coming home, hoping deep down to make everything right. Instead, he was only making them worse the longer he stayed.

The time had come to go. Simple as that.

He slapped the pendant into Campbell's hand. "I *did* hold up my end of the deal, and this time, you better hold up yours. Because this is the last round I'm playing, one way or the other." He turned, hands in his jacket pockets, and headed back across the prairie to his Jenny.

Chapter 38

WALTER SLID DOWN from the back of Papa Byron's farm truck. Not because he wanted to, but because it was easier than staying there and having everybody pay attention to him. He stared across the field.

Seemed like the whole town had driven out to the pilots' camp to celebrate. Bonfires spotted the darkness, framing a square floor of wooden planks hammered together for dancing. The town band was pumping out "Rose of Washington Square," with the drum and the trumpet pretty much drowning all the other instruments. Half a dozen long tables had been set up on the far side of the dance floor, and every lady in sight seemed to be carrying something to set on it.

His stomach growled. He hadn't eaten anything all day, except for a hunk of cheese he'd taken when he stole out of the house before breakfast. But out of all the punishments he deserved right now, being hungry was the least little bit of it. The pinched feelings inside of him squeezed harder.

He stood next to the automobile, arms slack at his sides. The rest of the family straightened their clothes—with lots of scolding from Mama Nan—and headed toward the party.

Jael, in a sleeveless dress of black lace, looked around and spotted him. She cocked her head to the side, almost frowning. "You are coming?"

He shrugged and stayed put.

She didn't know what had happened this morning—not any of it. Unless maybe Hitch had told her about Taos getting captured. But she didn't act like it. She'd been mostly cheery all afternoon.

She didn't seem all that sad her home had crashed. Maybe she hadn't been as happy up there as she had been here with them.

When she came home this afternoon, she seemed tired and a bit thoughtful. But then she looked at him and Aurelia and Molly and suddenly smiled her sparkly smile and started laughing.

Little pinched lines still edged her eyes, but her bones must not be hurting her anymore because she twirled Molly all around the girls' bedroom and hugged Aurelia. "We have won!" she said.

That was something anyway. *She* deserved to be happy.

The rest of the family went on ahead of him to the party, but Jael walked back to him.

She set her hand on his shoulder. "What is wrong?"

What he'd said to Hitch this morning was the first thing he could remember saying out loud in a long, long time. But he'd been right before: it was easier to keep still.

His cheeks burned, and he shrugged.

"Come to party." She brushed his hair off his forehead. "It is good thing to celebrate. We have fought, and we have won."

She had fought. She and Hitch. All he'd done was mess everything up.

He pasted on a smile and darted one look at her to make sure she saw it. Then he slipped out from under her hand and wandered across the field.

All over the place, people laughed and shouted. Practically everybody was here: Deputy Griff, the Berringer brothers, Col. Livingstone in his wheelchair with both legs bandaged, and the few pilots that were left. The smell of a roasting beef haunch wafted to him, along with wood smoke and leftover gasoline fumes from the planes.

What good would it do to see Hitch now? Probably Hitch hated him. Probably Hitch wished anybody but Walter was related to him. Walter kept his chin tucked and his eyes down.

He had deserved to be yelled at earlier. He'd tried to be brave, but he should have done like Mama Nan and everybody else wanted him to do. He should have stayed home, done his chores, and let the grown-ups handle it. That's what had finally captured *Schturming* after all anyway.

Far beyond the dancing floor, the towering silhouette of the airship flickered in the firelight. Sheriff Campbell's men had patched up the propeller and floated it out here, mostly so folks could see they really were safe again. Jael had said Sheriff Campbell was going to be personally guarding it all night, until they made sure Zlo didn't have any plans.

Hands in his pockets, Walter slipped past the crowded food tables—loaded with pies and fried chickens and big bowls of baked beans. His stomach growled again, and he tamped down on the feeling. No food for him tonight. No food and no party. But . . . maybe it'd be all right to have one look at *Schturming* up close.

Aunt Aurelia, in her violet party dress, stood next to the table and balanced a greasy roast beef sandwich on her lace-gloved palm.

She caught sight of him and turned all the way around. "Walter! They have pickles!" She kept turning. "Don't you want any? Where are you going?" She looked from him to *Schturming*. "Don't go out there." Her voice rose. "It's horrible."

He walked on.

The pirates were all in jail. The ship was tied to the ground.

Jael was right. The battle was over. So was the adventure.

He left the boundary of the firelight. Darkness stretched out to meet him. With his navy blue party suit, matching socks up to the knees of his short pants, and his black hair, he probably blended right in. Nobody'd be able to see him now anymore than they could hear him speak.

Maybe that was a secret power.

Or maybe it was just dumb. He was a dumb little kid who only opened his mouth when he had bad things to say.

Twenty feet away from *Schturming*, he stopped.

Lanterns surrounded the ship at intervals, marking the positions of the men guarding it. Sheriff Campbell stood beside the open front doors, talking with one of the guards. He jingled something brass in his hand.

In the dark, the moon gleamed against *Schturming*'s big balloon. She creaked against her tethers. But it was more like groaning than creaking, as if she was alive and sad because they'd caught her and tied her to the ground.

Walter's stomach turned over. It wasn't her fault the bad men had stolen her and made her do bad things.

Of course, unlike him, she wasn't really alive. She couldn't make her own decisions. She couldn't try to be a hero. The corners of his mouth turned down, and he bit his lips together. Maybe you *couldn't* try to be a hero. You just were, or you weren't.

He wasn't, that was plumb clear.

Ever since the bad day, when he'd nearly let Evvy and Annie drown, he'd been on the watch for a way to fix it all, a way to be a hero. And then Hitch Hitchcock—his very own uncle—had come, right out of the sky, and shown him how.

This had been his big chance, all right. But it was plain as plain he never would be any sort of a hero. He'd grow up to be like Papa Byron, only even silenter. He'd stay on the ground and stand back and watch while other people did brave and amazing things. He'd maybe have a farm. But he wouldn't have a dog.

His mouth pulled harder, and he blinked back hot tears.

Behind Walter, running footsteps tromped through the grass. A man blew right past him, not more than six feet away. He had a beard and wore a long coat down to his knees. He opened his mouth, and something glittered where his teeth should have been.

Zlo. It was the pirate leader Zlo.

But . . . it couldn't be. He was locked up in jail.

"*Skoree*, Seb!" Zlo bellowed. "*Vremya prishlo!*"

Behind him ran dozens more men, some of them brandishing revolvers.

They *couldn't* have broken Zlo out of jail. Everybody'd said Sheriff Campbell had captured all of them.

And yet here they were. Zlo must have left some of them off the ship when they'd been hiding by the Bluff. And they'd come back into town to rescue Zlo from jail?

In the darkness ahead, things started thudding. Some of the lanterns winked out.

Walter's breath caught in his throat. He pulled his hands from his pockets.

Zlo kept right on going, headed toward Sheriff Campbell. The sheriff barely had time to look up and around. The running shadow smashed into him and started bashing on him.

Two seconds later, Zlo shot to his feet and lofted his hand above his head. The brass thing glinted between his fingers.

Walter dropped to his knees, so even the white of his face would be hidden behind the grass. Now what was he supposed to do?

Already, Zlo's men were sawing loose the tethers and clambering aboard. *Schturming* floated a few feet up off the ground, held by only one tether at her front and one at her rear. The propellers started cranking.

This was his chance! He got his feet up under him, hands still on the ground. He could make everything right. Run back, tell Hitch and the others. It'd all be okay again. Except for Taos, of course.

He turned back toward the party.

Behind him, a dog barked.

His heart crammed itself so far up his windpipe it hurt. He whipped back around to look.

A small light pierced the dark hole of the main doors. Men ran around, most of them hauling themselves aboard. Some of them carried heavy loads—maybe things they'd hidden on the ground before Hitch captured *Schturming*. One of the loads wriggled.

If that was Taos, then Walter could make *everything* right again. And please, let it be Taos. Please, please, please.

All he had to do was sneak up there. He *was* practically invisible. If he was fast, he could find Taos, set him free, then still have time to run back to tell Hitch and the others. It could work. Zlo and his men wouldn't be able to see him, like they had earlier today. This time, Walter knew about them, but they didn't know about him.

He filled his lungs and tensed his calves, ready to run.

Behind, more footsteps swooshed in the grass.

"Walter? Waaaalter?"

Aunt Aurelia. Oh no, no, no. His throat clamped around his heartbeat again. He darted a look back at her.

She zigzagged in his general direction, both arms swinging, like she did when she was bored. "Waaaaalter, where are you?" She walked right past him, halfway to *Schturming*.

He looked at the ship.

The pirates had all gone still as a green sky before a tornado.

This was bad. He crouched lower. If she figured out what was going on, maybe she could run for help. But if she didn't figure it out . . . who knew what Zlo would have his men do to her.

Walter hissed at her and gave his hand a little wave. *Go back,* he wanted to shout. *Go back to the party and tell everybody!*

She stopped and looked straight at him. "Oh. There you are. What are you doing?" When he didn't respond, she raised her voice. "What—are—you—doing?" She walked toward him.

He held his breath.

The pirates seemed to hold their breaths too. For two seconds.

Then Zlo ran right at Aunt Aurelia.

No! Walter shot to his feet.

Aunt Aurelia whipped around to face Zlo. "You! No—" She screamed.

Zlo clapped one hand over her mouth and pinned her arms against her sides. He spun her around so he could scan the field.

"Are you there again, boy?" he said.

Walter's feet grew roots. He stood, hands fisted at his sides. Just like this morning—just like that day at the creek with the twins—he couldn't move.

Zlo shrugged and turned back to the ship, dragging Aunt Aurelia with him.

Not again. Not one more time could Zlo take something Walter loved *because* of Walter.

A scream built up inside of his head, louder and louder. It was like his eardrums were popping from the inside out. Who cared about being a hero? Who cared about being brave? This was about something else.

He opened his mouth and let the scream loose. He ran. His feet pounded the ground. He reached Zlo almost before the man could turn around to see him. Hot tears burst down his cheeks. All the air filtered out of his chest. But he kept right on screaming.

"*Chevo? Zatknis!*"

Walter dug his fingers into Zlo's arm and hung on. He kicked Zlo's leg, first with one foot, then with the other. Zlo lifted him clear off the ground, but he still kicked. His toes landed higher, leaving bone to thwack into the heavy meat of the thigh.

Zlo snarled and shook him off, like a dog shaking off a rat. "*Vozmite ego tozhe!*"

Hands reached out of the darkness and grabbed him. They hauled him away. Someone slapped him on the side of the head. Someone else held his mouth shut.

Pain swirled in his head, and he blinked hard. His lungs heaved for air, but, on the inside, the scream ran on and on. He would kill these men! He would kill them all!

In Zlo's grip, Aunt Aurelia stared at him, eyes huge.

Zlo looked up from Walter and surveyed the distant glitter of the party. Then he nodded to whoever held Walter. "*Otpustite nas.* It is time to go."

CHAPTER 39

GOODBYES WEREN'T USUALLY worth bothering with. So usually, Hitch didn't bother. But this time was different. He looked up from topping off the Jenny's gas tank, by the light of Earl's flashlight, and turned toward the glitter and the music of the celebratory party. That's where Jael would be.

"You sure you're sure about this?" Earl asked. "Wouldn't hurt nothing to stay another couple of days."

A few yards off, Livingstone worked on turning around his wicker wheelchair, so he could head back to the party himself. "But of course, he's sure." He flashed a grin. His top half was immaculate as always—from white Stetson to waxed mustachios—which put the contrast with his lower half somewhere between ridiculous and pitiful. Both legs stuck straight out, swathed in rock-solid plaster casts, his swollen toes poking from the ends.

Livingstone seemed unaware of the disparity. "You did a most excellent job, my boy," he said. "Our minor disagreements aside, I couldn't have done it better myself in the end. I have true appreciation for your stepping in for me in the hour of my calamity."

Earl huffed.

"I am truly proud," Livingstone went on, "to welcome you"—he offered half a glance to Earl—"and your valuable associate to the Extravagant Flying Circus."

What Livingstone really meant was he was happy to snap up the hero of the day and any resultant publicity. But what difference did it make? It got Hitch and Earl a job, and now that the dirigible was solidly out of Livingstone's grasp, it was a good job at that.

So Hitch just nodded.

Livingstone set both hands on the chair's wheels and started pushing himself toward the party. "I thank you for traveling on ahead of me and ensuring the circus's good name is upheld until my wounds allow me to rejoin you." He cast one more look back at Hitch, his gaze shrewd. "We will, of course, discuss the specifics of your contract more closely in the future."

And no doubt that contract would have plenty of clever little clauses designed to keep Hitch firmly under Livingstone's thumb. But that was a battle for another day. Lord knew, there'd certainly been enough battles for this one.

"Sure thing," Hitch said.

He watched Livingstone go.

The Jenny was already packed, fueled, and ready to head out. But before he could leave town, the one thing he absolutely *had* to do was tell Jael about the pendant. She'd probably be mad about it, but at least that'd make the goodbye part easier.

He cleared his throat. "Reckon I'll go say my goodbyes."

When Earl didn't respond, he glanced over.

Thanks to his own cast, Earl couldn't cross his arms, but his whole posture sent out the same attitude of skepticism.

"You sure you're up to flying?" Hitch asked.

"I'll fly out of here with you. I always do, don't I?"

"What's that supposed to mean? You want to stay?"

"Didn't say that."

Hitch glared a little. "Then save both of us the time and just say what you do want to say."

Earl shrugged. "Nothing *to* say."

"Good."

"Except—what you're doing here is runnin'. You know that, right?"

Hitch stared at the party—at the happy swirl of simple country folks, dancing and singing and eating just because they had people to hold onto at the end of a fright.

"I know it," he said and started walking.

He crossed the field and elbowed through the loud, swirling

crowd. Every few steps, someone hallooed him and wanted to shake his hand and tell him what a brick he was and how the whole durn town was indebted to him. He smiled and nodded and pulled his hand free as quick as he could. Sure, tonight he was a hero. Tomorrow, he'd be the black sheep again.

He reached the dancing platform and scanned the couples waltzing to "Goodbye Girls I'm Through." On the far side, Griff danced with Jael. He was smiling at her—about the first and only smile Hitch had seen on his face since coming home.

Hitch's stomach jigged a little. *If only . . .*

So many *if onlys.*

He shoved aside the swirl of regret and crossed the platform to reach them.

Griff turned, and Jael came into view.

Somebody'd given her a dress, a sleeveless black lace affair that swirled below her knees. With her short hair crimped into waves, she looked as keen as any society belle—except still Jael. A society imp maybe.

No wonder Griff was smiling at her. And *Hitch* was leaving her, doggone it. He'd come to say goodbye, tell her he'd pawned her pendant to Campbell, and then take off. His stomach jigged again. What kind of an idiot was he anyway?

Jael saw him and started to smile. But then she faltered under his stare and blushed prettily.

He groaned on the inside. Criminy, but she wasn't like any woman he'd ever known. Beautiful and brave, stubborn as all get out, and savvy right down to the ground in spite of her occasional naïveté. If he had half a brain, he would have seen that from the start. But no, he'd done everything he could to make sure he could leave her behind as easily as he left everything else.

Maybe he was losing his touch. Because this sure wasn't feeling none too easy.

Griff looked over his shoulder. His gaze met Hitch's, and his smile hardened to stone. He murmured something to Jael and inclined his head to her in half a gallant bow. Then he released her hand and left her to Hitch without a backwards glance. That much ran in the family, evidently.

Jael held out a hand. "Your brother is teaching me how you do this dance."

Hitch came forward to take her hand in his and pull her to him. He cleared his throat. "Last I knew, Griff was the one who needed somebody teaching him."

She floated in the circle of his arm, her steps light, if not quite correct. No wincing and no limping, just fluid grace with that vibrant energy that always seemed to be boiling right under the surface. She leaned her head back to smile up at him—and exposed that long, white sweep of her neck.

He cleared his throat again. "How'd Griff come to be here? I thought Campbell had everybody pulling guard duty tonight."

She shrugged her bare shoulders. "He *is* pulling this duty. He is only taking what he is calling 'break.' Campbell and others are all with *Schturming* now."

"Oh. Right."

The music jingled along, and they danced a few more steps.

He should tell her. Do it and get it over with. The confession only got a little harder every moment they danced like this, with the lace under his hand shifting against the small of her back.

He opened his mouth. "I like the dress."

She grinned. "It is belonging to Lilla. Nan did not approve."

"Yeah, well, Nan wouldn't." His voice dropped a note or two, in spite of himself. "But I do."

They danced on. His tongue forgot how to talk. He watched her, and she watched back.

Her smile faded. Her eyes deepened into that studying look once more, except this time she seemed to think she'd seen all there was to see.

Another *if only*.

The music stopped, and they stopped with it.

Now or never. He took a breath. "Look. There's something I have to tell you. Come for a walk?"

He kept her hand in his and led her off the platform. They made their way back through the party, toward the Jenny. From the looks of it, Earl had gone off to say his own goodbyes.

Jael wrapped her fingers tight around his hand, like she didn't want him to let go any more than he did.

What he *wanted* was to pull her into the shadows, take her by the shoulders, and kiss her like she'd never been kissed before and never was likely to be again. He clenched his teeth to keep back another groan.

Con*found* it. He couldn't possibly have been so stupid as to fall in love with her, could he? He knew better. He'd warned himself—Earl had warned him—the Berringers had warned him. Everybody had. Was he the only one who'd failed to realize how much he *hadn't* had this thing under control?

But maybe that wasn't *all* bad. Just because he had to go didn't mean she couldn't come too. Maybe she'd forgive him about the pendant. Her heart was big enough for it, Lord knew.

They reached the plane, and he did pull her into the shadows. But he didn't take her by the shoulders, and he didn't kiss her.

They stood in the darkness, facing each other. The silence grew. He shifted his weight and opened his mouth.

She beat him to it. "Have you said any words to Walter?" Her voice was clear and level. If she was anywhere near as confused and upset as he was, it sure didn't show. "He has distress about something."

Walter was someone else he couldn't leave without talking to.

"About that," he said. "That's my fault, I reckon."

"Well, you will say something to him?" She came a step nearer. "He thinks you are hero."

"I'm no hero, Jael."

She moved nearer still. "Yes, you are. I think you are." A smile pulled up the ends of her words. She raised her face. The flickering light from the bonfires slanted across her features and deepened her eyes impossibly. "You have done good things here, Hitch. Things no one else could have done."

"Kept you away from Zlo, I reckon. But I didn't get you home. I'm sorry for that." Sort of.

She lowered her voice. "I am glad you did not. If we had not stopped Zlo, I would have duty to go back. But I find I do not want to go back now. My decision is that I am staying here."

"Here?" Exactly what he'd been afraid of. But why not? She was starting to fit right in. Her English was getting better all the time; even her accent wasn't quite so thick.

She lowered her gaze from his eyes, to his mouth. Her lips parted.

Dear Lord in heaven, why did this have to be so hard?

The corner of her mouth curved up, half-smiling. "I would not slap you. Maybe."

And why did it have to be this *easy?* He lowered his face to hers. He touched her cheek and pulled her to him. Kiss her and have done with it. Get at least that much to carry with him, even if she *did* decide to slap him after he told her all of it.

But he couldn't. Before his mouth could reach hers, he made himself say it.

"Jael, I already decided. I'm still leaving."

For a second, she remained as she was. Then she flicked her eyes back up to his and drew her eyebrows together. She leaned away. "Why?"

"Because I should never have come home, and that's the truth." He shook his head. "Campbell says we're even, but we both know he can still chuck me in jail anytime I don't do what he wants. I had to give him your pendant."

"You found it? Under *Schturming?*"

"If I don't do what he tells me, then people get hurt. People I care about. Including you."

Her features remained still, like she was waiting to hear it all before judging.

"I've done nothing but cause more trouble since I came back here. I've raked up all of Nan's hurt over Celia's death and Griff's hurt over my leaving the first time. I upset Walter when he needed somebody to be on his side more than ever." He looked away. "Got my dog killed."

She nodded, slowly, realization dawning. "You are flying away."

He turned back to her. "I am sorry."

She shook her head. "I forgive you—about pendant. I understand why you did what you did. You were protecting people, and you did not have choice. I do not blame you for that."

From the sounds of it, she blamed him for *something*.

She sighed. "But . . . you are leaving."

His heart flipped. If *that* was all, then maybe this thing could still end happily.

He touched her arm. "Come with me. Fly around the world on my wings. You were born for that life as much as I was."

"You would be leaving more than just me."

"They're better off without me."

"That is *not* true."

"They can't wait for me to leave. You can read it on their faces."

She pulled her arm free. "That is excuse. They are your family! It is not for them you are leaving. It is for *you* that you are *running away*."

His guts twisted. He took a step back. "If I knew how to do it any different, I would."

She looked him in the eye. "You do know. I heard you tell Walter."

He waited.

"You said . . . to be brave, you only have to pretend."

He had said that to a scared little kid who didn't yet know what he was capable of. Hitch wasn't a kid any more. He'd been to the limits of himself and back again more times than he could count. Pretending didn't work anymore. Or at the least, it was a fool's game. He was what he was, and he only knew how to do what he knew how to do.

He started to shake his head. "I'm sorry—"

From beyond the party, deep in the field, a woman screamed—and then the scream was cut off.

Jael turned. "That was Aurelia."

The band kept playing. A moment ticked by.

And then another scream jagged through the night—on and on, higher and higher. It sounded strange, reedy, unused.

Hitch's neck burned cold. It sounded like Walter.

Chapter 40

ITCH AND JAEL started running at the same time. They headed for the back end of the field, toward *Schturming*. He overtook her, in her party shoes, almost immediately. Already the deep thrum of *Schturming*'s engines rumbled in his chest.

He shoved through the party. "Move! Get out of the way!"

His brain scrambled to catch up with his legs. Campbell had launched the thing? Why? Campbell had nothing to prove to these people. And he wouldn't hurt Aurelia or Walter. Hitch had done what Campbell'd wanted. Campbell didn't have a single reason to hurt them. His heart exploded energy through his body with every stride.

Ahead, the white cloud of *Schturming*'s envelope floated up from the ground. She was aloft, the bright moon showing every detail. The tethers had been cut, the propellers already repaired thanks to Campbell. She powered right over the top of the party.

People started looking up. They pointed. Some of them laughed and waved. But then uncertainty swept over them. Conversations ceased. The dancing stopped. A second later, even the band petered into silence.

Above, the engines cut out.

Hitch stopped, panting. Behind him, Jael skidded to a stop.

From above, a voice shouted down: "You are enjoying your party, yes?"

Zlo.

Rumbles of astonishment and confusion washed through the crowd.

How had this happened? Campbell *knew* Zlo had some

gambit up his sleeve. He had men on guard. Surely, Zlo couldn't have hidden away enough people to overpower them all. Hitch balled his fists. Or maybe he could. Maybe in allowing *Schturming* to be captured, what he had really done was cleverly get rid of all his deadweight—all the people from *Schturming* who'd disagreed with him. That would leave him with just those men who were loyal to him and his notions of what he wanted to do with the *dawsedometer*.

Hitch looked skyward—up and up, until *there*. Zlo and half a dozen other shadowy figures stood on the railed walkway atop the envelope.

Zlo laughed. "You tried your best, and you have lost. And now again, we are going to play this game by rules I give you. Except this time, you need *motivation* maybe. I have two of your people as my passengers."

"*Gospodi pomiluy*," Jael breathed.

"Say your names," Zlo said. "So your people know who they will lose." He shook one of the shadows flanking him. "Say it."

A whimper floated down. Then: "Aurelia Honoria Smith—and Walter."

The party erupted. People started shouting and screaming. Mothers started running for their children, husbands for their wives. Standing near the food tables, J.W. shook his fist.

"Two of your people," Zlo's voice deepened. "One each for two days—tomorrow and the next day. You have until then to give my ransom. Wave red flag on top of your bluff when you are ready." He turned to the shadows of his men. "*Otpustite nas!*"

The engines throttled up. The propellers started pummeling the air.

This whole thing was another setup. Zlo wouldn't give Aurelia and Walter back, no matter what the town did from now on. He'd chuck them overboard at his own good pleasure and in his own good time, just to show who was boss.

Walter and Aurelia's only chance was a rescue right here, right now.

Hitch turned and ran to the Jenny. He stopped at the rear cockpit long enough to stick his hand inside and feel for the fuel switch.

He turned back, and Jael practically smashed into him.

"What do you think you're doing?" he demanded. But he already knew.

"I am coming with you."

Protesting would be a fat lot of useless at this point. So he just plain didn't. Besides, a little help would be more valuable than not about now.

"Get in! You know what the magneto switch is on the panel? As soon as I tell you, flip it."

She kicked off her heeled pumps and jumped from the wing into the front cockpit. "All right!"

He raised his leg, like a pitcher ready for the game of his life, and cycled the propeller. "Contact!"

"Contact!" she hollered.

He hand-propped it again. The engine roared to life, and he ran back to swing himself into the rear cockpit. Feet on the rudder pedals and the stick in his hand, he opened the throttle and taxied the plane around to take off into the darkness. The wings caught air, and he pitched for a maximum rate of climb.

Ahead, *Schturming's* inner lights winked through her portholes. Paired with the moonlight, that would have to be enough. So long as they were in sight, he could find the ship. The moment those lights winked out, she was as good as gone.

He puffed in breath after breath, his lungs working too frantically. Calm down. Think. He regulated his breathing. First thing that had to be done here was to keep *Schturming* from gaining altitude too fast. The lower it stayed, the better the chance it wouldn't get away from him. He opened the throttle and careened past the airship, all the way to its prow.

Next thing would be to somehow get Walter and Aurelia out of there. Another of the rope ladders he and Rick used for car-to-plane transfers—like the one they'd used to clog *Schturming's* propellers earlier today—was already secured and rolled up under the wing, just waiting to be of use. If he matched speed with *Schturming*—and if Zlo still had his hostages up top—maybe Jael could climb down the ladder and help them into the plane. It was risky. Insane, actually. But it was better than nothing.

He knocked his fist against his windshield and waved his arm until he got Jael to look back at him. Then he mimed unfastening the ladder and climbing it.

The Jenny reached the front of the dirigible. With a yell, he slipped her in closer than was good for anybody's nerves. He nipped right under the front of the envelope, athwartships, and practically right over the top of the bow. The wind pressure shifted momentarily, and the sound of people yelping in surprise made it to his ears.

Ever so slowly and ever so slightly, *Schturming* edged down and to port.

Wasn't much. But it *was* something. He allowed himself a tight grin.

He swung the Jenny back around to the stern. They'd make one pass over the top to scope things out. Then, with any luck, Jael would get the same idea and chuck the ladder over the side.

He swooped in low, barely twelve feet above the envelope. The Jenny's forward bulk kept him from seeing straight ahead, so he kept the walkway under his left wing where he could monitor it.

In the front cockpit, Jael leaned over the side to see past the lower wing.

He held his breath and strained his eyes.

Nothing but white and more white. Maybe Zlo had already taken Walter and Aurelia down to the ship.

Then Jael stood up so fast the whole plane flinched.

He looked from her to the walkway. *There.* A large blot of black separated itself into half a dozen smaller shadows. Six pale faces looked up toward the Jenny.

Hitch bared his teeth. "Got you now."

That was when Zlo's men threw both Walter and Aurelia over the railing.

Every vein in Hitch's body seemed to explode. The Jenny roared on past, and he whipped his head back to see over his shoulder.

For an instant, they both clung to the railing. Walter was better visible against the envelope, thanks to his dark suit and his dark hair. He seemed to be reaching for Aurelia. She was slipping, slipping. He was grabbing for her hand, trying to pull her back. But her weight was too much for him. Both of them lost their grip and skidded down the side of the envelope.

"No!" Hitch shouted.

Zlo and his men glanced from the empty railing up to the Jenny. Then they turned and ran back down the walkway, headed inside.

Still standing in the front cockpit, Jael waved her arms and moved her mouth. But the wind swept away her words.

Hitch's mind spun in blank circles. His hands and feet seemed to operate entirely on their own. He turned the Jenny around and made another pass down the side of the envelope.

The mountain of white stretched forever. And then—the two shadows appeared against the endless envelope.

He exhaled hard.

Somehow, by some outright miracle, Walter and Aurelia had caught one of the ropes that were still slung over the top of the envelope from when Campbell had moored her earlier that evening. The rope must have caught on something on the other side, but it wasn't secure. Walter and Aurelia were descending: a few inches every minute. Twirling, they clung—Walter above Aurelia's head. Even if the rope could hold, *they* couldn't.

In front of him, Jael flung first one stocking and then the other out of the plane.

For the love of Mike, what now?

Then she stood up, and it all made sense. His heart kept right on galloping. But if anybody could pull this off, she could.

The ladder was their only chance now. If he could get the ladder within reach, maybe Aurelia and Walter could grab on to it. *Maybe*. He growled. That kind of trick was scary enough with a seasoned professional, much less an addled woman and a little boy.

Jael gripped the cabane struts holding up the top wing. She swung out first one bare foot and then the other. As soon as her toes touched the canvas, she leaned forward and grabbed the guy wires. Hand over hand, she passed herself from the wire to the strut near where the ladder was affixed. She looked a whole lot more like a monkey than that society belle she'd been imitating earlier.

She unfastened the ladder and it exploded out into the wind.

He applied opposite stick to compensate for her offsetting the center of gravity, then eased the Jenny around for one more pass. All he had to do was get the ladder in close enough for Jael to help Walter and Aurelia onto the ladder—and then keep the plane steady while he matched pace with *Schturming*.

Sweat trickled down the side of his nose into his mouth. He licked it away.

Walter and Aurelia still clung to the rope. They'd already slid halfway down the envelope. That rope could give at any second.

He rammed the Jenny in close to the envelope. And then closer yet.

Only Jael, crouching on the wing, held steady. Her skirt whipped around her thighs. She gripped the heavy strut with one hand, then swung herself under the wing and down onto the ladder.

Let her make it, just let her make it. Hitch held his breath.

Between the wings, Aurelia blinked into view.

Hitch throttled back just a little and rose until Aurelia was beneath him, hopefully right where Jael could reach her and guide her hand onto the ladder. Nope, too much. He gunned the engine the tiniest of smidges, then held steady.

Aurelia's wails filtered to him. Jael shouted something.

Aurelia rose out of view above the top wing.

That was bad. *Schturming* was climbing. Hitch nudged the stick back and added a little power to match the climb. Ahead, the sky was a black wall. If he lost *Schturming* in this, that'd be it for good and all.

Once more, the Jenny's wingtip hung steady beside Aurelia.

Still wailing, Aurelia pried one hand loose from the rope and lowered it toward Jael. Immediately, she slid a good five feet down the side of the envelope.

Hitch pitched down and reduced power to keep up with her. She reached again—and let go of the rope with her other hand. His heart somersaulted in his throat for a second.

But then the Jenny took the full brunt of Aurelia's weight on the ladder. Jael had caught her. The plane's whole frame shuddered. Hitch overcompensated, and the Jenny yawed hard left, away from the dirigible—and Walter.

Hitch fought with the controls. The weight beneath him swung around, first one way, then the other.

Jael had to get Aurelia under control, or they were all in big trouble.

He gritted his teeth. "C'mon, c'mon, c'mon, baby."

The Jenny howled for all she was worth. She shook beneath him. The stick bucked like a wild thing in his hands, and he strained against it.

A bare thousand feet off the ground, Jael suddenly heaved herself up onto the wing in front of Hitch. She gripped the forward cockpit's rim and crouched to reach back down for Aurelia.

Hitch hauled on the stick. Every muscle and sinew in his arms felt like it was tearing.

Jael hooked her elbow over the cockpit rim for extra leverage and leaned back, straining to pull Aurelia up. She threw her head back, and her mouth opened in a silent shout.

Hitch's heart stopped beating altogether. The wind rushed cool against the sweat on his face. His own breaths whistled, echo-like, in his head.

On the wing, Jael had gotten her feet under her. She crouched, one arm still hooked over the cockpit, the other pulling at Aurelia. She moved her mouth. She was talking, trying to calm Aurelia no doubt.

But if Aurelia heard any of it, she was too fear-crazed to listen. Hanging half off the wing, she kicked both legs and flailed with her free arm. She hit Jael, she hit the wing, she hit the fuselage. She was slipping.

"No!" Hitch shouted. What they'd just done in catching her was a miracle. They couldn't lose her now. "Aurelia, don't you do this!"

He looked around. Find a relatively flat place to land. Aurelia might break her legs, hanging off the wing like that. But it'd be a sight better than breaking her neck. Ahead, the pale dust of a road blinked faintly in the darkness. That'd do. It'd have to do. He pointed the Jenny in its direction.

As the plane turned, Aurelia's scream cut through the wind. For the second time, her hand yanked free of Jael's.

She fell.

Hitch froze.

Aurelia tumbled backwards. Her violet dress spread around her like broken wings. Her white face blinked in the darkness. Her eyes stared straight at him, her mouth open and round.

And then the Jenny sped on past. Darkness engulfed everything. *Aurelia . . . gone.*

For an instant, his mind was a vast empty space that held only those two words.

In front of him, Jael crouched on the wing. The night swallowed her black dress, leaving nothing but the dim outline of her arms and legs and face. She didn't move.

He looked up. The night sky stretched, punctuated only by icy stars. No *Schturming*. No Walter. A scream of pain and rage built in his chest. But he kept his mouth shut and trapped the power of it deep inside. He couldn't let it out. If he did, it would tear him apart.

He breathed in, a huge breath, until his lungs felt as if they would burst.

He waited until Jael collapsed back into the forward cockpit.

Then he raised the Jenny's nose to the sky and climbed. He wouldn't find the ship. And, even if he did, the chances of Walter remaining safe that long were next to hopeless. By now, the boy would have fallen too.

There would be no going back from this night. But he had to try. He'd fly until the engine choked from lack of fuel. Then he'd land, refuel, and fly again.

God help them all.

CHAPTER 41

THE AIRFIELD BLAZED in the darkness, but not with the warm lights of home. It was closer to looking like the mouth of hell.

The Jenny had been running on fumes for the last couple of miles. Wind howled behind her, a storm coming in fast and hard. Her engine finally cut out right above the field, and Hitch brought her in for a deadstick landing.

His arms felt like they had hundred-pound weights dragging at them. His chest and his abdomen ached, and his feet tingled with the cold. For hours, he'd circled higher and higher—and seen nothing but stars. And half of those were probably from straining his eyes so hard.

The Jenny dropped her tail to the ground and skidded to a stop. For an instant, the buzz in his ears filled his head with a noisy silence. Then that faded out too, leaving only the noise.

People swarmed everywhere. Most of them headed straight for the plane.

He sat and watched.

In the front cockpit, Jael bowed her head into her hand.

While they'd been up in the air, at least there'd been a small kind of hope. Maybe—miraculously—they'd find Walter. Maybe—miraculously—Aurelia would have survived her fall. Maybe it'd all been a dream.

But as always, the dreams had to stay in the sky. On the ground, there were only cold, hard truths.

He exhaled the breath he'd been holding and pried his fingers off the stick.

"Hitch!"

The voice floated through his brain, and he turned woodenly.

Earl fronted the swarming crowd. He ran like a sprinter, his splinted arm banging against his chest with every stride. His ball cap blew off, and in the glare of the bonfires, his eyes looked wild.

"Get that thing back in the air, you idiot!" he shouted. "They're coming for you!"

The words managed to penetrate Hitch's brain, but that was about all they did. "What?"

Jael looked up, then stood up. "Hitch—"

Then he saw it too.

Campbell, a bandage around his forehead, stalked at the head of the mob. His face was constricted with rage—and also something else: guilt, and maybe fear. The man was on the hunt for a scapegoat, plain and simple.

Griff paced behind him, eyebrows drawn hard in concern.

The crowd caught up with Earl and engulfed him.

Campbell shoved Earl aside and jammed a finger at Hitch. "Arrest this man!"

"Arrest for what?" Jael demanded.

Hitch swung down stiffly out of the cockpit. "What is this?" If he was going to have to face down Campbell—tonight of all nights—then he was sure going to do it with both feet under him. A few sharp raindrops slashed at his face.

The crowd reached the plane, stopped for a second, then surged all the way around. It was mostly men, and every single one of them seemed to be white-faced and red-eyed. They hollered and shoved. Fists got shaken in his face. Someone grabbed at his sleeve, and he had to shrug away. It looked a whole lot like a lynching mob.

The fading adrenaline kicked in again. The black rage started rising out of his chest, into his throat.

He looked at Griff and fought to keep his voice level. "I'm under arrest for what?"

Griff hesitated, opened his mouth, then shook his head.

Whatever it was, he didn't look like he entirely agreed with it. That was a good sign. Probably.

"Well?" Hitch said.

Rick pushed forward to stand behind Campbell. Lilla hurried in behind him, biting her lip.

"You think we don't know what you've done?" Rick said.

"You were in on this with Zlo from the very beginning! You helped him escape!"

Whatever Hitch had been expecting, that wasn't it. "Are you kidding me?" The rage climbed a little higher. He spread his hands. "Why would I do that? That's crazy!"

Jael clambered down from the cockpit. "That is most crazy!" Her face was set like stone, except for a half-dozen red spots flushing her cheeks. She was practically shaking. "Hitch has been fighting against Zlo from beginning!"

"Is that so?" Rick pushed closer, almost nose to nose with her. He only had maybe three inches on her in her bare feet. "Then why does he consort with one of Zlo's own people!" He spun around to face the crowd and jabbed a finger at Jael. "She's one of them!" His voice turned shrill. "She's a spy! She and Hitch have been working together to help Zlo from the very beginning!"

She hurled herself at him. "*Dostatochno!*"

Campbell caught her and clamped both her wrists in one of his hands.

She yelped and whirled on him, her short hair flying into her face. Another second, and she'd start kicking him.

"Jael," Hitch snapped, low and quiet. "Hold off." He turned back to Rick. "You really going to do this? Just because your pride couldn't take the truth?"

Rick lifted his chin and glared. "Who's the liar now, huh? People died because of *you*. Even your own sister-in-law. Did you know that?"

The last bit of hope choked out of him. He jerked forward a step, then turned to look at Griff instead of Rick. "She's dead? You found her?"

Griff barely nodded.

"Walter?"

Griff hesitated, then shook his head. "We didn't find him. We looked all around where we found Aurelia, for miles in every direction."

"But you can be sure his death's on your head too," Rick said.

Lilla grabbed his arm. "Stop it! How can you say that?"

Rick tried to push her aside. "Because it's the truth. Stay out of what you don't know anything about."

"I know what it's about—and it *isn't* the truth!"

He glared at her. "Just shut that big, stupid mouth in that big, empty head of yours."

Her jaw dropped. She narrowed her eyes. "*You*. You insufferable . . . insufferable *person*!" She turned to face the crowd and stood on her tiptoes. "He's lying! He's always lying! Hitch didn't do anything!"

Campbell growled. "Get her out of here."

With a scowl, Rick snagged her sleeve and dragged her away.

She started beating on him with both hands. "You want to know how stupid I really am? I was going to marry *you*, that's how stupid!"

"C'mon." Campbell looked at Griff. "Get it done. Arrest him."

Griff hesitated again, his mouth half open, like he wanted to say something, but didn't yet know what it was. He looked at Campbell. "We haven't got a lick of proof."

"C'mon, son!" Campbell said. "It's plainer than the noses on our faces. He's got a criminal record as long as your arm."

Griff frowned. "What are you talking about?"

"Why do you think he left you all in such a hurry back when? I had him dead to rights for thieving and smuggling."

Disbelief flickered across Griff's face.

So maybe he hadn't written Hitch off completely—yet.

Griff stared at Campbell. "Then why didn't you arrest him as soon as he showed up in town?"

"I ain't one to stir up old troubles. But he was at it again within the week. Bootlegging."

The rage exploded inside Hitch. He moved toward Campbell. "You think I'm going to stand here and let you say this? Not this time. I'll kill you where you stand before I let you do this to me again!"

Griff slapped a hand against Hitch's chest and pushed him back. "Shut up and let me handle this." He looked Hitch in the eye. "Tell me the truth, for once. Did you do any of what he's saying?"

"No!" Jael said. "These are halves of truths!"

"Then you did do it," Griff said.

"I did not let Zlo out tonight," Hitch insisted. "I had *nothing* to do with that."

"Were you bootlegging like he said?"

Hitch hesitated. Too late now. He exhaled. "Yes." If there was ever a time to tell the truth about his involvement with Campbell, this was it. "But you got to understand."

"Then you *tell* me why." Griff breathed hard. "Tell me why, Hitch. Make me believe you."

Campbell's mouth went flat and dangerous. He jerked Jael closer. His eyes bored into Hitch, their message clear.

Against the far sky, chain lightning slashed the darkness.

Jael caught Hitch's eye and gave her head a sharp shake. *Don't do this for me,* she seemed to say.

And she was right. He couldn't. Not this time. The truth had to come out sooner or later.

He turned to Griff and stepped back. "You want to arrest somebody here, you arrest Campbell, you hear me?"

"Don't be a raving idiot," Campbell said.

Griff shook his head. "Do this right for once, Hitch. If you're *not* guilty, it'll all work itself out."

Hitch took another step back. "I'm doubting that." This was about to end up in another fight, and this time it'd be a whole lot more serious than yesterday's spat. He tensed.

Then, on the edge of the crowd, a woman wailed. People looked back. A path opened up.

Nan staggered through it and flung herself at Hitch. Her face was slick with tears. She was sobbing so hard she was wheezing.

"I don't understand! I don't—understand. How could you let this happen? Aurelia's dead." She leaned against his chest, like she wanted to be held.

Instinctively, he brought his arms up around her.

With one fist, she beat feebly against his shoulder. "And Walter—to Walter of all people, how could you let this happen? Hitch!"

His heart twisted. "Nan . . ." He looked up, over her head, and saw Campbell.

A new light entered the sheriff's eyes. He cocked his head. "Well. Miz Carpenter, maybe you got only yourself to blame. Maybe if you'd told him how things really stand, he'd've taken better care."

Hitch set his hands on Nan's shoulders and pushed her back. He kept his gaze on Campbell. "What do you mean?"

"I mean," Campbell said, "I don't think they ever got around to telling you the truth, now did they?"

His heartbeat started to pound in his ears. "What truth?" He looked down at Nan. "What's he talking about?"

The deluge finally reached them. Open lanterns winked out.

Under his hands, Nan's whole body trembled. "Walter's not my son. He's Celia's—and yours."

And just like that, Hitch's world imploded. The wide vault of the sky seemed to lean down upon him and crush him with its cold, vast weight.

He had a son.

And tonight, he'd lost his son.

CHAPTER 42

ALL AROUND WALTER, cold wind wailed. He lay as still as he could on the wooden shelf that had stopped his fall. He kept his eyes shut. If he didn't move, he couldn't fall. And he didn't want to fall. Never, never again. A sob clogged his throat, but he forced it back.

How long had he been lying here? He eased his eyelids open. Darkness pressed in all around—except up top, where the white of the balloon loomed. Surely it had to be about time for the night to be over. He slanted his gaze to the side, trying to see the horizon. But, no, it was still dark.

He clamped his eyes closed again and strained his ears for the thousandth time. But no putter of the Jenny's engine broke through the wind and the thunder of *Schturming*'s propellers. It was too dark. It had been too long. Hitch wouldn't be able to find him, not now. Maybe he and Jael had crashed too. The whimper worked its way up.

Nobody was going to save him. It didn't make any kind of sense that they would. He *had* to be smart now. And brave.

So the first sensible question was: How far was he from the edge? He spread his fingers against the wood on which he lay. Inch by inch, he crawled his fingers away from his body.

After only about seven inches, they dropped right over the edge.

All the air left his lungs. He yanked his hand back. That's how close he'd been. All this time! Seven inches more and he'd have fallen straight to the ground, instead of catching himself here.

After Aunt Aurelia fell and Jael and Hitch had dived after her, Walter had kept clinging to the rope. But it slipped and slipped—until it wasn't just slipping, it was plunging. He'd skidded down the side of the balloon, clawing at the taut fabric. There had to be something, anything, to grab onto. But there was nothing . . . until the balloon disappeared and both his outstretched hands slapped into something hard.

He'd jammed to a stop. Everything hurt. For a second, he'd just hung there. Maybe Hitch would come back. Maybe he'd catch him, like they were catching Aunt Aurelia.

But, no, that was stupid. His arms trembled. He'd fall before they could make it back. He'd have to save himself. So he'd hauled himself over the edge and rolled to a stop. He lay there in the space between the balloon and the ship. The darkness was too thick to see what was on the inside edge of the ledge. Maybe another drop. He'd just have to wait for Hitch to come back.

But it was getting about as clear as Molly's looking glass that Hitch wasn't going to be able to come back anytime soon.

Walter spread the fingers on his other hand and inched them out—and out and out, until he stretched his arm all the way away from his body. The wooden ledge on that side extended as far as he could reach. At least he wasn't going to roll over in that direction and fall clean off the face of the ship.

He eased himself over onto his shoulder, then his stomach. Pains shot through his arms and legs—especially his arms—but he pushed himself up onto his hands and knees anyway. Then he started crawling.

After a few minutes, lights shone up ahead. To his right, a square hole—dark, but a lighter shade of dark—appeared. Voices echoed out of it.

If people were in there, then it'd have to lead to a safe place where nobody could fall. But if the people in there saw him, they'd probably throw him right back out. His arms trembled, and he bit his lip. Maybe just a look. He could always crawl back out.

He reached the few feet up to the hole and touched a strip of cold metal on its floor. He moved his hand to the other side of the hole and found another strip just like it. The strips were both wider on the top and grooved in the middle, kind of like railroad tracks.

The cannon! This was how they got the cannon in and out of the ship.

He stood up all the way and reached above his head until his hand bumped the top of the tunnel. It was maybe only four feet high. Not hardly big enough for anybody but him to fit in.

Once inside, he slid down the tunnel on his belly—as slow as a snake, and hopefully as silent.

Ahead, the orange light flickered, like it was off to the side of the tunnel somehow, maybe not inside of it at all. Around a slight bend, the light glared, full-strength. It lit up a huge, dark shape smack in the middle of the tunnel.

His heart jumped, and he stopped short.

The cannon. It was only the cannon. Good sweet angels.

For a second, he closed his eyes. Then he made his arms drag his body forward a little more.

The big ol' metal tube, on its wooden wheels, loomed over his head. It filled up almost all of the tunnel, facing away from him. But maybe he could crawl over the wheels first, then duck down under the cannon to get past.

In the tunnel's right wall, a trap door hung open from the hinges at its bottom. That where the light was coming from. Shadows moved across the opening.

He leaned against the wall and peeked an eye around the corner.

Inside a huge room, giant pistons pumped up and down. The wind blew the sweet smell of warm grease and the sharp smell of cold rain against his face. In the middle of the room stood a big tarp-covered something, about the size of Mama Nan's bureau—the one she never let him and the twins climb on.

The shadows blocked the light for an instant. The voices moved nearer, loud and growly. They said words like Jael sometimes said.

A man in a round hat, with a big bird on his shoulder, strode toward the tarp.

Zlo.

Walter ducked back and nearly banged his head against the trapdoor's sill.

Another shadow crossed the room. A man with a youngish voice muttered, *"Pozhaluista, otpustite nas."* He sounded like he was begging.

"*Zatknis*!" Zlo's bellow rumbled all through the room. "*Mi podozhdem poka svershitsya moi plan.*"

The floor of the tunnel shifted underneath Walter's hands and knees. What was happening? Had Hitch come back? Was he fighting *Schturming*? Maybe he was knocking it out of the air? Walter tensed his arms and legs.

The slant of the floor held steady.

No, what was happening was they were *turning*. They were going back. To Scottsbluff. His heart leapt. But . . . why? Zlo had said everybody in town had two days to pay the ransom.

Walter peeked around the corner once more.

The younger man, in a red coat, stood back from Zlo and fidgeted one leg. He kept looking around the room, like maybe he wanted a magic door to appear and take him away.

Zlo reached up and swirled the tarp to the floor. A machine almost as tall as Zlo himself, made of brass and tin and polished wood, sat underneath. It hummed through the dozen or so brass pipes sticking up from its backside.

This was the weather-maker. It had to be.

Zlo started poking at the round buttons set flat beneath three shiny panels that tilted upwards. The machine whirred harder.

The red-coated man clasped his hands and threw his head back, a little like he was praying. "*Pozhaluista, mi dolzhni idti!*"

Zlo stopped poking buttons and reached into his coat pocket. He came out with Jael's pendant, turned its little crank with the leaf-shaped handle, and fit it into a slot beside the panel of buttons.

"*Pozhaluista—*" the other man said again.

Without looking at him, Zlo grabbed a brass lever—about the size of a baseball bat—and shoved it forward.

The machine's hum became a quiet roar. It vibrated all through the tunnel's floorboards and buzzed in Walter's sore shoulder joints. The hair on his head stood straight on end. He touched it, and it crackled.

Outside, thunder rumbled.

Zlo turned away from the machine and looked at his friend. The bird on his shoulder cawed and ruffled its feathers. Zlo parted his lips, and the silver caps on his teeth glinted in the lantern's light. He didn't say a word. He looked mad, but not one bit afraid.

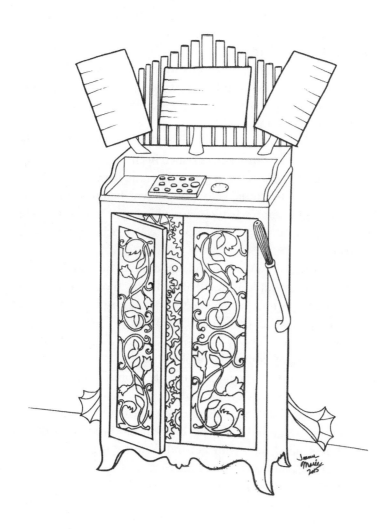

If Zlo wanted to, he could kill *everybody*. Walter's teeth started to chatter. After he got the ransom, Zlo could flood the whole valley to get back at Hitch and Sheriff Campbell for capturing him. And nobody would be able to stop him. Walter's stomach seemed to fall clean out of his body.

Zlo turned around. A long brass pipe had been secured lengthwise to the wall. It ended in a funnel, kind of like a megaphone. Zlo spoke into it. *"Derzhi kurs."*

After a second, a tinny voice answered. *"Tak tochno!"*

Zlo strode to his friend and clapped his shoulder, then pushed him around. They headed back across the room, leaving the lantern behind.

Right as they passed his trap door, Walter pulled back. He dropped onto his elbows and smashed his hands against the top of his head, trying to squash down his static hair.

Think. C'mon, think! Nobody down below—not even Hitch—could be sure what Zlo was planning. Only Walter. He was the only one who knew. And he was stuck up here, well and truly.

If Hitch hadn't crashed—and, of course, he hadn't—then he'd come back and look for Walter. But without the wing to mark *Schturming*'s hull, he wouldn't be able to find the ship. Unless . . . maybe Walter could mark it somehow.

But with what? Nobody'd be able to see anything in the dark.

Except light, of course. He looked up.

The lantern sat on the floor in the big room, beside the door Zlo and his friend had left through.

Time to pretend. Walter clambered out of the trap door and ran on tiptoe to grab the lantern. He glanced through the door.

Darkness filled the room beyond. Wind gusted through it and spattered raindrops against his face.

He looked up toward God. *Please don't let anybody be in there.* 'Cause if they were, they'd sure as spitting see him move the lantern.

He snagged the lantern's thin metal handle and darted back across the room. He shoved the lantern in first, then clambered after. His heart hammered all the way through his body.

The cannon filled up almost the whole tunnel, so he had to

lift the lantern over its wheel, then slither over it himself. He pushed the lantern ahead of him, on the floor, and scootched under the barrel. Good thing he was so scrawny. Any bigger, and he'd've been stuck right there. A line of sweat trickled heat down his forehead. He swiped it aside with the back of his arm.

The black tunnel stretched out in front of him. Somewhere down there, maybe he'd find a window. If he could put the lantern in the window, maybe *just maybe* Hitch'd be able to see it.

He started crawling, and he kept right on crawling—until he heard a dog's muffled whine. Goosebumps scattered his skin, and he stopped short.

Taos. Could that be Taos?

Walter's heart jumped with the first happy thought since Zlo had taken Aunt Aurelia.

Maybe, just maybe everything could still be all right. *If* Taos was here and *if* Hitch could somehow come save them both, maybe everything could be all right after all.

Chapter 43

HITCH STAGGERED THROUGH the doorway into the cellblock. They were way up on the fourth floor of the brand new court-house the county had built for Campbell. Rain rattled against the roof. Griff's hand against his shoulder guided him toward a cell.

Another deputy pushed a handcuffed Jael to keep her walking on by.

As she passed Hitch, she reached out and brushed her fingers against his.

His body reacted on instinct, his head moving in her direction.

She looked straight at him, her eyebrows furrowed hard at that crossroads somewhere between outrage and concern.

Her look pierced him. He snapped awake, out of the chaos of his jumbled thoughts, and drew a shuddered breath.

"You are not all right?" she said.

Who cared if he was *all right*? At this moment, the only thing he needed to figure out was how all this had happened. How could it be true? He had a *son*? And that son was Walter—who had probably fallen to his death only a few hours ago? Dear God in heaven.

"Did you know?" he asked her.

She shook her head. Her bedraggled, wind-whipped hair flailed against her cheeks. "No. I would have told you." She gave Griff a sidelong glare. "*They* should have told you."

The deputy assigned to her pushed her forward. "Come along."

She turned her glare on him instead. "And what am I in custody for?"

"Sheriff says you're an accomplice."

Like enough she didn't know what an accomplice was, but she tossed her hair back. "Your sheriff is criminal."

Still, she let him herd her away. She was limping again, whether from the storm or her bare feet or something she'd pulled during her aerobatics earlier in the evening.

Griff touched Hitch's elbow and guided him down the corridor. "This way."

Almost every cell was packed with the *Schturming* refugees who had been left behind when Zlo's men had broken him out.

Hitch let himself be guided. His mind churned in a nauseating blur of exhaustion and new adrenaline. He had a son. He was a father. Celia'd had a son. He and Celia had had a son together . . . and nobody'd ever told him.

He clamped his eyes shut as he walked. The past week scrolled through his head like a moving picture. Walter running through the cornfield as the Jenny zipped overhead. Walter peeking underneath the fuselage the day they met, when he'd wanted so bad to bum a ride. Walter playing with Taos. Walter holding that sign advertising rides. Walter sitting in Hitch's lap during his first flight, his hands clamped tight on the stick. Walter turning somersaults afterwards.

Of course the kid was his son. Whose else? He'd even thought how, if he'd had a son, one like Walter wouldn't have been too far off the mark.

And then there was Walter saying the first words he'd said in years—and saying them to *him*. And Hitch had sent him running like a whipped pup, as if Taos could have mattered more than him.

A groan tore up his chest.

Tonight, for the first time, he was a father.

No, scratch that, he'd been a father all along. For eight years. Tonight was maybe the first time in all those years he *wasn't* a father anymore.

If he'd been faster tonight—if he and Jael had gone for Walter first, instead of Aurelia—if he hadn't lost his temper with Walter after Zlo had taken Taos—if he hadn't come back home—if he hadn't left. All these useless ifs. At the end of every single one of them, Walter was still unaccounted for and probably dead.

He stopped short of his cell, yanked his elbow out of Griff's grip, and turned to the wall. He smashed his hand into it once, then again. His knuckle split open and streaked blood across the wall.

Griff grabbed at him. "Hitch. Hitch—stop it. This isn't doing anybody any good."

Hitch spun on him, fist still clenched. He nearly swung at Griff's head.

But what good would that do at this point? Another fight. One more for the history books. What good had any of those fights done? What had they proven? That he was right and his brother was wrong? What good would a fight do Walter now?

He dropped his fist and stepped backwards, into the open cell. He watched Griff the whole way. "Why didn't anybody tell me?"

Griff watched him right back, but his expression wasn't so certain anymore.

"You didn't think I had a right to know something like that?" Hitch said.

Griff reached for the cell door. His hand trembled. "You left. You left your family. You lost your rights when you did that."

"You think I wouldn't have come back if I knew?"

Griff's gaze charted Hitch's face. Slowly, he shook his head. "We thought it was best for the boy."

"That he never knew his father?"

"He thinks Byron's his father." He wouldn't look Hitch in the eye. "Are you really going to tell me you'd have come back, settled down, given him a home? You're telling me the life he would have had, getting dragged around the country, living hand to mouth would have been a better upbringing than what he's getting with Nan?"

Yes! The boy was his *son*.

But the words caught in his throat.

He *would* have come back, picked up his swaddled infant, and flown right back out. Griff was right about that.

So then what?

He'd spent the last nine years chasing freedom through the skies. A baby would have chained him down as sure as a farm. Walter was nobody's fool. He'd have figured that out. He would have realized a long time since that his father was no hero. Hitch Hitchcock was just a no-account wanderer. He had no roots, no responsibilities, no convictions.

Griff inhaled. "I'm not saying what we decided was right. I'm just saying . . ." He watched the floor.

Then he clanked the door shut. "What you said back there about Campbell being the one we should arrest . . . That true?" His mouth stayed hard, but something in his face was vulnerable, searching.

Hitch looked him in the eye. "What do you think?"

Griff opened his mouth, then closed it and nodded. "You're stuck here for now—probably until a hearing. But I'll see what I can do." He left. His footsteps thudded down the corridor.

Hitch backed up, one step after the other, until the low bunk hit his legs. He sank down on it. His hands bumped into the thin mattress beside his thighs, and he left them there, limp. He leaned back until his head hit the wall. Overhead, rain hammered against the ceiling. Shadows shifted in the corners.

Walter was out there somewhere, either up with Zlo or dead on the ground.

Please let it be Zlo. His throat cramped, and he closed his eyes. Never thought he'd pray for that. But please let it be.

Because, God help him, he didn't know what he'd do if it was otherwise.

He had a son, and hadn't something in him known it all along? He loved the kid already. He'd loved him from the first time he'd met him. Taos had known. Somehow the dog had seemed to see it all before Hitch had even gotten a clue.

If things had gone the way he—and Griff and Nan—had wanted them to, he'd be on his way out of the state right now. He'd have left without even knowing.

That wasn't even close to being all his fault. They'd had no right to keep this from him. They'd misjudged him every step of the way, never even tried to understand where he'd been coming from, what kind of wrath he'd been trying to stay clear of.

But they were right about one thing: he *had* been that close to leaving his family one more time. Dear God. Just like he'd done before. He'd given it all up without a second thought, because it was hard, because he was afraid, selfish, too downright blind stupid to see.

He raised his head and let it fall back against the wall. Pain splashed through his skull.

And now it was too late.

He thumped his head against the wall again—and again.

———————

Hitch must have slept, because after what seemed an ageless wandering through gray and frantic dreams, he woke up and peeled open his sticky eyelids. He was still hunched against the wall. Cramped muscles held his spine in a curve. He raised an arm, and pain jagged through his shoulders. He let the arm fall.

The rain still pounded on the roof; it had pounded all the way through his nightmares. A trickle of light spilled down the corridor and cast a man's shadow slantways across the cell's floor.

Hitch looked up and up, until he found the craggy face, shadowed under a fedora, a toothpick in the corner of the mouth.

Campbell. Come to twist the knife, no doubt.

Anger heated Hitch's stomach. He let the heat growl up into his throat. But he stayed slouched against the wall. No more games. Campbell always won those.

This wasn't a game anymore anyway. Somewhere along the line—maybe as long ago as the beginning—this had become a war.

Campbell pulled the toothpick from his mouth. He looked old, the lines around his eyes strained, as if he hadn't slept all night. But his jaw was granite.

"I reckon you know why you're here," he said.

"Because you let Zlo take *your* town right back from you. Can't hardly lock yourself up, can you?"

If possible, the set of Campbell's jaw got harder. "You'd best not climb on a high horse. There ain't a sheriff in this country'd say you're a model citizen."

"What do you call a model citizen?"

"A man who abides by the rules."

"You mean your rules."

"That's what I mean."

Hitch shoved himself away from the wall. Pain slashed through his cramped back, and he stifled a wince. "What do you want?"

Campbell tapped the toothpick against the crossbar. He rasped a whisper, even though few of the men in the surrounding cells spoke English. "I want you to know that if you finish telling your brother what you started to last night, it makes no matter to me."

"What?"

"Who do you think the judges around here are going to believe?" But a flicker in his eye said he wasn't as sure as all that. Maybe.

Hitch stood up from the bunk and took a couple steps toward the bars. "You don't really think I'm going to sit in here and take the rap?"

"I don't see that you have a choice." Campbell investigated the chewed tip of his toothpick. "But you could earn one."

"How's that?"

"I still got a job opening for an enterprising flyer. I'll get you out of jail. Give you back your wings."

"You don't say?" Hitch took another step toward the bars. Less than a foot separated him from Campbell. "From threats to bribes. Seems like maybe you haven't got this town as sewn up as you'd like me to think. If that's the case, I don't need your help to get out of here, do I?"

"Either you stay locked up in jail for the rest of your life—or you get one chance to go back out there." Campbell pointed down the corridor, toward the door. "Under the sky and in the wind, with your plane in one hand and your life in the other. Leave town, fly anywhere in this country. That's what you want. We both know it. Locked up here in a jail cell, sitting in one place every day for the rest of your life, that ain't your style."

Freedom. Sweat itched in Hitch's palms. He could be back in the air and out of this mess in the space of one word. That's what Campbell was offering.

No. That's what Campbell wanted him to *think* he was offering.

That road was a whole lot of familiar by this point. That road had led him here.

"You think I'd leave?" His throat tightened around the words. "Now that I know about Walter?"

"The boy's dead. It's a shame, but there it is."

"No." He rubbed his hands against his pants. "They haven't found him yet, and until they do, he's not dead and I'm not leaving."

Campbell narrowed his eyes. "You make the call to stay in here, and I guarantee you're going to stay for the rest of your sorry life."

Hitch let out another laugh, just to taunt him. It was about the only weapon he had right now. "If I get out of here, the first thing I'm going to do is find my son. The second thing I'm going to do—the second thing is to come back here and find you."

The crags of Campbell's face went rock hard. He lowered the toothpick. "Now, that'd be a mistake."

"I didn't do it a long time ago. That was the mistake."

Campbell's mouth worked. Finally, he drew in a deep breath and bellowed over his shoulder, "Milton, bring the keys!"

A young deputy hurried down the corridor.

Campbell stepped back. "Let him out."

Hitch frowned. "What?"

"They're burying your sister-in-law today—before the rain turns the ground too soft." Campbell glowered. "Reckon you ought to be there, see a little of your handiwork, don't you think? And maybe the citizens ought to see what I do to folks who don't play by the rules."

Aurelia. His stomach panged. He'd almost forgotten she was gone. All the words drained out of him.

Deputy Milton opened the door and cuffed his wrists.

At the door, Campbell stopped Hitch, one broad hand against his chest. "Enjoy your outing." His whisper sounded like gravel underfoot. "And you be thinking about all this. Else it'll be the last time you'll see the sky for a long, long while."

The wooden coffin bumped into the bottom of the grave with a splash audible even twenty feet back, where Hitch stood with his deputy guard.

Campbell had sent Jael out too, just for the spectacle of it, no doubt. She stood another twenty feet away from Hitch, still in her now-ragged party dress. She hunched her shoulders against the rain. Her bare feet moved restlessly in the mud, like it hurt her to stay still.

Rain poured down on them out of a sky thick with clouds. All the graveyards around here were built on high ground, since the water level was only three feet under in most places. But the way this rain was bucketing down, it wouldn't be long before even the hilltops were flooded.

Behind Hitch, motorcars packed the road, chugging out of the valley. Folks were leaving in droves. They were under siege for real now, and this time there was no one left to stop Zlo.

Overhead, a few patched-up planes flew low, staying beneath the overcast. They were headed out as fast as they could fly.

Yesterday, he would have been flying with them.

For all the good his staying was doing anyone now. His gut tightened, and he flexed his wrists against his manacles.

He had to get out of here. The only way to help Walter, or Jael—or anyone—was to get in a plane and fly. Finding Zlo again was a chance in a million, but the only way to win this was to somehow take the fight to *him*.

The preacher was saying words now—fast words probably, since every minute the grave was open was another pail of water on top of the coffin. Nan and her family stood around the hole, slickers belted over their black clothes. They bowed their heads and hung onto each other.

Nan kept glancing up at him. Probably, she wished she'd kept her mouth shut last night.

He looked around. One crooked row of headstones away from him, his father's name was visible on a granite stone: *Robert Hitchcock, 1864-1915*. Beside him would be Hitch's mother. *Elsie Griffith Hitchcock, 1869-1900*. Beside her: *Celia Smith Hitchcock, 1890-1912*.

Why folks wanted to come out and stand over their loved ones' graves and talk to them had never made any kind of sense. The spirits were long flown. The bodies were gone to corruption. Might as well speak into the stars, for all practicality's sake.

But standing here, with the rain dripping down the back of his coat collar and plastering his trousers around his knees, the urge hit him like a sledgehammer between the eyes.

He stared at his father's headstone—the one he hadn't been here to help plant.

This time he was going to see things made right—for them, for Walter and Jael, for Griff and Nan, for himself. They had his word on it. Somehow, God willing, he would find a way. Let Zlo flood the valley. Let Campbell lock him away. Let days and months and years pass. Didn't matter. Everything that had happened—everything that had been done—everything he had done—it did not end here today.

Movement caught the corner of his eye, and he turned back.

Nan walked through the mud, straight toward him. Her eyes were dark pits in her pale face. She'd clamped her mouth in a hard line, but tear tracks still scarletted her cheeks. Wet wisps of hair escaped the black kerchief tied under her chin. She stopped in front of him.

He braced himself. "Nan. I'm sorry. Aurelia didn't deserve this. I'm sorry for whatever part I played in her getting caught up in it last night. Her and"—he made himself hold her gaze—"Walter."

She pulled her mouth a little to the side and nodded. Then she looked at Deputy Milton. "Would you give me a few minutes' speech with my brother-in-law?"

Milton touched the brim of his hat. "I don't know about that, ma'am. Sheriff Campbell didn't think it was right to have him talking to—"

"My sister has just died. He's family. I *need* to talk to him. I know the sheriff wouldn't deny me that right now."

"Well . . . Of course, ma'am." Milton backed off about ten feet, out of hearing.

Nan glanced down the row of headstones, toward Celia's, then back at Hitch. "I . . . I don't think she even knew she was carrying Walter yet, when you left. She'd surely have told you, if only to try to get you to stay."

Nan was giving him an explanation, as easy as that? He'd half-expected to have to pry it out of her.

"Why didn't she write me afterwards?" he asked.

"I don't know. To punish you, I suppose. She took sick not long after Walter was born. She was gone before we even thought about death being a possibility." She stared at the ground. "Even I didn't take her serious. She was always complaining about something being wrong with her health. You know how she was."

Yeah, he knew. But his heart still twisted.

"After she was gone, you still weren't back." She took a deep breath and raised her head. "So Byron and I took in the boy. He was just a baby, so he never knew the difference. Even Molly was too young to really understand he wasn't her brother."

The flash of anger burned again. They'd had no right to rob Hitch of eight years of his son's life. Maybe, as things had turned out, *all* of his son's life.

She met his gaze, slowly. Tears welled. "I am sorry, Hitch."

"It's done now." He swallowed. Griff had been right. "It wasn't the right decision, but I can't say it was the wrong one either."

The corner of her mouth trembled. She bit her lip. "I—I judged you right harshly all these years. But it wasn't all your fault." Her eyes grew huge, luminous with more tears. The tears finally welled over, streaking down her cheeks. "It was mine too. You weren't here, but I *was*. I saw her every day, and I should have known. I should have known—when you had no way of knowing—that something was wrong, that she was dying."

He shifted in the mud. "That was not your fault. That wasn't truly anybody's fault. It was just something that happens."

"I tried to be a good mother to Walter, for her sake."

"You were a good mother."

She shook her head. "I wanted to love him like he was one of my own. But I looked at him, and I didn't see Celia." She closed her eyes. "I saw you." She opened them again. "That's why he doesn't talk, you know."

Ah, that. He'd wanted to know, of course. But before now, he'd never had a right to ask. He waited.

She stared down at where she'd clenched her hands together. "He hasn't talked since he was five. My twins—they were just

388 – K.M. WEILAND

babies then, just barely walking—and he'd taken them down to the creek. They fell in—Evvy nearly drowned." She looked up. "I was scared out of my mind, and I said things to him. Things I didn't mean. Things I really meant to say to you." Her mouth pulled down, her chin trembling harder than ever. "And he never talked again."

"Nan . . ."

"I've hated you all these years. Maybe it was so I wouldn't have to hate myself."

He stepped toward her and raised his manacled hands, wanting to comfort her somehow. "God knows we all make mistakes. But you did things for him I never could. That much is gospel truth, and we both know it."

She licked her lips, trying to keep back the tears. "You asked me to forgive you before. Well." For the first time since he'd come back, the look she gave him was an honest one, open all the way down to the bottom of her soul. "If there's any way you could go up there and find Walter, bring him back—" One more tear spilled over and mingled with the raindrops. "Then I *will* forgive you. And what's more, I will beg your forgiveness."

He reached out with his cuffed hands and snagged her fingers. "You get me free, and I'll find a way. I promise you."

Milton's footsteps started slogging toward them.

Time to go then.

He kept hold of her hand. "Tonight."

She nodded. "Tonight."

Milton reached them. "Sorry, ma'am. But I really do got to take him back now."

"I understand." She pulled her hand free. "Goodbye, Hitch."

"Goodbye, Nan." He watched her leave. His throat tightened, but for the first time since yesterday afternoon, he was able to draw a full, cold breath into his lungs.

Milton took his elbow and turned him toward the car.

Another batch of planes roared overhead. The sound reverberated in his chest, and the old longing stirred. He could still fly away. Tell Campbell *yes*, get out, and never come back. Once he was gone, Campbell'd never find him.

On the other hand, if he stayed, and especially if this escape tonight worked, Campbell would prosecute him to the full extent he was capable. Like enough, Hitch *would* spend the rest of his life in jail.

That's what logic said.

But when you came right down to it, he'd never lived much of his life by logic.

Chapter 44

THE COMMOTION IN the jailhouse erupted about nine o'clock.

Hitch stopped pacing his cell.

It was hard to hear past the din of the rain pounding on the roof. But that thud had sounded a whole lot like a body hitting the floor.

Something clanged. Another thud.

A whisper shrilled through the empty corridor: "Dagnabbit! Did you have to drop him right on my big toe?"

"Never mind that. Now, son, just you move along. We don't want no trouble."

Hitch dodged into the far corner of his cell, where he'd have the best angle of sight down the corridor.

Three men appeared through the far doorway. The two in back, clad in overalls and straw hats, wore red bandannas over their noses and hefted shotguns.

The Berringer brothers. Of course. Who else was Nan going to recruit?

Hitch almost grinned.

They prodded Griff along in front of them.

"Now, git on." J.W. poked at Griff with his shotgun barrel. It wasn't cocked. "You think a jailbreak's supposed to take all night?"

Griff held up both hands. The key ring dangled from one thumb. His teeth were clenched hard, but his expression was more forbearing than upset.

Matthew clamped a hand on Griff's shoulder and looked back at J.W. "Hush your mouth. You want to wake the whole blamed place?"

"*Me* wake the whole blamed place? What about you knocking them fellers out and letting them smack into the floor? If you'd given me some warning, I'd've caught 'em and nobody would've heard a thing."

"What did you think I was going to do? Stand there and wait until they turned around and recognized us in these silly disguises?"

"These disguises are a common-sense precaution, and you know it."

"They're silly. Ain't going to fool nobody." Matthew rattled Griff's shoulder. "Fool you, son?"

Griff cleared his throat. "That . . . might depend on who's asking."

"See?"

J.W. snorted. "What's silly is this whole idea of a truce between you and me. I'd be in and out and have this job finished all by myself by now."

"Surely." Matthew didn't sound sure. He looked at Griff. "Now where's your brother?"

Hitch kept his mouth shut. Matthew and J.W. were already making so much noise, it was a miracle nobody had heard what was going on. The *Schturming* refugees in the other cells just stared slack-jawed and muttered amongst themselves.

Griff led the Berringers to Hitch's cell and looked Hitch straight in the eye as he stuck the key in the lock.

Hitch gave him a nod. No doubt Griff had his own reasons for letting him out. Whatever they were, the results were a heap better than all the fighting and stonewalling they'd been doing ever since he'd got back.

Hitch looked at Matthew. "Thought you'd never get here."

J.W. crooked his elbow around his shotgun. "Can't hardly do a jailbreak in broad daylight."

"Hush," Matthew said. "Now, Hitch Hitchcock, you stop your wisecracking and listen to me. This whole thing's rash, and I hope you know it. But it's the only chance most of us got—including you. So if you're brave enough to take that contraption of yours up tonight, God bless you. Your mechanic's got it fueled and ready for takeoff, right outside of town. He's been keeping it dry under tarps all this time."

Griff opened the door.

Hitch grabbed his leather jacket off the bunk and stepped into the corridor. "What about Jael?"

"Hmm." J.W. scratched his nose above his bandanna. "Where do they keep lady prisoners anyway?"

Griff headed down the corridor without needing even a single prod from Matthew. "This way."

The cell Griff led them to was empty and dark.

Griff frowned. "She's supposed to be here." He unlocked the latch and stepped inside the cell.

"This a trick?" Matthew said.

The words were barely out of his mouth when something streaked down from the corner and hit Griff in the head. He toppled forward onto his knees.

Hitch lunged to catch him. "What—?"

With a grunt, Jael fell out of the ceiling. She landed in a crouch, next to the short log she must have somehow snagged and smuggled in under her skirt when they'd been at the graveyard that afternoon.

Hitch caught her bare arm. "What do you think you're doing?" He looked from her to the ceiling. "How'd you get up there?"

She scrunched her face in a wince and straightened up. "I climbed."

"And wedged yourself up there?" The girl was a consarned monkey.

Matthew pushed past Hitch to help a bleary Griff back to his knees. "What'd you hit this poor boy for?"

"Don't you know a rescue when you see one?" J.W. said.

"This is rescue?" She looked at Hitch, then down at Griff. "Oh." Then, sympathetically: "*Oh.*" She knelt and gently patted Griff's cheeks.

Hitch scrubbed his hand through his hair. "How come I didn't get all this nursing whenever you hit *me*?"

"*You* were not rescuing."

"Yes, I was . . . some of the times."

She slanted him a glance that looked downright reproachful.

"Yeah, well, anyway. I'm about to beat it. Breaking jail's a crime in itself, so if Campbell catches up to me, it'll mean about twice as much trouble as before. You can come on out if you want, and the Berringers or somebody will take care of you." He glanced at Matthew for a nod of confirmation. "But you just might be better off staying here. It's your choice."

She stood and faced him. "You are going after *Schturming*. In this weather?"

"Yes, to find Walter and stop Zlo."

"I will go with you."

"*No.*" The word came out fast. He took a breath and slowed himself down. "I don't want you up there tonight. Flying in weather like this is . . . well, it ain't recommended. I could crash as easy as not, and that'd be the end of it."

"You will never be finding *Schturming* without me. Now that Zlo has changed the *dawsedometer* to on again, I can feel where it is. You cannot."

"Jael—" How to say this? And in front of Griff and the Berringers too.

He'd been a fool last night, for a lot of reasons. One of those reasons was how close he'd come to walking away from her.

But now everything was different. He was either going to die tonight or end up in prison for an awful long time. Whatever chance he had of making things the way he wanted them to be with her was long gone.

He *needed* her to be safe. But he needed to find Walter too. She was right about his chances of locating the dirigible without her. But . . . He shivered. What if it got her killed too?

He reached to hold her shoulders at arm's length. "I don't want you to do this."

She raised both eyebrows. Her eyes were deep and steady. "But you have need of me to. So do not be wasting your time telling me this."

His heart flip-flopped—partly because she'd said yes and partly because . . . she'd said yes. God help them.

"Thank you." His voice sounded hoarse.

She reached for his hand and took a limping step. "Let us go."

He paused to help Griff up. "I don't know if you did this 'cause the Berringers strong-armed you or—"

Groggily, Griff looked him in the eye. "Good luck, Hitch."

It wasn't precisely a reconciliation, but it was enough for tonight.

"Hustle yourself," Matthew said.

Hitch gave his brother a nod, then pulled away.

They made it all the way down to the ground floor and started looking for the exit. Then they turned the wrong corner—and ran straight into Campbell coming out of his office.

The sheriff stopped shuffling papers and gaped. "What—"

So much for the clean getaway.

Hitch wheeled around, hauling Jael with him.

"This way!" J.W. hollered from the far end of the hall.

Ahead, double doors glinted.

Behind, Campbell started shouting orders. His heavy footsteps pounded the hallway.

Hitch kept running.

Beside him, Jael grunted pain with every stride.

He circled her waist with his arm and half-dragged her after him.

"Stop!" Campbell shouted. "You stop where you stand, or I'll put you all in the ground!"

He probably would too.

"Sheriff!" That was Griff's voice.

Just shy of the door, Hitch skidded to a stop, and looked over his shoulder.

Campbell had stopped too. He stood only about twenty feet off, his revolver in his hand.

Up the hallway behind him, Griff ran after them. He held out a placating hand. "Just wait. They need to go. This is our only chance—"

"You're part of this, Deputy?" Campbell swung around and smashed his big fist square into Griff's nose.

Griff staggered back and crashed into the wall. He exhaled hard. Blood spluttered from his face.

"No!" Hitch started back.

Jael snagged his sleeve. "We have to be going! Griff wants us to go!"

Campbell filled his hand with Griff's shirtfront and glared down the hallway at Hitch. "You stay, you hear me? Or your brother gets everything in your place. You want to live with that on your conscience for the rest of your life?"

Hitch tugged free of Jael's grip.

Griff shook his head. He left his arms hanging slack at his sides, not fighting. More blood drenched his face, already flooding his shirt. But his blue eyes stared straight into Hitch's.

Frustration welled up in Hitch's belly. It roared up out of his mouth.

Leave, and who knew what'd happen to his brother? Stay, and he'd lose his son for sure. It was the devil's own choice, but there was only one answer at this point. Griff knew it. Hitch knew it.

Still roaring, he turned and ran out through the door after Jael.

In the street, J.W. pumped the crank on the front of his jalopy. The engine rattled and coughed to life, and he ran around to the passenger side to throw open the doors. They all piled inside.

A gunshot cracked through the night.

Hitch shoved Jael's head down and ducked himself. In the driver's seat, Matthew hit the gas, and the jalopy careened away. Another shot exploded and pinged against a back fender.

Hitch looked up.

Silhouetted in the courthouse's columned doorway, Campbell cracked off his revolver. The muzzle flashed yellow through the rain, but the shot must have gone wide. He shot again—and again—until the jalopy lurched around the corner.

"This ain't good," Hitch said through clenched teeth. He let up on the back of Jael's head, so she could straighten. "Griff shouldn't have helped with this. We should have grabbed another deputy."

Matthew hunched over the wheel, peering through his spectacles. The roof was up, and the wavering headlights lit the road only dimly. "He wanted to be a part of it. That was his call."

Hitch flopped back against the hard seat. *All right, little brother.* But this time, God help him, he *was* coming back. He had to take on Zlo if only so he'd live long enough to come back and beat Campbell into a pulp.

"Here." J.W. passed a bundle back over the seat to Jael. "Clothes. We done the best we could. Britches, boots, and a coat."

"Those are just the correct things." She slumped down on

the seat. "Now, I will have all of you look at road."

They all turned studiously forward.

That didn't keep Hitch's ears from hearing her grunts—and something that came right close to being a whimper—as she wriggled into the breeches.

He dared a glance over and found her buttoning the pants underneath the skirt of her party dress. "You sure you're okay?"

In the dark, her face was only a pale blur. "It is hurting. Worse than before. But that is good, yes? Means I will find *Schturming* for you."

Maybe. If she didn't pass out first. If she was hurting this bad now, it was only going to get worse the closer they got to *Schturming*. He reached for her hand and squeezed it.

She squeezed back.

"All right, you two." J.W. hauled another bundle off the floorboards and into his lap. This one clattered. "Now for the good stuff. Can't have you going into enemy territory unarmed and defenseless." He looked in Jael's direction. "Know anything about using a gun, missy?"

"Only Enforcement *Brigada* are allowed."

He grunted. "Well, then. Maybe a knife for you. I know you can handle that just fine."

She took the knife and leaned forward to slit the dress's skirt from hem to hips. She cut it all the way around her waist, until all that was left was the top part, like a shirt. Then she shrugged into the leather jacket J.W. had given her.

Matthew stomped on the brakes. "Here we are then."

Rain plinked against the little rear window behind Hitch.

Ahead, in the faint glare of the headlights, the Jenny's red skin glinted through a crack in the tarp that covered it. Earl stepped around in front and waved his good arm. He and the Berringers had parked the plane right in the middle of an abandoned road. It'd give Hitch a straight takeoff into the wind—which was about the best that could be hoped for at the moment.

J.W. handed Hitch a pistol. "You always favored a .45, as I remember."

Hitch pocketed it in his jacket. "That'll do."

Here they went, then. This was for real. A tremble of adrenaline passed through him.

He looked over at Jael. "You ready for this?"

"Yes." The sharp little exhale before the word said she was nervous. The soft, firm way she spoke the word itself said she *was* ready.

"Then let's go." He popped the door and pushed it open.

Matthew leaned back over the seat. "Hitch."

"Yeah?"

"I want you to remember something." He looked at Hitch over the top of his specs. "I know you're doing this 'cause of your boy—and that's fine. But this ain't only about him. You got yourself a whole valley of farmers that are going to be in pretty bad shape if you can't do nothing to help them."

Hitch made his tight throat swallow and his stiff neck nod. "I know it. I'll do my best."

"You'll have lots of folks saying their prayers for you."

"Wish they'd started that about fifteen years earlier."

Matthew let out a small grin. "Maybe they did." He cocked his head toward the plane. "Now get on."

"Right." Hitch slammed the door after him and ran to the plane.

Jael was already bundled up in the front cockpit. Her white face peered out at him.

J.W. stood ready at the propeller.

Earl met Hitch halfway and handed over his helmet. "You ready for this?"

"No."

"Did tonight really have to be the first time in your life you admit that?"

Hitch pulled his helmet over his ears and buckled the strap snug under his chin. He looked into the black swirl of the night sky. "First time for everything, right?"

CHAPTER 45

THE WIND TOSSED the Jenny around like she was a handful of dice in an all-in craps game. Which she was, actually. Hitch braced his hands against the heaving stick. His fingers had gone numb after the first fifteen minutes. He was only hanging on now because his fingers were too cold to unfurl.

Rain, hard as gravel, peppered him from all directions. The wind snarled and cursed in his ears, drowning out even the roar of the engine. The only thing letting him know the Hisso was still running was the thrum rattling up through the stick and the seat of his pants. That was pretty numb too, come to think of it.

The Jenny was trying her heart out, no question. But she couldn't take much more of this, even if he could keep his fingers curled around the stick. Sooner or later, the turbulence would break the airplane—or he'd just plumb lose track of which dark blot was the sky and which was the ground.

Every now and then, Jael would raise her arm and wave the white scarf Earl had given her. She'd motion him one way or the other. But everywhere they turned, darkness surrounded them. Felt a whole lot like flying in big goldurn circles.

His heart beat so fast it was one great lump of pressure in his throat. *C'mon, c'mon*, he prayed. This couldn't all have been for nothing. When a man made up his mind to risk his life in a one-chance-in-a-million venture, he was resigned to dying. But seemed like he was at least owed *one* chance.

Up ahead, Jael's scarf flashed, a tiny blur of not-quite-black in the darkness.

Which way this time? He leaned forward and squinted.

The Jenny rocked, but not from the wind. Jael must be wiggling around.

He fought the stick. "Hold still, durn it."

More wiggling. The scarf flashed again, followed by three more pinpoints of pale—her face and her waving hands.

Oh, for crying out loud . . . Was she really standing up again, in the middle of *this*?

She waved wildly. The faintest buzz of her screamed words wafted back to him.

"*What?*" he shouted.

And then he saw it too: a flash of light, almost like a star. Except there were no stars tonight. Just the infernal darkness of this hammering wind.

Schturming. It had to be. Nothing else would have a light.

He eased back on the stick and lifted the Jenny's nose. "Come on, sweetheart. Just do this one last thing for me."

She did it, and she didn't even so much as balk. With a mighty roar of that blessed Hispano-Suiza, she lifted her snub nose into the storm and chewed right on through the wind. She might be a saucy little tramp most of the time. But tonight she was a warrioress, a Valkyrie.

The light flickered. For an instant, he half thought both he and Jael had only imagined it.

Then it shone out once more, hard and dazzling. It grew brighter and bigger. And then—the great bulk of *Schturming*'s white envelope loomed from out of the clouds.

He squeezed the stick until red-hot pinpricks pierced the cold in his finger bones. He nudged the Jenny down, below the envelope, toward the cargo bay in the bow end.

Just please let the doors be open.

He'd landed there once before. He could do it again. The glimpse he'd gotten inside the ship had showed a long corridor that seemed to stretch all the way through the entirety of the bottom level. It was wide enough—barely—for the Jenny, and it just might be long enough to get her stopped without crashing back out through the other end.

More light—a great square hole of it—flashed, not so bright as the smaller one. He almost forgot to breathe.

The doors were open. And . . . full of men. White faces turned up in their direction. Half a dozen lined the opening, watching the storm, no doubt.

So be it. Beggars couldn't be choosers. He lined the Jenny up with the doors and killed the engine. Too much momentum and he wouldn't be able to hold her steady enough to thread the needle down the length of the bay.

The men in the doorway scattered.

Just as well, since hitting them would have ripped up the wings and the landing gear good and plenty.

The wind clobbered the plane from above, and she plunged straight down, losing altitude. Without the thrust to keep her speed up, she would pitch into a dive any second now.

Just a few more feet. That's all they needed. "C'mon!"

Her windmilling propeller entered the bay, and for four long seconds, she floated inside the dirigible. Along the ship's walls, its supplies—boxes, barrels, crates—protruded from the fastenings that kept them from rolling about in the wind and the turbulence. The Jenny's wingtips had no more than two feet of clearance on either side.

The wheels bumped the floor, and her tail started to sag. Her wheels bounced up, then came back down to skid. A few inches, just a few inches more—and then, *bwack!* The tail thumped down.

He dared a look over his shoulder.

The howling black hole of the storm engulfed his vision, only fifty or sixty feet back. By the time he looked back around, the rest of his body was already telling him the Jenny had come to a complete stop. A bare thirty feet separated the propeller from the dividing wall in front of them.

All the air left his body in a great whoosh. A wing and a prayer. That's what that had been. Literally.

Adrenaline and cold shook through his hands, but he made himself yank his safety belt loose and find the revolver in his pocket. Zlo's men had all either fled for their lives or thrown themselves face down on the floor. Judging from the blood on one's face and the way his mouth was hanging open, he'd clunked his head on something.

The others started looking up and shouting.

"*Oni ƶdes!*"

Somebody ran to a speaking tube on the back wall and started hollering into it. "*Eto* pilot!"

This was where he and Jael advanced from dying in the storm to dying at the hands of indignant pirates. Great.

Hitch stood in the cockpit, braced the revolver in both hands, and cracked off two shots.

The baddies hit the deck again.

"Jael!" he shouted. "Can you move?"

She wallowed around in the front cockpit. This close to the *dawsedometer*, her pain level had to be near crippling.

He took another shot and maybe winged a guy, judging from the pained cry. He swung out of his cockpit on the far side of the plane and reached for Jael with both hands. "C'mon!"

Her pinched face appeared over the edge, and she let him half-drag, half-swing her over. She landed hard on her knees, and barely managed to claw herself to her feet, using the fuselage on one side and his hand on the other.

Keeping the Jenny between them and Zlo's men, he backed toward the engine room door in the far corner. "We'll shut the *dawsedometer* off. It's just around the corner. It'll be all right."

She managed a nod and staggered after him.

Except it wasn't all right.

The door to the engine room swung open, and half a dozen men burst out, all of them packing Webley revolvers. One look at the plane in their cargo bay and their eyes got big and their mouths fell open.

Hitch faced them and fired another shot.

The bullet caught one of the men in the side, and he spun around in a spray of blood. The others started shooting back. Fortunately, none of them were very good at it. Bullets splatted and zinged against the ceiling and the walls. A rope holding a wooden crate near the ceiling snapped and spilled its load of potatoes all over the floor.

Jael tugged his hand, pulling him in the opposite direction. "This way!"

They ran to the back of the plane. Lashed by wind from the gaping bay doors, he vaulted over the fuselage behind the rear cockpit. He popped a warning shot at the thugs in the corner, then reached back to haul Jael after him.

She landed in a heap on the floor but started crawling even before he pulled her back to her feet.

She crashed into a door in the wall, fumbled with the latch a second, then shoved it open. "Hurry!"

The men rushed across the room, all of them shouting.

Hitch backed through the doorway and blasted off his last shot. Then he grabbed for the edge of the door and hurled it shut. "Please tell me this thing's got a lock?"

She struggled to lift a wooden crossbar. "Here!"

Footsteps pounded outside the door. The men roared garbled words. Several shots smacked into the heavy wood, then the doorknob started to turn.

Hitch grabbed the crossbar and slammed it into place. The door opened just enough to bang into the bar before his own momentum knocked it shut again.

Panting, he surveyed the crossbar, then turned back to Jael. "Now where?"

She headed down the corridor, pulling herself along with one hand on the wall. Lamps, fixed at intervals in brackets near the ceiling, offered a dim, flickering light. The place smelled of ozone, mixed with dust and grease and some kind of spicy incense.

He jogged after her, reloading out of his pocket as he went. "You all right?"

"I will be." The way she gasped her words didn't offer much conviction. "As soon as we turn off *dawsedometer*."

Which, at the moment, they were running away from.

He clenched his teeth. "Right."

Halfway down the corridor, she reeled to a stop and raised her head.

He clicked the revolver's cylinder back into place and looked around. "What?"

"I hear . . ." She drew in a sharp breath. "They're coming. Through other door!" She pointed to the far end of the corridor.

"Oh, great." They would be like tin ducks in a shooting gallery. He looked around. "Get behind me." He'd have to get on his knees, try to pick off Zlo's men as they came through the door. At least there'd be a bottleneck.

She caught his hand and pulled him forward. "No, wait! We can get out here!" She slid her hand against the wall, and suddenly there was no wall. Just that same howling darkness. "It is observatory deck!" She ducked outside.

He followed before he had time to think about it. They banged the door shut, just as the other door burst open.

Darkness engulfed his vision. Icy wind shrilled all around him. He leaned back and bumped into a waist-high iron railing. "Now what?"

Her teeth chattered. "Wa-a-a-it?"

"Yeah, until they realize where we are—and then we're really stuck." He looked around. "I don't suppose there's any other way out of here?"

Through the storm, something whispered.

He cocked his head and concentrated. There it was again. "Do you hear that? It sounds like . . ."

Her hand slapped out through the darkness and caught his sleeve. "Dog! It is dog!"

"What?"

"Maybe it is Taos!" She jerked his arm. "Look!"

He looked up.

About ten feet overhead, a light shone against the darkness.

Their guiding star. It had to be.

The light blinked out for a second, and then something hit him in the face. He slammed back into the railing once more. The thing hit him again, soft and tickly and snake-like.

He reached for it. "A rope."

"It is Walter!"

He jerked another look up.

The silhouette of a small, dark head gleamed against the backdrop of the light. Then a dog's head appeared beside it—a dog with one floppy ear.

A wave of dizziness washed over him. "Walter. Are you hurt?"

The boy shook his head.

In the corridor, footsteps stomped.

Wouldn't take more than a minute for those mugs to check this door.

"Okay." He tried to make his brain work again. He tied the

rope around Jael's waist. "I'll climb up, then pull you up after me."

"Yes," she said.

"Please tell me you think you can hang on."

She didn't respond.

"Where's your scarf?" He found it in her pocket and looped it under her arms, then used it to tie the rope snugly against her chest. "That'll help, but you've got to hang on, you hear me?"

"I am hearing you."

"Good."

He took hold of the rope, climbed atop the railing, and started over-handing himself up the thing. The wind tore at him, and his numb fingers burned like match-struck gasoline all the way up.

He'd tell himself not to look down, but there was nothing to see down there anyway. It was not *thinking* about what was down there that was the trick. His dislike of heights swarmed him, rolling his stomach over and over. Funny that it would bother him out here, but not in a plane. Pretend he was in a plane, that's all he had to do. He gritted his teeth. Easy as pie.

Finally, he reached the light, framed in a porthole. Walter caught his elbow and helped him over the top. The room was tiny, a storage closet from the looks of the tarp-covered boxes and bits of machinery stacked all around. A lantern sat near the windowsill.

Somehow he couldn't quite make himself look at the boy. Like if he looked too hard, it'd all turn out to be a dream.

"We've got to pull Jael up," he managed.

Together, they hauled her up and over.

She landed on the floor with a thump and lay there for a second, gasping.

Then she looked up at Walter, and a grin broke through the pain on her face. "Walter." She pried her fingers from the rope and, still lying on her side, held out an arm for him. "You are in safety. I am so happy you are in safety."

Walter dropped to his knees and folded himself into her arm. With both hands, he helped her sit up, and the two of them clung to each other for a second. He snuck a look, out of the corner of his eye, at Hitch.

Hitch stood back. His hands seemed to be entirely in the

way. They didn't want to hang at his sides, fit in his pockets, or wedge under his elbows. His jaw cramped, and his tongue stuck to the roof of his mouth.

He needed to say something. Anything. Tell the boy he'd never been gladder to see anyone in his entire life. Tell him he was sorry. Tell him he was never going to let him out of his sight again.

His heart pounded, and the words all crammed in his throat, too big to get out.

Taos frisked around his feet and let out an excited little yip.

Hitch dropped to a crouch and pulled the dog up, so Taos's front paws rested against his knee. He fondled his dog's ears and watched his son.

Jael opened her eyes and looked, first at Hitch, then at Walter. She sat back and pushed Walter away. With a little nod, she directed his attention to Hitch.

Walter turned, slowly. He still wore his party suit: a dark blue jacket and shorts and a string tie. Both socks were ripped, and his dark mop of hair fell in his eyes. He tucked his chin and peered up at Hitch, like he still wasn't quite sure what to expect.

Hitch cleared his throat. "I'm real glad you're all right. You saved us just now, you know."

Walter scuffed his toe, then shot a glance at Taos.

Still about the dog then. Hitch's heart just about split clean in two.

He dropped to his knees and pulled Walter to him. "He's just a dog. He doesn't matter a lick compared to you. You hear me?"

Two skinny little arms wriggled up around his neck.

"I'm sorry." He tightened his hold around this boy—this incredible, brave, loyal, determined little boy who was his own flesh and his own bone. His son. He wanted to press him right into himself, until they were bonded, until Walter could never leave him again.

He could barely get the words past his cramped throat. "Do you hear me? What I said was wrong, and I didn't mean it. Taos getting caught wasn't your fault. You're a hero, Walter. You found *Schturming*. We'd never have captured it without you." He eased back a little, so he could see the boy's face.

Tears streaked Walter's cheeks, but his chin was firm. He nodded.

Hitch opened his mouth to tell him the truth, all of it: you're my son, I love you, I'll be the father you need me to be, I promise.

But now wasn't the time. The first thing they had to do was escape. If they lived to touch ground again, then he'd tell him.

"It's going to be all right," he said. "I'm going to get you out of here, and it's going to be okay. You got that?"

Walter nodded. Then he swallowed, and the corner of his mouth tilted up.

Hitch looked over the top of Walter's head.

Propped up on one hand, Jael stared back at him. Her eyes shone in the flickering lamplight. She smiled and gave him a nod.

She knew what he'd just promised, even if Walter didn't yet.

"All right, then." Hitch breathed deep. "Let's bring this bird down and go home."

CHAPTER 46

ITH A PICKAX from the supply closet in one hand and a limping Jael hooked in the crook of the other arm, Hitch elbowed through a final door into a dim room. Two clusters of brass pipes ran through the center of the room, entering through one wall and passing right out through the other. One cluster hung a foot from the ceiling; the other was mounted a foot off the floor.

In his experience, the best plans were the simplest ones. And this one was about as simple as it got:

Sneak over to the maintenance room.

Smash the mainline pipes that, according to Jael, powered the thing.

Sneak back to the plane and get three people and a dog on board.

Fly away.

Watch said airship crash in a big ball of flames.

He looked down at Jael. "Is this it?"

Maybe he'd even be so big a hero the grateful townsfolk wouldn't let Campbell get at him.

She eased herself away from him and lurched a few steps toward a valve on the top pipes. "Yes. Top one takes gas to *aerostat.*" She pointed up, toward the envelope. "Turn it off, then knock away valve, so they cannot change it back if they find it."

He hefted the pickax first. "And the bottom one is for carrying steam for the engines?" That one he'd just plain smash. He glanced back to where Walter and Taos stood in the doorway. "You stay out there and keep watch. I don't want you in here if something goes wrong." He glanced at Jael. "You too."

She wobbled into the corner by the door and nodded.

One swing of the pickax was all it took. Its point bit into the soft metal, and the steam erupted in a fountain of white. He dodged back so only hot drops of water flicked against his face.

He glanced at Jael. "Reckon they heard that?"

Behind him, Taos yipped.

"Hitch!" Walter yelled.

Footsteps ran down the corridor.

Jael met Hitch's gaze. The gray of her eyes turned to flint. "They have heard."

He lunged across the room to the valve on the gas pipes. He twisted it—one turn, two, three, tight. Then he hooked the tip of the pick into the circular handle and torqued it up. The valve stuck fast. He leaned into it, using the pick as leverage.

It wasn't going to give. They were sunk. The engines might quit, but *Schturming*'d still be all safe and cozy above the clouds.

In the corridor, Zlo shouted at his men. Another second, and they'd all be in this room.

And then—*pop*. The valve's handle snapped off. He staggered forward and nearly hit his head against the pipes. Instinctively, he darted out his free hand and caught the handle before it could clang against the floor.

Taos started barking his head off.

"Hitch!" Walter shouted, then yelped.

Hitch juggled the handle for a second, then pulled it in and passed it to Jael.

With a nod, she eased it down to the floor and toed it into the corner.

He turned, pickax raised, just in time for three men to tackle him.

They threw him to the ground, hard enough to rattle stars through his head. Almost before he could blink his vision clear, they flipped him onto his stomach, found the revolver in his pocket, and bound his hands behind his back.

Booted feet stomped into his view. "*Derzhite ego.*"

Zlo.

The men wrenched Hitch to his feet.

Jael and Walter were already in the corridor, their hands tied behind their backs. Walter stared, agonized, as Taos got his muzzle tied with a strip of cloth.

Jael had to lean one shoulder against the wall to stay upright, but her face was going red in spots, like it did when she was spitting mad.

Zlo grabbed Hitch's chin and forced his gaze away from Walter and Jael. "You should be looking at me, flying man." He had shed his hat and coat and wore a leather vest over a faded striped shirt. His hair was buzzed as short as his beard, the same brown-blond color.

He flashed his silver teeth in a grin, but his eyes were dark. Dangerous. "So you come onto my ship"—he extended his free hand to gesture about; in it, he held a fat-bladed knife—"and think you are winning. You are not winning." His grin faded, and that look in his eyes glared harder. "Now you are trussed like pig. And maybe like pig I will gut you."

Hitch snorted. "*Your* ship here went undetected for sixty years until *you* took control. You already got yourself caught once. And guess what?" He clucked. "You're charting a straight course in that direction again."

"You, I think, would live longer with no tongue." Zlo balanced the knife in his palm. "I will tell you, I am impressed you have flown into my ship. But I will tell you something else." He leaned closer, as if imparting a secret. He tapped the point of the knife to the underside of Hitch's chin. "Although you are unexpected prize, I have no use for you. Except maybe to send messages to your people below."

Okay, not good. Hitch did himself a favor and kept his mouth shut.

Zlo removed the point of the blade from Hitch's chin. "I will skin you like rats and throw you back to your friends." This time, he touched the knife to the meat of Hitch's shoulder. He looked straight at Hitch. What he was going to do was plenty clear before he even started.

Hitch braced and stared right back.

The blade sunk into his skin. Pain razored all the way down to his fingertips, sharp at first, and then just as deep. Warm blood welled up against his jacket sleeve.

410 – K.M. WEILAND

The pain gathered in his throat, stopped up his lungs. But he forced it back down, right to the hot center in his stomach. He kept his gaze on Zlo's.

The man curled his lip. He left the tip of the blade in Hitch's arm. "I see. You are very brave man? *You* feel no pain, is that it?" He looked over his shoulder into the corridor, then stalked across the room to where Taos lay hogtied. Zlo kicked the dog in the soft of his belly.

Taos's eyes whitened around the edges. He thrashed and cried past his gag.

Hitch lunged at Zlo.

One of the men holding Hitch turned the knife in his arm.

Pain ripped through him again, and this time he couldn't stop the yell.

Jael yanked away from her captor. "Stop it! *Ti zlode!*" She only got one step before her knee gave out under her. She twisted and caught her shoulder against the wall, then came back up glaring.

Zlo surveyed her. "Well, and what has happened to you?"

She jutted her chin.

He approached and grabbed her elbow. "You walk like old woman." He levered her hands up. Tied together behind her back like they were, they bent at a sharp angle that would have hurt even somebody with healthy joints.

She gasped and tried to wrench free.

Zlo pushed harder. He thrust his face into hers. "This is what you get, worthless *nikto*. You betray me? You choose Groundsmen over people of your own blood?"

"You wanted to bring me to death!"

"You have brought your friends to *their* deaths. I will let you watch maybe, before it is your turn." He pulled her arm up farther, then bent her fingers back.

A cry gurgled in her throat. She arched her back, teeth clenched.

With a scream, Walter twisted away from his captor. He hurled himself at Zlo's legs and landed two hard kicks.

Zlo shoved him back and someone caught him from behind.

Again, Walter twisted loose and dropped to his knees. He closed his teeth in Zlo's calf, so hard the click was audible across the room.

With a bellow, Zlo kicked him away. "*Parazit!*" He lurched at Hitch, ripped the knife free, and turned back to Walter.

The hot center in Hitch's belly exploded. Everything around him went red hot. Blood rushed in his ears. The hole in his arm seemed to ignite in a gout of pain. All of it funneled into strength.

With a roar, he jerked free of his captors. He hurled himself at Zlo and managed to hook his good shoulder in the small of Zlo's back, right where his kidneys should be.

Zlo's back arched, his head flinging back. He hit his knees and practically bounced. His head came back up, and Hitch brought his own down hard. He cracked his forehead against the back of Zlo's skull. More pain shattered through him, starting in his head and radiating down through his limbs. Blackness and stars swam in his vision.

But if Zlo was still conscious, Hitch would hit him again, so help him. He reared his head back for another go. He'd beat the evil swine's brains to a bloody mush, even if he had to beat his own out right along.

Hands scrabbled at his back and his arms. They hauled him to his feet, and his arm sockets screamed in protest. A few hard blinks cleared his vision.

Zlo had managed to prop himself on his hands and knees, but his head hung down and he swayed.

Hitch braced against his captors and jumped off the floorboards with both feet. His booted heels caught Zlo in the hip and spun him halfway around. The mugs hanging onto Hitch lost their grip for a second, and Hitch gained a few forward inches. Enough to land another kick square on Zlo's nose.

The man sprawled again.

Somebody jabbed fingers in Hitch's shoulder wound.

The whole room spun, and every thought in his head got smashed flat under the weight of pain.

When finally it let up, Zlo was dragging himself to his feet. He glared at Hitch, eyes huge and unblinking. He backhanded a wash of blood from under his nose and clenched his knife in the other hand. If ever anybody'd had homicide in his eyes, he did right now.

It was a look Hitch had seen a few times before, in barroom

brawls gone bad. But this was the first time he'd ever seen it while tied up and stabbed, with no Earl in sight to watch his back.

He kept his feet under him, fighting the restraining arms that held him.

Zlo reeled closer. He spat blood to the side. "Now, I *will* take out your guts."

"No!" Walter screamed.

Jael fought against the men who held her. "Zlo! Do not do this. You cannot do this! You said fault was mine. So kill me—kill me and let them go! They are no part of this!"

He kept coming.

Hitch looked him in the eye. "C'mon, then."

Beneath their feet, the floor heaved. The whole ship jerked like a tail-shot Jenny. It listed hard to port and bounced in the turbulence. In the corridor, everyone smacked into the far wall. Hitch pitched forward, and his guards clawed at his sleeves to keep their grip.

From far back in the ship, the propellers whined—and then *silence.*

It . . . worked? He had to forcibly tighten every muscle in his neck to keep from looking back at the busted pipes. In the excitement, Zlo and his pals hadn't noticed them. And now, with any luck, the damage would be good and done.

Zlo shoved back to his feet and hollered at his men. His gaze snagged on Hitch and he hesitated. He tightened his fist on the knife.

Then *Schturming's* tail end slewed again.

Zlo bared his teeth and waved the prisoners away. "And you," he said to Hitch, "you will get my blade, every bit of it, later."

At this point, later was almost as good as never. Hitch let a long breath fizz past his teeth. He looked at Jael.

She closed her eyes in relief and gave him a little nod.

They were bundled down the hall into what might be a navigation room, judging from the charts spread all over the high table in the center and the scrolls sticking out of racks along the walls.

Their guard—a fidgety kid in a striped coat—latched the

door from the inside and posted himself in front of it. He swallowed twice, then pointed at the floor. "You will sit to ground, all of you." He studiously avoided eye contact with Jael.

Wind whistled against the porthole in the far wall. The floor slanted prow-ward now, and the ship bucked in the gale like a fresh-broke colt.

Walter scootched down against the wall beside Hitch. He cradled Taos's head in his lap.

"Are we going to crash?" he whispered.

That was a mighty good question. "Of course not." Hitch exchanged a look with Jael on his other side.

She shook her head.

This was *not* how the plan was supposed to go. Of the two present options—get gutted by Zlo or crash in a fireball—neither was too appealing. He glanced sidelong at Walter. This was supposed to have been a rescue. At the moment, it looked a whole lot more like Custer's last stand.

Walter stared up at him.

Hitch forced a tiny grin. "It's going to be okay."

The boy snuggled into the crook of his arm.

Without looking at Jael, Hitch crawled his hand across the floor until he found her icy fingertips.

She gave him a little squeeze back. But she didn't look at him either. "I am sorry," she whispered. "You are here because of me. Both of you."

"The only way somebody gets someplace, bad or good, is if he takes himself." He craned his head around to see her face. "I'm here because of me."

She looked at him for a long moment, her eyes charting his face. Then she smiled, just a smidge. "Thank you. For very little it is worth now, I thank you."

Hitch looked at their guard and cocked his head toward Jael. "Can't you get her a chair? You can see she's hurting."

The guard glanced uncertainly over his shoulder, then back. "That is not orders—"

"Just get her a chair. What's it going to harm at this point?"

The guard hesitated, then shuffled across the room, headed for a round-backed chair.

Hitch let him get the chair and he let him come back. But as soon as the guard was in front of him, he drew back a leg and kicked the kid right below the knee, as hard as he could.

The leg buckled.

The guard wailed and staggered forward. He whacked his chin on the chair's seat, and, for a second, his eyes rolled up into white.

Hitch lunged forward and threw a leg over the guard's back. He sat, facing the kid's feet. Swallowing back the pain in his shoulder, he groped until he found hair.

The guard moaned and raised his arms, trying to push himself up.

"Just don't." Hitch pulled the guard's head back by his hair and gave it a good thwack against the floor. And then another for proper measure.

"Oww . . ."

"Oh, shut up," Jael said.

"Yeah, please," Hitch said. "And listen close, because I'm going to tell you how this is going to go."

CHAPTER 47

AS SOON AS Jael and Walter were free, they got Hitch's shoulder wound packed and bandaged. It hurt like the devil's ugly face, but it wasn't bleeding too much and he still had pretty good flexion. At least Zlo had missed hitting anything too important, like arteries and tendons.

As best he could with one and a half arms, he snugged the ropes around the guard's wrists. Then he gave the kid's head an extra bonk on the floor—just because. The guard's eyes rolled white again, and he moaned against the gag—Taos's gag—stuffed in his mouth.

Schturming fishtailed in the wind, and the floor slanted even more.

Hitch groaned and stood up. "Now let's get out of here. And I do mean now." He looked at Jael. "How do we get to the wheelhouse?"

She had buttressed herself with one hand on the chart table and the other on Walter's shoulder. "It is on next level up. There are stairs in engines room." She eyed him, her face crimped with pain. "What are you going to do?"

He clamped his bad arm against his stomach and extended the other one, herding her and Walter toward the door. "I'm going to find Zlo. Then I'm going to find his knife. And then I'm going to stick his knife right in his black heart."

"But ship, it is crashing. We have to exit."

"Also part of the plan."

They hustled down the corridors, following Jael's directions. She kept them mostly to the back routes, clear of the traffic. And there was plenty of traffic.

Every juncture they passed was crowded with men, running and shouting. Heavy boots clomped against the canted floor. Lights flickered through the doorways and cast mutating shadows across the floors. In the distance, a klaxon blared.

A faint breeze blew through the hallways, carrying a whiff of smoke. A fire under a gas bag. Just what they all needed.

"They are evacuating," Jael whispered. "With elevators."

Hitch looked down to where he was supporting her in the crook of his good arm. "They're not even going to try to fix the engines?"

She lifted a shoulder. "We have damaged maybe more than we thought. Or they are too afraid of fire."

"Well, that's something."

Whether it was a good something or a bad something remained to be seen. He firmed his mouth. At least if they all had to die in a fireball, they'd take the infernal ship with them.

Walter trotted along at his side. He peered up at him. "Are we . . . evacuating?"

"You bet your buttons, kiddo."

They passed the observation balcony where he and Jael had gotten trapped earlier. At the end of the corridor, he raised the bar from the entrance to the cargo bay, then eased open the door. The room lay in darkness. The big doors to the storm had been closed, and without the propellers thunking away in the engine room beyond, the only sounds filtering in were the muffled shouts of Zlo's crew.

"All right, c'mon," he said.

He hauled Jael through the door and halfway across the room, all the way to the Jenny—which Zlo, fortunately, hadn't had the foresight to chuck overboard. In fact, somebody had cleared the boxes away from it enough to turn it around, and then they'd tied it down so it hadn't gotten tossed around when the dirigible swerved. Looked like they thought they'd found themselves a prize.

He pushed Jael on ahead. "Go on to the engines. I'll meet you there."

She knit her brows, but staggered on anyway.

He turned to Walter and knelt to eye level. "Everybody's got a part in this plan, you hear me?"

Walter nodded, tight-lipped.

"I need you to keep Taos here while Jael and I take care of a few things. If Jael comes back and tells you to, I want you to help her start up the plane, like I showed you the other day, okay? You remember where all the switches are?"

Walter frowned, but he nodded again.

"Of course you do." Hitch's heart bumped up into his throat. He opened his mouth to say more, but there was way yonder too much. He helped Walter into the rear cockpit. Then he directed Taos into the front.

If something went wrong and he couldn't get back to them before the fire spread too far, Jael would never get the doors open by herself. So he took five precious seconds to heave them open, one-handed. Rain-flecked wind swirled in.

When he turned back, Walter was watching him. The boy had his face all scrunched up and his head cocked to the side, like he used to do when he was trying to ask a question.

Hitch headed for the engine room and reached to touch Walter's head as he passed.

"Wait." Walter swiveled in the cockpit. "Aren't you going to come back?"

Hitch stopped and looked over his shoulder. "You just wait there. I'll be back as soon as I can." Then he started walking.

This time, the only way to come back was to leave.

Jael had already made it into the engine room. She huddled over the *dawsedometer* and its steady hum, clicking away at the buttons.

Hitch hustled toward her, looking around as he came. Wonder of wonders, nobody else was here. If she was right about the evacuation, they could be flying an empty ship now, for all they knew.

The ceiling creaked. Footsteps? Or the wind?

She looked up at him, mouth tight. "*Yakor*—my pendant—it is gone. Zlo must have taken it."

"But you don't need it to shut it off, right?"

"No." Still, a muscle in her jaw twitched. She'd fought a long time to keep that thing from Zlo. Had to rankle a little to know he'd gotten it in the end, even if maybe it didn't matter anymore.

"How long will it take to shut down?" he asked.

"It is all the way on this time. It takes ten *minuti*, maybe more."

"As soon as you get that thing off, you hurry on back to Walter. I'll join you as soon as I can. Then we're all going home." He headed on past her, toward the spiraling metal stairs that would lead him to the upper levels. If Zlo was still up there, they'd do this the hard and final way. If not, at least maybe he could give a shot to figuring out how to maneuver *Schturming* for a survivable landing.

"Hitch."

He stopped at the bottom of the stairs and looked back.

She leaned one trembling hand against the *dawsedometer*. This close to the machine had to be murder for her. In the lamp-lit darkness, her pupils looked huge, her eyes almost all black.

She shook her head. "Hitch, I do not think this is good plan. We should go, all of us now. Let Zlo crash."

"And if he doesn't crash? Or if he crashes this thing on top of a house with a family and kids in it?" He dug down deep and found his cockiest grin. It felt a little false, even to him. "It's going to be okay." He stared at her. "Jael . . ."

Now or never.

He walked back to her. "I just want you to know . . ."

She tilted her head all the way back to look up at him.

"I just want you to know I could never have done this without you—any of it." He touched the back of his hand to her face. "You're the most incredibly brave person I've ever met."

The corner of her mouth crooked up. "That was my thought for you."

He let his hand slide down off her chin. "Stay alive, okay?"

Her breath shuddered. "You too, Hitch Hitchcock."

He turned away.

He ran up the stairs, three at a time, then all the way down the empty corridor to the bow and up another flight of spiral stairs.

The wheelhouse lay in a flickering half-darkness, lit only by lanterns secured near the ceiling. He stopped five steps from the top, with his head still below the railing. He peered around the corner.

Big paned windows lined both walls, looking out onto more observation balconies. The room tapered to a point, where another window, half again as tall as the others, revealed the night ahead of them. The sky looked maybe a hair less black than the last time he'd seen it, but lightning glimmered, building up inside the clouds, no doubt on the remaining juice of the powering-down *dawsedometer*. They'd been up here for hours. Surely, the time had to be getting along about sunrise.

Beneath the front window, the ship's wheel spun drunkenly. No one manned the helm.

Maybe Zlo really had abandoned ship. The man was no fool. But if he left now, it would mean he'd given up on his dreams. *Schturming* was the only life Zlo knew, and the *dawsedometer* was the best resource he'd ever have. If he let the ship crash, he'd lose both in one fell swoop. And judging from that gleam he'd had in his eye, he wanted both a little too much to let go.

Hitch climbed another couple of steps and looked over the railing.

Behind the spinning wheel, a small shadow moved. Golden eyes gleamed. Feathers ruffled.

The bird. Maksim. Would Zlo have left him behind?

A blast of wind clouted the ship, and the wheel whirled to starboard. The whole ship banked.

If *Schturming* flipped too far over, that certainly couldn't be good. And if she decided to tilt bow-ward, the Jenny was likely to fall right out of the bay and take Walter and Taos with her.

Hitch looked around once more, then stepped all the way up into the wheelhouse.

He made it two strides toward the wheel.

From behind, an arm closed around him. Hot air whooshed against the back of his neck, and a sticky blade creased his throat.

He thrust himself backward and threw his arms wide, trying to break the bear hug. His torn shoulder flared pain. No good.

The hot breath panted harder. "*Ti vonuchaya zhaba*, you are crashing my ship! For that, I will kill you twice."

Hitch hammered his good elbow back and found ribs.

Zlo woofed an exhale. His grip loosened.

Hitch thrust his elbow back again and twisted, both to lever more power into the blow and to squirm free.

Even as Zlo lost his balance and spun away backwards, he stabbed Hitch.

The tip of the blade bit into the buttoned-up front of Hitch's jacket. It tore through leather, past his shirt, and sliced a thin line of fire all the way across his stomach.

Instinctively, he doubled over and clamped his arm over it. Just as fast, he yanked the arm away to get a look. Underneath his torn clothes, blood seeped out of a long gash. Not too deep. Mostly, the blade had just chewed through skin. It hadn't punctured past muscle into the important stuff. But that didn't stop his heart from revving.

He looked up and glared. "Stop stabbin' me!"

Zlo had tripped face first into the stairwell railing and opened up his nosebleed again. He came up snorting blood and shaking his head, probably to clear his vision.

The ship lurched, stern down this time. More lightning gathered in the clouds outside, flickering ominously. Thunder bellowed, so loud Hitch could practically feel it against his skin.

Zlo fell back and skidded down the floor—right to Hitch.

Hitch caught one of Zlo's arms and spun him around. He hammered his fist into Zlo's nose. Bone, blood, and cartilage squished around like a crawdad under a boot. Probably, the nose had busted back when Hitch had kicked him in the face. But like Earl was always telling him, it paid to make *sure* a job got done right.

This man pitched women off his deck into the night, kidnapped little boys, and whipped dogs. So help him God, Hitch didn't need a knife to finish this filth. He'd do it with his bare hand.

He hit Zlo again—and again.

Zlo swayed back and forth and barely kept his feet. His eyes rolled around wildly. He opened his mouth and burbled out a desperate yowl.

"Yeah, scream." Hitch clenched his teeth. "Maybe God'll hear you."

With a screech and a flurry of wings, the eagle dove across the room, straight for Hitch's face.

He shot his arm up just in time. The talons skipped off his forearm, and the bird gouged at him with its beak.

Using both hands, Zlo wrenched Hitch's grip loose from his shirt.

Hitch punched Maksim square in the body.

With a squawk, the bird hit the deck, wings spread.

Zlo staggered backwards. Blood slicked his lips and chin, and his eye sockets were already starting to swell. He held the knife out one-handed, wobbling it all over the place. "You are fool." With his other hand, he scrabbled inside his vest.

Hitch eyed the knife. "Probably." The *dawsedometer* thrummed up through the soles of his feet. It was fainter now, but Jael still hadn't gotten it quite turned off.

"I never had argument with you." With every word, blood spattered from Zlo's mouth. "You are like me—like all of us here in *Schturming*. You fly. The sky belongs to you. You could have flown away from all of this. I would have let you go."

"You weren't what kept me here."

The ship lurched crazily again. It rolled to starboard, and the floor under Hitch's feet turned into a steep incline skidding him toward Zlo.

With a yell, Zlo yanked Jael's pendant from inside his vest. He turned for the window, for the lightning.

The crazy idiot. What was he trying to do? Pull in the lightning? Yes, of course, he was. Just as Jael had done: Zlo would pull in the lightning. But it wouldn't hit him. However it was the *yakor* worked, it would protect Zlo while Hitch got fried.

Adrenaline surged. Hitch managed to yank his bad arm up high enough to just barely smack away Zlo's knife. With his other hand, he grabbed at the pendant. He pitched himself forward, and his weight hit Zlo full in the body. They slid down the floor, straight for the windows.

He buried his face in the crook of Zlo's collar, and then they plowed through the glass. If nothing else, maybe the pendant would protect *both* of them. Cold wind slashed his hair. Rain and specks of ice splattered the back of his neck. Then just as suddenly, the ship rocked the other way.

The balcony railing smashed against Zlo's legs. He toppled over backwards.

Hitch hung onto the pendant.

It ripped from Zlo's hand, and with a shriek, Zlo plummeted over the railing.

Hitch barely let go of Zlo in time. He slammed into the railing himself and caught it with both hands. His elbows locked, straining to keep his weight back long enough.

Within the blue-black cloud, the glow of the lightning swelled. All around him, the air turned to electricity. The hairs on his neck and arms stood on end. The smell of the blood on his arms turned to burnt copper.

He loosed a yell from his own throat and hurled the pendant out into the storm. He hit the deck, hands over his head.

With a great clap, the lightning burst out. From the corner of his eye, he could see its blinding flash spear straight toward the pendant.

Beneath it, Zlo pinwheeled, screaming, into the darkness. The lightning ricocheted off the pendant in an umbrella of energy, shot toward Zlo, and cracked into him.

No more scream.

Beneath Hitch's feet, the floor finished straightening out. Still on his knees, he tilted back from the railing and rammed into the windowsill behind him. His whole body was shaking like it was in an earthquake. Everything smelled like burnt rain, but he was alive. He made himself turn around.

He'd done it. Zlo was dead. They'd won.

Behind him, warning sirens shrieked. The ship bucked and started to dive.

Death by gutting was no longer a threat. Time to focus on death by fireball.

He scrambled over the jagged glass in the window frame and ran for the wheel.

The view through the bow window showed the clouds breaking up. A faraway rim of scarlet lined the horizon and glinted against the raindrops spotting the glass.

He gripped the wheel and tried to steady it. The ship fought him, and she had a whole lot more weight to argue with than the Jenny'd ever had. The biceps of his good arm swelled with the strain. His wounded arm hung heavy and numb, pretty near useless.

He leaned to the other side, trying to see the ground. "C'mon, give me a reference point."

Another skein of clouds melted away. Lights gleamed through the murk below. City lights.

"Oh, gravy."

Schturming was headed straight toward town, and she was maybe only a thousand feet in the air.

No matter which direction he pointed her, she'd never completely clear the town in time to prevent casualties. And as for getting her back up, it was a good bet the crew hadn't paused to fix the gas stoppage before they'd all so thoughtfully evacuated.

The best anybody could do now was to pilot her where she'd do the least damage.

Sure appeared that anybody was him.

He looked around for the speaking pipe. It hung off the ceiling, about a foot from his mouth. He filled his lungs. "Jael!" Please let her hear him. He shouted her name again. Then once more. "Jae—"

"Hitch!" Her voice, tinny through the pipe, echoed back. "We are crashing! What is happening? Where is Zlo?"

"Zlo's dead, so never mind him. And you're right, we are crashing. I need you to climb in the Jenny with Walter and take him out of here. You got that?"

"What? No! We cannot fly. You are only one who can pilot!" Her exhale whuffed through the pipe. "I am not leaving you, Hitch. Do not be crazy, not now!"

"Jael, this ship *will* crash. You have to get Walter out of here. If I'm going to do this, then I need to know the two of you are safe. He can fly the Jenny, I know he can. It's not that hard, and he's a natural. You'll just have to handle the rudder for him."

"He is little boy!"

"He can do it. Help him. You've got a better chance of surviving in the plane than you will up here!"

"Hitch—" Her voice caught.

He could almost see her expression, halfway between crying and wanting to punch him in the face.

"You need to live," she said. "You wanted to start again. You wanted to be there for Walter. You cannot do that if you are dead."

"I *am* starting again." He looked out the window, his one good hand planted on the wheel. "This is my start."

CHAPTER 48

THE WIND BLARING through the big double doors in front of the Jenny made it hard for Walter to hear what Jael was yelling into the pipe telephone thing. But he caught the last part—about wanting Hitch to stay alive.

Her face twisted all up, and her eyes got big and scared. Whatever Hitch had told her, it must not have been him agreeing with her.

Hitch had told Walter to stay in the plane. But he couldn't now. He just couldn't. He grabbed the edge of the cockpit and scrambled over the side. They weren't going to leave Hitch, not ever. Hitch had come all this way to rescue him, even after what had happened to Taos. Hitch was his friend, and he—he—Heat burned in his throat, and he gulped it down.

Jael ran back across the big room. The floor was mostly steady under their feet now, and, ever since she'd shut off the weather machine, she was walking better.

In the front cockpit, Taos propped his front paws against the rim and started barking.

Jael caught Walter and stopped him, a hand on each of his shoulders. "We have to go! We have to go!"

"No!" He planted his feet and pushed on her wrists. "We can't leave Hitch!"

"We have to." She tried to turn him around to face the plane. "We are going to crash if we do not!"

"But then *he'll* crash! I don't want him to crash. We can't let him!"

"Walter." She caught his chin. Deep lines creased her forehead. The silver specks in her eyes practically threw sparks.

"Hitch is man of much bravery. He has to do this, and we—" Her voice faltered, and she firmed her jaw. "We must be letting him."

He kept shaking his head, but his stomach went all hard and cold. His stomach knew she was right. It was just that his heart didn't want to believe it.

She guided him toward the Jenny. "He wants you to fly us out of here."

That stopped him short again. His two lungs felt like wings, fluttering away in his chest. "But I can't—"

They reached the plane, and she helped him into the rear cockpit's cracked leather seat. She paused, one hand on the rim. "He says you *can* do it. He says you are natural."

Hitch had said *that?* Walter stared.

"So take breaths. Make yourself to calm down inside and remember all he has told you. You can do great things, Walter. And this *is* great thing."

He didn't believe he could do this. But if Hitch did—and Jael did—then that'd have to be enough. Little trembles rolled through his muscles. He'd do it for them. He clenched his fists to make the trembling stop. He'd do it for Hitch.

Jael untied the Jenny's wheels and tailskid, then ran around to the propeller. "Tell me what to do!"

He took the breaths, like she'd told him to, and squinted at the control panel. First, the fuel had to be on. Then the magneto switches had to be off—or was it on? Sweat prickled his skin all over. Off—it was off.

He swallowed hard and scootched around to sit on his bent legs, so he'd be able to see the top of Jael's head over the cockpit rim. "Okay!"

She cycled the propeller. Then she swung it again—and again.

Wait. Now the magneto switch had to be turned on. He leaned forward. His fingers were so slick with sweat he had to grab the switch twice before he could hang onto it. He flipped it.

She swung the prop again. With a snort, the engine blatted to life.

The floor slanted again. This time, the Jenny started inching straight for the doors. The engine started to fade out, like it was going to quit altogether.

No, no! He scanned the instrument panel. Now what? What had Hitch done now? The trembles came back and rumbled all the way through him.

Jael started running back to him. "Open throttle! Only small bit!"

She reached the rear cockpit and swung herself up and over. She dropped into the seat and scooted under him, so he was sitting on her lap.

"What do I do?" she asked.

"Put your feet on the pedals!"

She circled his waist with arms and clamped both of them in with the safety belt.

Thanks to the slant of the floor and the Jenny's own engine thrust, the plane was soon speeding toward the opening. The propeller passed through the doorway, then the wheels, and then—they were airborne.

His head spun. His hands froze on the stick.

The nose pointed toward the ground. The patchwork of buildings and roads was still far away, but it seemed close at the same time—so much closer than it should be.

"Take breaths, take breaths!" Jael hollered right in his ear. "The nose must come up!"

Right. The nose. He hauled back on the stick.

Please work! He wasn't a pilot. He was only a little boy.

But the magic worked for him just like it had for Hitch.

Slowly, the Jenny pitched up. She was almost level. She *was* level. She was flying!

Walter whooped, and Jael laughed. In the front cockpit, Taos raised his head and barked.

Only little spits of rain spotted the windshield. The wind must be stopping too, because the Jenny wasn't bouncing around like *Schturming* had been earlier.

"Bring her lower!" Jael shouted. "Be slow!"

He pushed the stick forward, just a bit. The Jenny bobbed down right away, like she'd been reading his mind all along.

Below, people packed the streets. They carried lanterns and torches—and guns and pitchforks. Their faces looked like little white dots as they peered upwards.

"Search for street that is empty!" Jael shouted.

He nodded.

Two streets over would have to do. He showed Jael how to use the rudder pedals.

"Are you knowing how to land?" she asked.

He shrugged.

Her hands tightened over his on the stick. "*Gospod pomogi nam.*"

That sounded like a prayer, so he said one too. *Please let me land. And please don't let Hitch crash.*

They guided the Jenny in. The plane glided—one hundred feet off the ground, then fifty, then maybe only ten.

Jael was hollering again. The engine sputtered.

His heart beat so hard it drowned out everything else.

How did you know when it was time to touch the ground? What did you do then? Sweat slipped over his eyebrows and stung his eyes. He blinked fiercely.

Then, just like that, a wheel hit the ground. They smacked so hard his neck about snapped. The whole world went fuzzy. But then, almost as quick, the Jenny hopped right back up—and down again. Something that looked a whole lot like a wheel bounced away to the side.

They were so close to the ground. They *couldn't* crash now.

Jael wrapped both her hands around his, and together they hauled back.

He yanked one of his hands loose long enough to cut the throttle.

Life crept by, one long breath after another. With every second, the Jenny's high tail end rose a little higher. She was going to flip right over.

But she didn't. Just when it seemed she couldn't get any higher, the tail fell. It whomped back into the ground. Mud showered everywhere. Walter was jerked back and his head walloped Jael's chin. Then he pitched forward and hit his forehead against the stick.

Lights speckled behind his eyelids for a second. Or more likely five seconds.

He opened first one eye, then another. His head throbbed on both sides, but that was about all that hurt. He craned a look back to Jael.

She clamped one hand over her bloody chin and stared at him, eyes wide.

She was alive. So was he. He looked over the edge of the cockpit. The plane had settled onto one wing, but she *was* settled. Taos scrambled out of the front cockpit and ran around the plane, barking.

They'd done it! Walter clawed the safety belt loose and piled out of the plane. His legs quivered like a still-wet calf's.

People ran up the street, shouting. Sheriff Campbell, a storm lantern in one hand, ran at their front. Earl ran behind him.

Walter looked back to where Jael was standing up in the cockpit. "I did it!"

She grinned. "You did it!"

"I did it!"

He jumped up and down once, then threw himself forward into the dirt to turn a somersault. The pain in his head banged away louder than Evvy and Annie playing with Mama Nan's pots and pans. But that didn't matter right now.

"I did it!" He opened his mouth, and, for the first time ever, yelled as loud as he could: "*I DID IT!*"

Hitch had been right about him.

Hitch . . . He craned his head back to see the sky. Where was Hitch? Clouds filled up every cranny of the sky. But no *Schturming*. He spun all the way around, head back as far as it would go.

The rumble of running feet drowned out any chance of sound.

People shouted and shrieked.

"The boy, he's safe!"

"Would you look at that?"

"Where's Hitch?" That was Earl.

"Everybody stand back!" Campbell shouted. He wore a bandage over his forehead, and the corners of his lips were pulled back, like a bear on the prod.

He stalked right up to Jael, still standing in the plane. He grabbed her arm and hauled her down. "This woman is under arrest!"

Earl looked about ready to spit. "Oh, for cryin' out—"

Walter ducked through the swarm of people and latched both hands onto Campbell's arm. "Let her go!"

Campbell stared, probably a little shocked Walter was talking.

But he dropped the lantern instead of Jael and used his freed hand to grab Walter's shirtfront. "Where's your rescuer now?" He turned back to Jael. "He gets you both stuck up there and then abandons you to your own devices, is that it?"

Walter clenched both hands around Campbell's fingers in his shirt and tried to pry them loose.

Jael stood up straight, like the storybook queens, and stared down her nose at Campbell. "You know that is not true." She faced the crowd. "Hitch stayed in *Schturming* to save us—to save all of you! So it would not crash and kill you!"

With a fluttery whistle—kind of like a tremendous kite— *Schturming* broke out of the clouds and passed over their heads. For an instant, its shadow blocked out the gray trickle of new morning light. Black smoke gushed from the cargo bay's open doors. The fire must have spread.

Earl spun to face the crowd. "Buckets? Hoses? You got a fire brigade in this town?" He turned around and jogged past Jael. His eyes found hers. "He ain't dead yet. If there's any chance at all, that ol' bushwhacker spirit of his'll get him out of this alive."

She started after him.

Campbell snarled and snatched her back. "*If* he's unlucky enough to survive this, he's going to be in more trouble than even he knows what to do with."

Walter finally yanked free. He glanced at Jael. He should stop and help her.

She caught his eye and shook her head. "Go!"

That was all he needed. He took off running. His feet, in his pinched party shoes, slapped through the sloppy mud of the road. He'd help carry buckets—or bandages—or anything, if it'd help Hitch stay alive.

CHAPTER 49

SCHTURMING WAS HOLDING altitude about as well as a lump of lead. Faint wisps of smoke trickled into the wheelhouse. Fire was gnawing at her from somewhere below decks. All it'd take would be one spark on one hiss of gas, and the whole thing would go up in flames.

Hitch ignored the blood trickling from under his shoulder bandage. No chance at all of getting completely clear of the city. Pretty near the only thing he could do now was find a crash site where she'd cause the least amount of damage.

And he knew just the place.

He muscled the wheel around, hand over hand, and managed to turn the prow a couple degrees. That'd be enough. They were almost there.

Schturming whisked over housetops, maybe only twenty feet above the chimneys.

Through the windshield, a two-story frame house with a dormer roof loomed on the edge of town. Campbell's house.

But not for long. Hitch spared a tight grin.

He hauled the wheel back to center. The bowsprit lined up with the dormer window like the sight on a .22.

Only thirty feet to go.

Didn't matter how hard that wheel spun now. *Schturming* couldn't help but hit Campbell's house. That was Hitch's cue to leave if he wanted any chance of surviving the crash.

He let go of the wheel and backed away two steps. Then he turned and ran.

He blasted across the wheelhouse, hurdled the stairway

railing, and landed halfway down the circular steps. He ran back down the length of the ship to the engine room in the stern and Jael's hidden closet next to the entrance. He yanked the door shut, dragged her thin mattress over him, and dropped to the floor in a fetal ball.

The whole ship shuddered. Then, almost as if the momentum had to catch up with the feeling, she slammed hard. That'd be her prow ripping through Campbell's roof.

His good shoulder thudded into the closet door. Hammers and wrenches from Jael's hanging bag clattered down on him.

The ship kept skidding. A sensation like fingernails against slate grated up the floorboards all through his body. And then she was pitching forward. He went weightless for a moment.

The prow battered into the ground and hurled him against the door. The latch gave way, and he hurtled down the floor's steep incline. Halfway across the room, he thumped into the *dawsedometer* where it was bolted to the floor.

The ship skidded even farther: another weightless sensation, followed by another tremendous thud. She toppled onto her port side.

Hitch caught hold of the *dawsedometer* and kept himself from toppling with her.

Any second now, she was going to burst into flames and burn like the devil's bacon.

He looked around. With the floor slanted like this, he'd never be able to climb back up to the door in time.

Thick smoke wafted in from the cargo bay and grated in his lungs. He coughed.

Out of the corner of his eye, gray daylight flashed. Only a few yards back from the *dawsedometer* was Jael's "door in floor." Without the pendant, he could hardly have unlocked it, but the crash had already done the work for him: the trapdoor hung open, its hinges completely busted.

That'd do—and *how*.

He scrambled around to the topside of the *dawsedometer* and barely managed to catch a handhold on the nearest of the engine's pistons. Every muscle in his body screaming, and his right arm refusing to hold his weight half the time, he dragged himself up. His hand found the edge of the trapdoor, and cool air wicked against the sweat on his skin.

He heaved himself over the ledge. This end of the ship had run aground in Campbell's yard, but the front end was still wedged in the roof. From the porthole, it was only a ten-foot drop. He hit the ground, lost all his breath, and got up dizzy.

Run. That was the only thought in his head. He sure as gravy hadn't made it this far to blow up with his feet on firm ground.

He spared one glance at the wilting envelope. Both arms pumping, lungs heaving, he ran across Campbell's yard, turned the corner around the picket fence, and sprinted down the road.

From behind, a sound whuffed, like a thousand birthday candles blowing out. Heat engulfed his back, the hairs on his neck singeing. Light like high noon splashed shadows everywhere. A great crackling blotted out every other noise, even the slap of his feet against the road.

In front of him, people packed the street. Half of them stopped and stared, shouting and screaming. Some turned and ran. They were probably out of range back there, but better safe than sorry at this point. A handful of men with sloshing buckets broke through the crowd, headed toward the wreck.

Earl, a bucket in his unbroken arm, led the charge. From across the road, he caught sight of Hitch and stopped to hang his head back in relief.

Hitch's lungs burned hotter than the fire behind him. He slowed up and looked back.

Sure enough, *Schturming* had plowed through Campbell's dormer roof. Three times as big as the house, she leaned upended in the yard. Fifty-foot flames chewed through the skeleton of the envelope. Right in front of his eyes, the whole structure crumbled into ash.

Without the gas to consume, the flames subsided. But they'd already crawled across the yard and up the side of Campbell's house.

Hitch crouched, hands on his knees, and rasped in breath after breath. Every single one made him want to cough, but he kept pulling them in.

"Hitch!" That was Jael's voice.

He jerked his head around, back toward the crowd.

Campbell had Jael by the arm and was stalking toward him.

Jael grinned. Walter ran beside her, lugging a bucket in both hands. She grabbed his shoulder and pointed at Hitch.

A smile split the boy's face. He jumped up and down, bucket and all, water splashing all over the dark front of his party suit.

Thank God. They'd made it. Hitch dropped to both knees. Thank God, thank God, thank God. And bless that crazy, cranky Jenny. Somehow, impossibly, she'd gotten them both back to the ground in one piece.

Campbell let go of Jael. "Hitchcock!" He looked like he wanted to barrel across the road and pummel Hitch. But every few steps, he had to stop and gape at his house.

Finally, he turned to Hitch and jabbed a finger at him. A pulse beat in his temple, and his jowls quivered. "I'll bury you for this!"

Hitch stood up. Blood from his shoulder wet the crevices of his fingers, but he left the arm straight at his side. The time for showing weaknesses was over.

Campbell grabbed his arm—the good one, thankfully—and leaned into his face. "You're going to wish you'd died in that crash, you hear me?"

"Stand down, Sheriff. I just did you the biggest favor of your life in saving *your* people from that thing."

"You arrogant flyboy! You think you can return here a hero? After what you pulled last night!"

"I think if you try even one single thing, I will bring this whole town down on your scurvy head."

"You try it, son."

Hitch shrugged out from under Campbell's grip. He turned and he walked away. Campbell'd never stand for that, especially not now. But let him make the first move. Better that way this time. The whole town would see their sheriff, and the whole town could draw their own conclusions about him.

Hitch made it two steps before Campbell's paw slammed down, this time right on his wounded shoulder.

Pain sliced through his vision. He staggered sideways and fell to his hands and knees. He tried once to get up, then caught himself on his good hand and shook his head woozily.

Around the corners of his blurred vision, he could see the crowd shifting. Their attention moved from the fire, toward him. Some of them muttered protests.

"Stay down," Campbell said.

Hitch raised himself onto his knees and faced the crowd. "He's going to arrest me. But before he does, you all need to know this man's got no business being your sheriff. He's been crooked for years!"

They started murmuring amongst themselves.

"Don't go there," Campbell growled, low and deep. "You can't win." He grabbed Hitch's good arm and twisted it up behind his back.

New pain exploded in his arm socket, and he groaned.

"That's enough!" a woman shouted.

The crowd closed in around them, some of them just curious, some of them repeating the dissent.

"How do you know this?" a man yelled at Hitch.

He raised his chin. "I know this because I've let him make me a part of it."

Jael clasped her hands and shook her head.

Hitch kept on going. "I've smuggled stolen goods and bootleg liquor for him, and when we downed *Schturming* the other day, I turned control of it over to him. I shouldn't have. But I did it because he's threatened my family time and again."

Brows started to lower. Mouths started to frown. At least they weren't dismissing him out of hand.

Campbell hauled him to his feet. "Not true, and you all know it. This here boy ain't the hero you want to make him out." But his hand on Hitch's wrist was starting to sweat a little.

The crowd's murmurs grew into an outright hubbub. A ripple moved up through the people, and they parted to let three men through: Griff, Matthew, and J.W.

Griff's nose was swollen, and dark bruises welled under each eye. He looked tousled and exhausted, but at least he wasn't in jail. Judging from the shotguns propped on the Berringers' hips and the smug determination on their faces, they had to be the reason.

Griff gripped a revolver as he crossed the distance. "What

my brother says is true. William Campbell, you are under arrest for malfeasance."

"Call it skullduggery and be done," J.W. said.

Campbell's jowls quivered. "Escaping after a lawful arrest, you think that's going to get you anywhere, Deputy?" He glowered at the Berringers. "Or your friends?"

"You can say what you want." Griff walked up to Campbell, handcuffs in hand. "We both know where this is going to end."

"You make any kind of case that I'm guilty, then your brother has to be complicit. You don't want that." With surprising speed, he snatched Griff's revolver away from him. His voice went deadly calm. "You don't run this town, boys. I do. And that isn't changin'."

Behind them, a second explosion erupted.

Hitch ducked. Specks of hot debris spattered against his back, and he twisted a look over his shoulder.

Campbell's green sedan had flipped all the way over and flattened the picket fence. The fire must have gotten to it. Campbell's big house and Campbell's big car—all in one fell swoop. Not bad for a day's work. But it wouldn't mean a thing if they couldn't get Campbell himself.

Hitch gathered his weight on the balls of his feet, ready to hurl himself against Campbell—and probably break his other arm in the process.

Like the rest of them, Campbell had jerked around at the sound of the explosion. Already, he was turning back. His eyes found Griff. The revolver rose.

From behind Campbell, a board from his own house smacked him right in the back of the head. A look of utter surprise dropped his mouth. Then his eyes rolled up, and he thudded to his knees. He stayed upright for one second longer, then toppled sideways into the mud.

Behind him, Jael held the board cocked over one shoulder, ready for another go. Right in front of all the town's ladies, she spat at Campbell's body. "*Eto pravosudie.*" Then she raised her fierce gaze to Hitch. The set of her mouth looked extremely satisfied.

Hitch's breath fizzled from his body, and he gave her a grateful nod.

Griff turned to the crowd. "C'mon, let's have four men to carry him to a car!" He turned his head, not quite looking at Hitch. "Campbell's right. I'm going to have to put you under arrest too. If I ask you to come along, will you do it?"

The adrenaline filtered out of Hitch. Everything started to hurt. He cradled his bad arm against his stomach. "Yeah, I'll come."

Jael frowned. "What is this? Wait—" She clenched the board harder.

Hitch touched her arm. "It's all right. Take care of Walter. Make sure he gets back to Nan."

She knit her eyebrows hard. "Hitch—"

He found he could smile, in spite of everything—or maybe because of everything. "It's all right, kiddo."

He turned to follow Griff.

Townspeople rushed on every side. The thirty-member volunteer fire department had arrived. People with buckets started to form lines, all the way down the street to Campbell's home. Maybe they'd even put out the fire before it could spread to any other houses.

He squinted upward. The clouds were drawing up higher into the sky. Here and there, a rim of gold edged a crack, and, on the brink of the horizon, the warm, red line of the summer sunrise reached out for him.

Chapter 50

FTER TWO WEEKS cooped up in that dad-blasted cell, waiting on a hearing, the sun felt mighty good. Hitch stepped out of the courthouse into the late August heat. Under a sky of perfect blue, the waning morning stretched as far as he could see, golden and dusty. Two weeks was plenty of time for Nebraska soil to suck up even a cataclysmic storm's moisture.

He paused on the steps to roll his shirtsleeves up to his elbows. Then he slung his jacket over his stitched-up shoulder. It was still stiff, but the doc said it'd mend fine in another couple of weeks.

He looked down the street on one side, then the other. Automobiles rumbled and honked along. Farmers in overalls and straw hats strolled the sidewalks, alongside women with their handbags over their arms and their shopping lists in hand.

Everything looked back to normal: back to boring farm-town life. And it all looked about as beautiful as anything he'd ever seen. It was good to be home. If he had said that when he'd first flown in here, nearly a month ago, he might have been lying. But right now, it was the gospel truth.

Of course, a little part of that might be the fact he was free to walk out here into the sun, rather than stay locked up in jail for the good Lord knew how long. His insides jittered at the thought of it, and he started down the steps.

Campbell was still stuck in there, eating jail food, railing about burying everybody in sight, and waiting for a trial that was sure to put him away for a good long while. Folks Hitch hadn't even known about were coming out of the woodwork, wanting to testify against him for everything from doctoring finances to extortion to criminal connections with his bootlegging buddies in Cheyenne and beyond.

Hitch got off easy. The judge let him go due to "considerations." After all, he *had* more or less saved the valley. And he had confessed and ratted on Campbell. Plus, it appeared the new sheriff had put in a surprisingly good word on his account.

A black Chevrolet, the top folded back, puttered up to the curb.

From under his fedora's brim, Griff peered up at him. "You're out then?" Against his suspenders, his new badge glinted.

Hitch sauntered down the steps. "Looks like."

Griff wet his lip. "Want a ride to camp?"

He lowered himself into the car and slammed the door. "Thanks."

Griff checked traffic and pulled into the street. He watched the road.

Hitch only pretended to watch it. Mostly, he watched his brother out of the corner of his eye.

What were you supposed to say in a situation like this? Seemed like the two of them had made up, more or less. But it'd be nice to know for sure. He couldn't just come out and ask, even though the answer mattered now more than ever, what with his new plans.

They passed the cleared lot where Campbell's house had once stood. The captured residents of *Schturming* had been released after their own hearings had proven they'd more or less been Zlo's hostages. Now, they rooted amongst the charred rubble, salvaging whatever they could of their belongings.

"Lot of folks without homes," Hitch said. "What happens to them now?"

"The town's doing what they can for them. Some of them want to stay, buy farms. Some of them want to rebuild their ship."

"And the town's going to let them?"

Griff shrugged. "They were cleared. Honestly, I wouldn't be surprised if they're not the only ones around here who try to build one of those things." He glanced sideways at Hitch. "Might be we'll have a whole fleet of them before we're done."

"No weather machine though?"

"No, that went up in the fire. Reckon we'll leave the weather to God. For now at least."

"Sounds good to me."

As they left the city limits, Griff cleared his throat. "So . . . what now?"

Hitch shrugged. "I don't have it all worked out. But I do know there's some things I've got to do yet. First thing is finding a job hereabouts."

Griff kept his eyes on the folded-down windshield. "Nothing glamorous around here. Right now, the only available jobs are on the farms or in the sugar-beet factory. You realize that?"

"I realize it. But I reckon we both know that's what needs to happen. At this point, staying and working a lousy job is a small price to pay. You were right." He waited until Griff looked him full in the face. "It would be a mighty poor idea to drag that kid all over the country in a plane—no matter how much we might both love it at first." He made himself say the words he'd been thinking ever since it had looked like there might be a chance he'd get out of *Schturming* alive. "It's time for me to stop roaming. Time to root. If I'm ever going to have a chance at a family, this is it."

Griff watched him for a second, seeming to digest the words. Then he faced the road again. He might even have dipped his chin in a small nod. "What's the second thing?"

Hitch laughed. "Don't you reckon that's enough for now?"

As a matter of fact, the second thing was somehow talking Jael into sticking around too. She had nowhere left to go, and she'd been wanting to stay before. But things had changed. Asking her to reconsider was another set of words he'd had stuck in his throat ever since *Schturming*'s crash.

They drove in silence for several miles more. Griff took the turn into the erstwhile airfield—shorn now of all but two planes: a red one and a red-white-and-blue one. Half a dozen automobiles filled in the gaps. Blankets had been spread on the ground and pinned down with picnic baskets.

Beside the biggest basket, Nan and Molly knelt, doling out potato salad and fried chicken—and swatting away the twins whenever they tried to stick their fists into the pitcher of lemonade.

Lilla, wearing a tremendously wide-brimmed yellow hat, swept in and grabbed a twin's waist in either arm. She looked up at the oncoming motorcar and released one of the girls long enough to raise a hand and wave. No Rick in sight. Last Hitch heard, Rick had skedaddled out of the state with Lilla swinging a broom at his backside. Good riddance.

The menfolk—Byron and the Berringers and a few others— stood back a ways with a handful of youngsters. Judging from the bats and worn leather gloves, they were getting ready for a ball game.

Griff bumped the auto across the field toward the crowd.

"What's all this?" Hitch asked.

"Celebration. Hopefully, it'll end a little better than the last one."

"No kidding."

Griff parked at the end of the row of motorcars and shut off the engine.

For a moment, they both just sat there. In front of them, the hot cylinders ticked. A meadowlark sang from atop a fencepost. The men's raised voices drifted across the field.

"Now, now," Matthew said, "why can't you let these boys play it how they want to?"

"They want to play it right or not?" J.W. jammed his hand into a glove and held out the other for Matthew's ball. "If they want to play it right, I reckon they better listen to the rules first."

Matthew passed over the ball. "The thing I can't figure is how you keep forgetting the *right* way and *your* way are not the same thing."

"And I s'pose *your* way is?"

"In this case—yes."

Hitch laughed. "Old buzzards."

Griff tilted the corner of his mouth. "They'll go to their graves arguing about something."

A stout older woman with a mop of frizzy red curls piled atop her head sashayed over to the Berringers. Whatever she said wasn't audible, but it sure did a number on them. In unison, they clammed up. Eyes got big. Matthew's face went beet red.

She laughed—no, giggled was more like it—then twirled her fringed parasol over her shoulder and flounced off, ample hips swaying.

"Who's that?" Hitch asked.

Griff let a grin slip. "Ginny Lou Thatcher."

"Wha-at? That's the girl they been fighting over all these years? And they're *still* fighting over her?"

"Not exactly. Anymore, I think they just fight 'cause it's easier than fixing things up." Griff's grin faded. "You know, everything that's gone under the bridge here lately . . ." He shook his head. "You're not the only one who's got things to be sorry for."

"You don't have to say that to me."

"Yeah, I do. You wanted me to forgive you, and I wouldn't."

"I don't blame you for that." Lord knew, he probably wouldn't have forgiven himself either. "I hurt you bad. I see that now, where I didn't before."

"That's the point. You always were a clueless lug." Griff studied the steering wheel. "I felt like you needed to be punished."

"I probably did."

"Well, it wasn't mine to do." He looked over. "I'm glad you're staying."

"Me too."

Griff smiled. "Yeah, well." He cleared his throat. "Shall we join the party?"

Hitch climbed out slowly and looked around.

On the far side of the baseball players, his Jenny burned red against the gold of the cropped grass. From the sound of things, she'd gotten pretty banged up in that last landing. Her skin was ripped in places and in need of mending. But she looked all of a piece. Earl must have been patching her up around the clock.

Next to the open engine cowling, Jael crouched. Walter hunkered beside her, watching intently as she fiddled with the carburetor.

Hitch shoved his hands in his pockets and started toward them.

Jael looked back and flashed him a grin. The sun glinted against the smudge of grease across one cheek. She was back in breeches and boots—with a red kerchief over her silver-streaked hair.

She looked like she belonged here. No more the bedraggled, wild-eyed ragamuffin who'd parachuted in front of his Jenny. She now looked about like a woman who had taken on pirates should look.

She was the reason for all of this. If it hadn't been for her, he'd have been on the far side of the country by now. He'd have left town without ever knowing about Walter, without ever making things right with Griff.

He smiled back at her. Someday he'd tell her that. And thank her for it. Maybe today, as a matter of fact. He lengthened his stride.

"Captain Hitchcock."

Livingstone. He winced and slowed up enough to look over his shoulder.

Still in his white suit and Stetson, Livingstone propped his walking stick across his lap and used both arms to wheel his chair toward Hitch. His bandaged legs stuck straight out in front of him on the chair's wicker leg rests.

That explained the other plane.

Hitch faced him. "Still here, are you?"

"Couldn't rightly leave the vicinity without laying eyes on our own true-blue hero, now could I?" Livingstone scanned Hitch from top wing to landing gear. He *almost* looked impressed.

"This isn't about the bet, is it?" Hitch asked. "'Cause it doesn't look like I'll be able to take that management position after all."

"Is that a fact?" Livingstone pursed his lips. "Well, then, might it be our purposes are coinciding without our even realizing it?"

"What do you mean?"

"I mean simply this." Livingstone wheeled a little closer and lowered his voice. "As you may know, the Extravagant Flying Circus has met with a rather tragic demise."

"Ah, yes." After Zlo's escape, all Livingstone's pilots had winged it out of the valley, intent on saving their planes while they still could.

"But," Livingstone said, "a new venture has come to my mind. Despite the recent tribulations, this area has proven itself ripe for the expansion of aviation. I am considering opening a flying school."

"A school?" Hitch frowned. "With one plane?"

"Or perhaps two." Livingstone glanced at Hitch's Jenny. "Knowing the art of good publicity as I do, I believe if I were able to advertise a flying instructor of some heroic notoriety, we could draw in quite a crowd."

Stay here—and still be able to fly? His mind started spinning with the possibilities.

Livingstone smoothed his mustache. "We could even put on a small circus hereabouts. A monthly affair, perhaps. I've already signed on your fair wing walker."

"Ah . . ." The words wouldn't come fast enough.

Livingstone smiled—a little too victoriously maybe—and started wheeling his chair back. "You think about it. Take your time. Let me know whenever you're sure."

Hitch was already turning to his Jenny—to Walter and Jael. "Oh, I'm sure." Saying so was a mistake, of course. Livingstone would use it against him when the time came to negotiate wages. But the words popped out, right from the bottom of his soul.

He started across the field toward the Jenny.

Earl hobbled over from the other direction, his roll of tools under his good elbow. The fingers poking out of his filthy bandage held a chicken thigh to his mouth.

He gave Hitch a grin and a nod, then turned and caught sight of Jael and Walter kneeling beside the engine. "Hey! What do you think you're doing? You two ain't grease monkeys yet, no matter what you think." He stomped toward them.

Jael and Walter both laughed and jumped up to run around the back end of the plane, practically daring Earl to chase them. He didn't, of course.

Hitch stopped a few yards off and waited for them to circle back around the front. He rubbed the sweat from his palms onto his pant legs. Almost involuntarily, he looked over his shoulder.

Still kneeling on her picnic blanket, Nan shaded her eyes with her hands and watched him. Her shoulders lifted in a breath, and as she let it out, she lowered her chin in a deep, consenting nod.

Walter rounded the front of the plane, without Jael, who

must have realized what was in the wind and backed off. He saw Hitch and danced over, eyes sparkling.

"Howdy," Hitch managed.

The boy grinned up at him all the harder.

"What's this? Don't tell me you're back to not talking?"

Walter shrugged. He seemed to think about it, then said, "Howdy."

"That's more like it. 'Cause, you and me, we got things to talk about." He knelt and set his hands on Walter's shoulders.

Every minute in that jail cell, he'd been trying to figure the best way to say this. Nan and Byron had promised to prepare the way for him.

He wet his lips. "What would you think if I were to start being your dad?"

Walter cocked his head and raised his eyebrows. He looked intrigued.

Hitch kept going. "What would you think if it turned out I *was* your dad? And maybe, one of these days, if you wanted to, you could come live with me?"

Walter kept staring. If anything, the look rising in his eyes seemed to be one of hope. He flung himself against Hitch's chest, wrapped his arms all the way around, and hugged him.

Hitch's breath ripped right out of him. How could anybody forgive that fast? Or trust that easy? He didn't deserve it, that was sure. But here it was, like a gift someone had slipped into the palm of his hand. And he'd almost missed catching it altogether.

Walter stepped back from Hitch's arms and looked up at him, fairly glowing.

Then J.W. hollered, "Hey, kid, you playing or not?"

Walter glanced over, then again at Hitch, eyebrows raised, asking for permission.

Hitch nodded. "Go along. We got more to talk about, but it'll wait."

He stayed on his knees and watched Walter scamper off.

So help him God, he was going to make good this time. He'd be there for Walter, every single day of his life. He'd accept this gift, and he'd do his best to take care of it like it deserved to be taken care of.

Beside the plane, Jael stood with her hands in her back pockets. She grinned.

He pushed up to his feet and joined her. "I hear Livingstone offered you a job?"

She inclined her head.

"Me too." He took a breath. "I don't have any kind of right to ask you to stay, after everything that's gone down. But just in case it might mean anything to you, I am promising *I'm* going to stay."

Her grin faded. She stitched her eyebrows together and pursed her lips. She'd never seemed to have much trouble making up her mind about things. But right now, she looked downright indecisive.

He tried again. "I reckon you don't have to say anything right now."

"It is not that." She moved a step closer. "It is that I am not knowing right word for . . . this." She set her palm on his chest. Without so much as a blush this time, she leaned in and kissed him right smack on the mouth. Then she pulled back, shook a few loose tendrils of hair out of her face, and grinned wickedly.

He blinked. "What? No slap this time?"

She shrugged one shoulder. "Not this time, I think."

"What about this time?" He cupped a hand around the nape of her neck and pulled her back in.

From behind him, voices started hollering.

"What kind of umpire are you?" J.W. demanded.

"The boy was safe," Matthew said. "I make the calls the way I see them."

"Well, maybe the fact you're wearing *spectacles* is a hint you shouldn't be umpire!"

"And maybe the fact you're *not* wearing them is a hint why you weren't voted umpire in the first place."

Hitch stopped kissing Jael, but kept her close, and looked over his shoulder.

Livingstone wheeled his way over to where Matthew and J.W. stood nose to nose. "Gentlemen, gentlemen, was this not supposed to be a friendly ballgame?" He turned to Hitch. "Perhaps our resident flight instructor might be persuaded to give free rides instead?"

Hitch looked at Jael. "What do you say?"

She tilted her head all the way back to see into his face. "I have lived in sky for as long as my life. Take me home, Hitch Hitchcock."

"My home too." And he didn't mean just the sky this time.

He stepped away from her. "All right, who wants a ride?"

Several people whooped, Walter loudest of all.

Hitch hopped up into the rear cockpit. Almost before he'd settled, Walter scrambled into his lap. Taos jumped right in without so much as an invitation—barking his head off, of course—and somebody coaxed Nan and Molly into the front cockpit. Jael perched herself on a wing, while Earl swung the propeller. The Jenny couldn't take off with all of them, but Hitch could taxi them around the field.

"Contact!" Earl shouted.

Hitch flipped the magneto switches. "Contact!"

Earl swung the prop again, and the engine started chugging. Inch by inch, the Jenny lurched forward, until she was bumping across the field. The wind touched their faces with the scent of cut grass.

Walter leaned back against Hitch's chest, one hand on the stick, the other on Taos's ruff.

Hitch glanced over at Jael, on the wing, and she laughed, delighted.

His stomach got that same old weightless feeling. He faced forward again, feeling the Jenny's rhythm beneath him. Flying a biplane, especially one as rickety as a war-surplus Curtiss JN-4D, meant being ready for anything. He just hadn't ever expected "anything" could turn out to be quite this good.

Note From the Author: Thanks so much for flying along with me on *Storming*! Did you know reviews are what sell books? If you've had fun reading this book, would you consider rating it and reviewing it on Amazon.com? Thank you!

Join the discussion: #Storming

Don't want the fun to end?

CLAIM YOUR FREE BOOK!

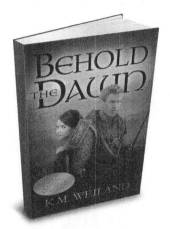

From internationally published and award-winning author K.M. Weiland:

The vengeance of a monk.

The love of a countess.

The secrets of a knight.

For sixteen years, rogue knight Marcus Annan has remained unbeaten on the field of battle, but waiting for him in the midst of the Third Crusade is the greatest enemy he has ever faced . . . his past.

"Meticulously researched and so beautifully written, it reads like poetry."

kmweiland.com/resources/free-e-book

Want more?

Use the following link to visit a hidden webpage, designed especially for fans of *Storming*:

kmweiland.com/storming-extras

Access exclusives such as:

Desktop Wallpaper

Story Soundtrack

Deleted Scenes

Character Interviews

Research Notes

Story Outline

And more!

Acknowledgements

WRITING A BOOK is something one does alone. The finished draft is a solitary accomplishment. But a good book? That is the result of a generous collaboration of intelligent minds and wide-open hearts. I am blessed to have a good many such minds and hearts in my life—and it is the owners of these important organs that allow me to share my novels with you.

As I finish yet another literary journey, I must pass out rounds of espresso, dark chocolate truffles, and tremendous thanks to the following people who guided, encouraged, and joined me on the trip.

My chief writing buddy Linda Yezak: who brings all that red-headed verve to cheering me on and, occasionally, helping me fight my battles.

My editor CathiLyn Dyck: who gives me no nonsense and the confidence I'm on the right track.

My proofreader Steve Mathisen: who is so much more than that with his continual encouragement and fellowship.

My critique partner London Crockett: who is secretly much more brilliant than I am.

My beta readers: Lorna G. Poston (for whom I created Taos), Daniel Farnum (who gave me Snoopy as my writing mascot), Braden Russell (who is also secretly much more brilliant and —not-so-secretly—much funnier than I am).

My aviation experts: Chuck Davis (who actually drew up blueprints of *Schturming*!) and Matthew Gianni (who talked me into cutting all my favorite scenes and making the story much more plausible).

My family: who really are the best writer's family I have ever heard of.

My illustrator and cartographer: Joanna Marie (who has been working with me since *Behold the Dawn* and who phenomenally outdid herself this time around).

My translator: Alex Shvartsman (who made the completely unfair trade of checking all my Russian translations in exchange for my reviewing his awesome book).

Wordplayers everywhere: What a community you guys have created! Thank you for showing up every day on my blog and social sites and reminding me why readers are the best people on the planet.

Thank you!

K.M. Weiland
November 2015

About the Author

K.M. WEILAND LIVES in make-believe worlds, talks to imaginary friends, and survives primarily on chocolate truffles and espresso. She is the IPPY and NIEA Award-winning and internationally published author of the medieval epic *Behold the Dawn* and the portal fantasy *Dreamlander*, as well as the bestselling *Outlining Your Novel* and *Structuring Your Novel*.

When she's not making things up, she's busy mentoring other authors through the award-winning website Helping Writers Become Authors.com. She makes her home in western Nebraska. Visit her website km.weiland.com/news for bi-weekly updates about her books and her adventures as a writer. You can email her at kmweiland@ymail.com. Join her mailing list for news of upcoming books.

Also by K.M. Weiland

*What if dreams
came true?*

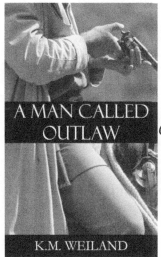

*One man stood up unafraid.
One man fell alone.
One man's courage became a legend.*

www.kmweiland.com